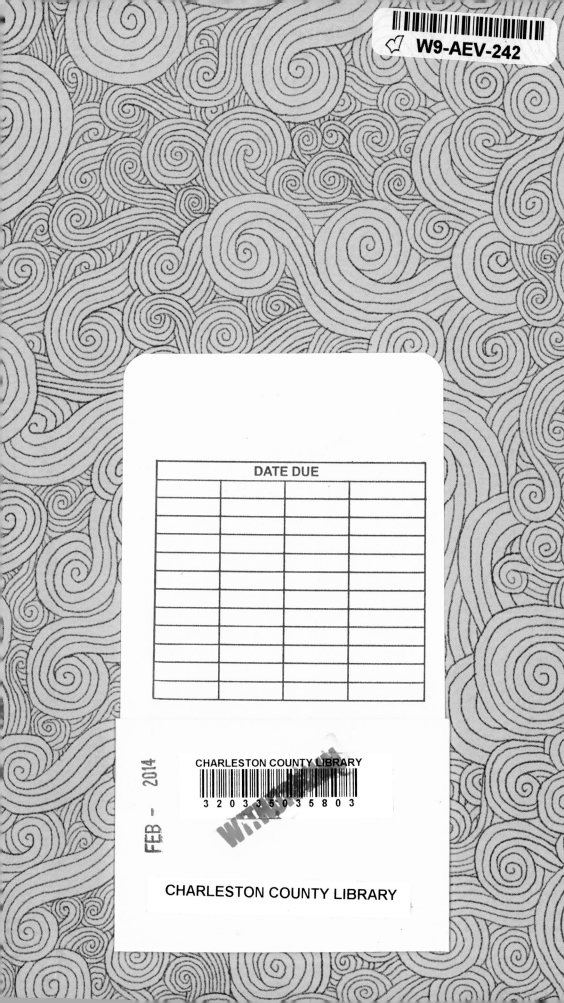

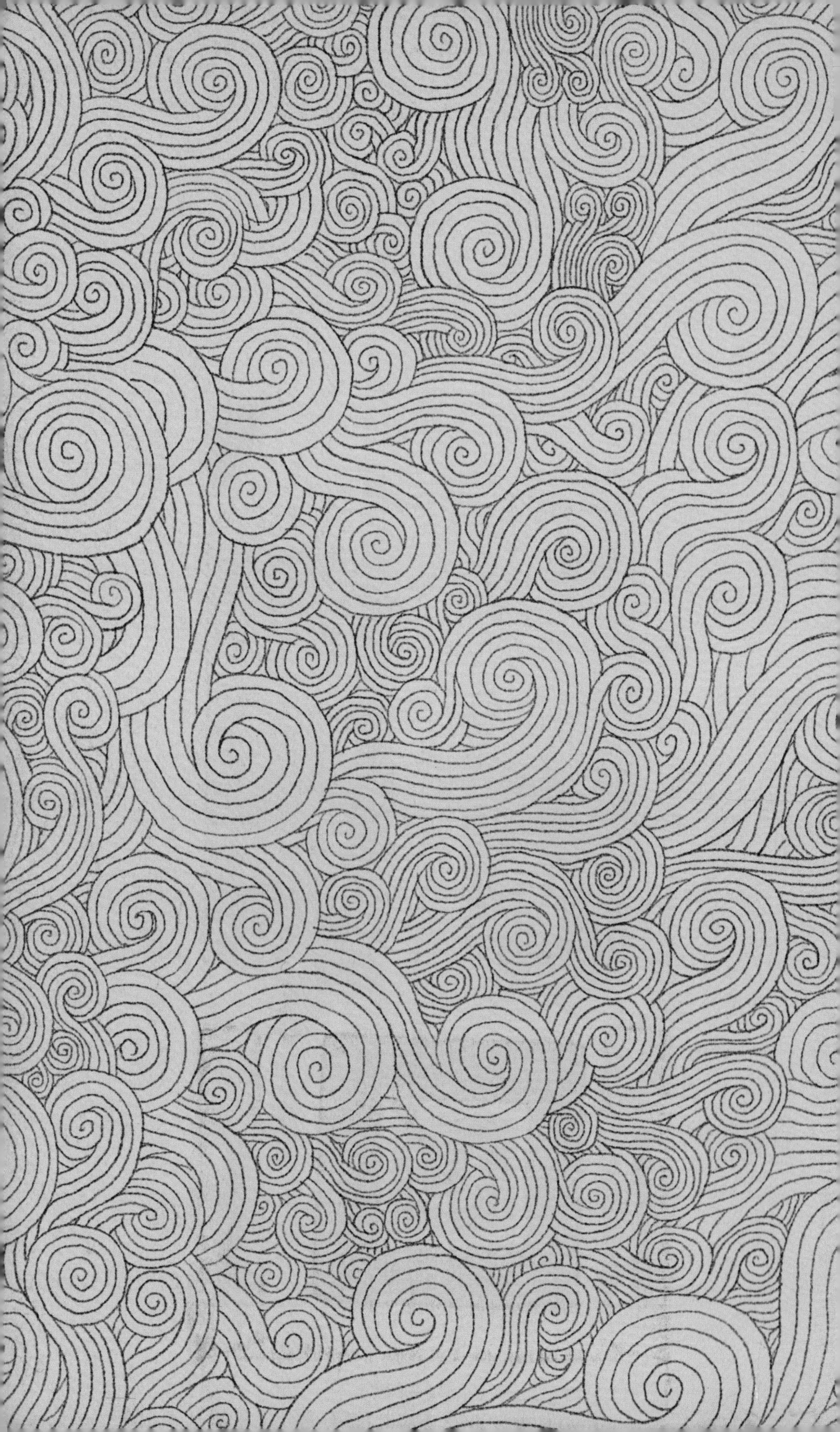

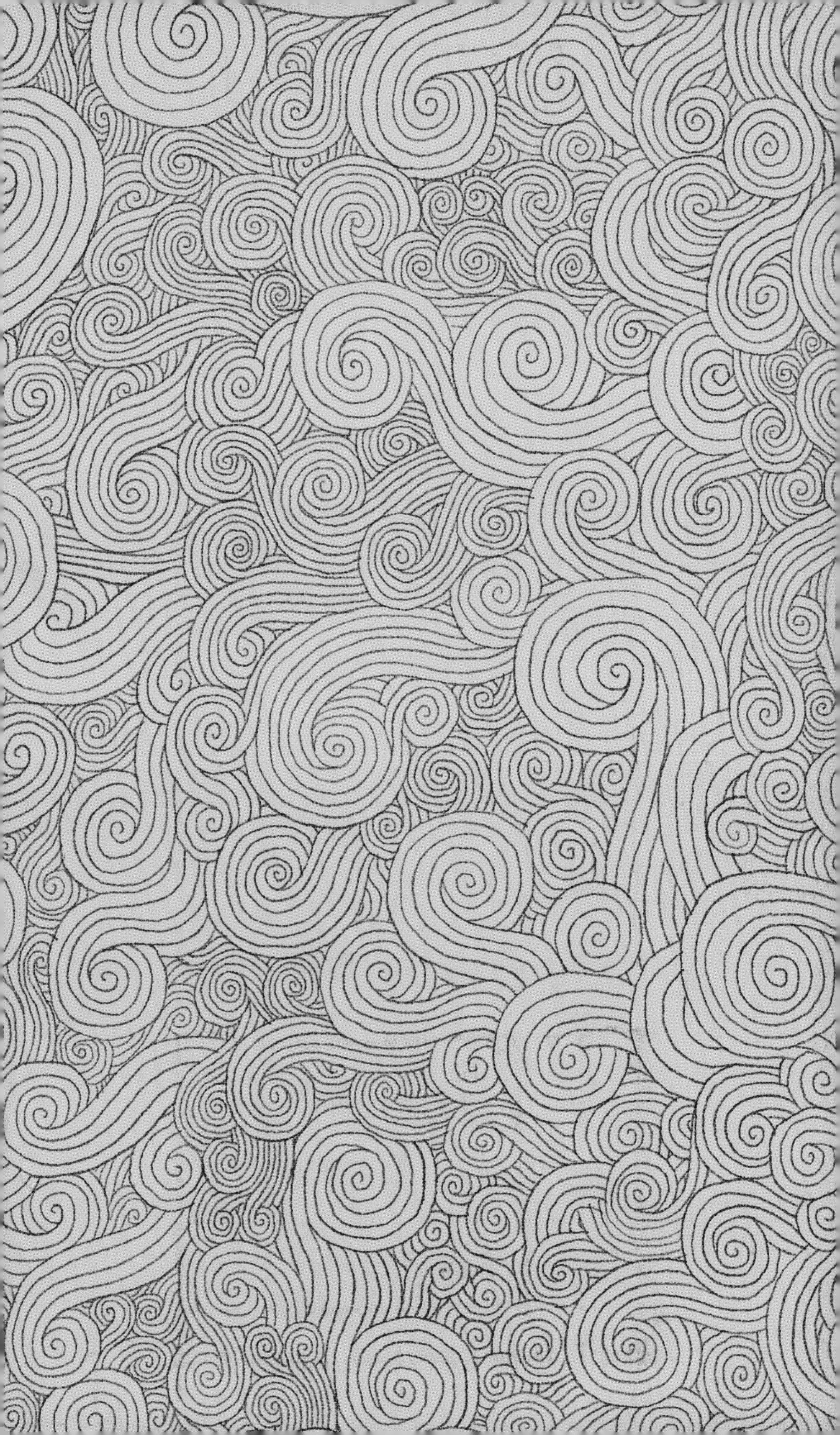

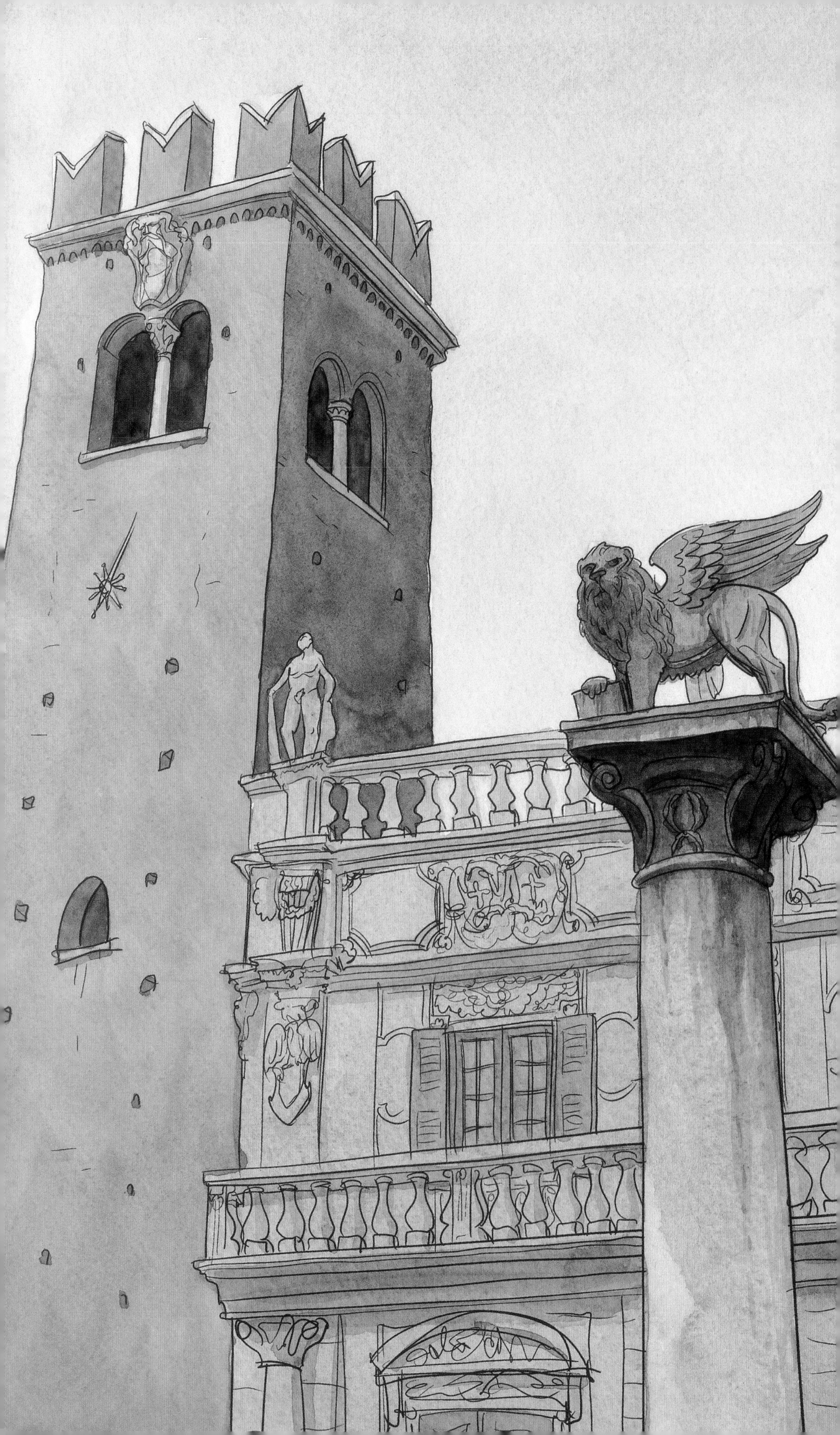

The Most Excellent and Lamentable Tragedy of

Romeo & Juliet

a play by William Shakespeare

adapted and illustrated by Gareth Hinds

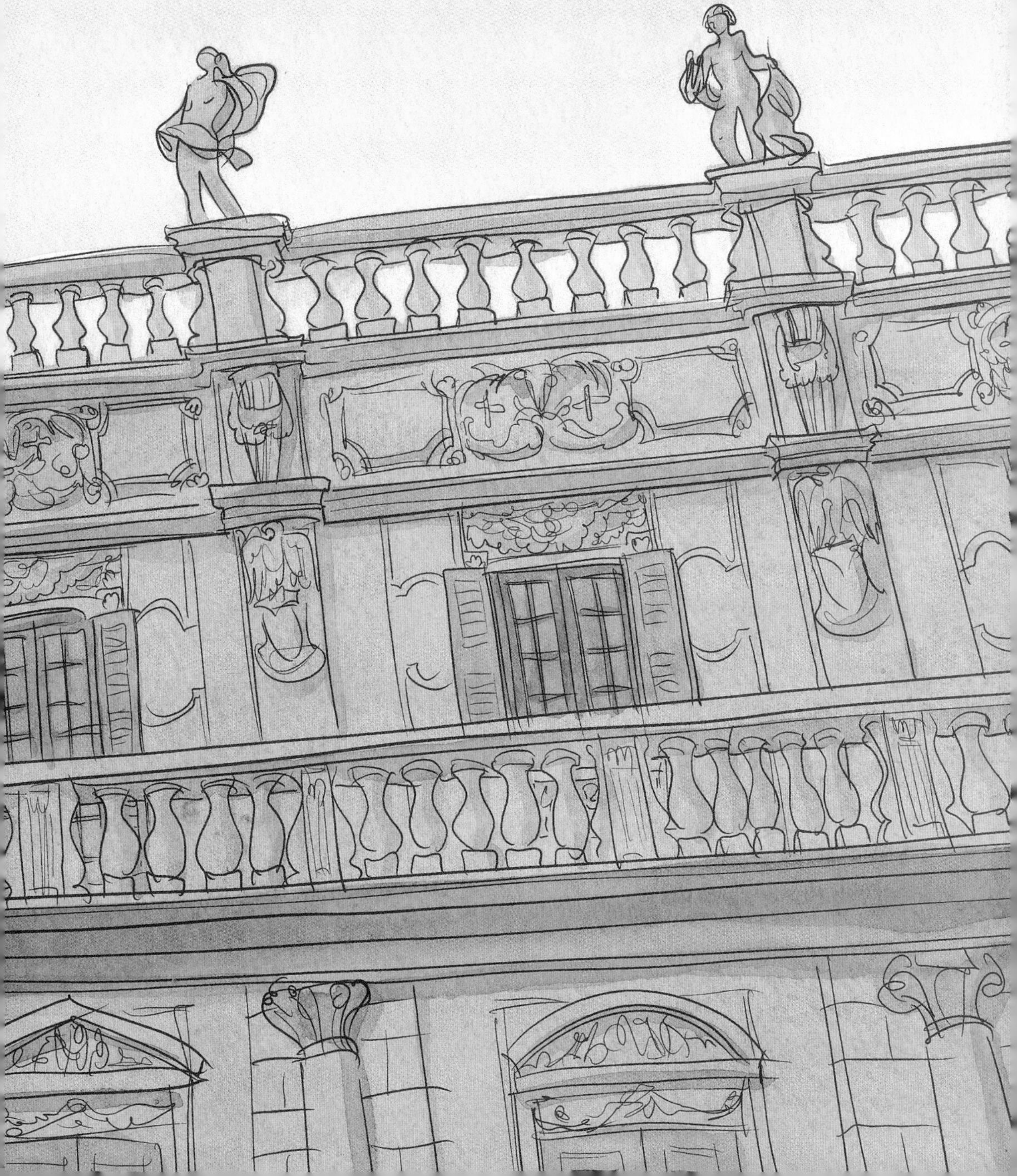

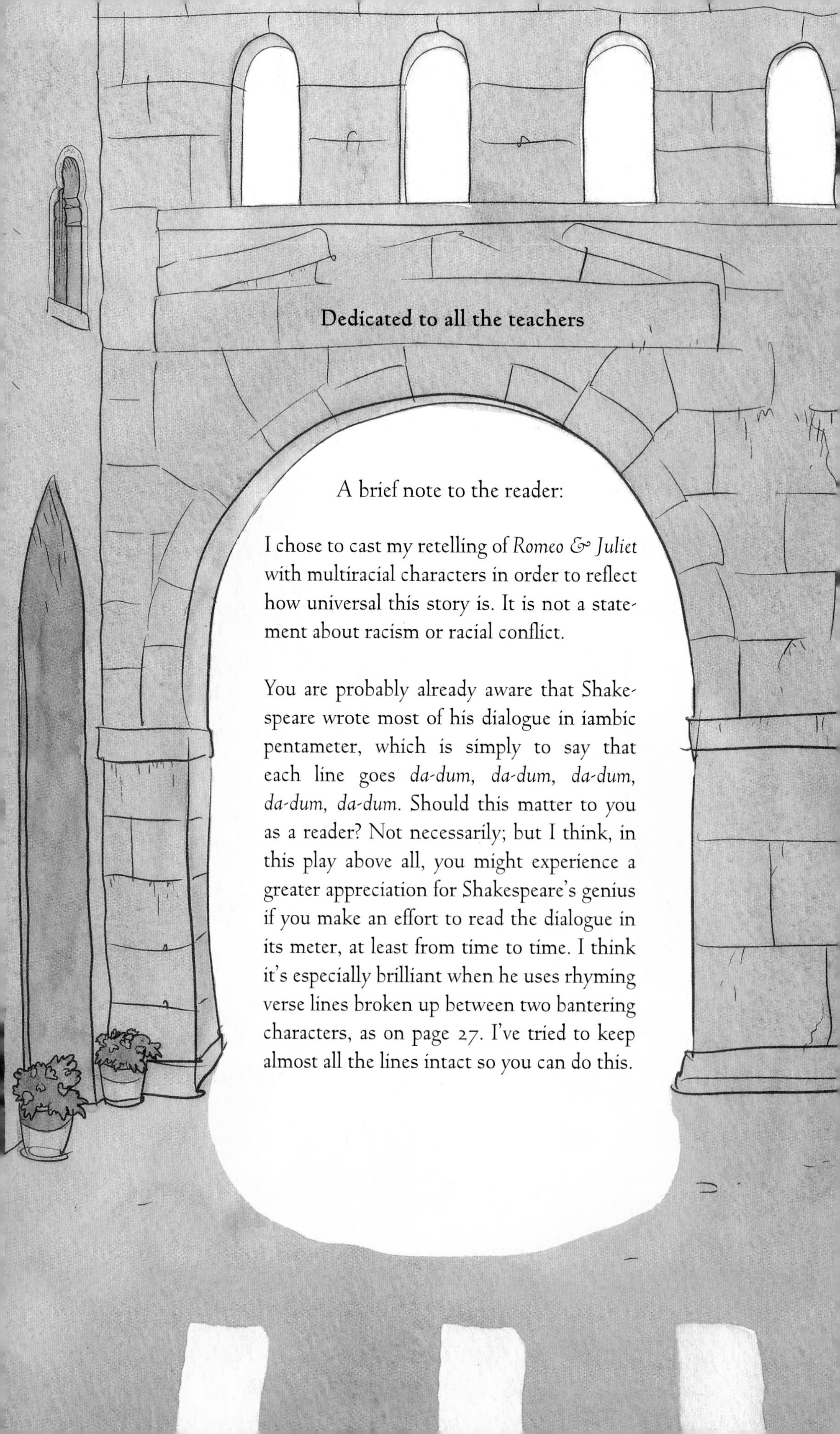

Dedicated to all the teachers

A brief note to the reader:

I chose to cast my retelling of *Romeo & Juliet* with multiracial characters in order to reflect how universal this story is. It is not a statement about racism or racial conflict.

You are probably already aware that Shakespeare wrote most of his dialogue in iambic pentameter, which is simply to say that each line goes *da-dum, da-dum, da-dum, da-dum, da-dum*. Should this matter to you as a reader? Not necessarily; but I think, in this play above all, you might experience a greater appreciation for Shakespeare's genius if you make an effort to read the dialogue in its meter, at least from time to time. I think it's especially brilliant when he uses rhyming verse lines broken up between two bantering characters, as on page 27. I've tried to keep almost all the lines intact so you can do this.

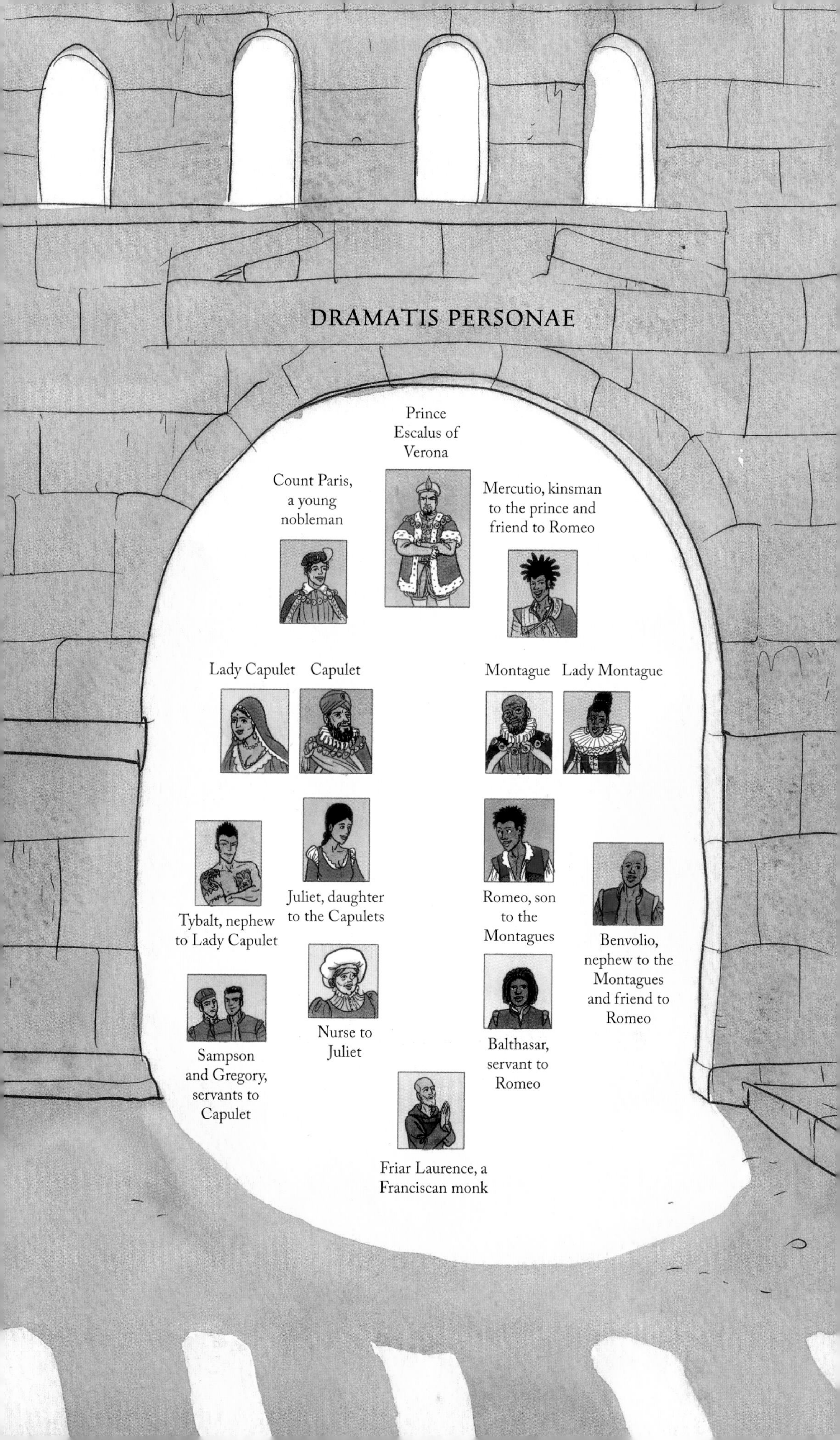
DRAMATIS PERSONAE
Prince Escalus of Verona
Count Paris, a young nobleman
Mercutio, kinsman to the prince and friend to Romeo
Lady Capulet
Capulet
Montague
Lady Montague
Tybalt, nephew to Lady Capulet
Juliet, daughter to the Capulets
Romeo, son to the Montagues
Benvolio, nephew to the Montagues and friend to Romeo
Sampson and Gregory, servants to Capulet
Nurse to Juliet
Balthasar, servant to Romeo
Friar Laurence, a Franciscan monk

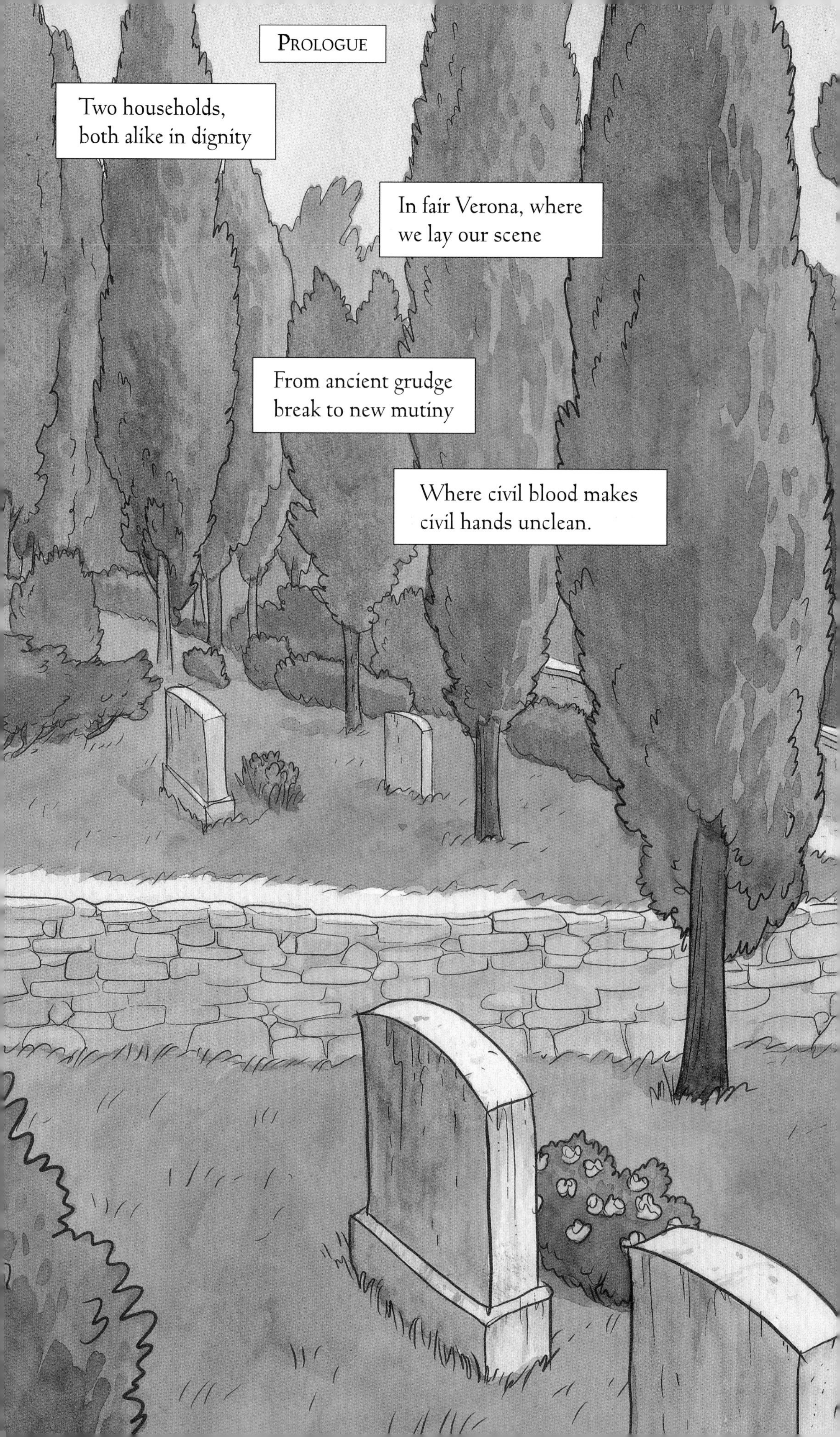

PROLOGUE
Two households, both alike in dignity
In fair Verona, where we lay our scene
From ancient grudge break to new mutiny
Where civil blood makes civil hands unclean.

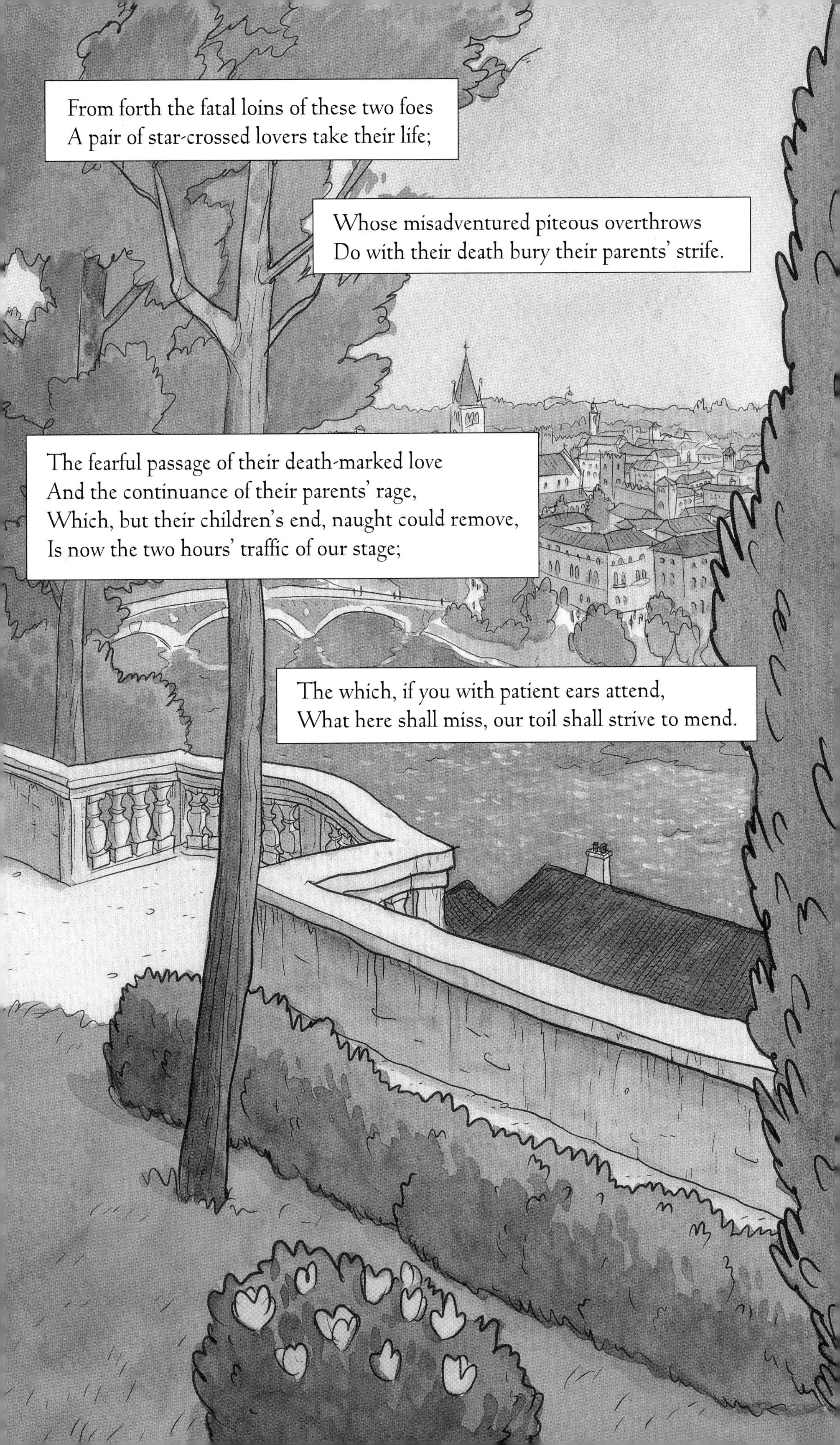
From forth the fatal loins of these two foes
A pair of star-crossed lovers take their life;
Whose misadventured piteous overthrows
Do with their death bury their parents' strife.
The fearful passage of their death-marked love
And the continuance of their parents' rage,
Which, but their children's end, naught could remove,
Is now the two hours' traffic of our stage;
The which, if you with patient ears attend,
What here shall miss, our toil shall strive to mend.

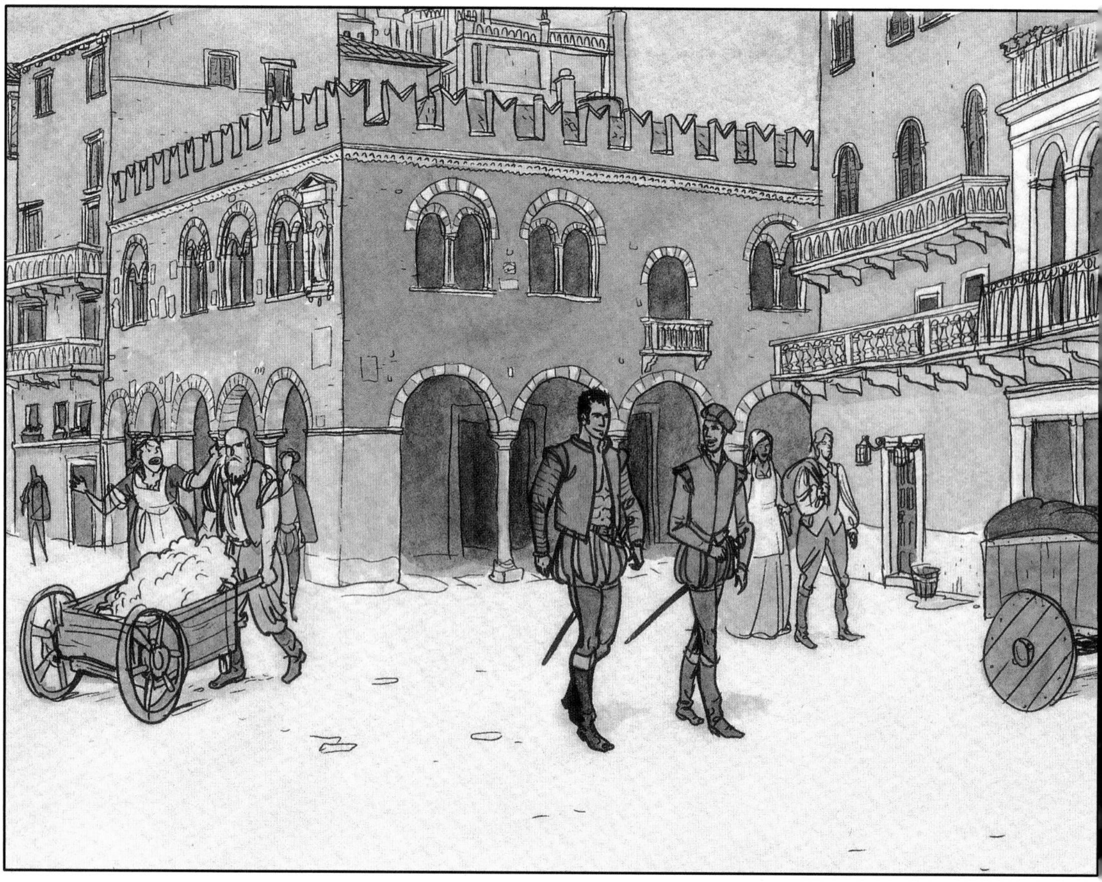

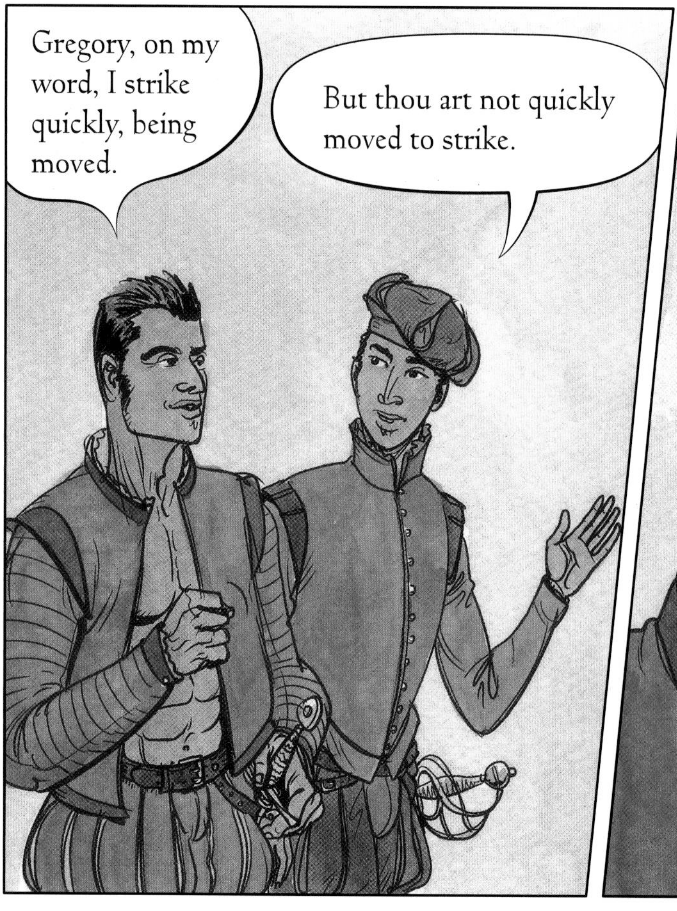
Gregory, on my word, I strike quickly, being moved.
But thou art not quickly moved to strike.

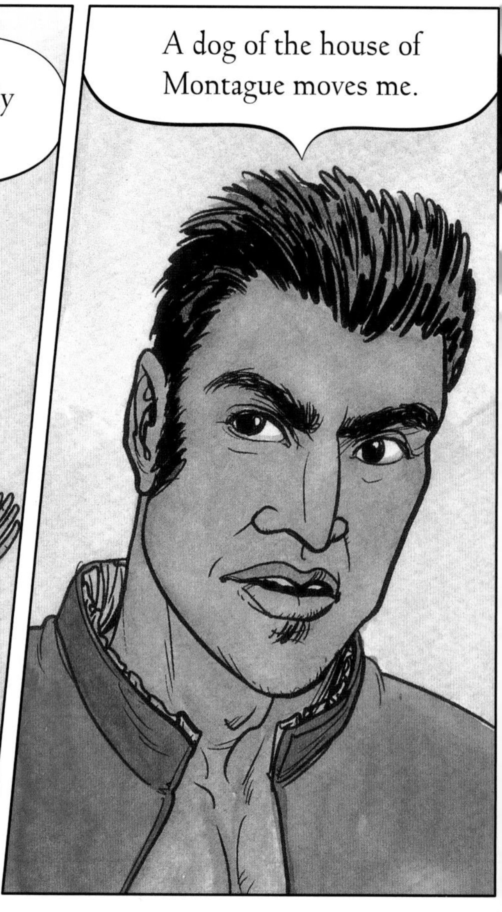
A dog of the house of Montague moves me.

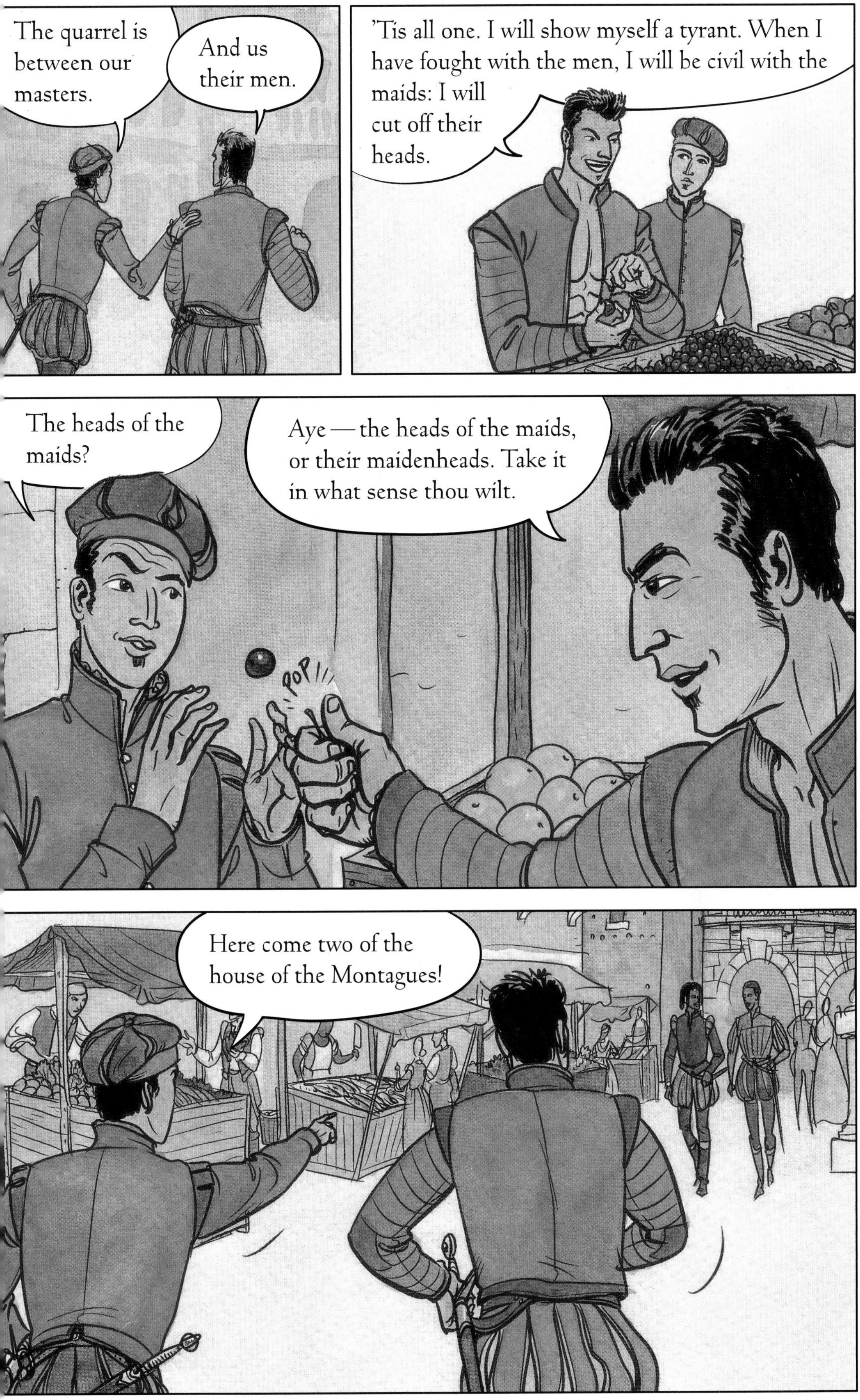
The quarrel is between our masters.
And us their men.
'Tis all one. I will show myself a tyrant. When I have fought with the men, I will be civil with the maids: I will cut off their heads.
The heads of the maids?
Aye — the heads of the maids, or their maidenheads. Take it in what sense thou wilt.
POP
Here come two of the house of the Montagues!

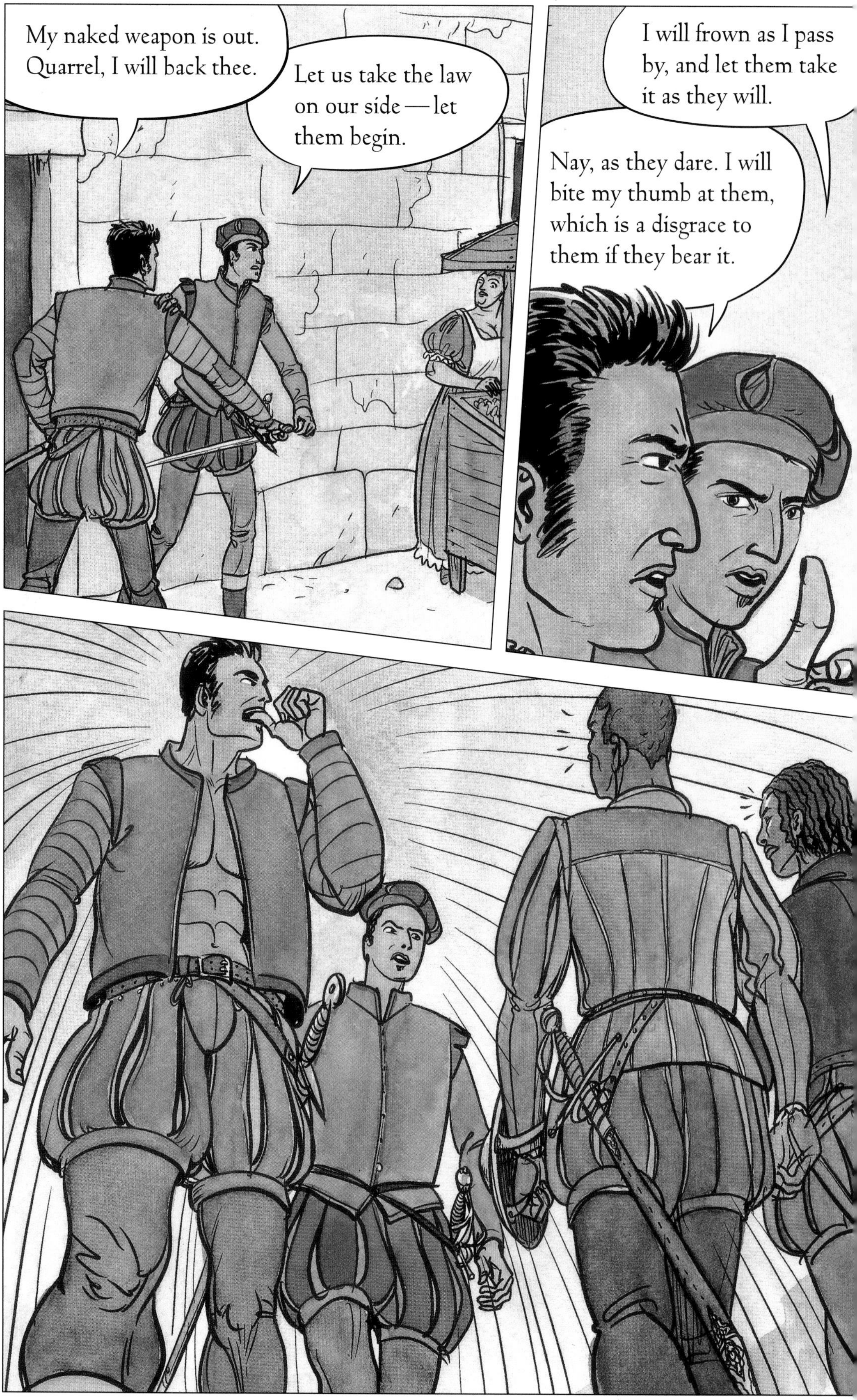
My naked weapon is out. Quarrel, I will back thee.
Let us take the law on our side — let them begin.
I will frown as I pass by, and let them take it as they will.
Nay, as they dare. I will bite my thumb at them, which is a disgrace to them if they bear it.

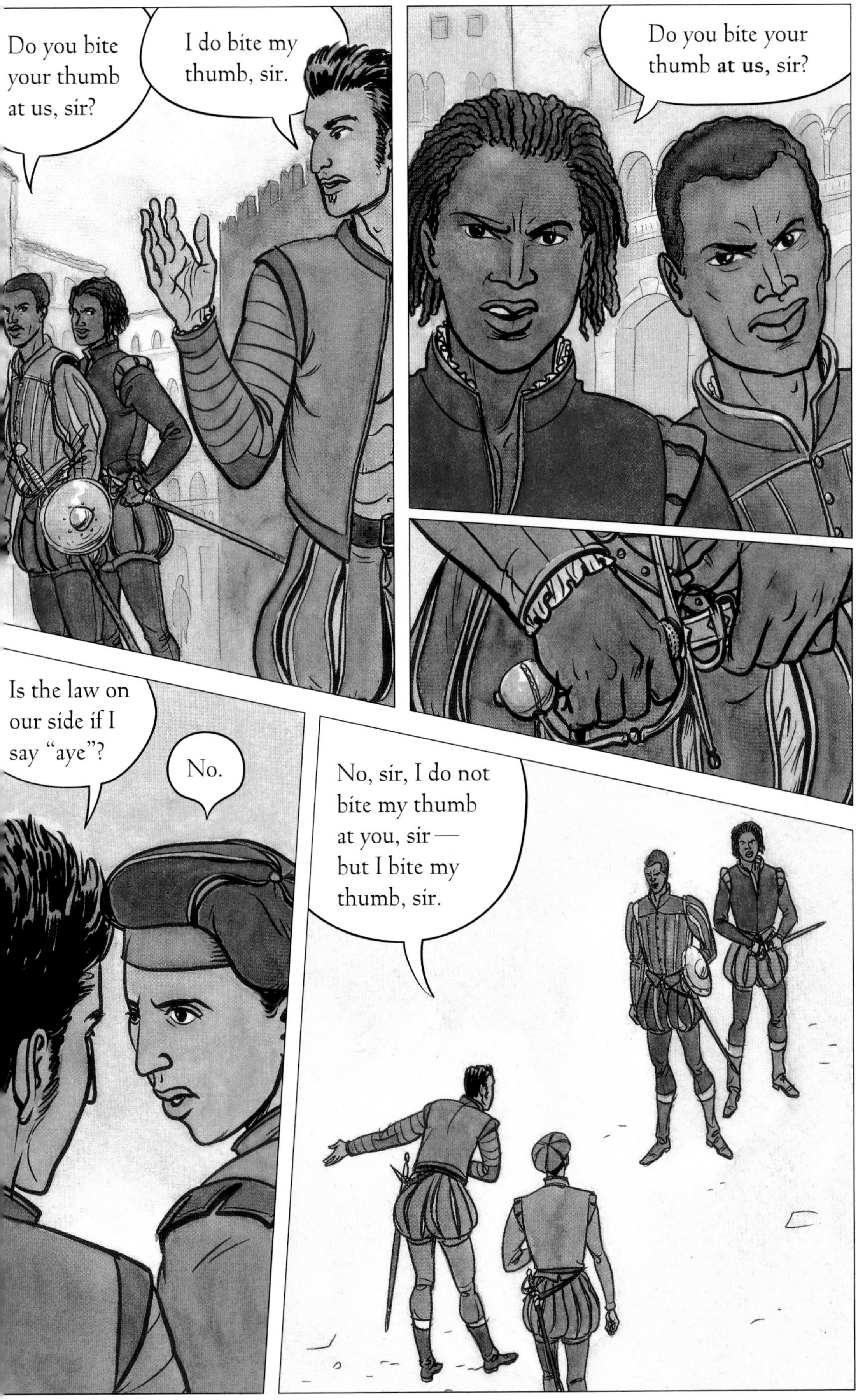
Do you bite your thumb at us, sir?
I do bite my thumb, sir.
Do you bite your thumb **at us,** sir?
Is the law on our side if I say "aye"?
No.
No, sir, I do not bite my thumb at you, sir — but I bite my thumb, sir.

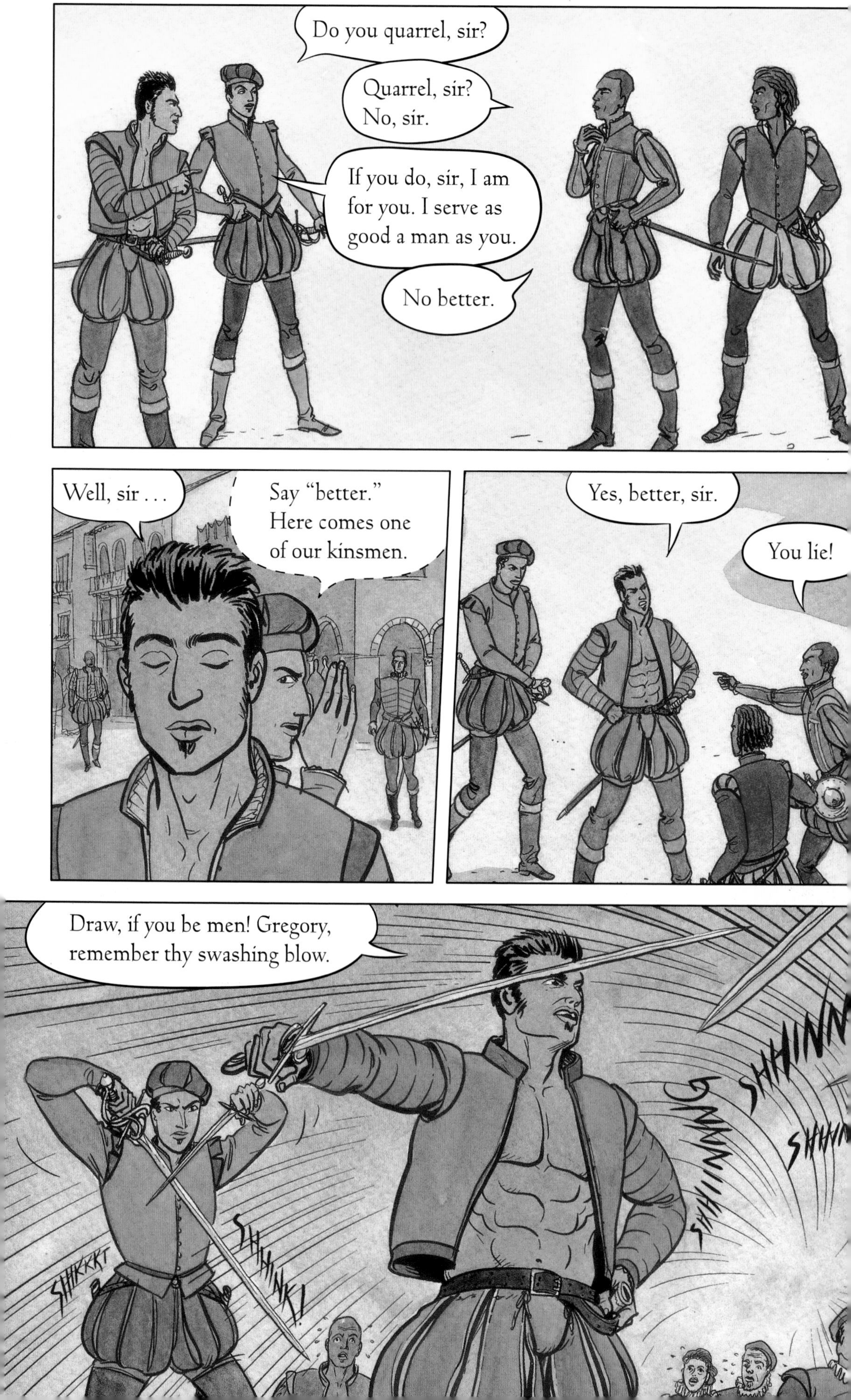
Do you quarrel, sir?
Quarrel, sir? No, sir.
If you do, sir, I am for you. I serve as good a man as you.
No better.
Well, sir . . .
Say "better." Here comes one of our kinsmen.
Yes, better, sir.
You lie!
Draw, if you be men! Gregory, remember thy swashing blow.
SHKKKT
SHHINK!
SHHINNNNG
SHHINN

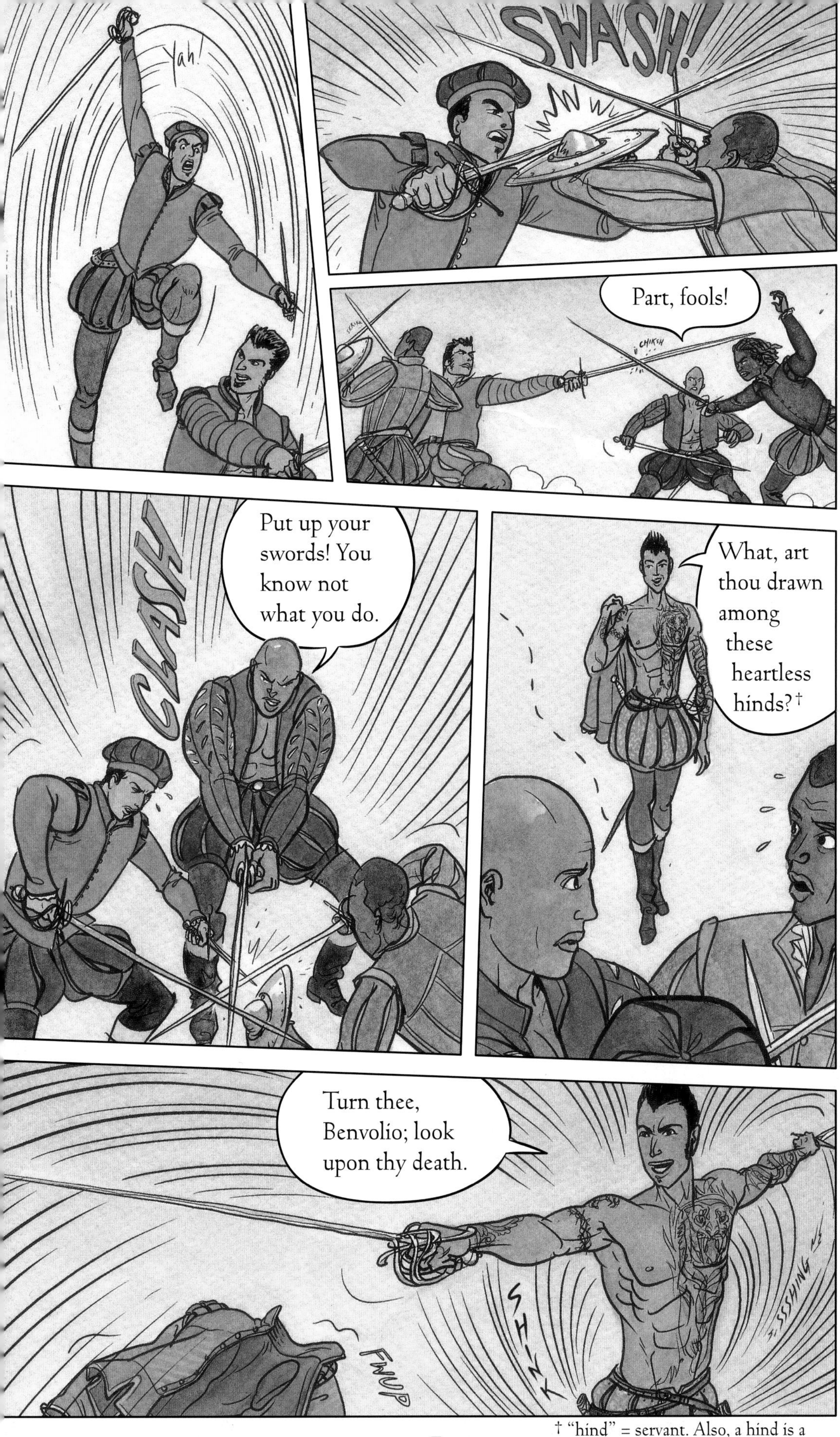
Yah!
SWASH!
Part, fools!
CHIKSH
CLASH
Put up your swords! You know not what you do.
What, art thou drawn among these heartless hinds?†
Turn thee, Benvolio; look upon thy death.
SHINK
SSSHING
FWUP

† "hind" = servant. Also, a hind is a female deer, and a hart is a male deer, so "heartless" is an added pun.

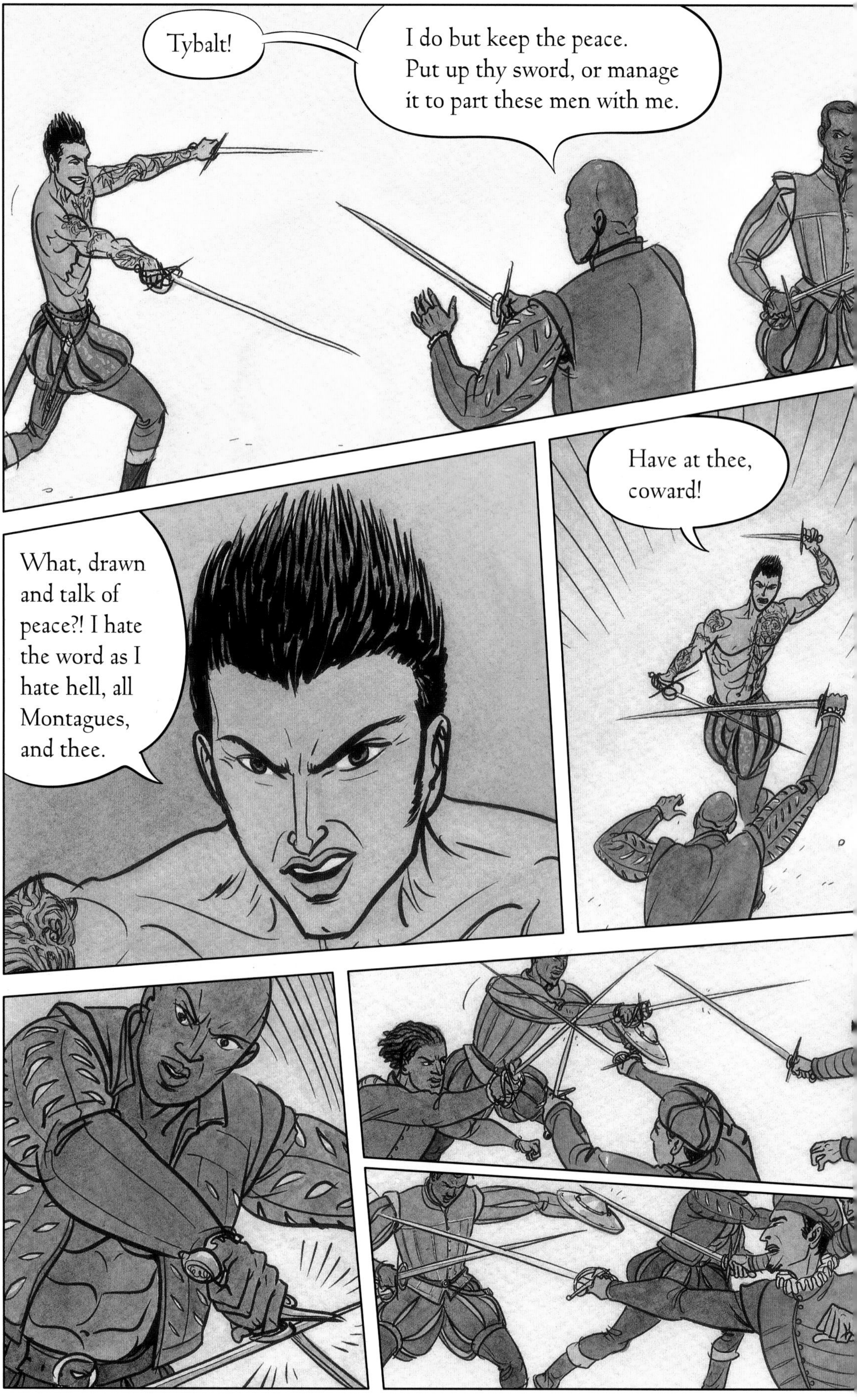
Tybalt!
I do but keep the peace. Put up thy sword, or manage it to part these men with me.
What, drawn and talk of peace?! I hate the word as I hate hell, all Montagues, and thee.
Have at thee, coward!

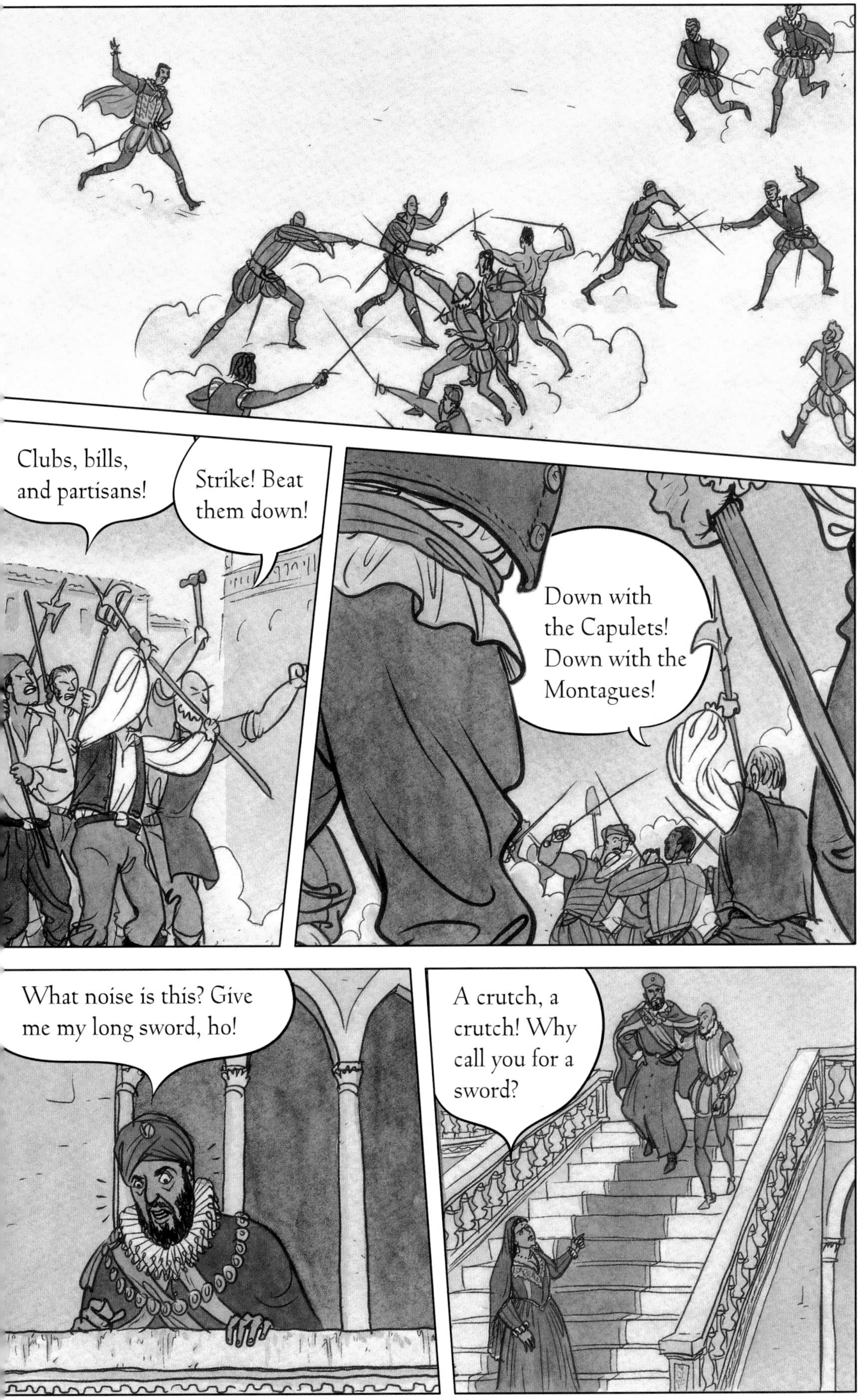
Clubs, bills, and partisans!
Strike! Beat them down!
Down with the Capulets! Down with the Montagues!
What noise is this? Give me my long sword, ho!
A crutch, a crutch! Why call you for a sword?

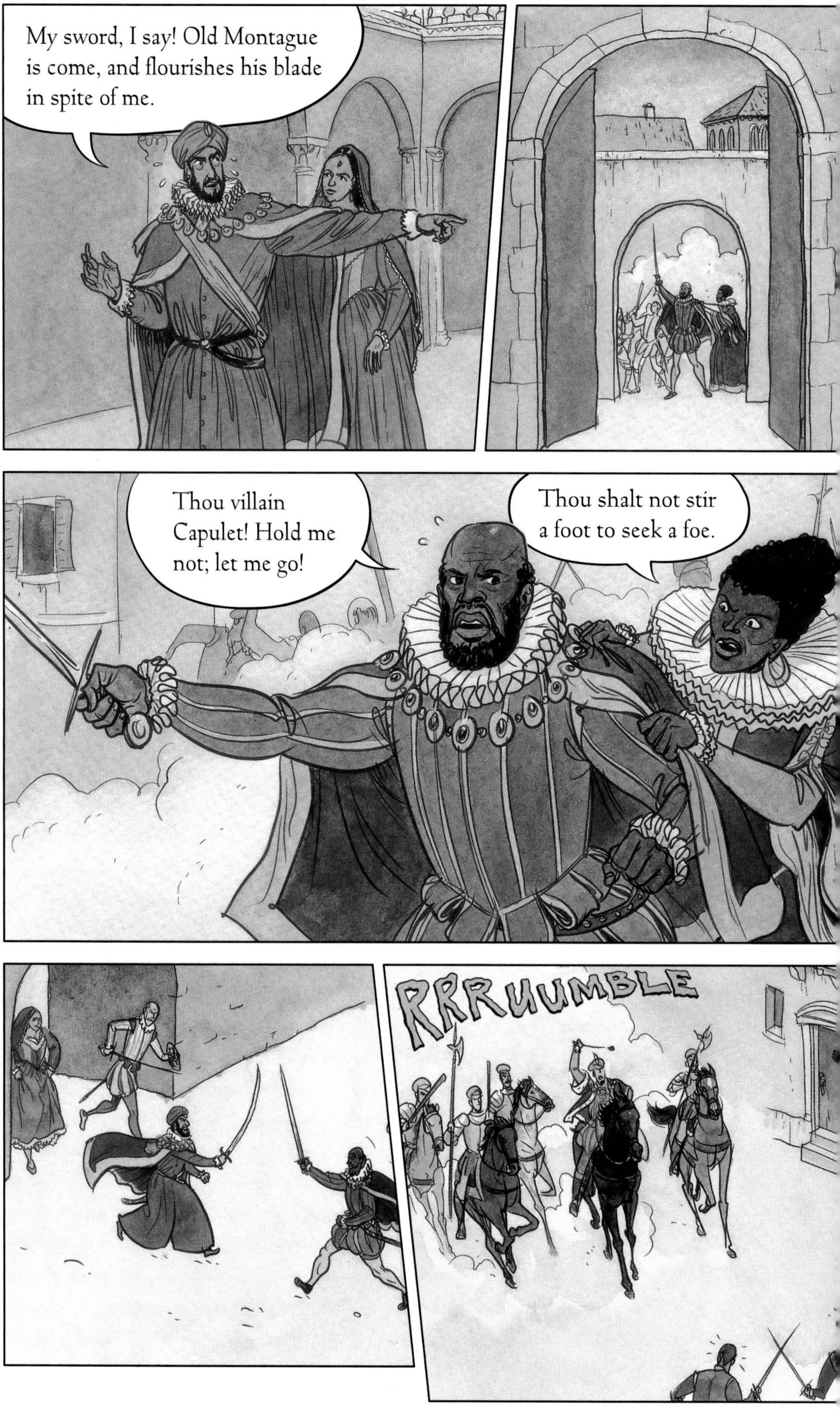
My sword, I say! Old Montague is come, and flourishes his blade in spite of me.
Thou villain Capulet! Hold me not; let me go!
Thou shalt not stir a foot to seek a foe.
RRRUUMBLE

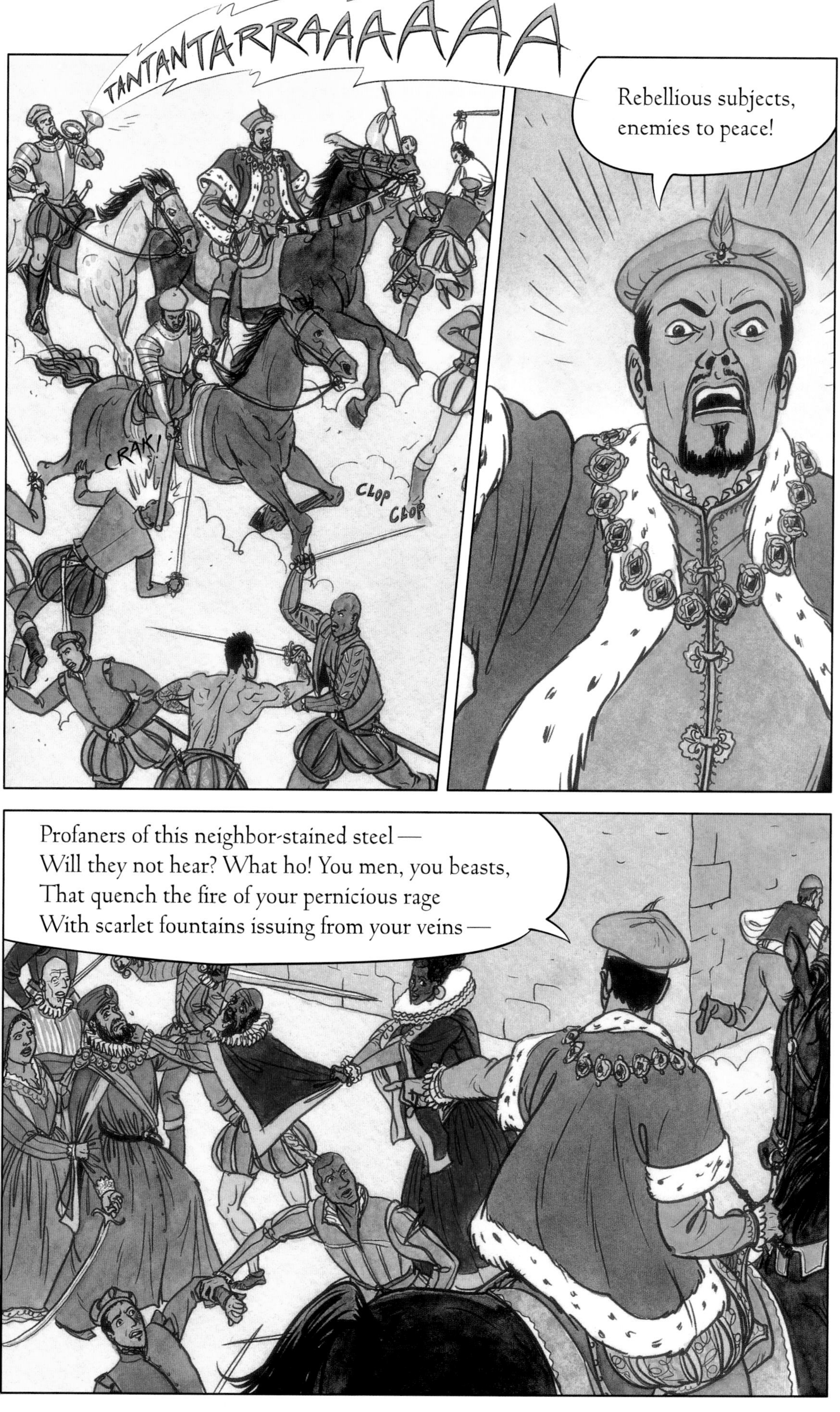
TANTANTARRAAAAAA
CRAK!
CLOP
CLOP
Rebellious subjects, enemies to peace!
Profaners of this neighbor-stained steel—
Will they not hear? What ho! You men, you beasts,
That quench the fire of your pernicious rage
With scarlet fountains issuing from your veins—

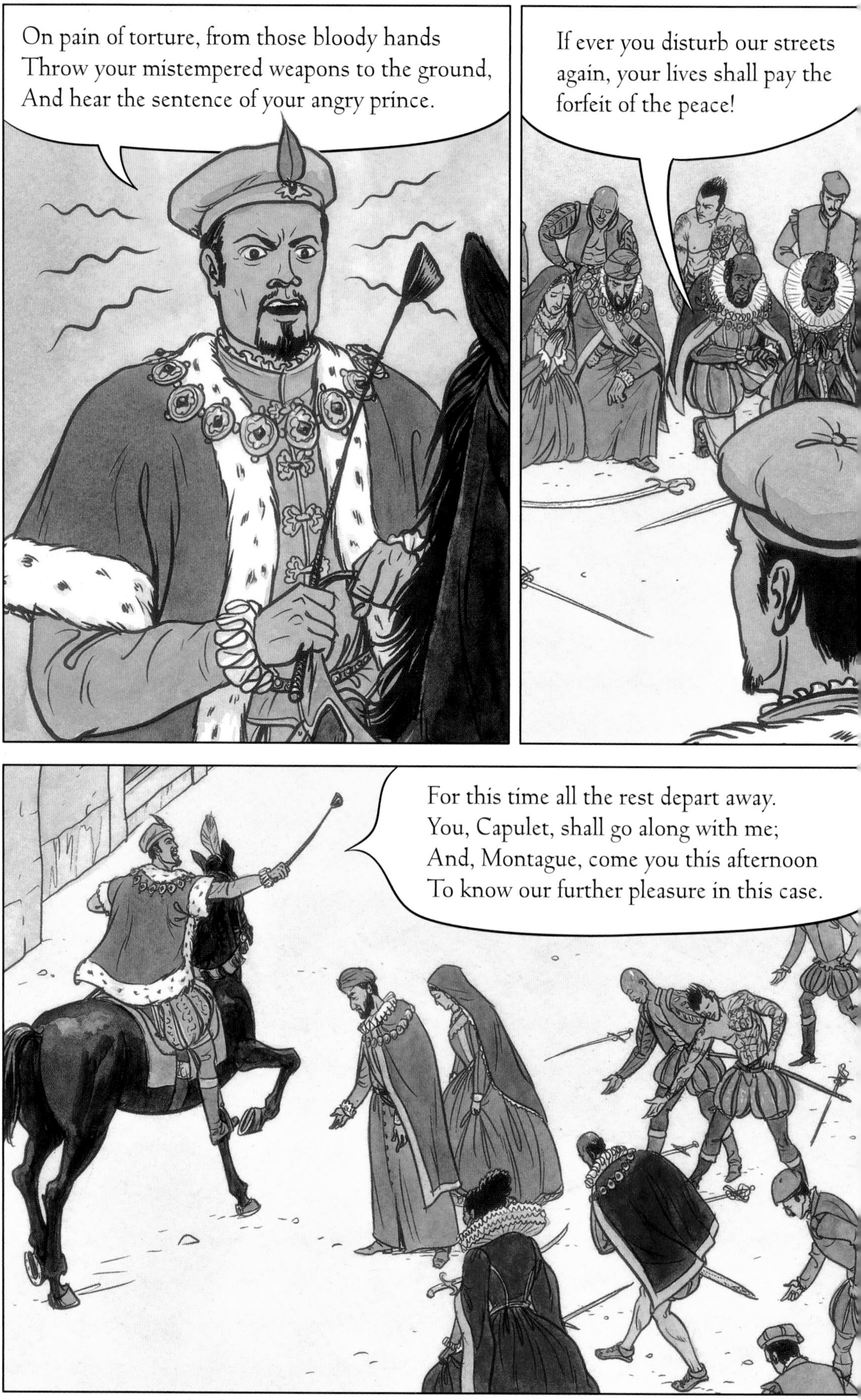
On pain of torture, from those bloody hands Throw your mistempered weapons to the ground, And hear the sentence of your angry prince.
If ever you disturb our streets again, your lives shall pay the forfeit of the peace!
For this time all the rest depart away. You, Capulet, shall go along with me; And, Montague, come you this afternoon To know our further pleasure in this case.

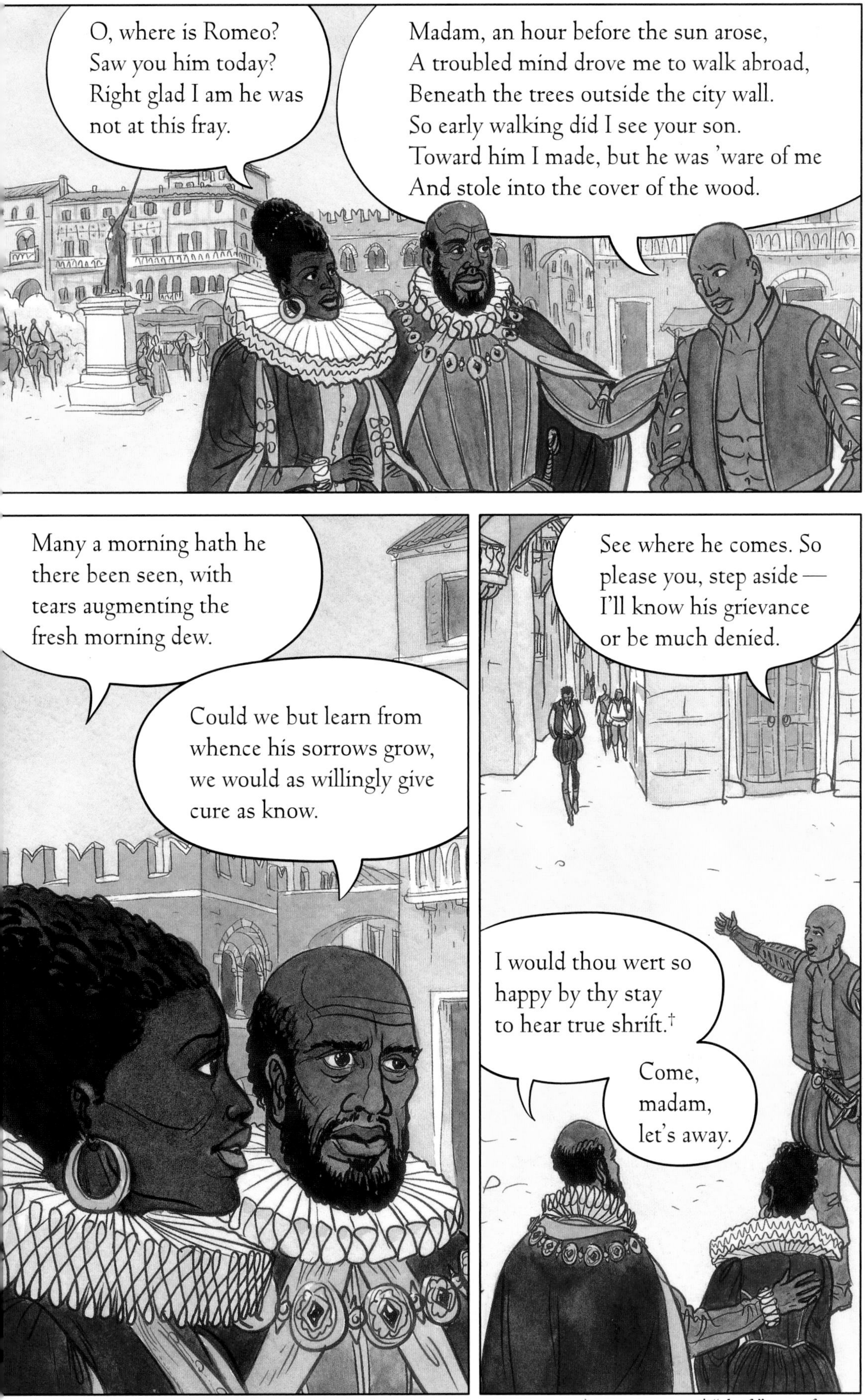
O, where is Romeo? Saw you him today? Right glad I am he was not at this fray.
Madam, an hour before the sun arose,
A troubled mind drove me to walk abroad,
Beneath the trees outside the city wall.
So early walking did I see your son.
Toward him I made, but he was 'ware of me
And stole into the cover of the wood.
Many a morning hath he there been seen, with tears augmenting the fresh morning dew.
Could we but learn from whence his sorrows grow, we would as willingly give cure as know.
See where he comes. So please you, step aside — I'll know his grievance or be much denied.
I would thou wert so happy by thy stay to hear true shrift.†
Come, madam, let's away.

† "shrift" = confession

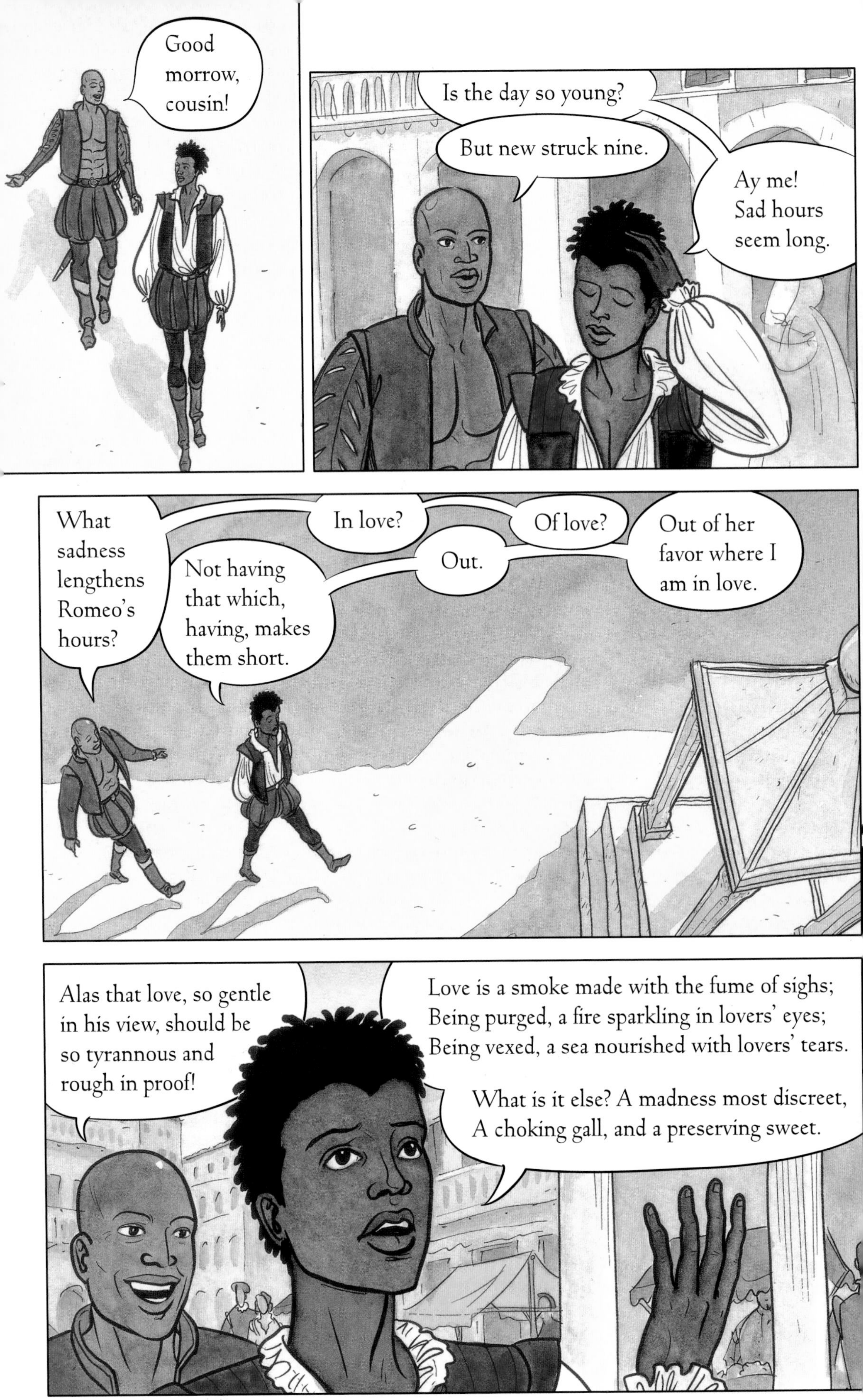
Good morrow, cousin!
Is the day so young?
But new struck nine.
Ay me! Sad hours seem long.
What sadness lengthens Romeo's hours?
Not having that which, having, makes them short.
In love?
Out.
Of love?
Out of her favor where I am in love.
Alas that love, so gentle in his view, should be so tyrannous and rough in proof!
Love is a smoke made with the fume of sighs;
Being purged, a fire sparkling in lovers' eyes;
Being vexed, a sea nourished with lovers' tears.
What is it else? A madness most discreet,
A choking gall, and a preserving sweet.

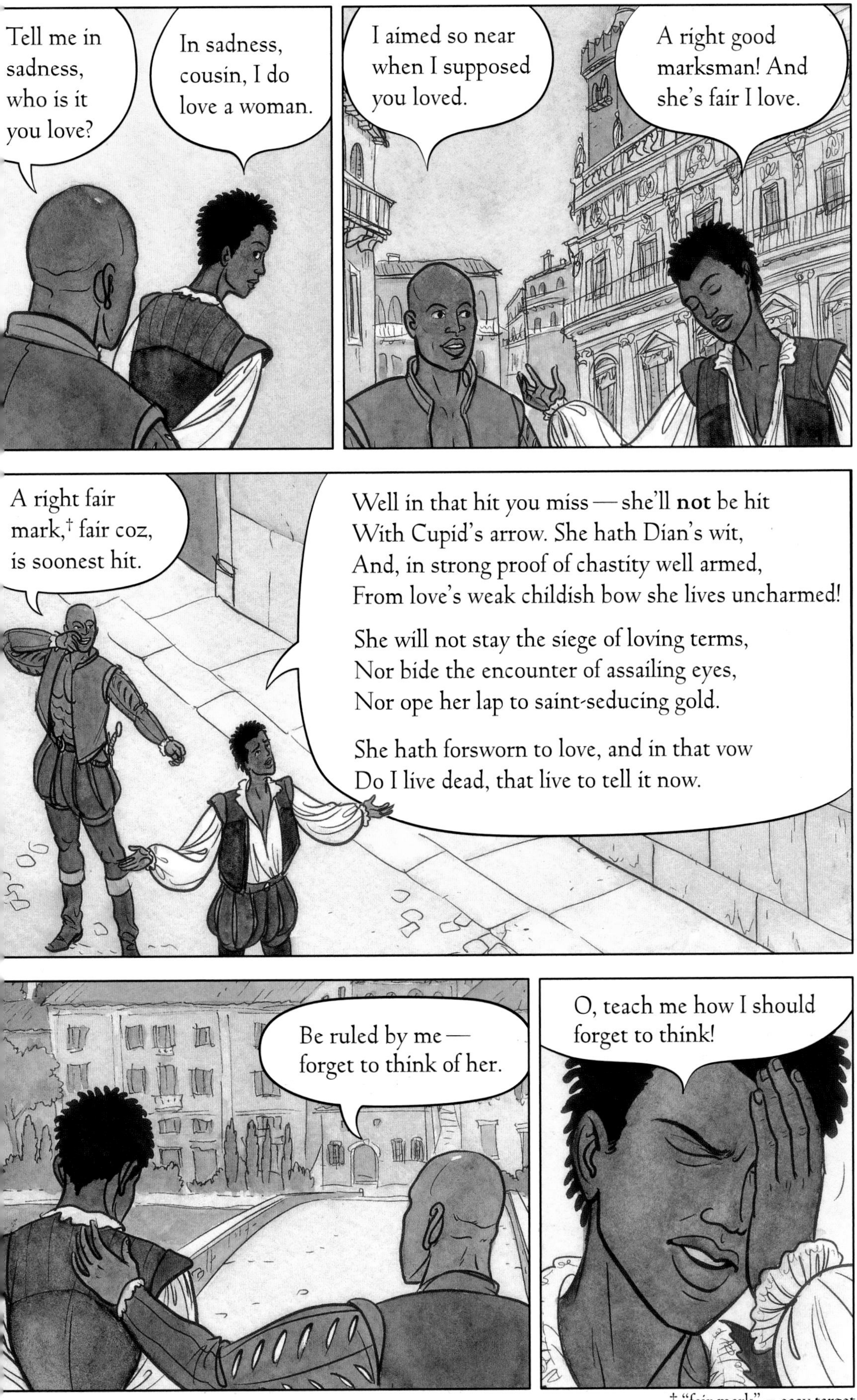
Tell me in sadness, who is it you love?
In sadness, cousin, I do love a woman.
I aimed so near when I supposed you loved.
A right good marksman! And she's fair I love.
A right fair mark,† fair coz, is soonest hit.
Well in that hit you miss — she'll **not** be hit
With Cupid's arrow. She hath Dian's wit,
And, in strong proof of chastity well armed,
From love's weak childish bow she lives uncharmed!
She will not stay the siege of loving terms,
Nor bide the encounter of assailing eyes,
Nor ope her lap to saint-seducing gold.
She hath forsworn to love, and in that vow
Do I live dead, that live to tell it now.
Be ruled by me — forget to think of her.
O, teach me how I should forget to think!

† "fair mark" = easy target

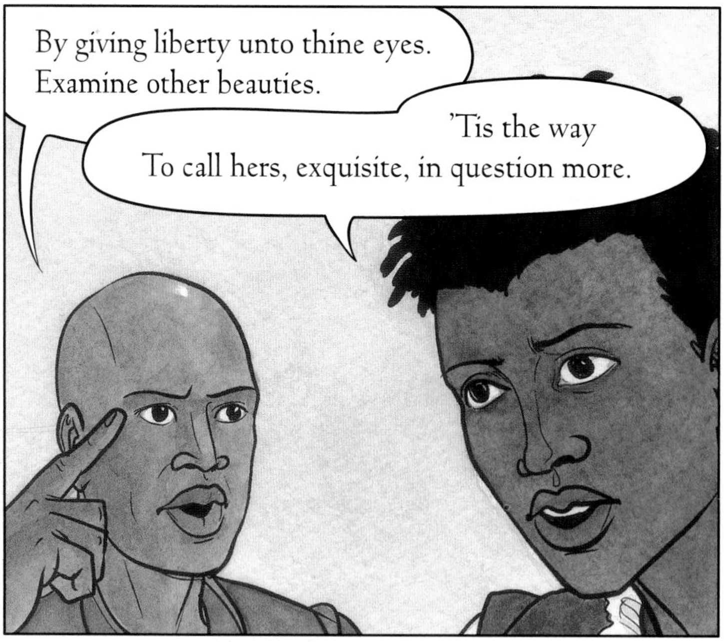
By giving liberty unto thine eyes.
Examine other beauties.
'Tis the way
To call hers, exquisite, in question more.

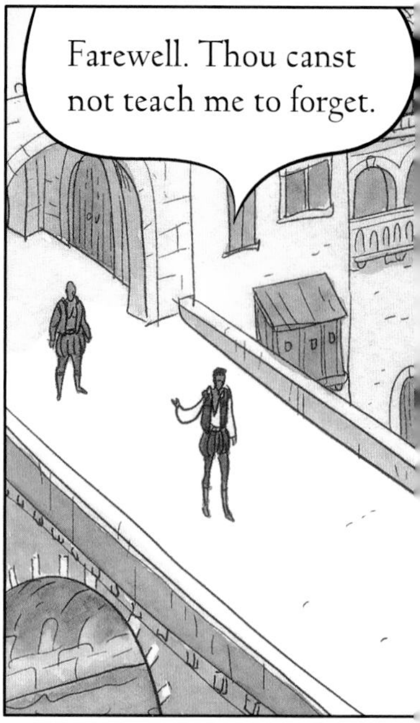
Farewell. Thou canst not teach me to forget.

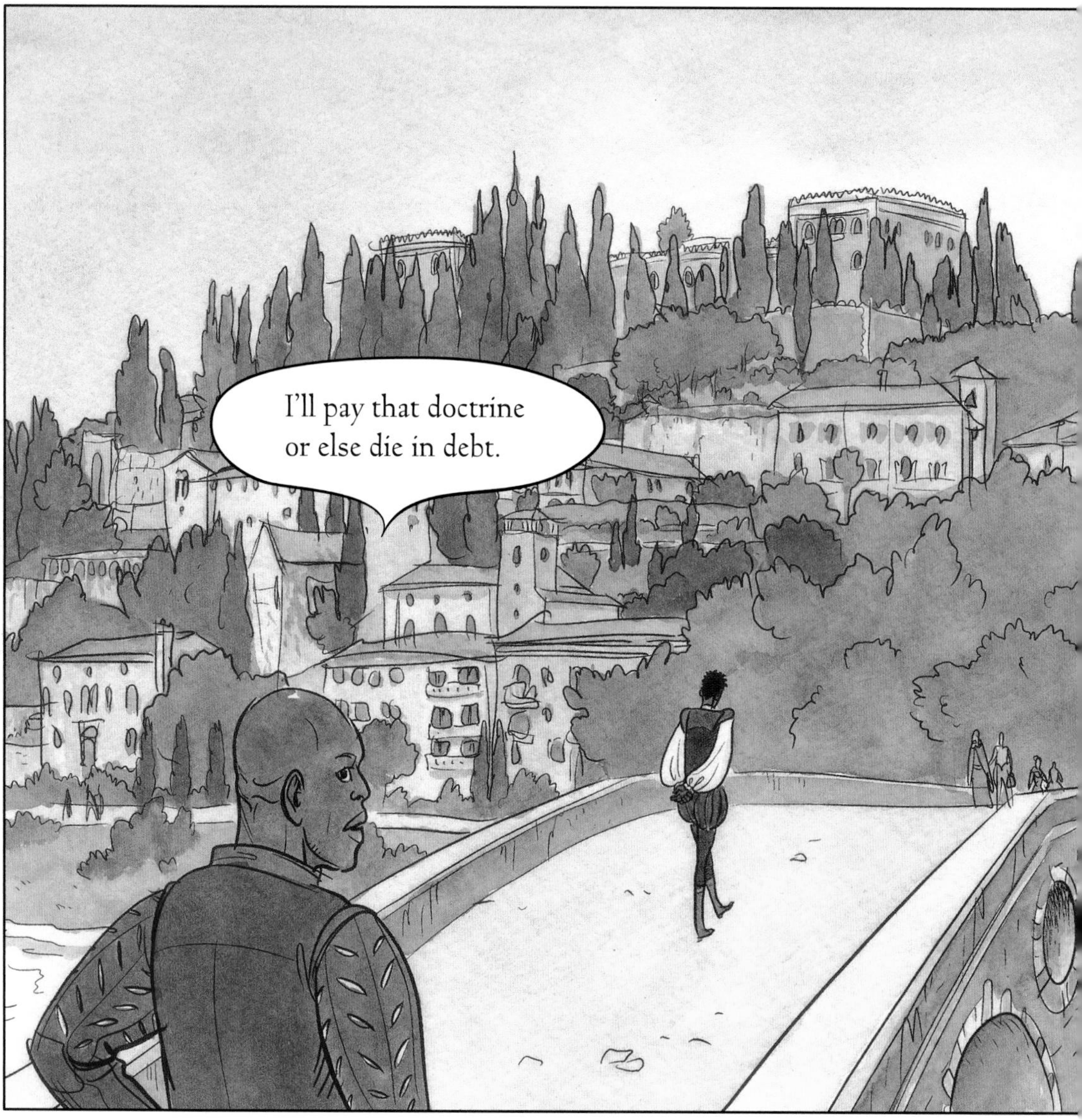
I'll pay that doctrine or else die in debt.

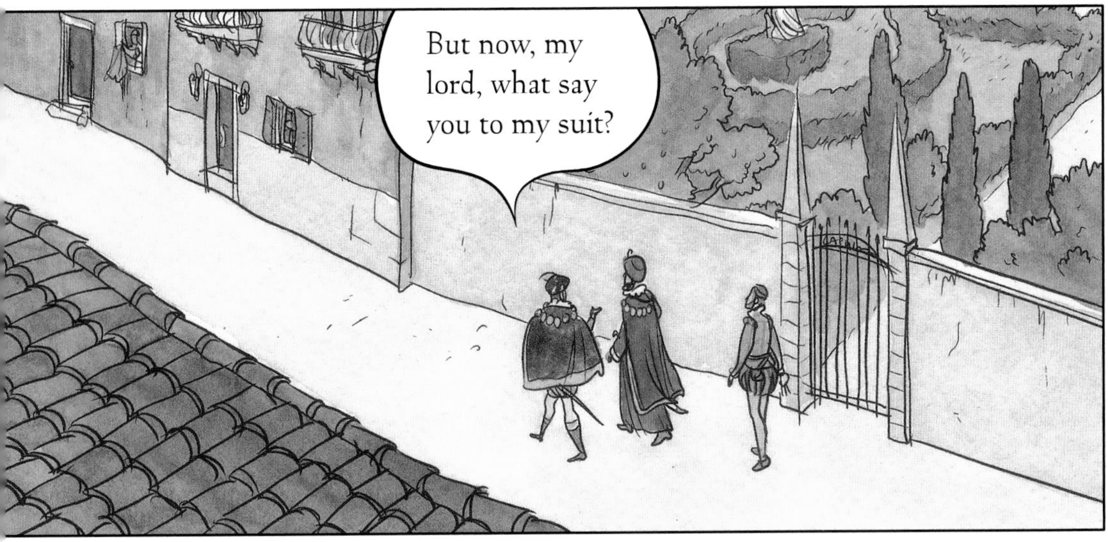
But now, my lord, what say you to my suit?

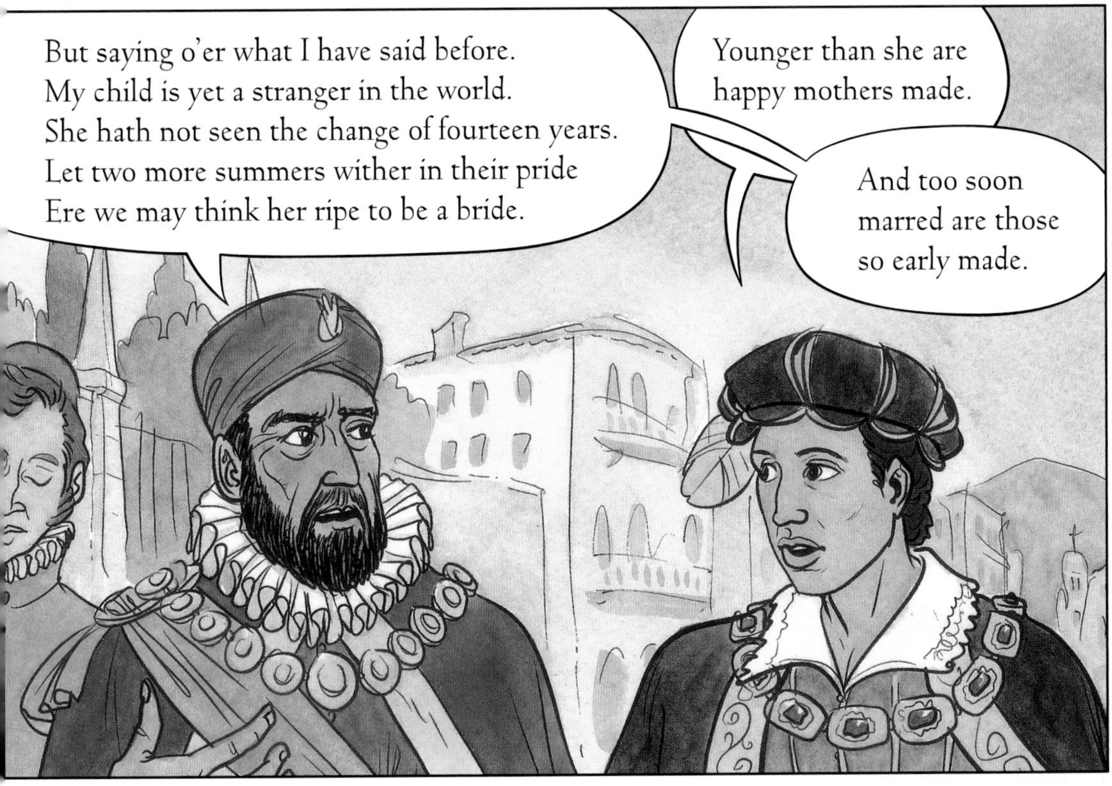
But saying o'er what I have said before.
My child is yet a stranger in the world.
She hath not seen the change of fourteen years.
Let two more summers wither in their pride
Ere we may think her ripe to be a bride.
Younger than she are happy mothers made.
And too soon marred are those so early made.

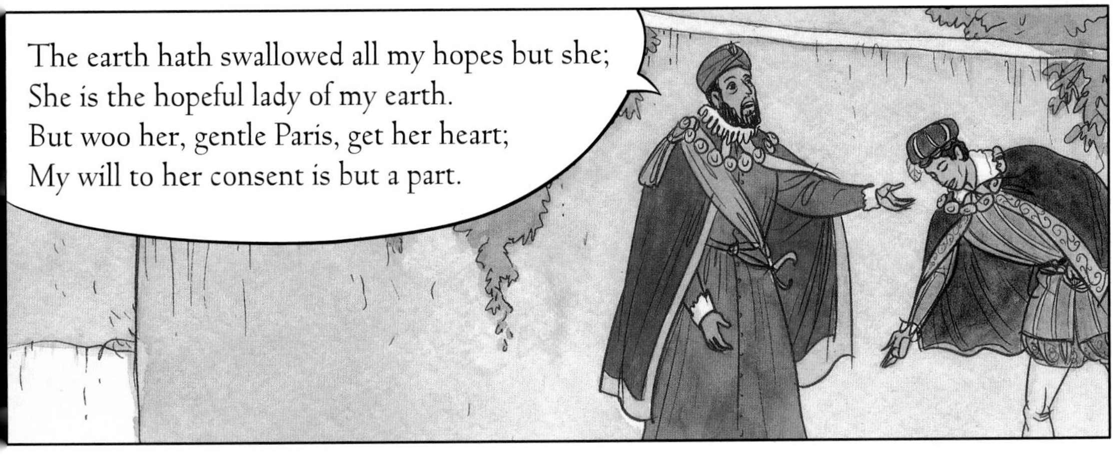
The earth hath swallowed all my hopes but she;
She is the hopeful lady of my earth.
But woo her, gentle Paris, get her heart;
My will to her consent is but a part.

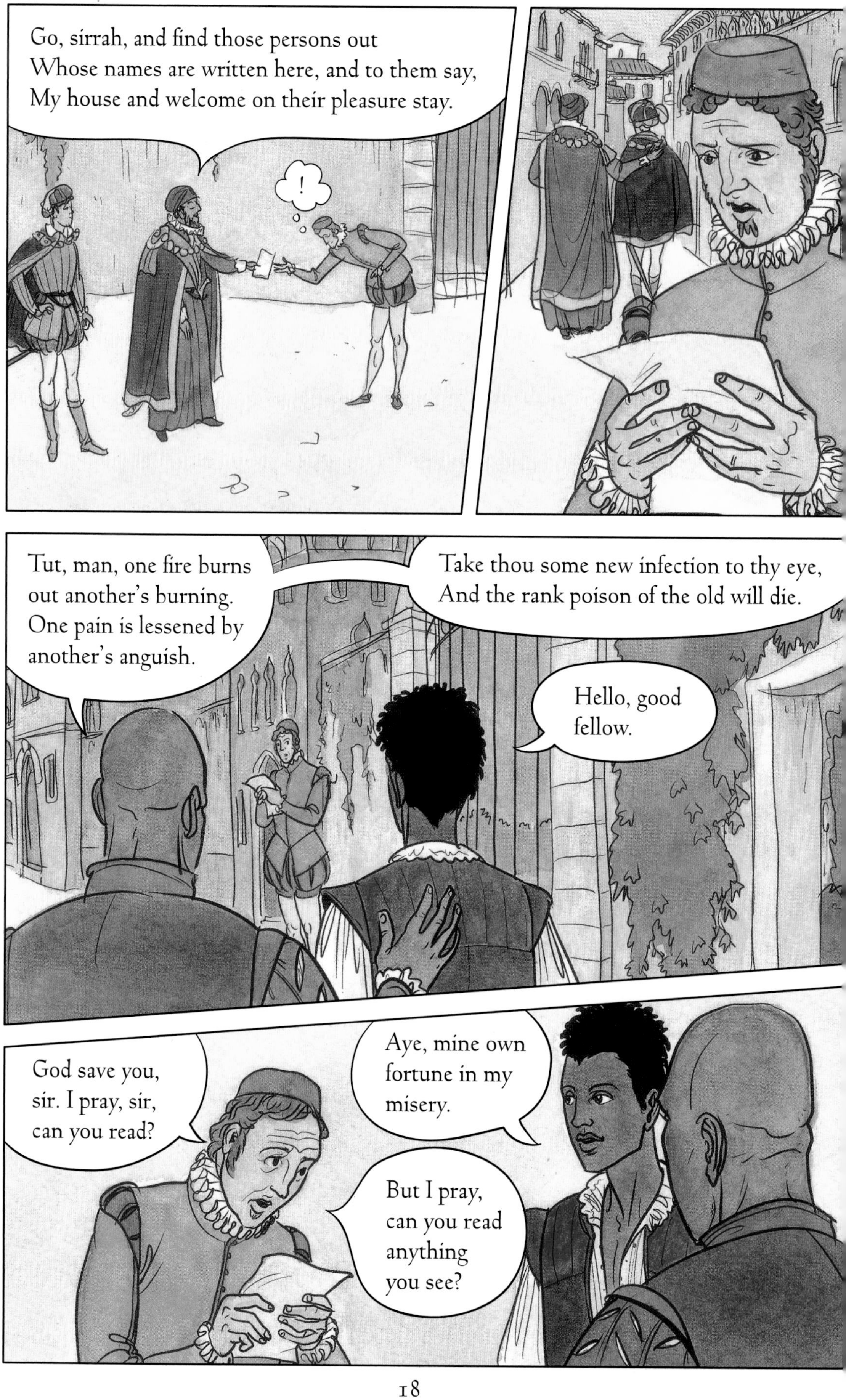
Go, sirrah, and find those persons out
Whose names are written here, and to them say,
My house and welcome on their pleasure stay.
!
Tut, man, one fire burns out another's burning. One pain is lessened by another's anguish.
Take thou some new infection to thy eye, And the rank poison of the old will die.
Hello, good fellow.
God save you, sir. I pray, sir, can you read?
Aye, mine own fortune in my misery.
But I pray, can you read anything you see?

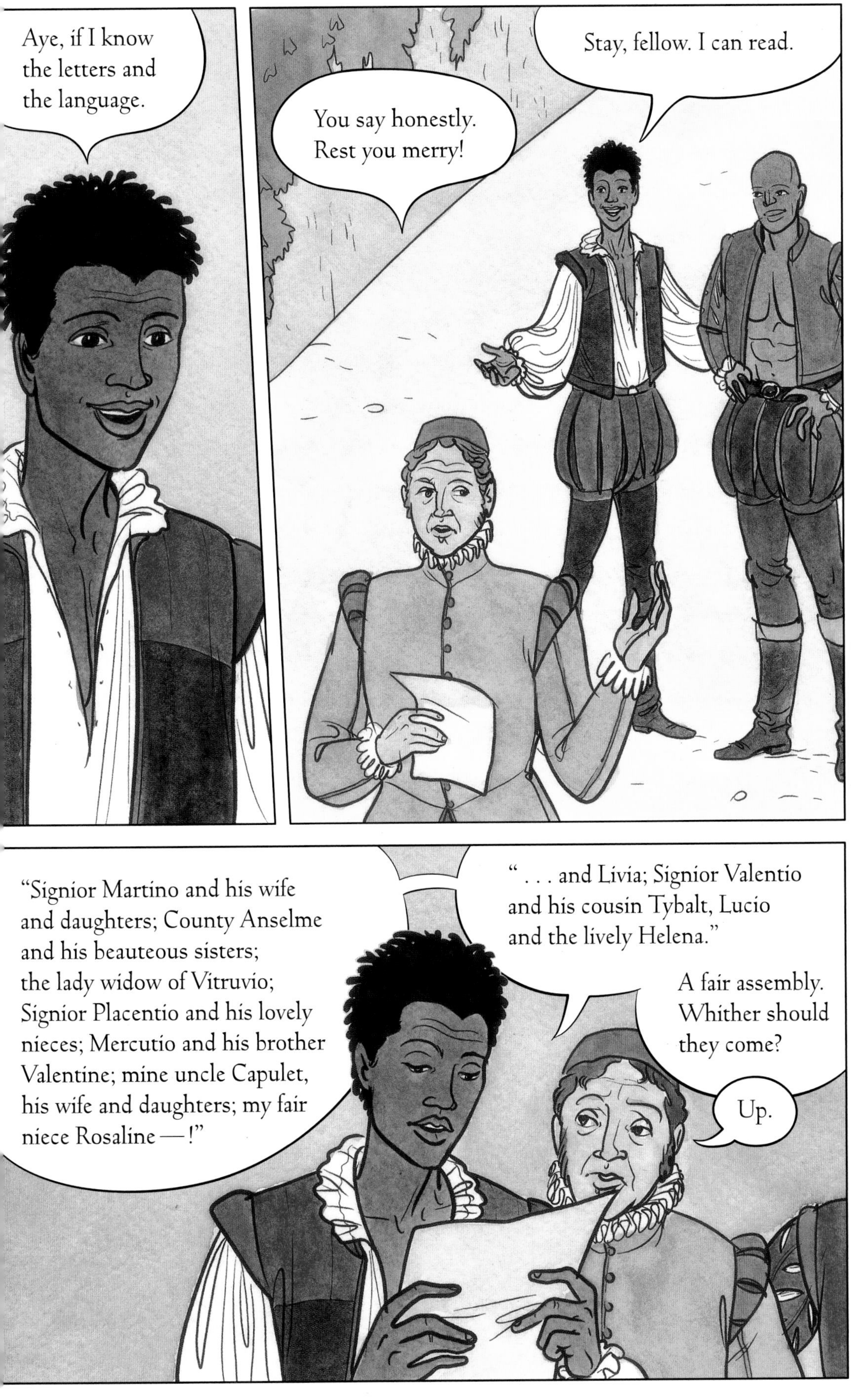
Aye, if I know the letters and the language.
You say honestly. Rest you merry!
Stay, fellow. I can read.
"Signior Martino and his wife and daughters; County Anselme and his beauteous sisters; the lady widow of Vitruvio; Signior Placentio and his lovely nieces; Mercutio and his brother Valentine; mine uncle Capulet, his wife and daughters; my fair niece Rosaline —!"
" . . . and Livia; Signior Valentio and his cousin Tybalt, Lucio and the lively Helena."
A fair assembly. Whither should they come?
Up.

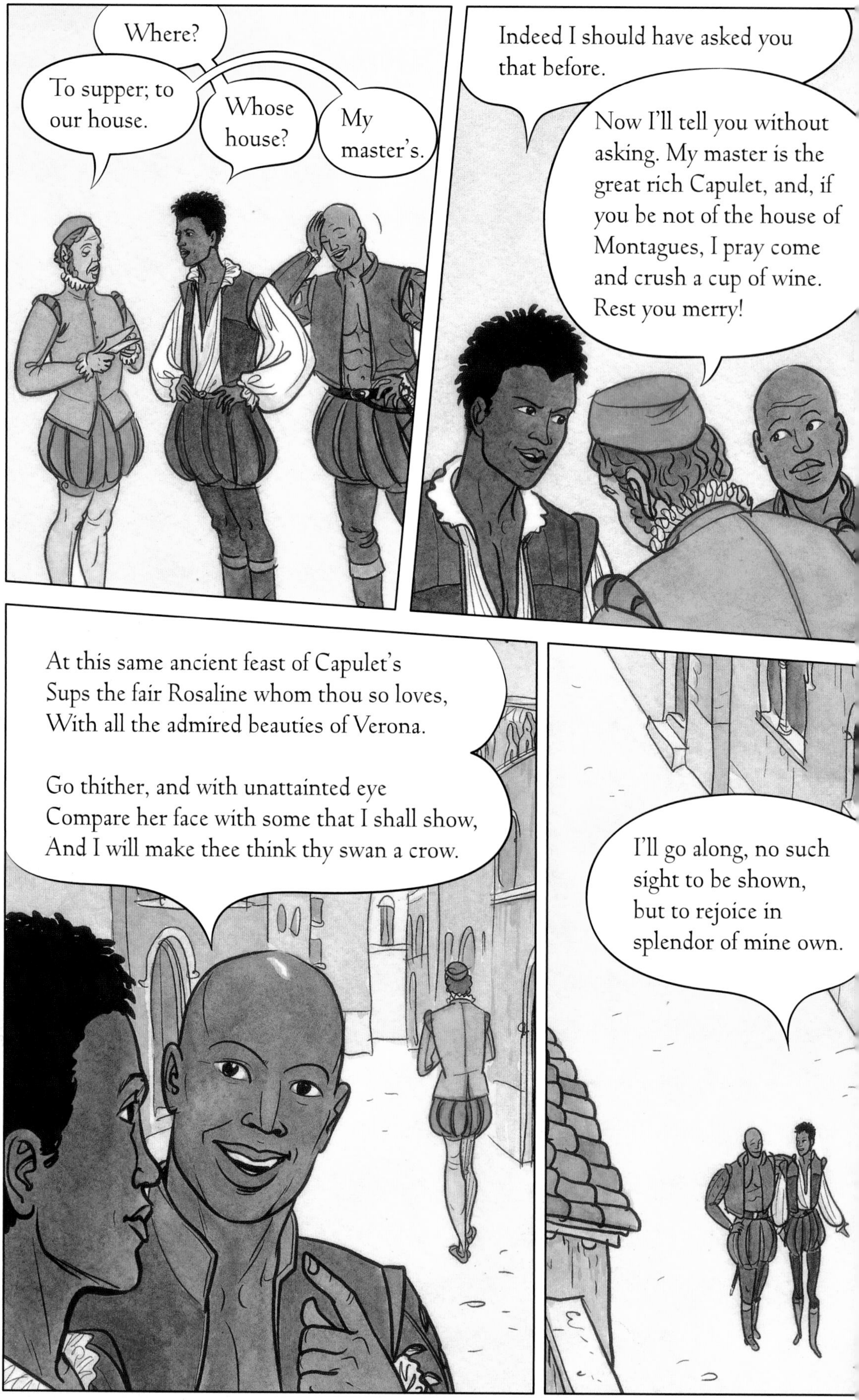
Where?
To supper; to our house.
Whose house?
My master's.
Indeed I should have asked you that before.
Now I'll tell you without asking. My master is the great rich Capulet, and, if you be not of the house of Montagues, I pray come and crush a cup of wine. Rest you merry!
At this same ancient feast of Capulet's
Sups the fair Rosaline whom thou so loves,
With all the admired beauties of Verona.
Go thither, and with unattainted eye
Compare her face with some that I shall show,
And I will make thee think thy swan a crow.
I'll go along, no such sight to be shown, but to rejoice in splendor of mine own.

Scene 3 : Capulet's House

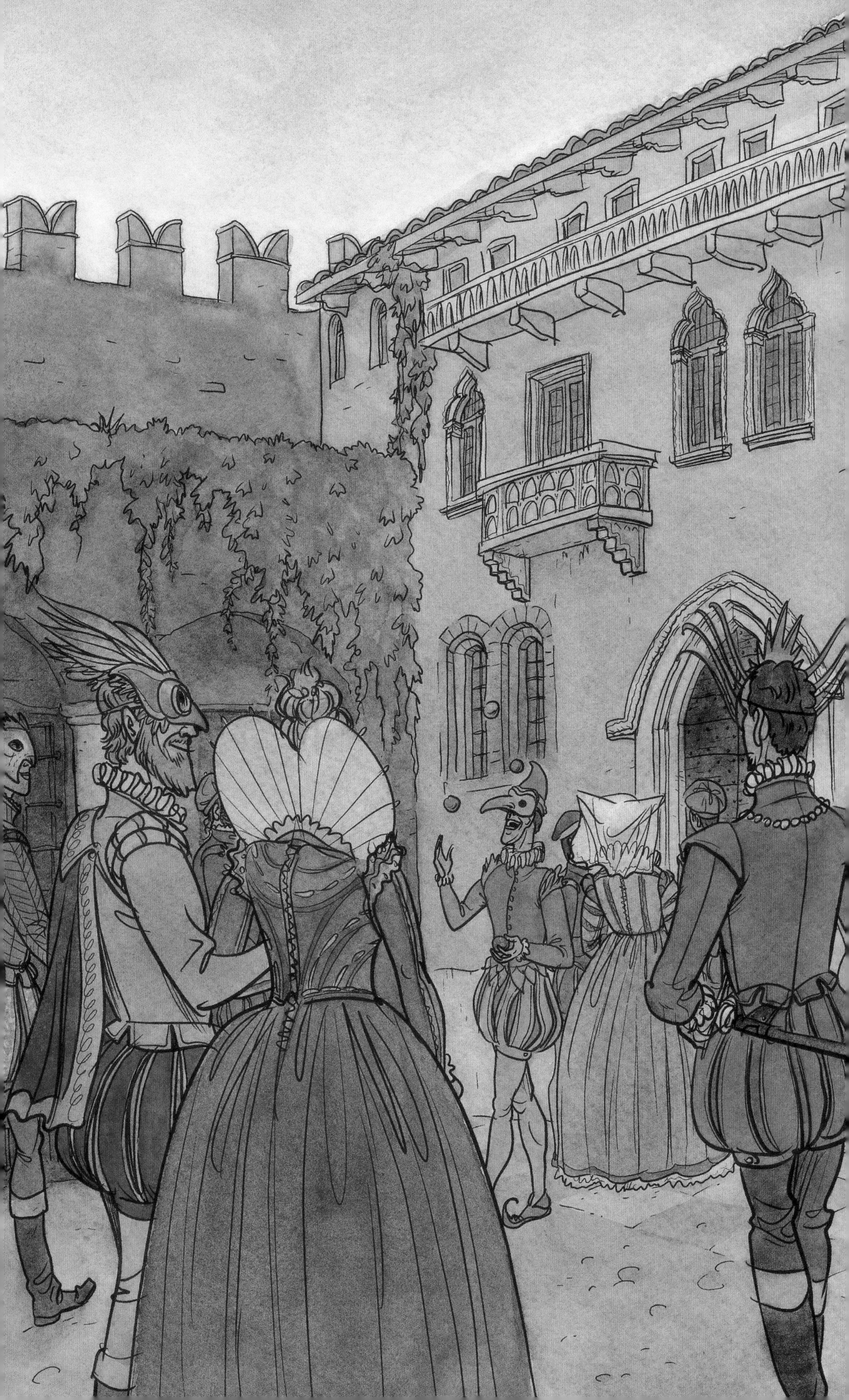

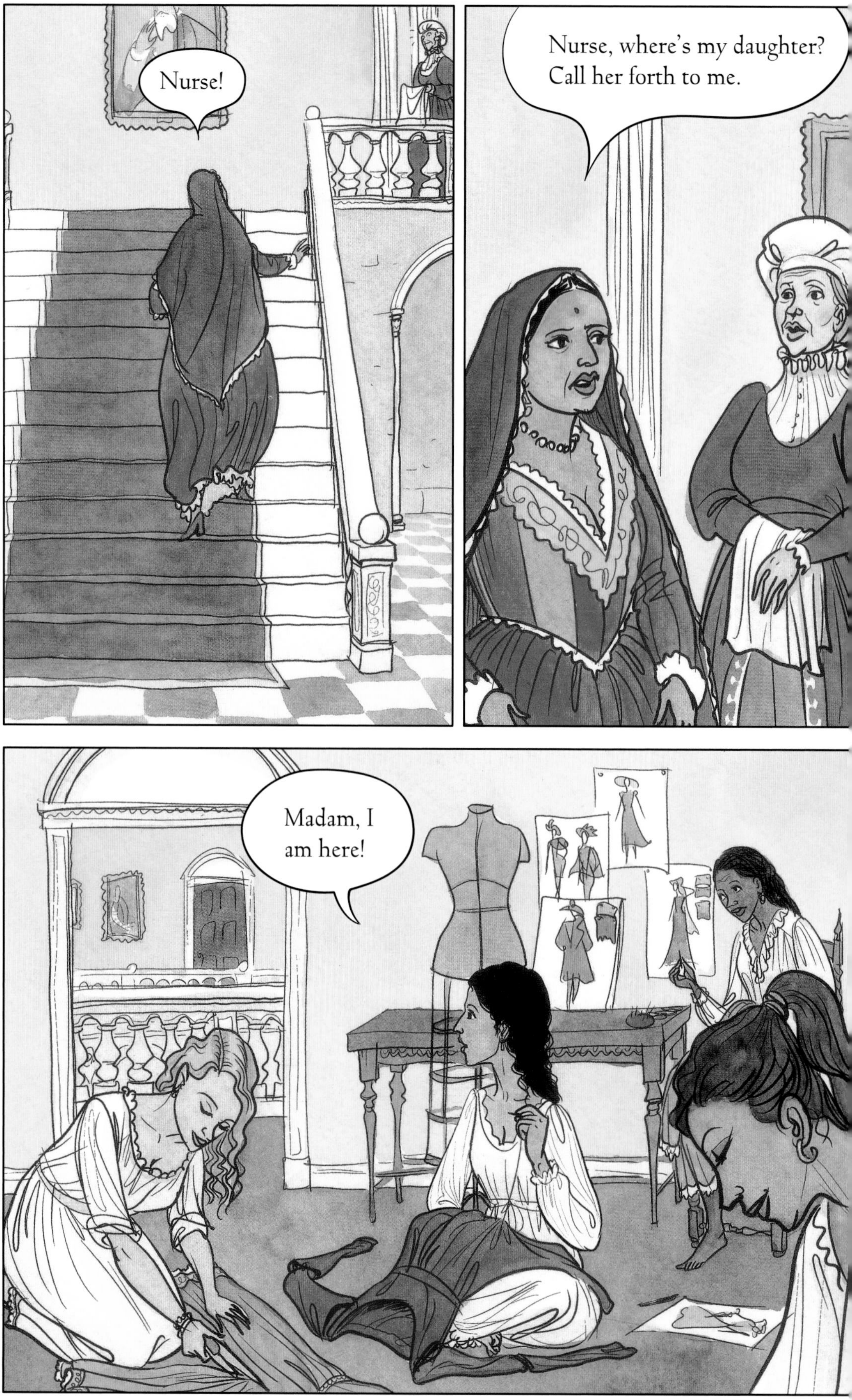
Nurse!
Nurse, where's my daughter? Call her forth to me.
Madam, I am here!

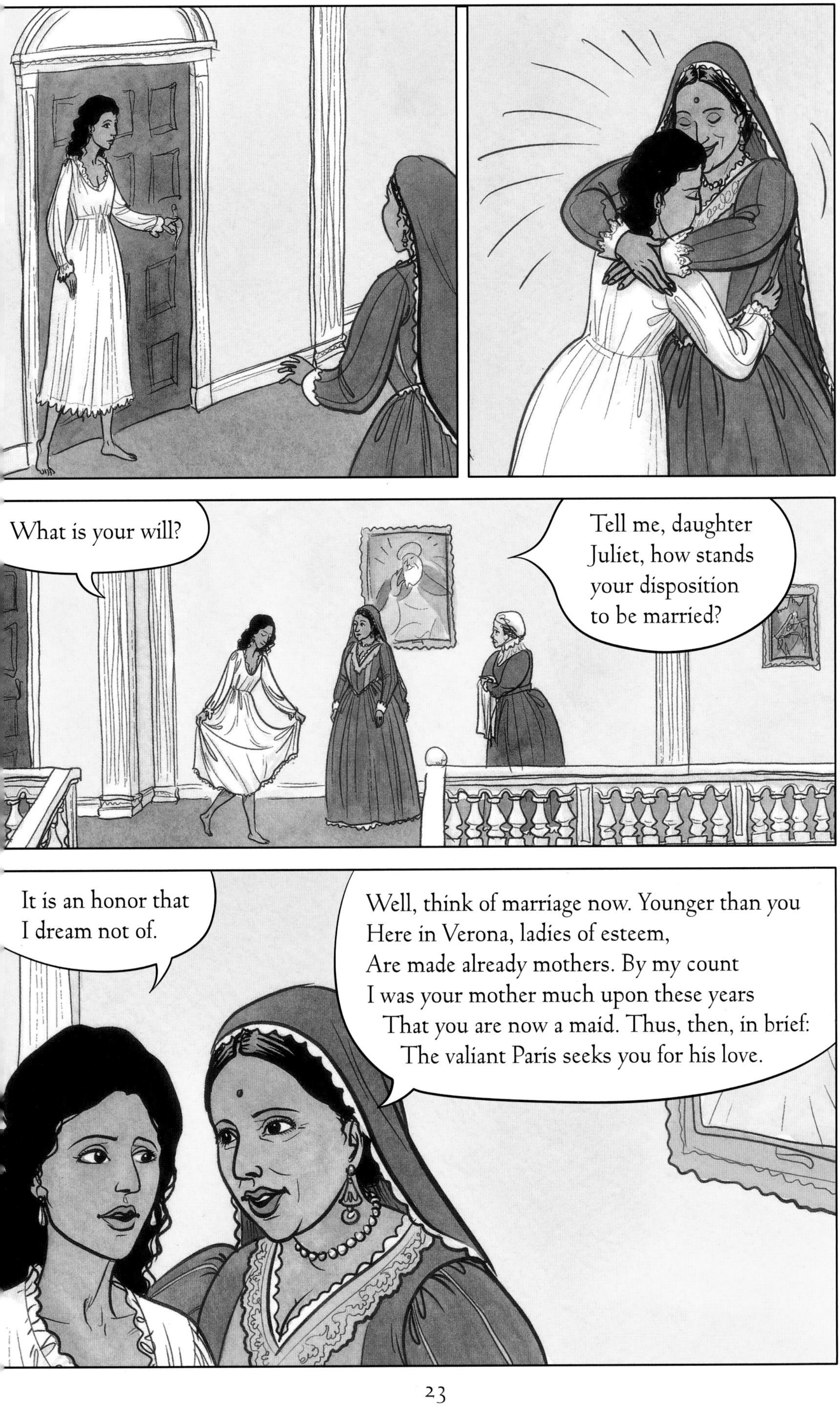
What is your will?
Tell me, daughter Juliet, how stands your disposition to be married?
It is an honor that I dream not of.
Well, think of marriage now. Younger than you
Here in Verona, ladies of esteem,
Are made already mothers. By my count
I was your mother much upon these years
That you are now a maid. Thus, then, in brief:
The valiant Paris seeks you for his love.

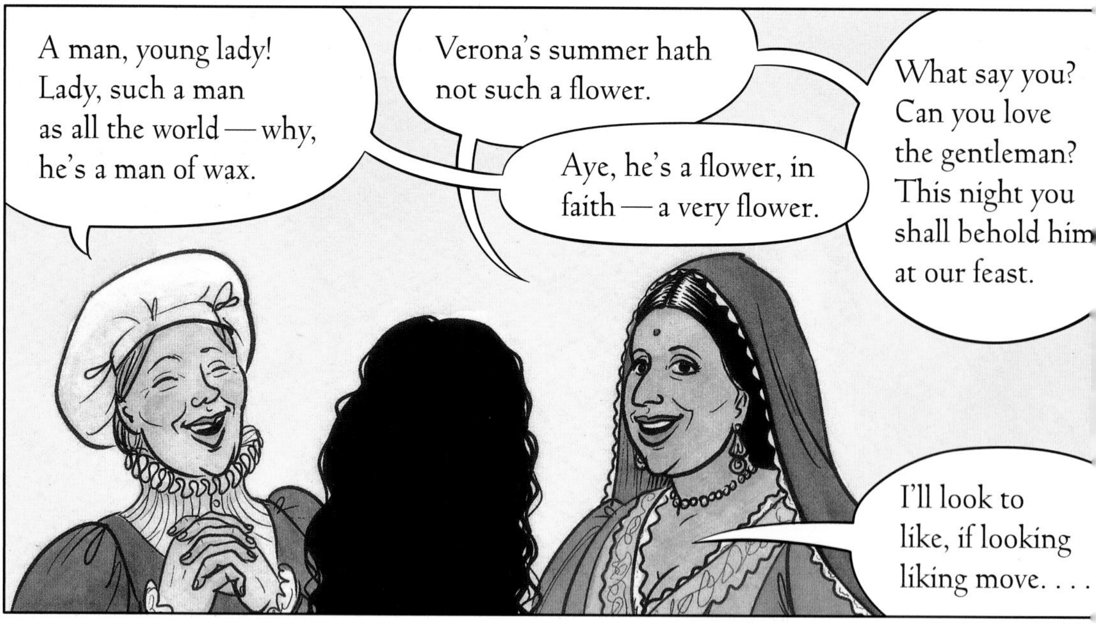
A man, young lady! Lady, such a man as all the world — why, he's a man of wax.
Verona's summer hath not such a flower.
Aye, he's a flower, in faith — a very flower.
What say you? Can you love the gentleman? This night you shall behold him at our feast.
I'll look to like, if looking liking move. . . .

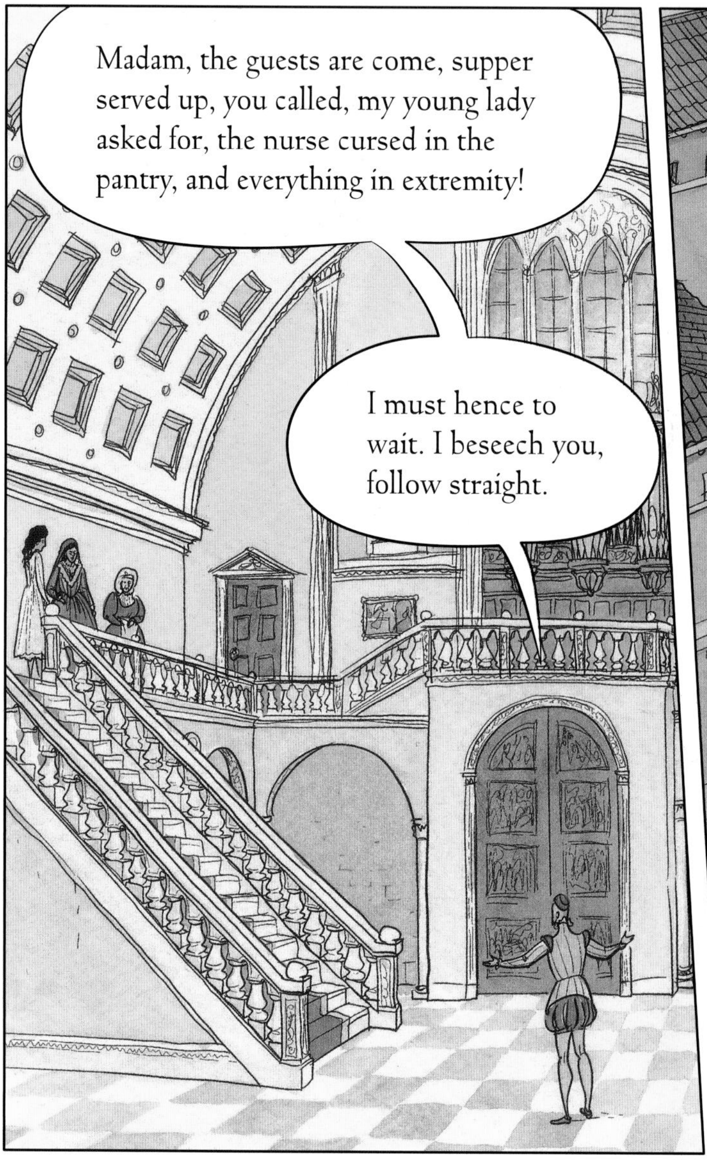
Madam, the guests are come, supper served up, you called, my young lady asked for, the nurse cursed in the pantry, and everything in extremity!
I must hence to wait. I beseech you, follow straight.

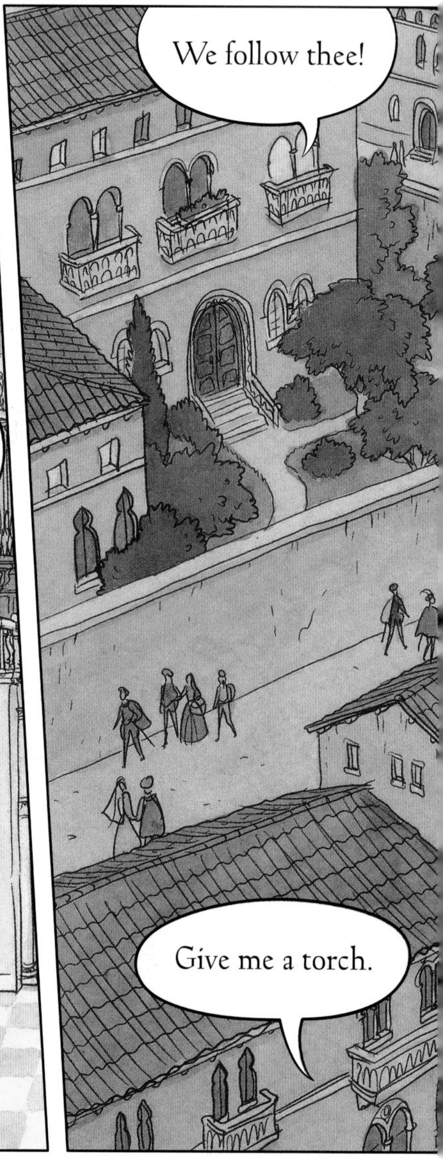
We follow thee!
Give me a torch.

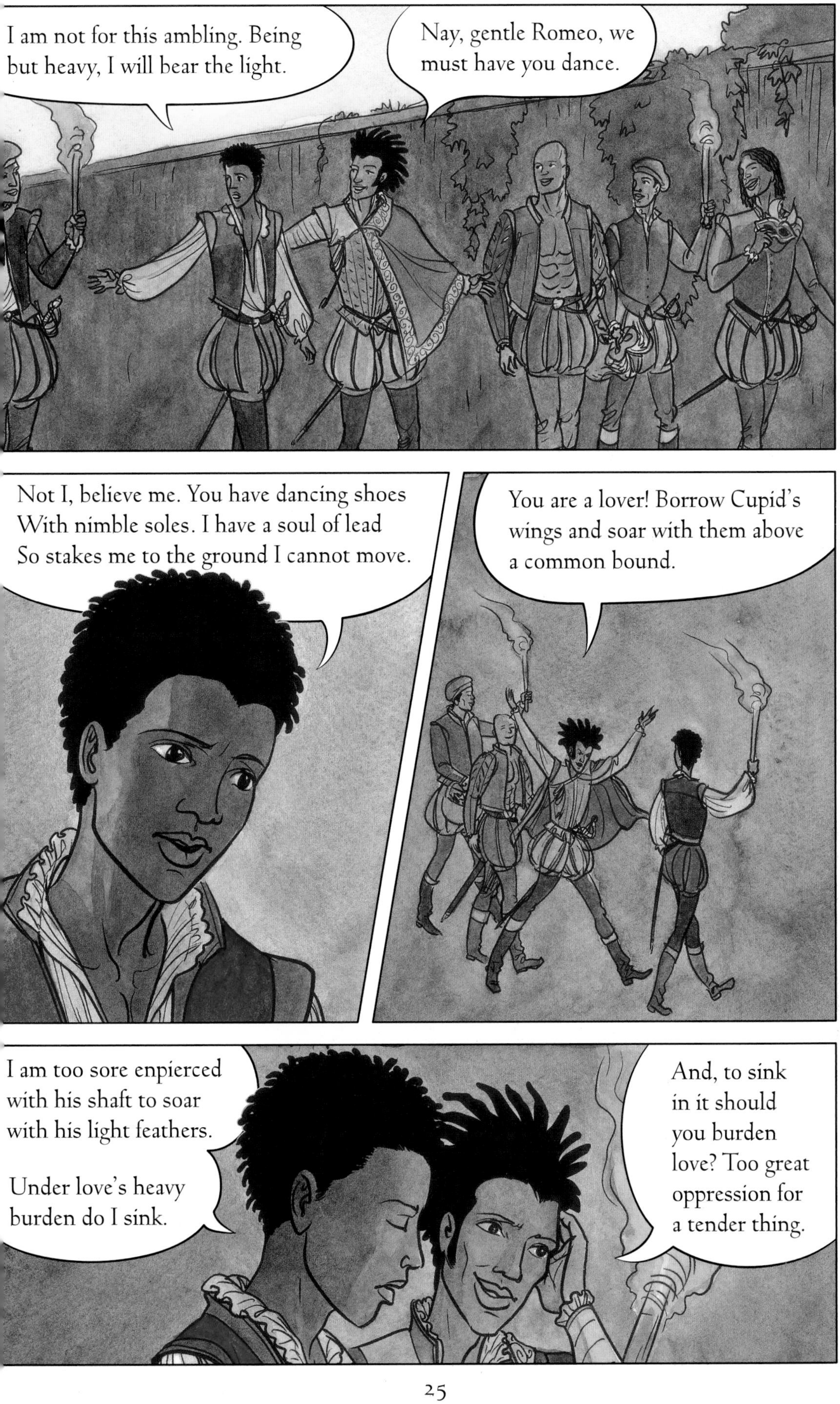
I am not for this ambling. Being but heavy, I will bear the light.
Nay, gentle Romeo, we must have you dance.
Not I, believe me. You have dancing shoes With nimble soles. I have a soul of lead So stakes me to the ground I cannot move.
You are a lover! Borrow Cupid's wings and soar with them above a common bound.
I am too sore enpierced with his shaft to soar with his light feathers.
Under love's heavy burden do I sink.
And, to sink in it should you burden love? Too great oppression for a tender thing.

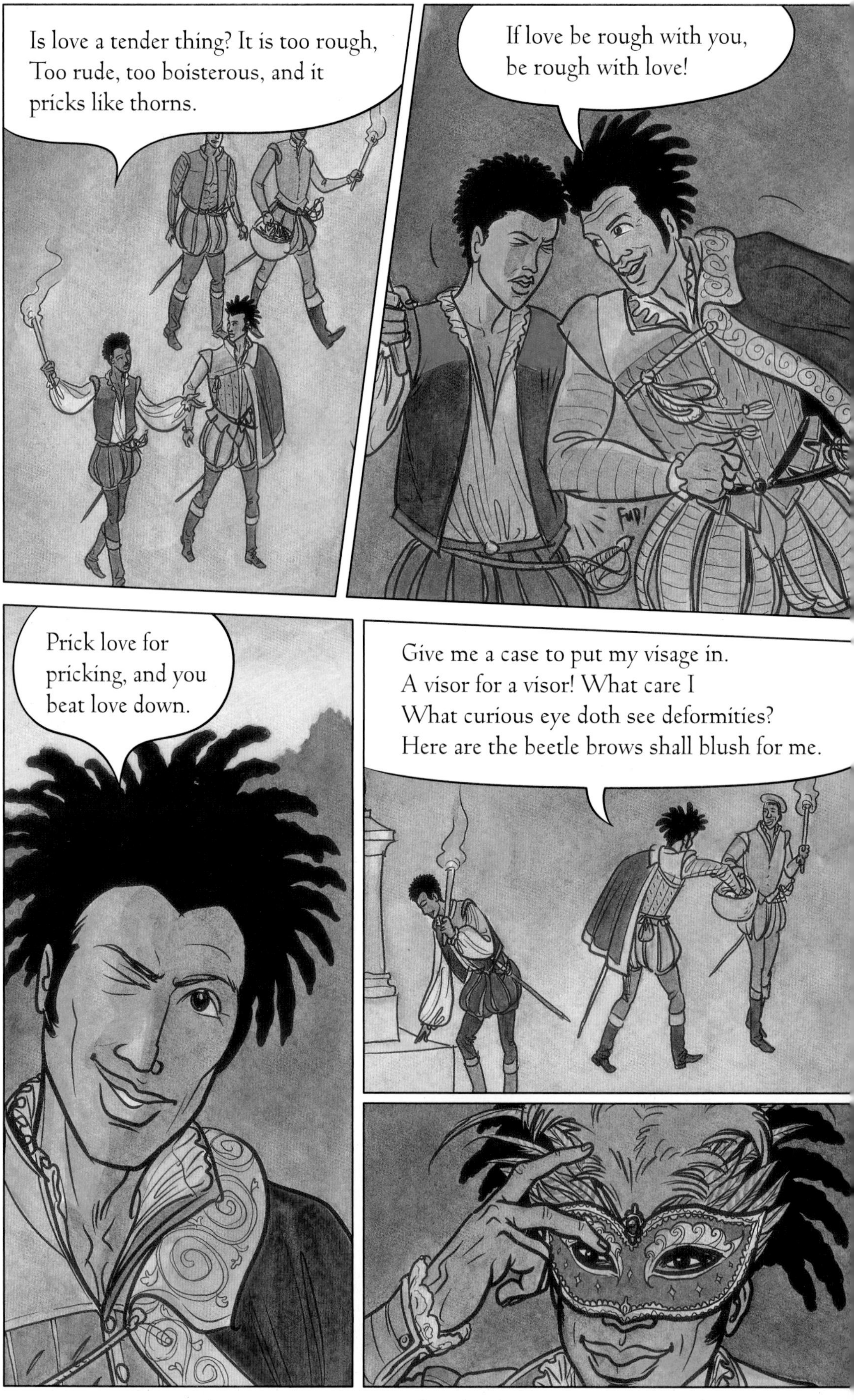
Is love a tender thing? It is too rough, Too rude, too boisterous, and it pricks like thorns.
If love be rough with you, be rough with love!
FWP!
Prick love for pricking, and you beat love down.
Give me a case to put my visage in. A visor for a visor! What care I What curious eye doth see deformities? Here are the beetle brows shall blush for me.

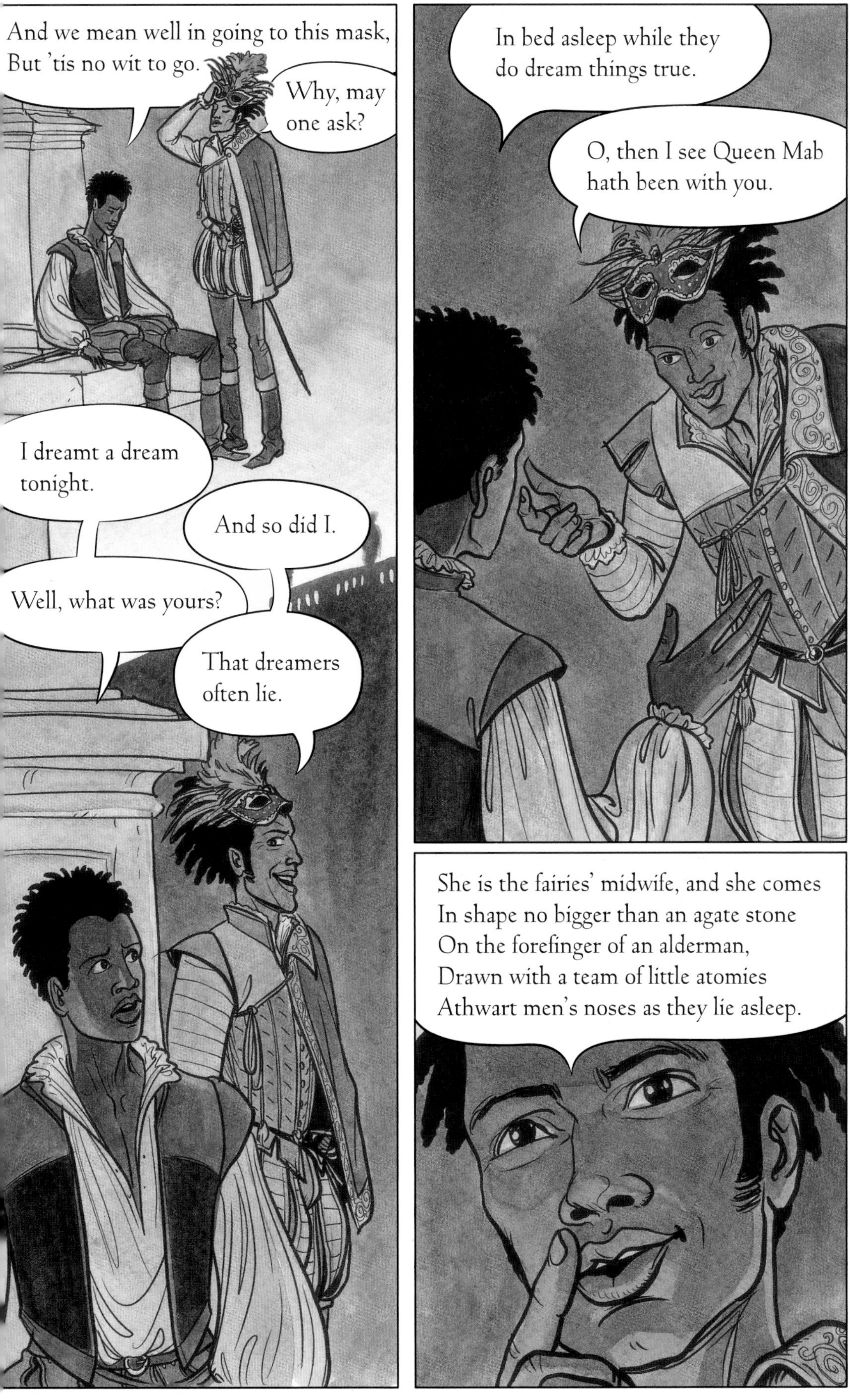
And we mean well in going to this mask,
But 'tis no wit to go.
Why, may one ask?
I dreamt a dream tonight.
And so did I.
Well, what was yours?
That dreamers often lie.
In bed asleep while they do dream things true.
O, then I see Queen Mab hath been with you.
She is the fairies' midwife, and she comes
In shape no bigger than an agate stone
On the forefinger of an alderman,
Drawn with a team of little atomies
Athwart men's noses as they lie asleep.

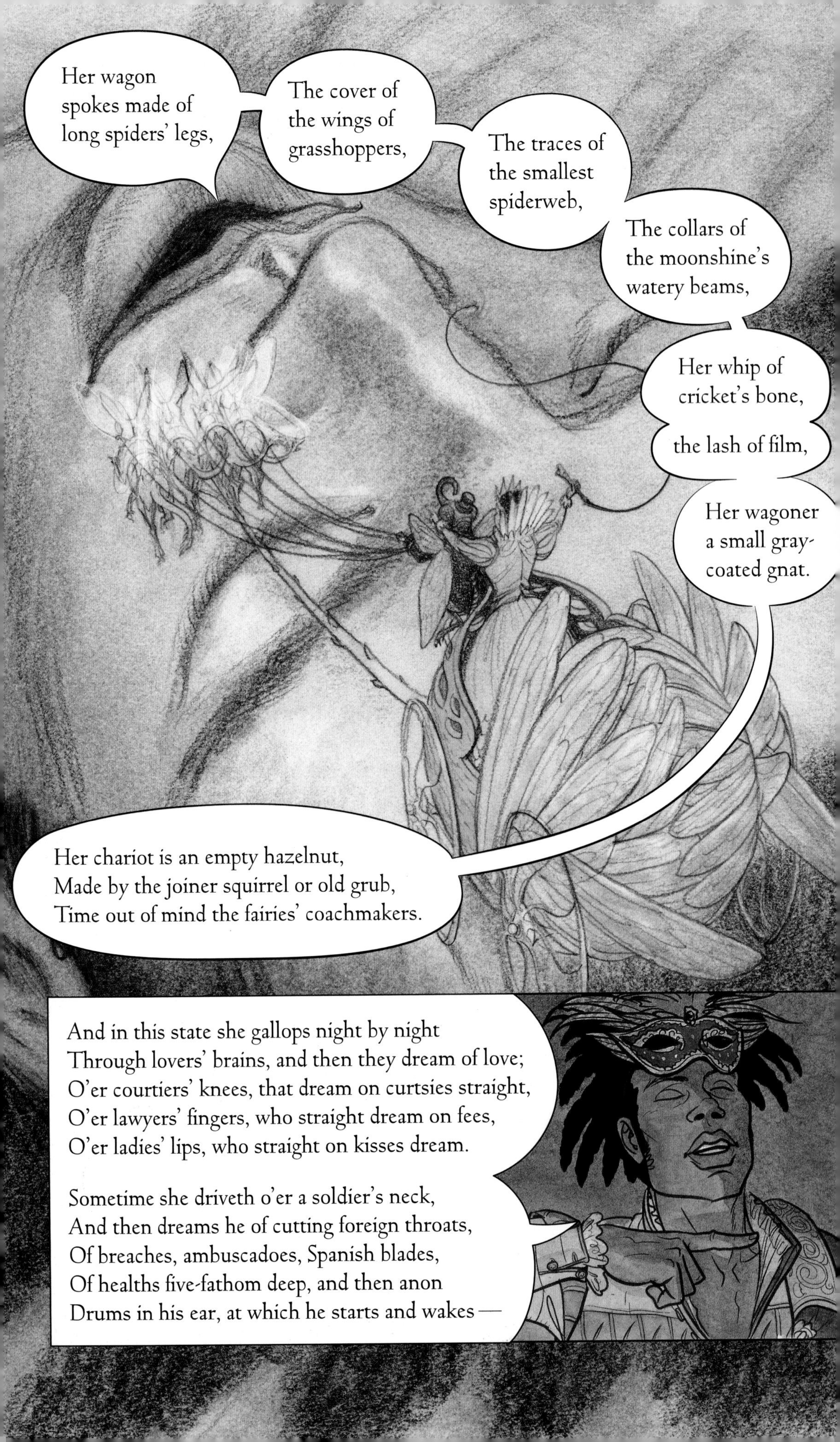
Her wagon spokes made of long spiders' legs,
The cover of the wings of grasshoppers,
The traces of the smallest spiderweb,
The collars of the moonshine's watery beams,
Her whip of cricket's bone,
the lash of film,
Her wagoner a small gray-coated gnat.
Her chariot is an empty hazelnut,
Made by the joiner squirrel or old grub,
Time out of mind the fairies' coachmakers.
And in this state she gallops night by night
Through lovers' brains, and then they dream of love;
O'er courtiers' knees, that dream on curtsies straight,
O'er lawyers' fingers, who straight dream on fees,
O'er ladies' lips, who straight on kisses dream.
Sometime she driveth o'er a soldier's neck,
And then dreams he of cutting foreign throats,
Of breaches, ambuscadoes, Spanish blades,
Of healths five-fathom deep, and then anon
Drums in his ear, at which he starts and wakes —

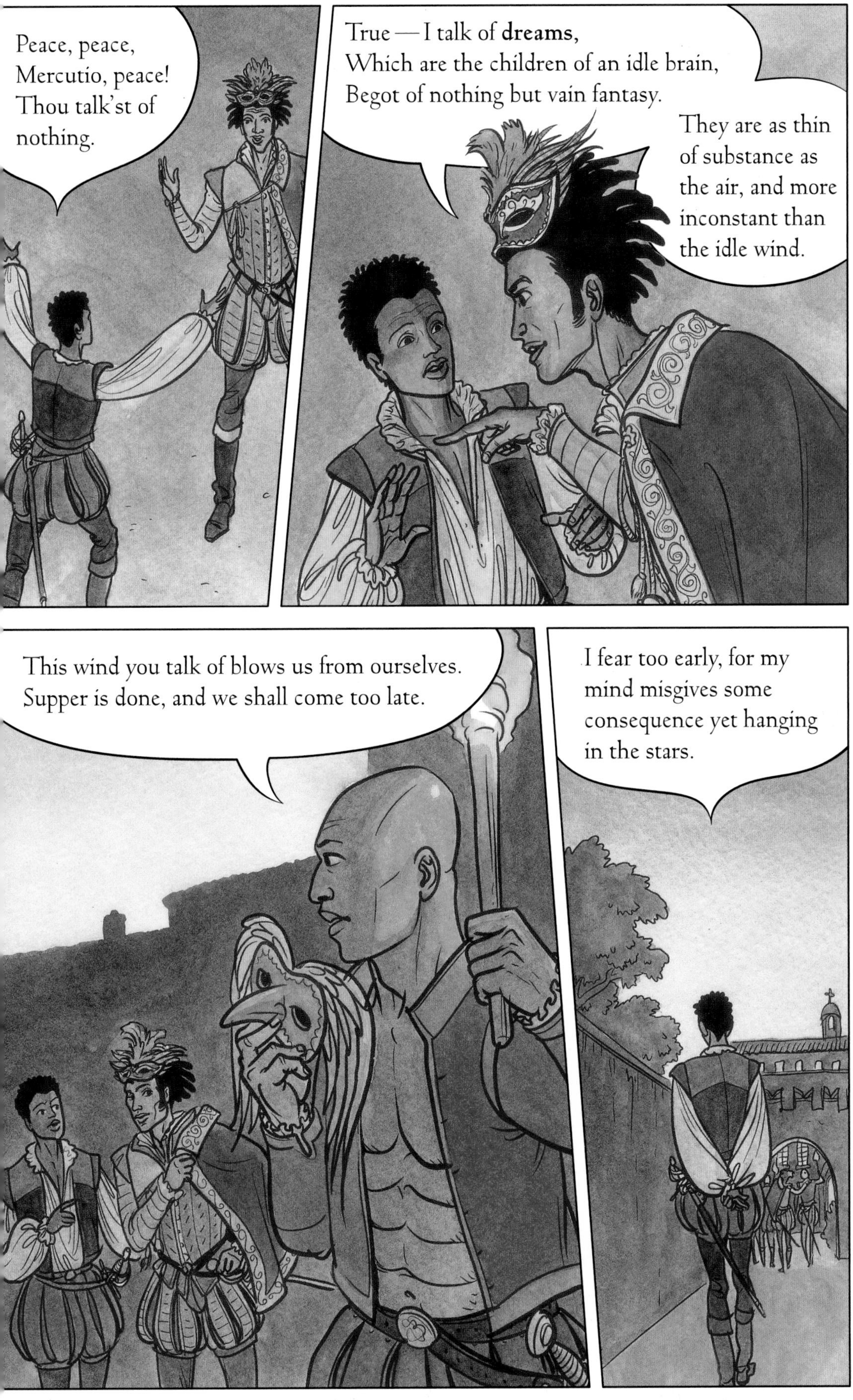
Peace, peace, Mercutio, peace! Thou talk'st of nothing.
True — I talk of **dreams**, Which are the children of an idle brain, Begot of nothing but vain fantasy.
They are as thin of substance as the air, and more inconstant than the idle wind.
This wind you talk of blows us from ourselves. Supper is done, and we shall come too late.
I fear too early, for my mind misgives some consequence yet hanging in the stars.

Scene 5 : Capulet's House

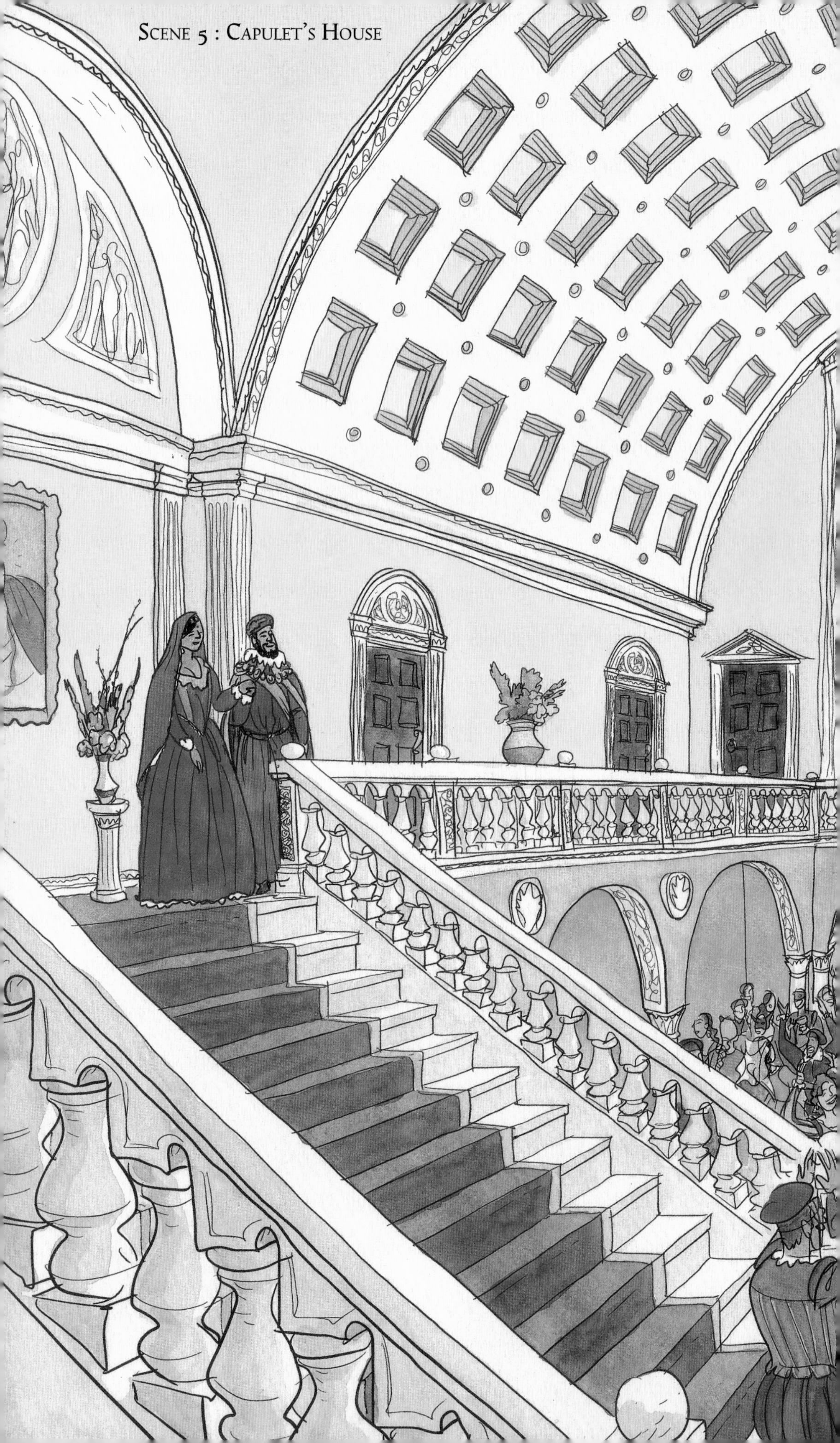

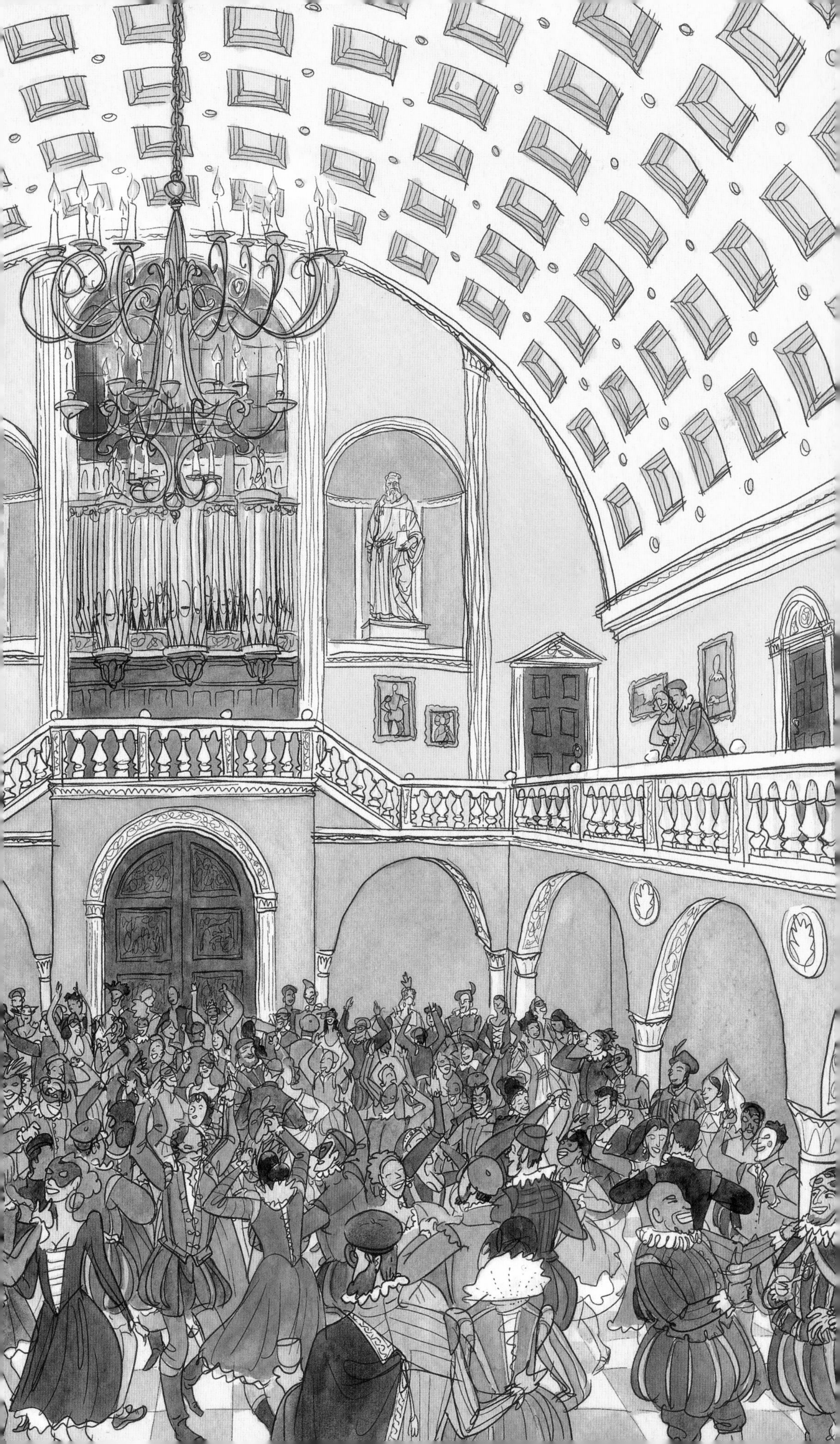

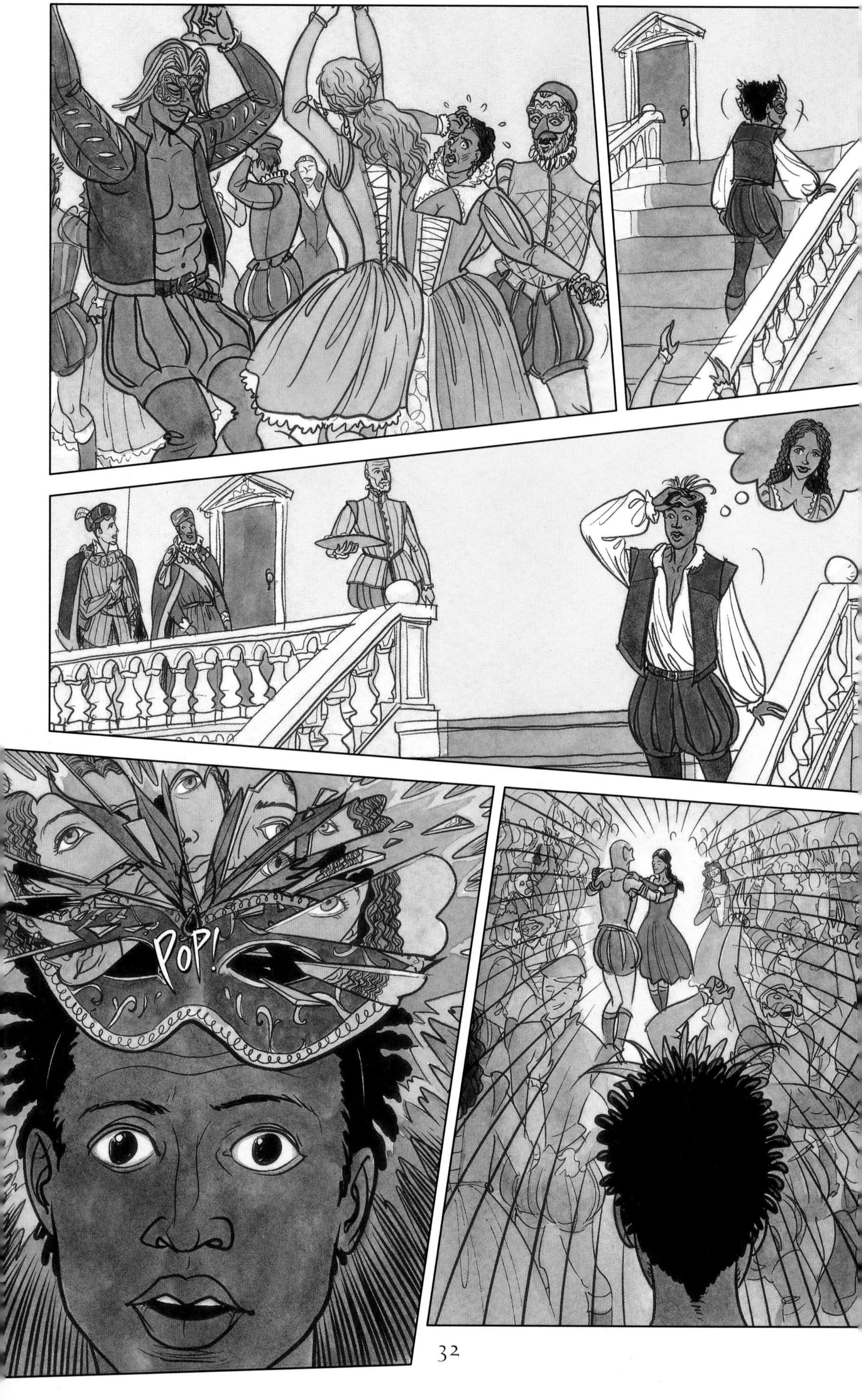
POP!

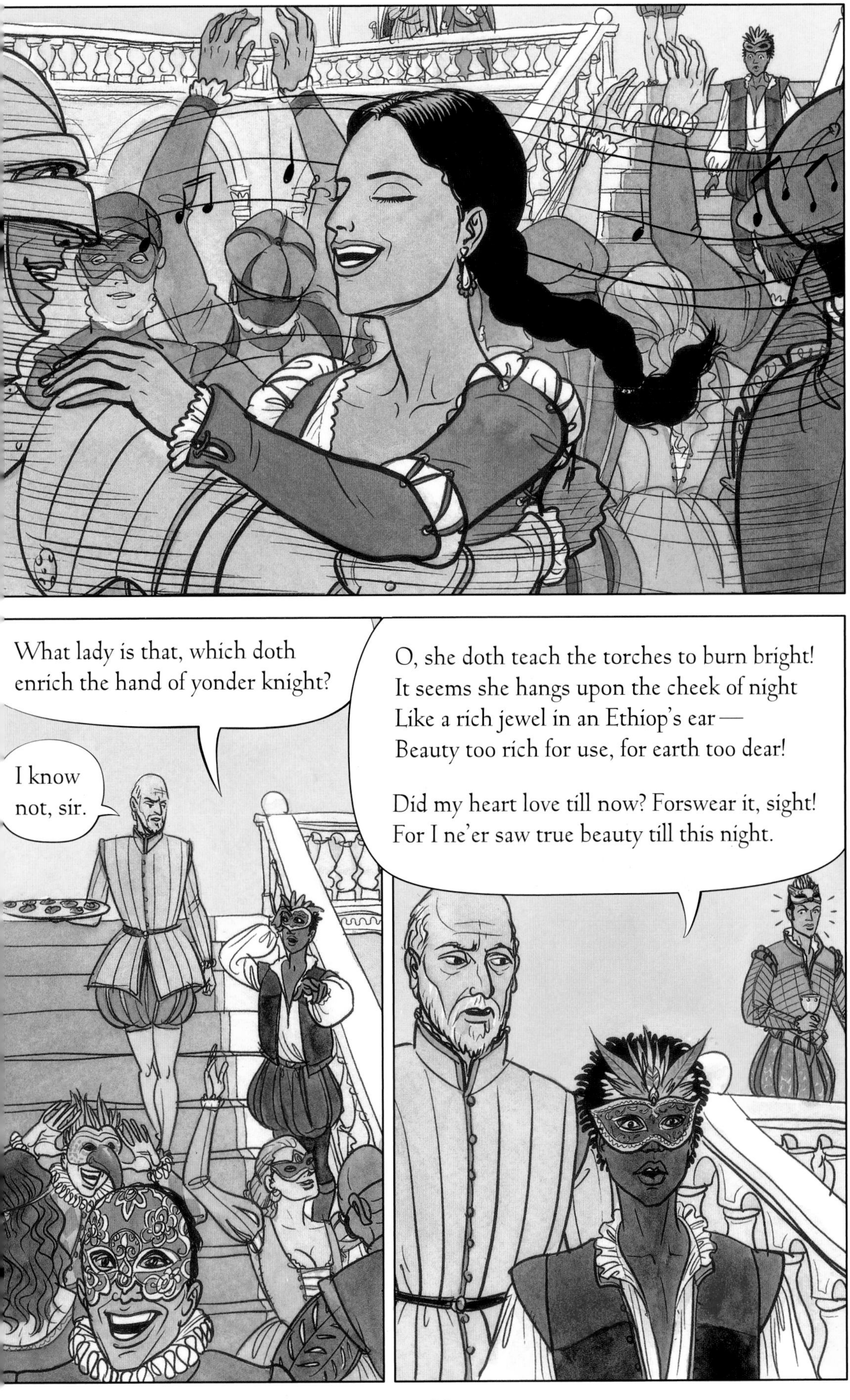
What lady is that, which doth enrich the hand of yonder knight?
I know not, sir.
O, she doth teach the torches to burn bright! It seems she hangs upon the cheek of night Like a rich jewel in an Ethiop's ear — Beauty too rich for use, for earth too dear!
Did my heart love till now? Forswear it, sight! For I ne'er saw true beauty till this night.

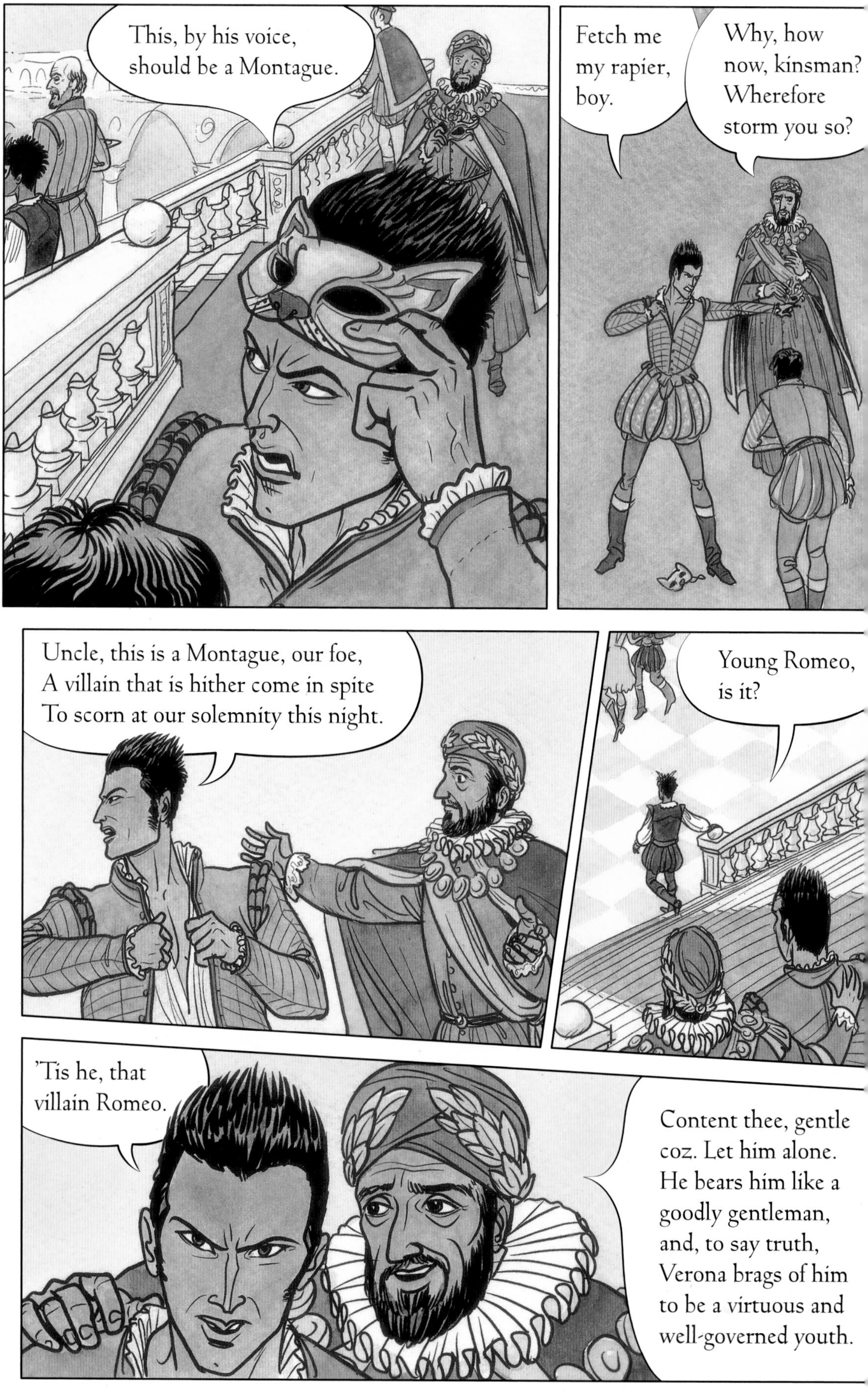
This, by his voice, should be a Montague.
Fetch me my rapier, boy.
Why, how now, kinsman? Wherefore storm you so?
Uncle, this is a Montague, our foe,
A villain that is hither come in spite
To scorn at our solemnity this night.
Young Romeo, is it?
'Tis he, that villain Romeo.
Content thee, gentle coz. Let him alone. He bears him like a goodly gentleman, and, to say truth, Verona brags of him to be a virtuous and well-governed youth.

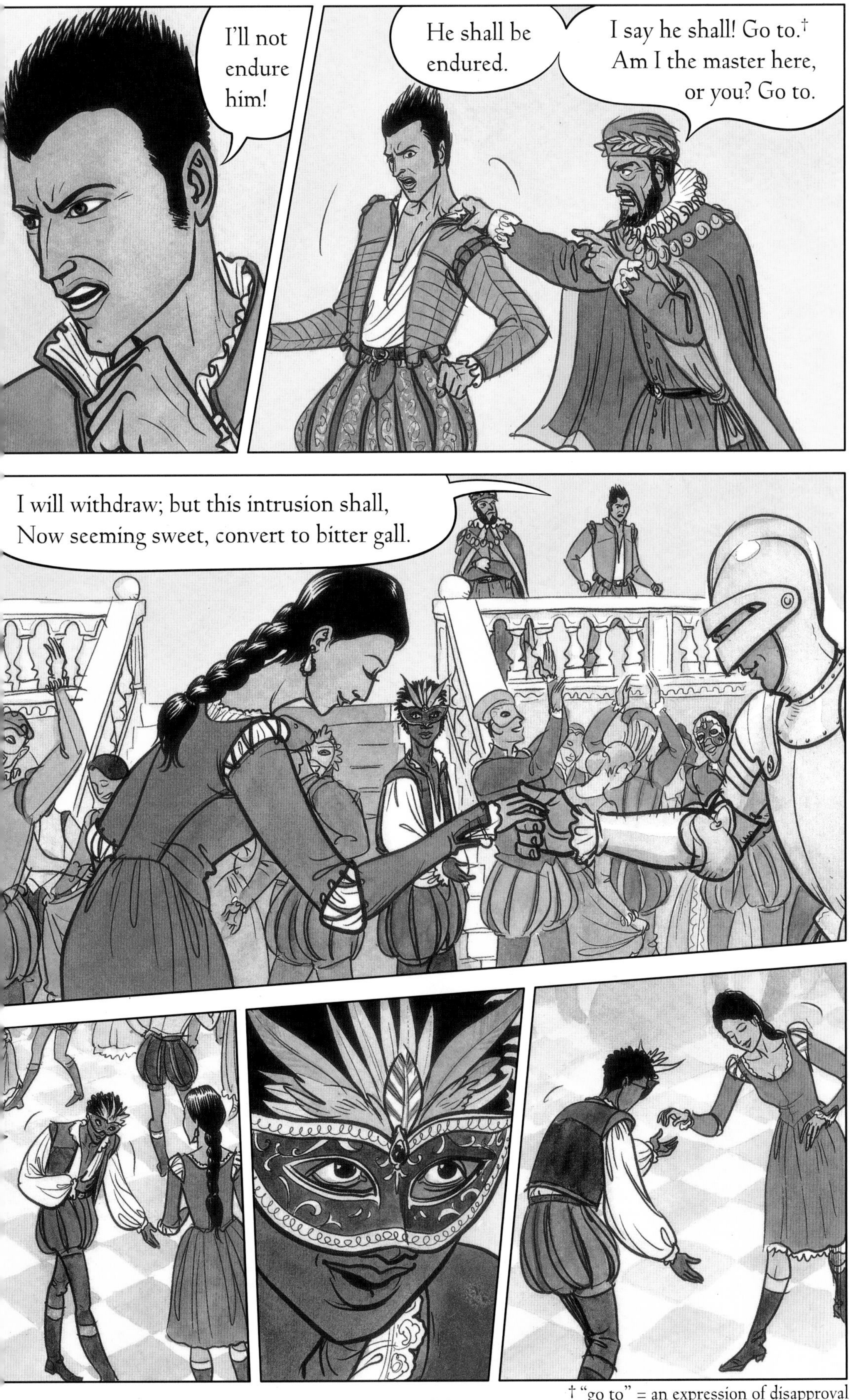
I'll not endure him!
He shall be endured.
I say he shall! Go to.† Am I the master here, or you? Go to.
I will withdraw; but this intrusion shall, Now seeming sweet, convert to bitter gall.

† "go to" = an expression of disapproval

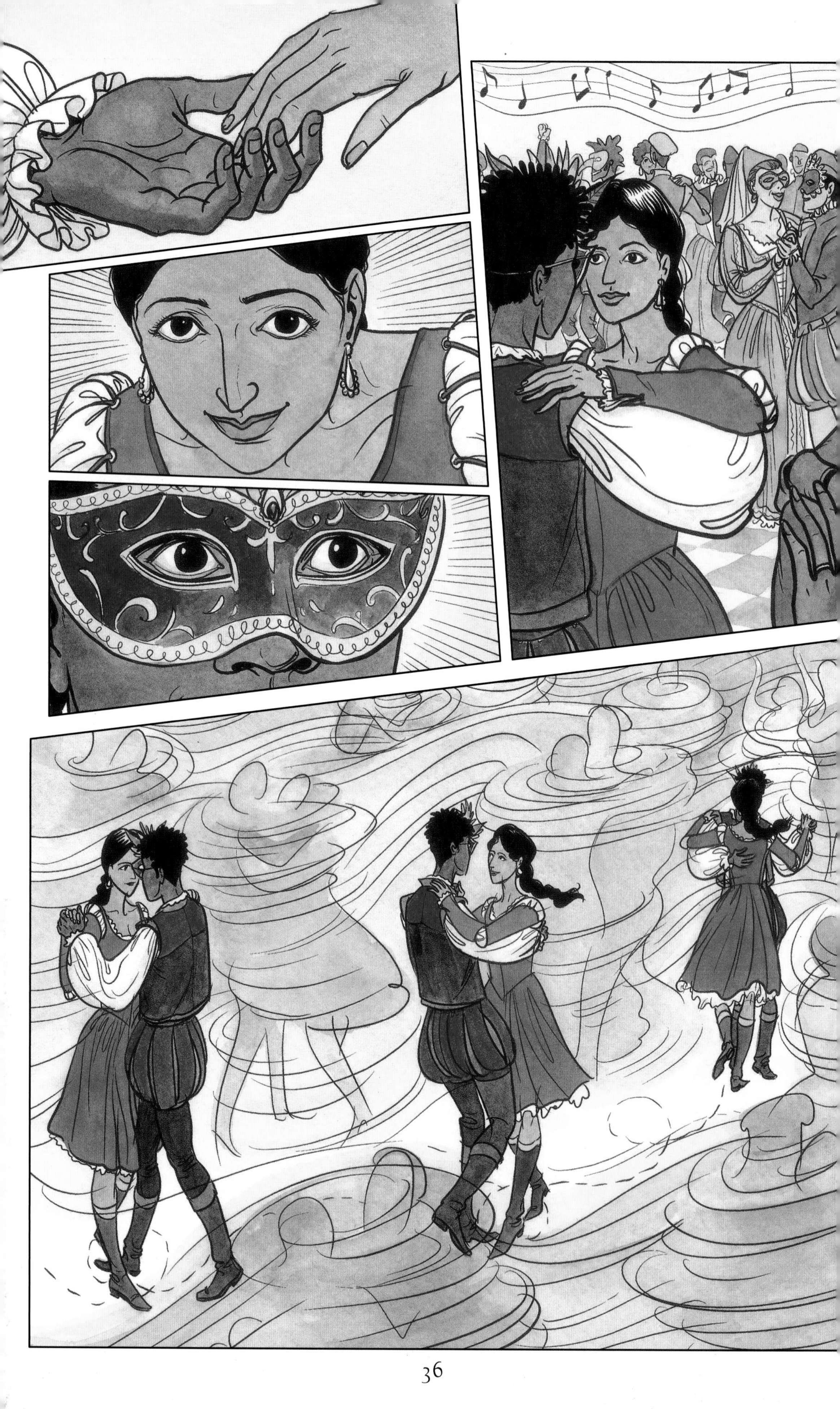

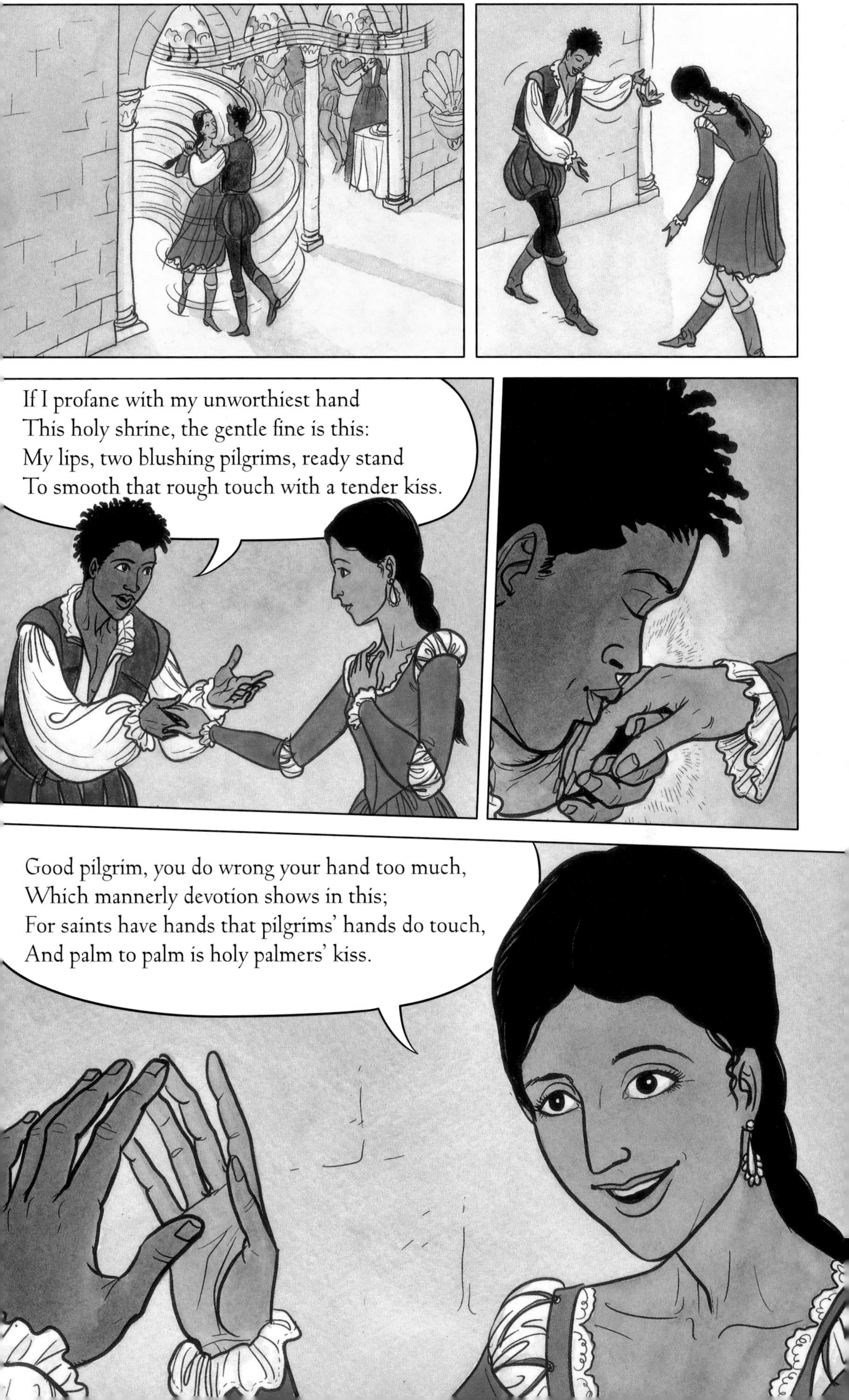
If I profane with my unworthiest hand
This holy shrine, the gentle fine is this:
My lips, two blushing pilgrims, ready stand
To smooth that rough touch with a tender kiss.
Good pilgrim, you do wrong your hand too much,
Which mannerly devotion shows in this;
For saints have hands that pilgrims' hands do touch,
And palm to palm is holy palmers' kiss.

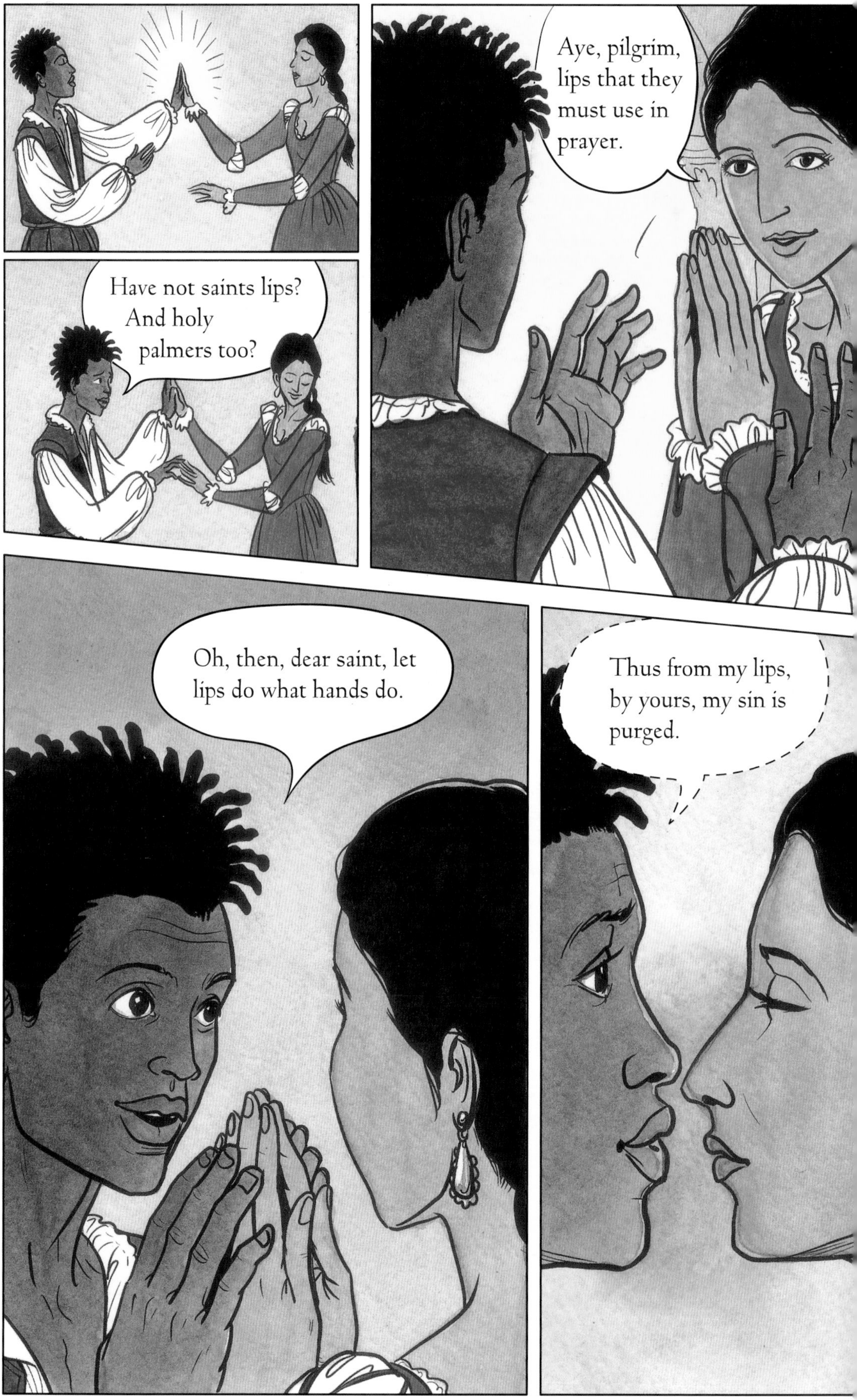
Have not saints lips? And holy palmers too?
Aye, pilgrim, lips that they must use in prayer.
Oh, then, dear saint, let lips do what hands do.
Thus from my lips, by yours, my sin is purged.

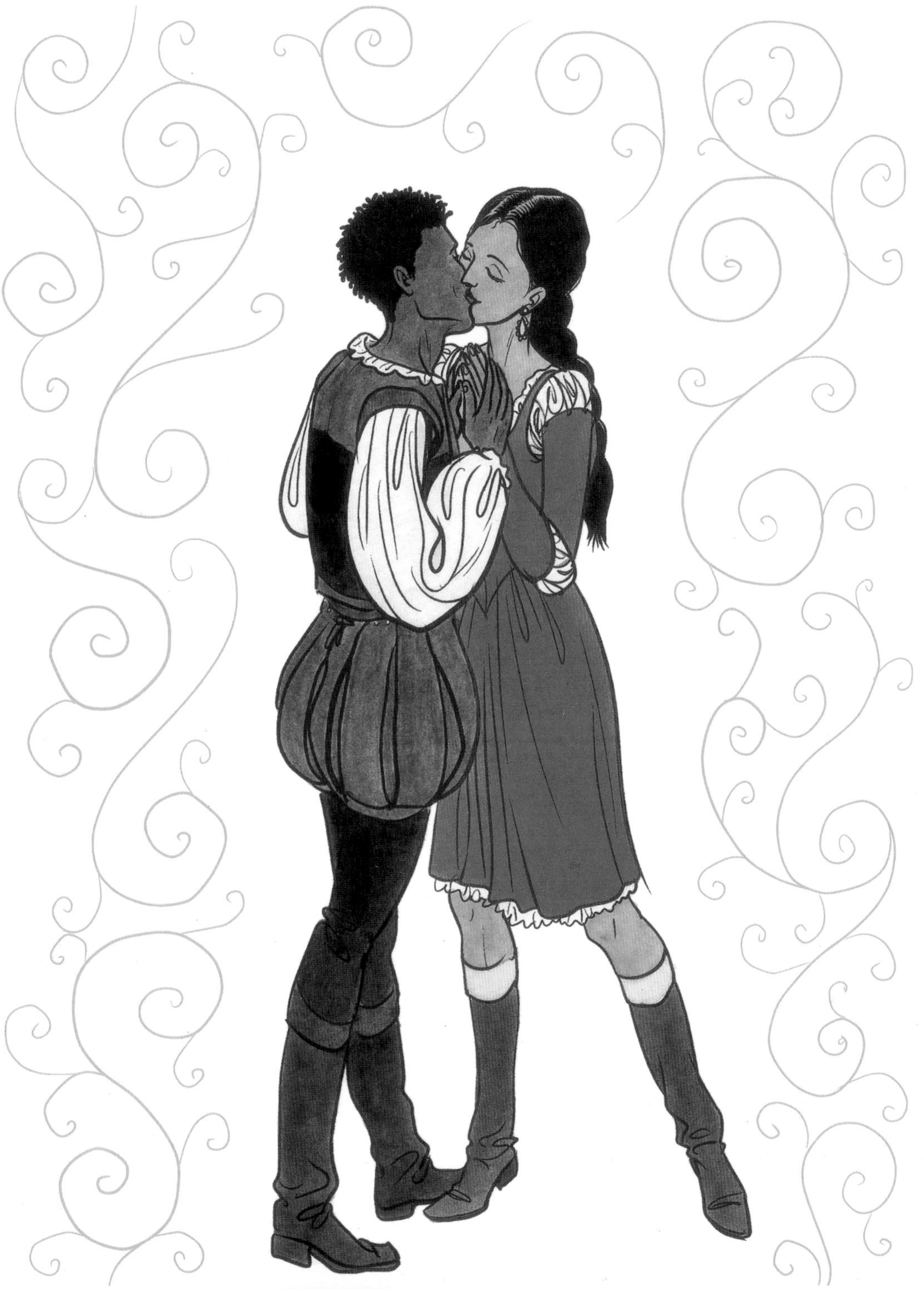

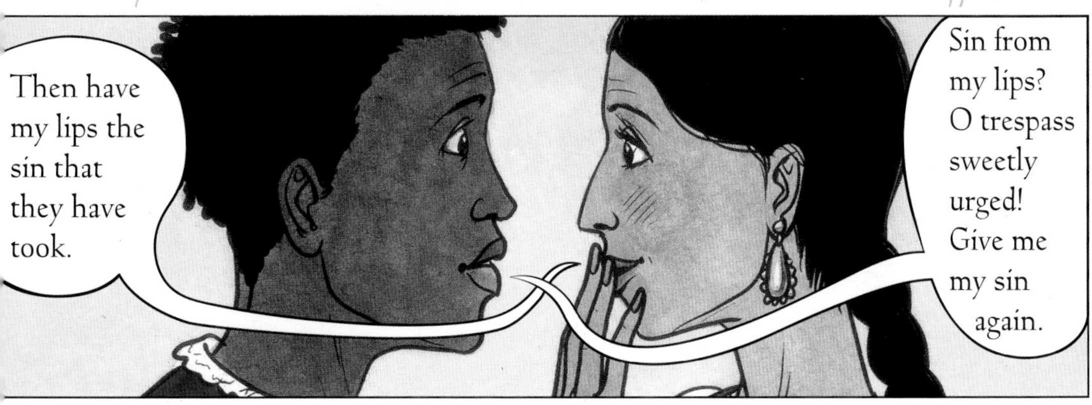
Then have my lips the sin that they have took.
Sin from my lips? O trespass sweetly urged! Give me my sin again.

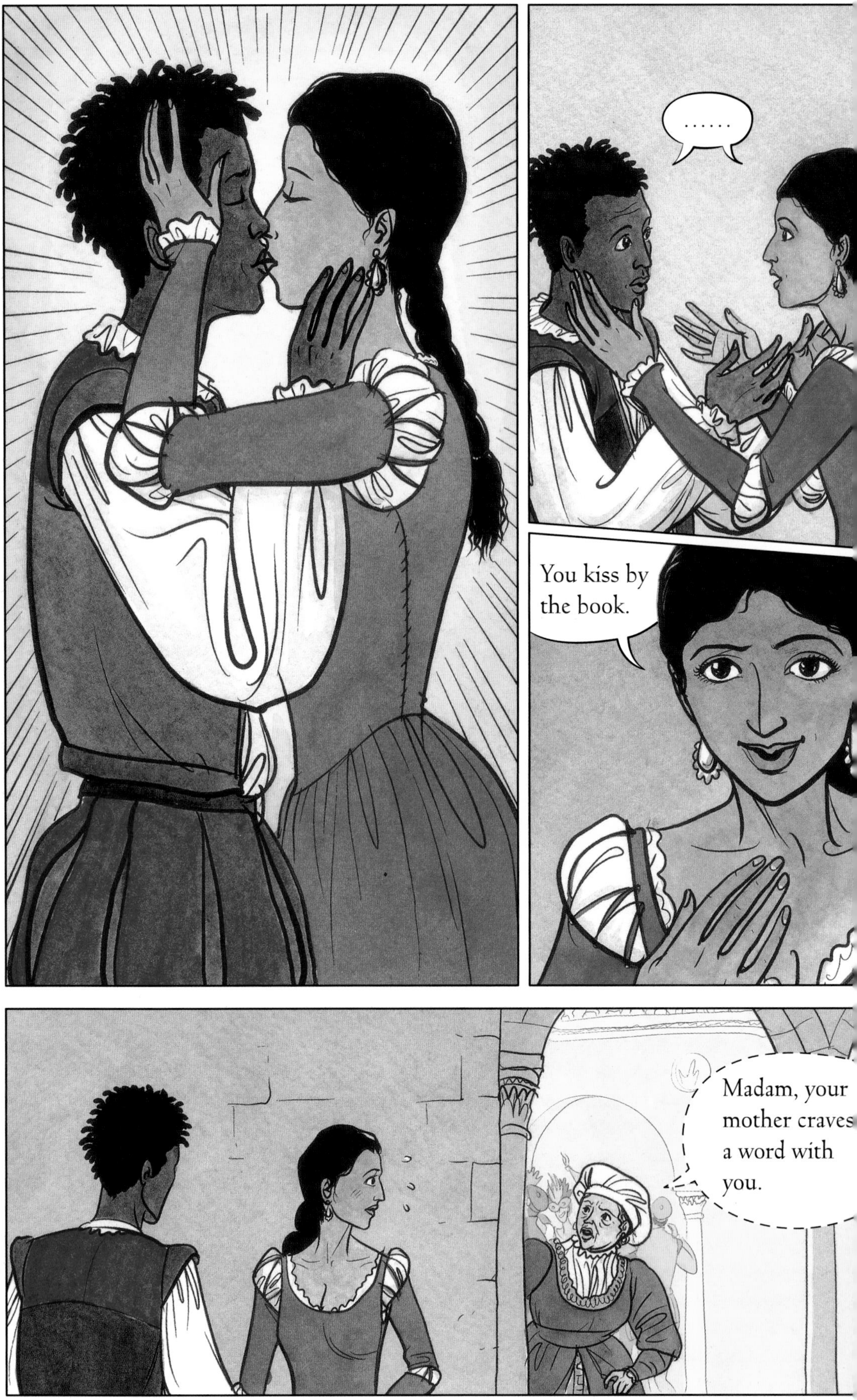
......
You kiss by the book.
Madam, your mother craves a word with you.

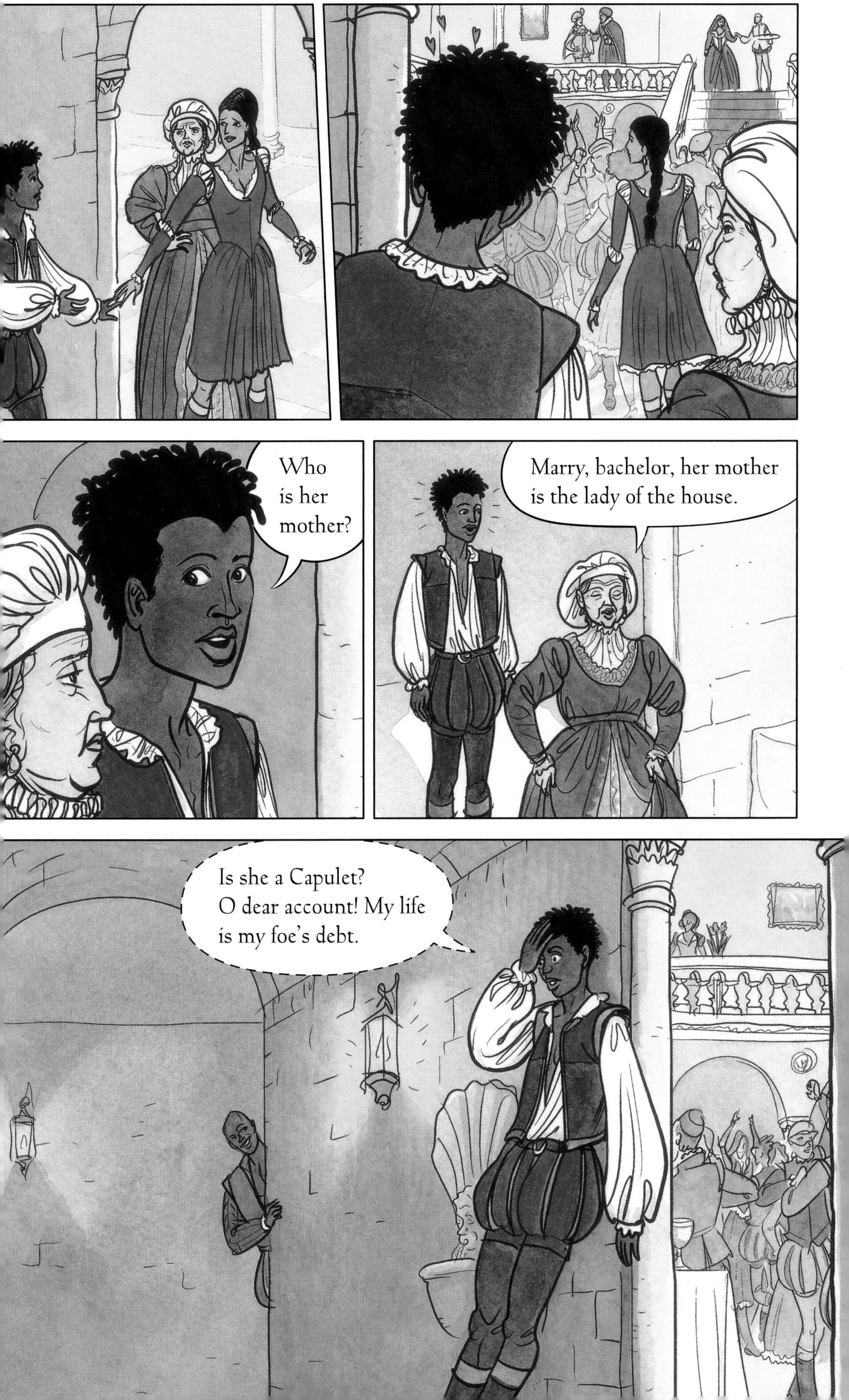

Who is her mother?
Marry, bachelor, her mother is the lady of the house.
Is she a Capulet? O dear account! My life is my foe's debt.

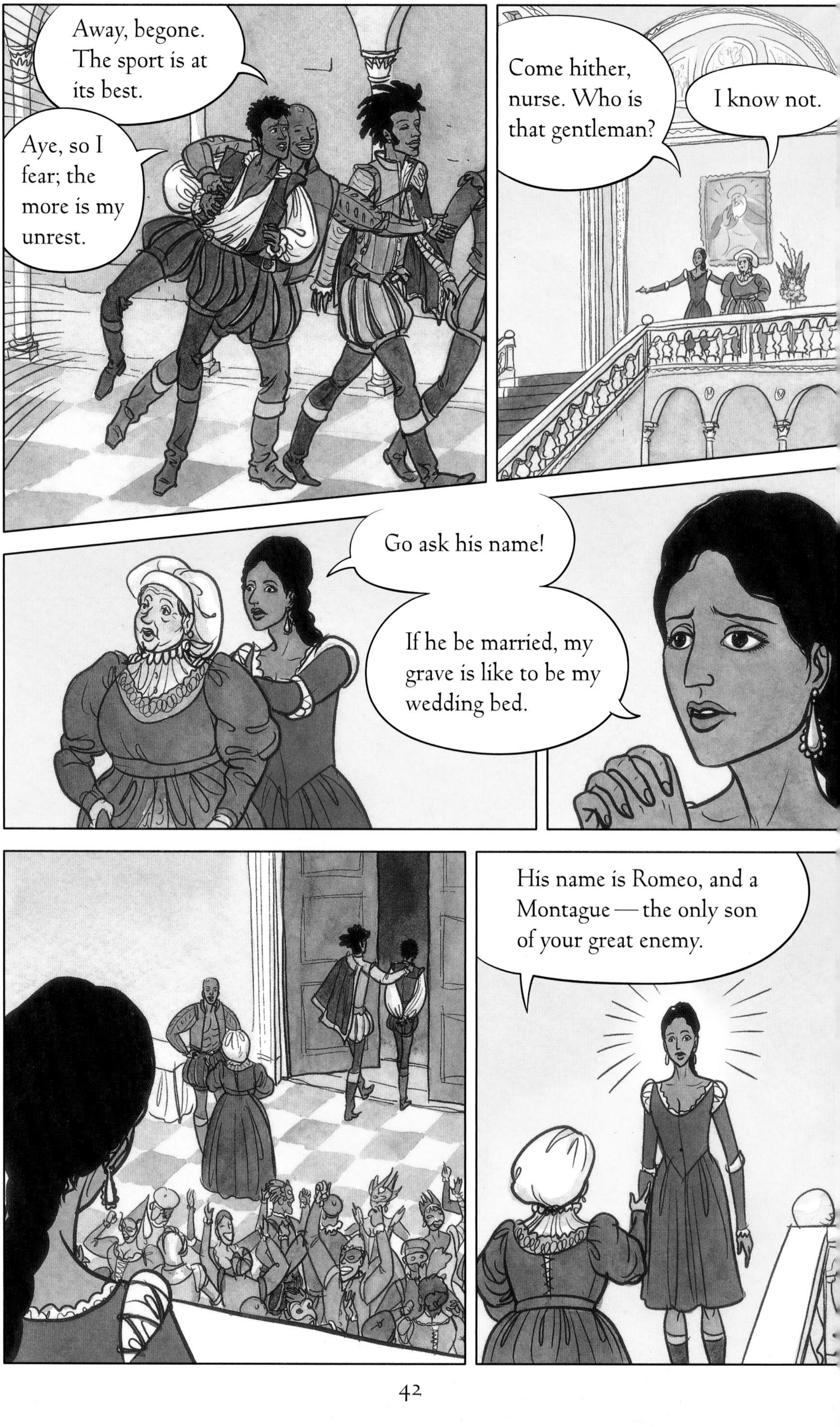
Away, begone. The sport is at its best.
Aye, so I fear; the more is my unrest.
Come hither, nurse. Who is that gentleman?
I know not.
Go ask his name!
If he be married, my grave is like to be my wedding bed.
His name is Romeo, and a Montague — the only son of your great enemy.

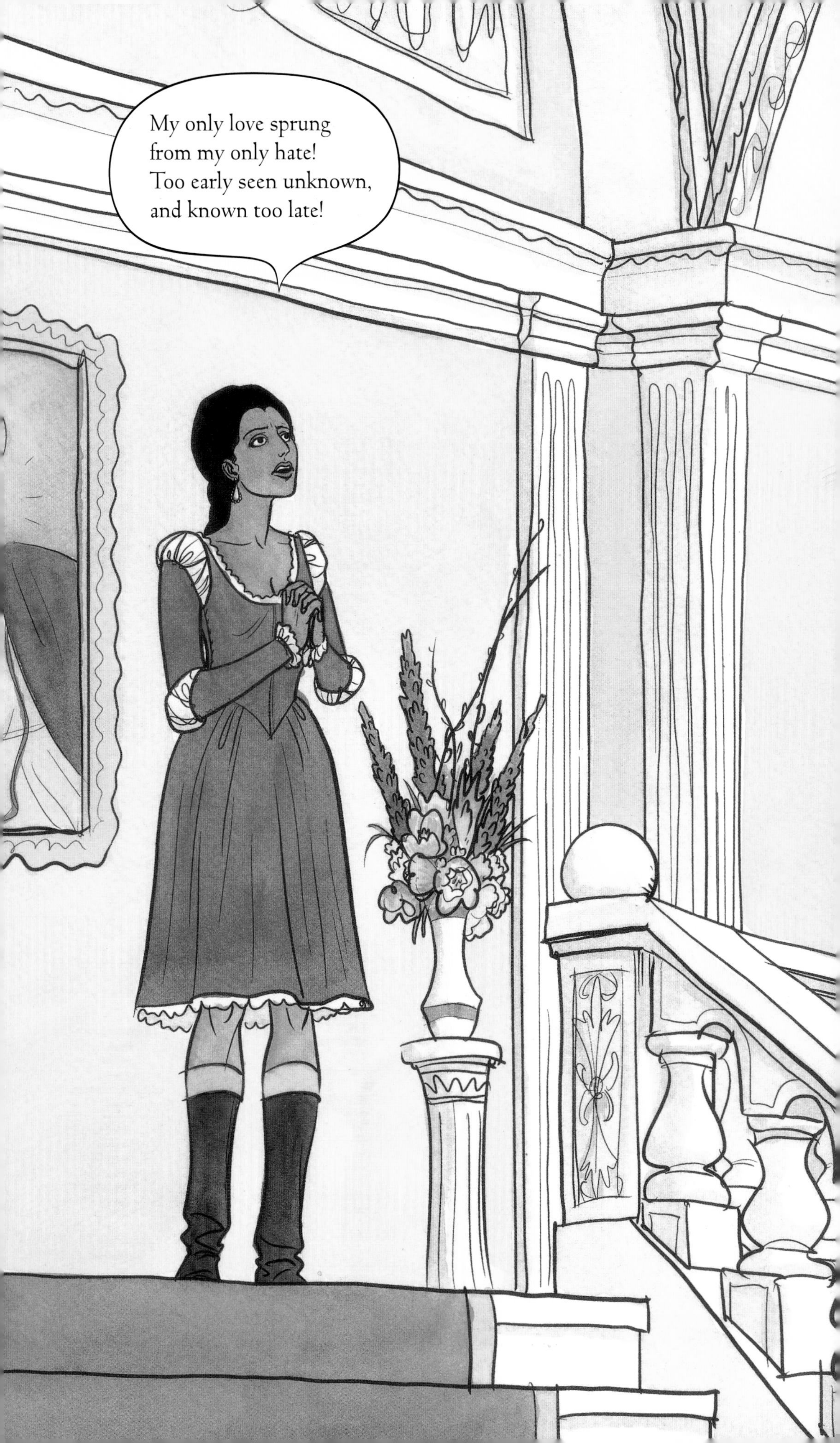
My only love sprung from my only hate! Too early seen unknown, and known too late!

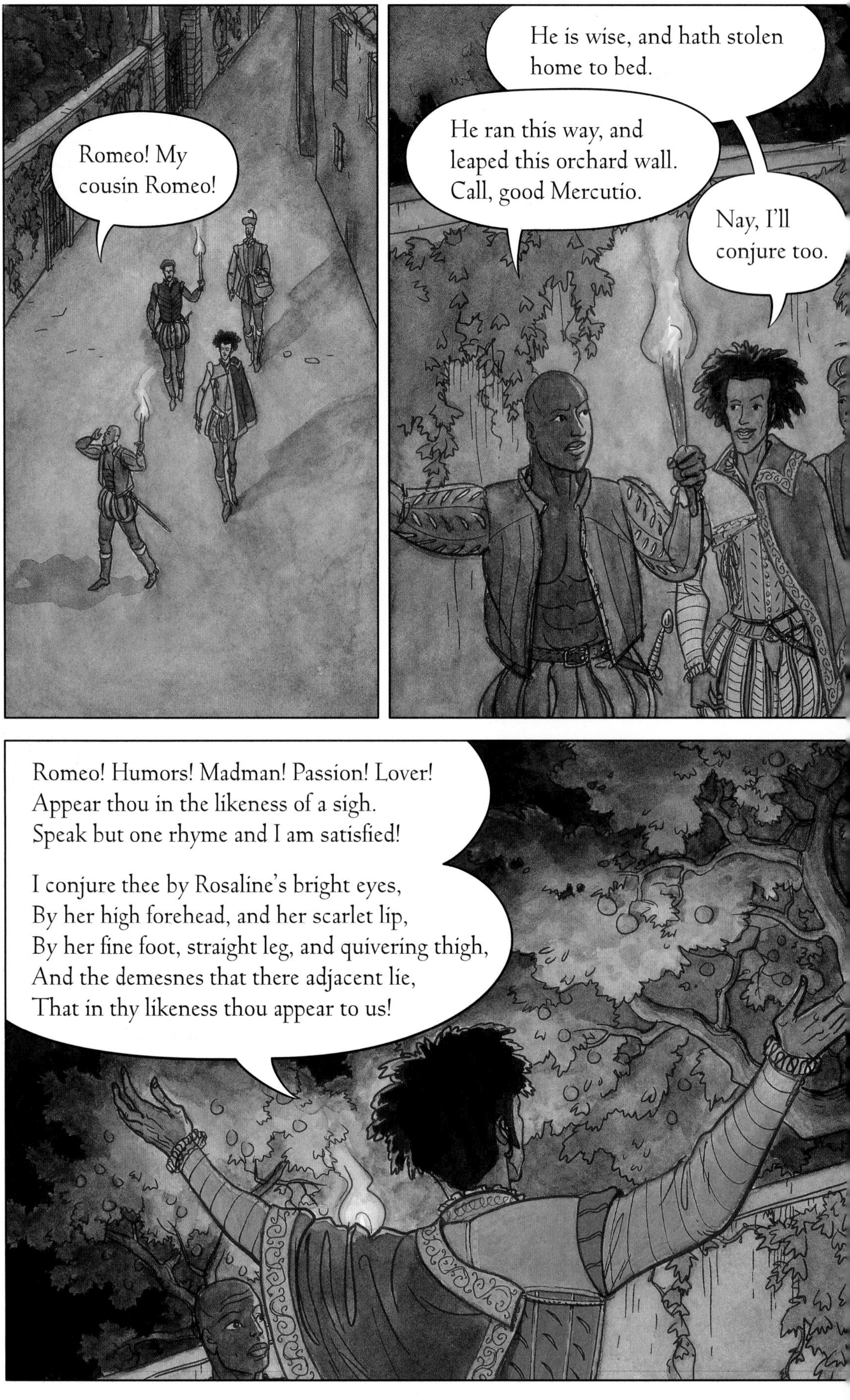
Romeo! My cousin Romeo!
He ran this way, and leaped this orchard wall. Call, good Mercutio.
He is wise, and hath stolen home to bed.
Nay, I'll conjure too.
Romeo! Humors! Madman! Passion! Lover!
Appear thou in the likeness of a sigh.
Speak but one rhyme and I am satisfied!
I conjure thee by Rosaline's bright eyes,
By her high forehead, and her scarlet lip,
By her fine foot, straight leg, and quivering thigh,
And the demesnes that there adjacent lie,
That in thy likeness thou appear to us!

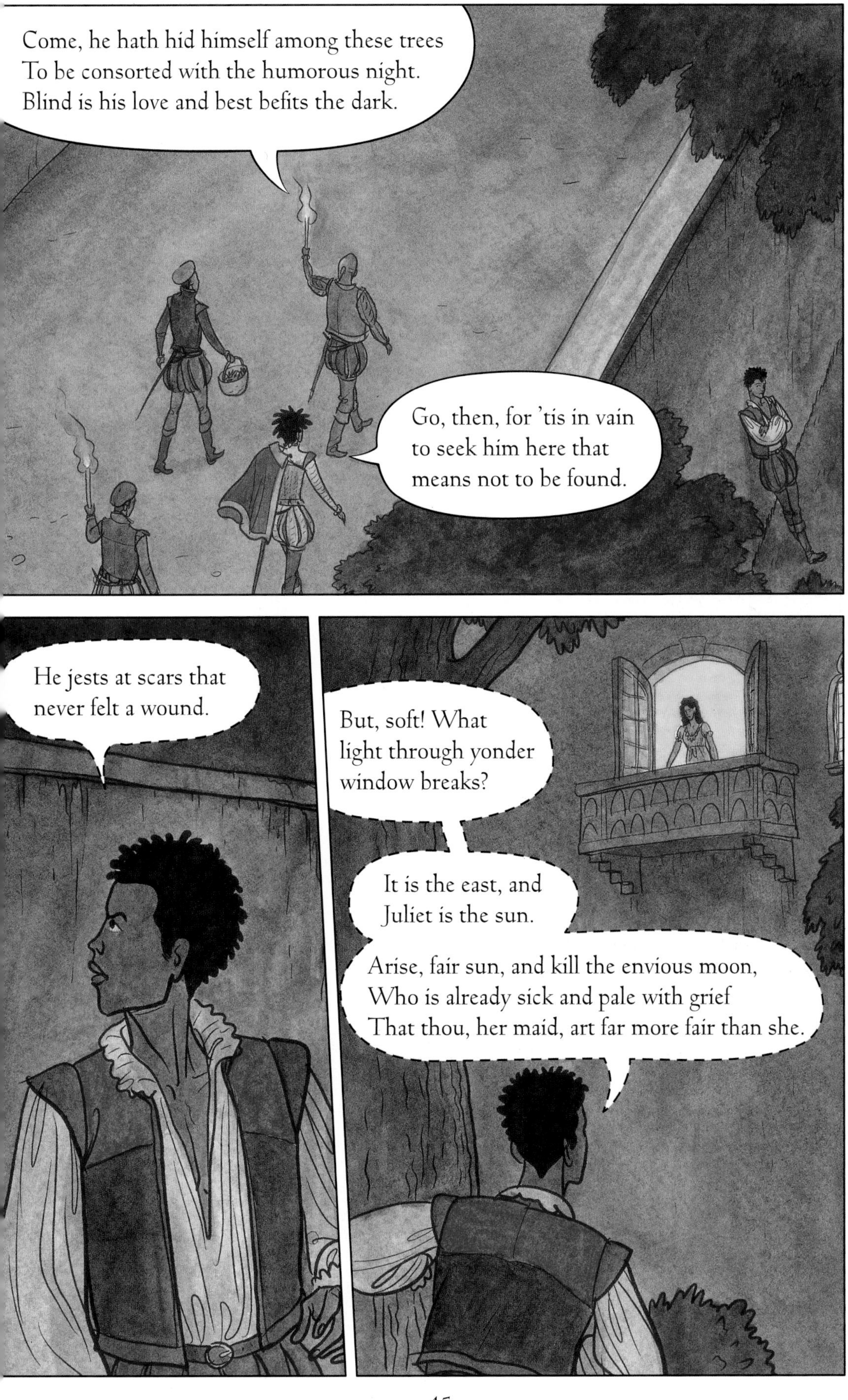
Come, he hath hid himself among these trees
To be consorted with the humorous night.
Blind is his love and best befits the dark.
Go, then, for 'tis in vain to seek him here that means not to be found.
He jests at scars that never felt a wound.
But, soft! What light through yonder window breaks?
It is the east, and Juliet is the sun.
Arise, fair sun, and kill the envious moon, Who is already sick and pale with grief That thou, her maid, art far more fair than she.

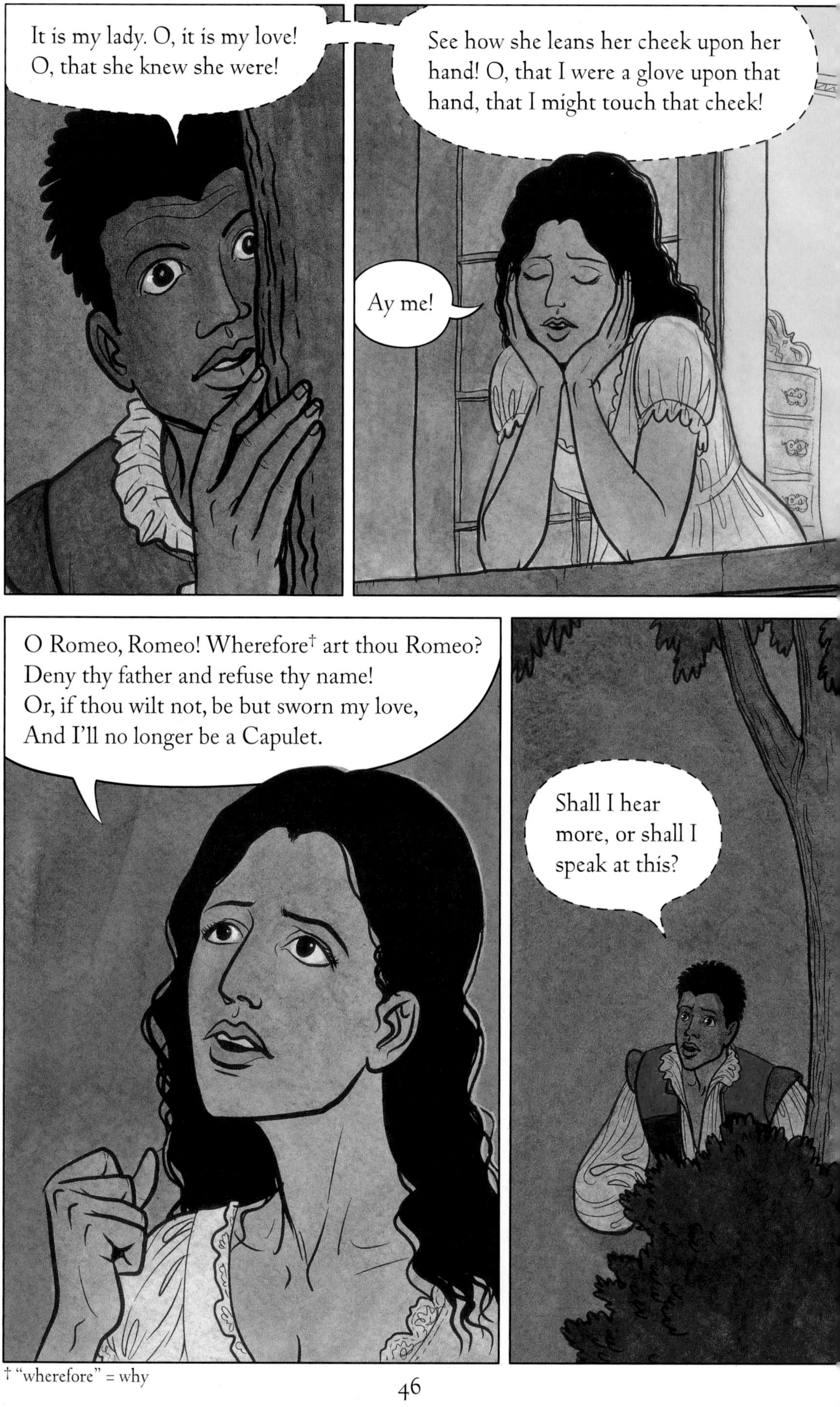
It is my lady. O, it is my love! O, that she knew she were!
See how she leans her cheek upon her hand! O, that I were a glove upon that hand, that I might touch that cheek!
Ay me!
O Romeo, Romeo! Wherefore† art thou Romeo? Deny thy father and refuse thy name! Or, if thou wilt not, be but sworn my love, And I'll no longer be a Capulet.
Shall I hear more, or shall I speak at this?

† "wherefore" = why

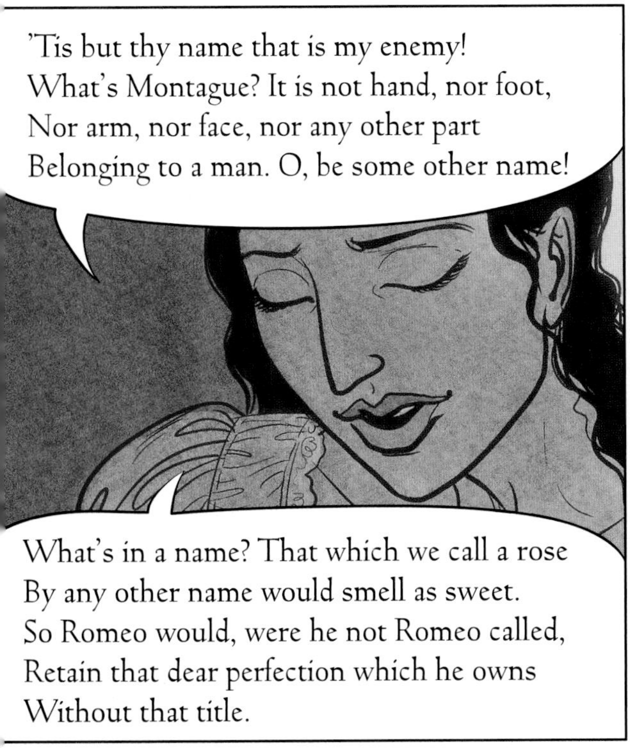
'Tis but thy name that is my enemy! What's Montague? It is not hand, nor foot, Nor arm, nor face, nor any other part Belonging to a man. O, be some other name!
What's in a name? That which we call a rose By any other name would smell as sweet. So Romeo would, were he not Romeo called, Retain that dear perfection which he owns Without that title.

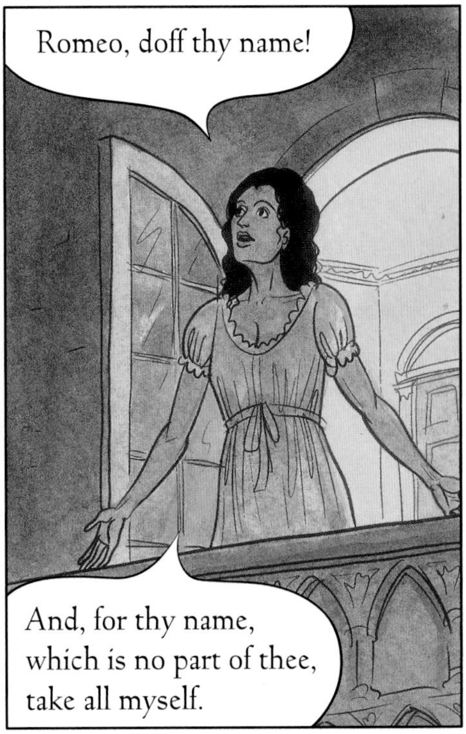
Romeo, doff thy name!
And, for thy name, which is no part of thee, take all myself.

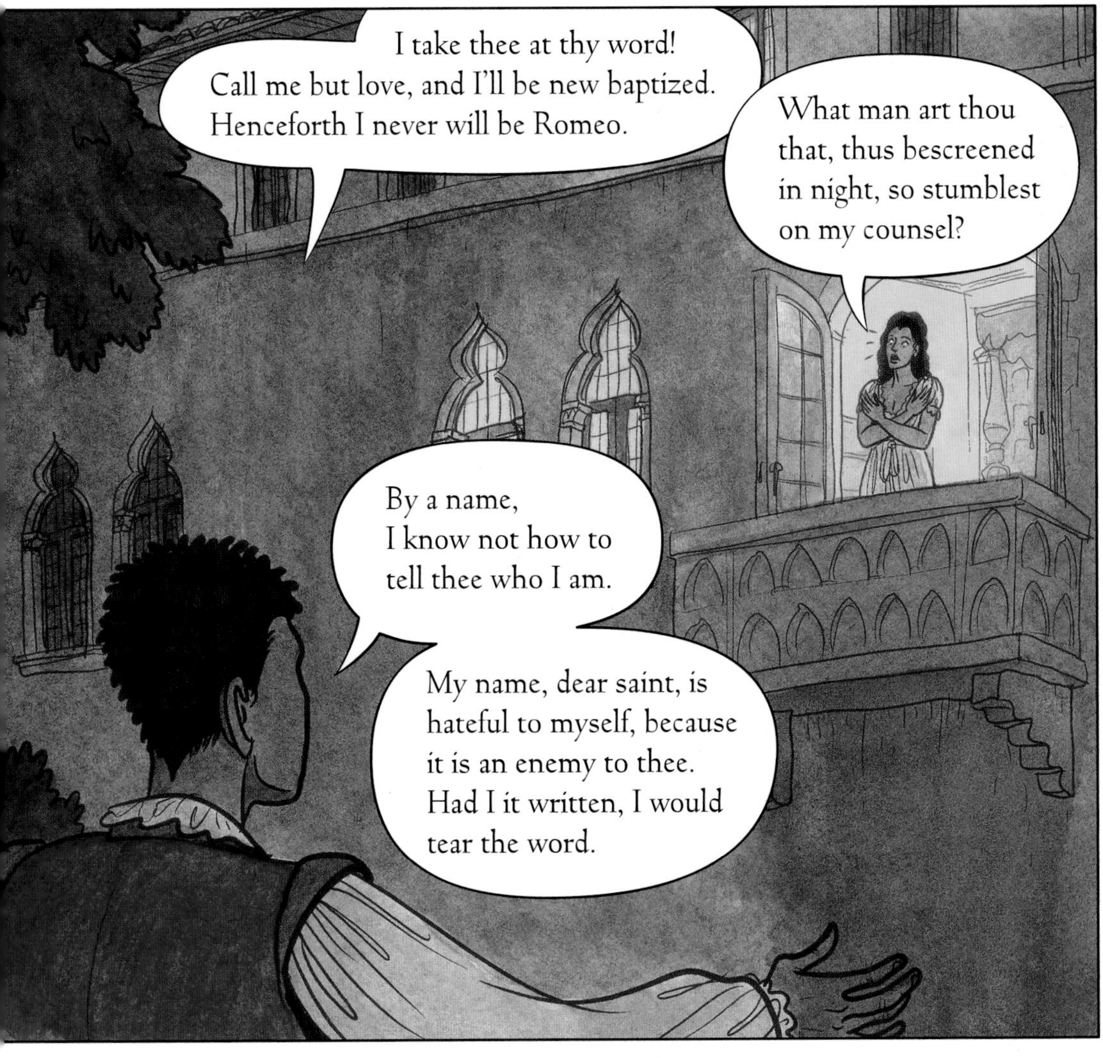
I take thee at thy word! Call me but love, and I'll be new baptized. Henceforth I never will be Romeo.
What man art thou that, thus bescreened in night, so stumblest on my counsel?
By a name, I know not how to tell thee who I am.
My name, dear saint, is hateful to myself, because it is an enemy to thee. Had I it written, I would tear the word.

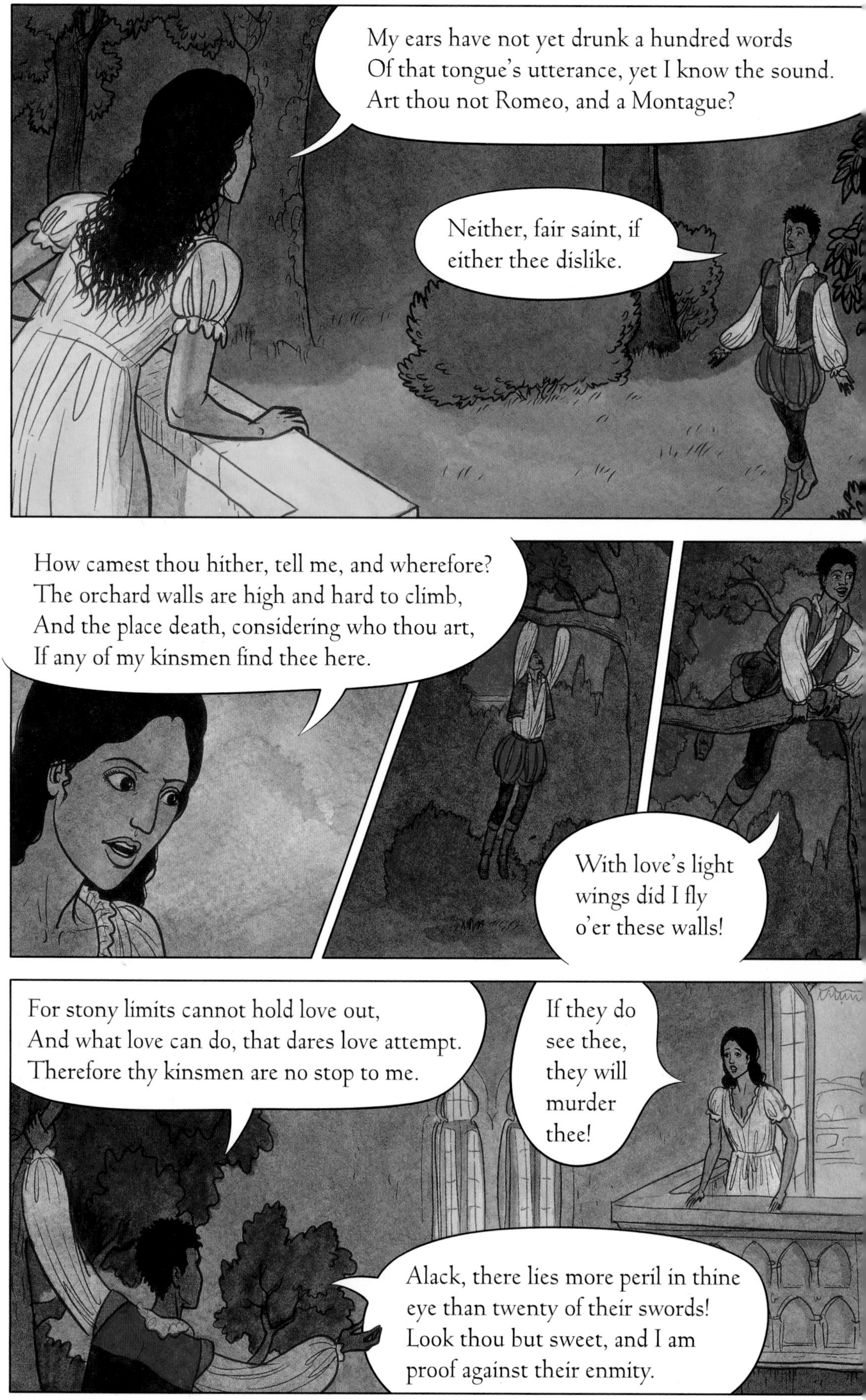
My ears have not yet drunk a hundred words Of that tongue's utterance, yet I know the sound. Art thou not Romeo, and a Montague?
Neither, fair saint, if either thee dislike.
How camest thou hither, tell me, and wherefore? The orchard walls are high and hard to climb, And the place death, considering who thou art, If any of my kinsmen find thee here.
With love's light wings did I fly o'er these walls!
For stony limits cannot hold love out, And what love can do, that dares love attempt. Therefore thy kinsmen are no stop to me.
If they do see thee, they will murder thee!
Alack, there lies more peril in thine eye than twenty of their swords! Look thou but sweet, and I am proof against their enmity.

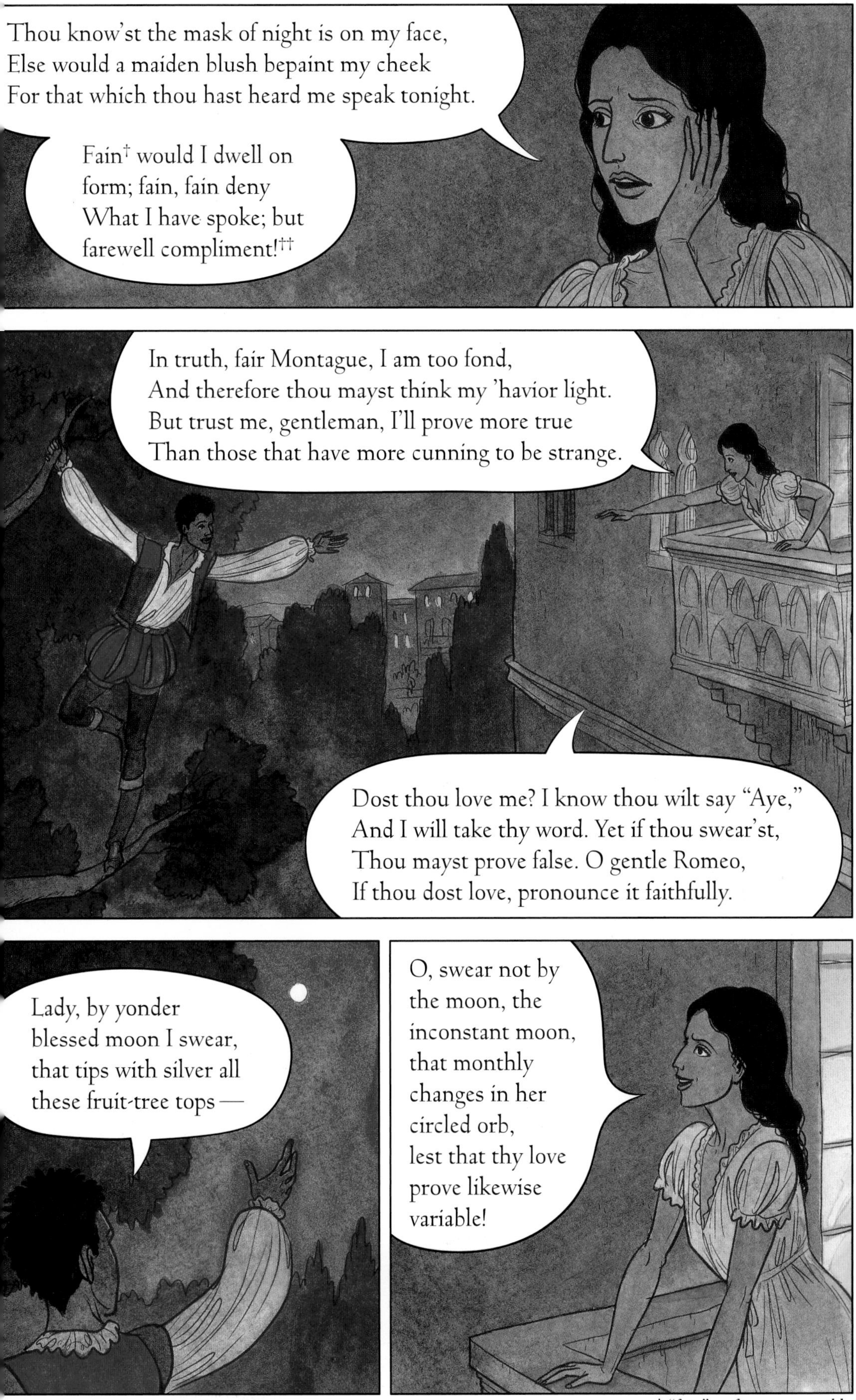
Thou know'st the mask of night is on my face, Else would a maiden blush bepaint my cheek For that which thou hast heard me speak tonight.
Fain† would I dwell on form; fain, fain deny What I have spoke; but farewell compliment!††
In truth, fair Montague, I am too fond, And therefore thou mayst think my 'havior light. But trust me, gentleman, I'll prove more true Than those that have more cunning to be strange.
Dost thou love me? I know thou wilt say "Aye," And I will take thy word. Yet if thou swear'st, Thou mayst prove false. O gentle Romeo, If thou dost love, pronounce it faithfully.
Lady, by yonder blessed moon I swear, that tips with silver all these fruit-tree tops —
O, swear not by the moon, the inconstant moon, that monthly changes in her circled orb, lest that thy love prove likewise variable!

† "fain" = if it were possible
† † "compliment" = formality

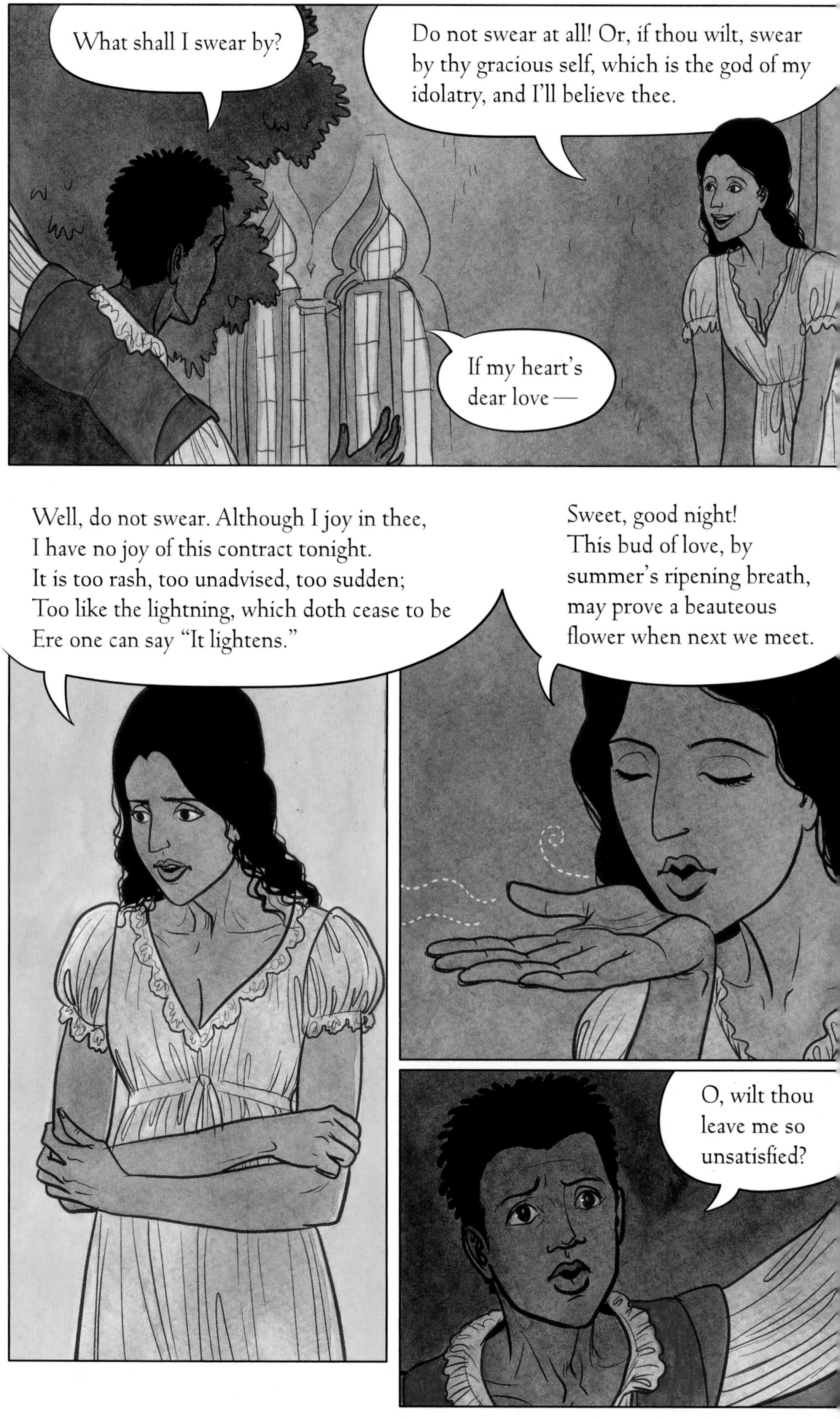
What shall I swear by?
Do not swear at all! Or, if thou wilt, swear by thy gracious self, which is the god of my idolatry, and I'll believe thee.
If my heart's dear love —
Well, do not swear. Although I joy in thee, I have no joy of this contract tonight. It is too rash, too unadvised, too sudden; Too like the lightning, which doth cease to be Ere one can say "It lightens."
Sweet, good night! This bud of love, by summer's ripening breath, may prove a beauteous flower when next we meet.
O, wilt thou leave me so unsatisfied?

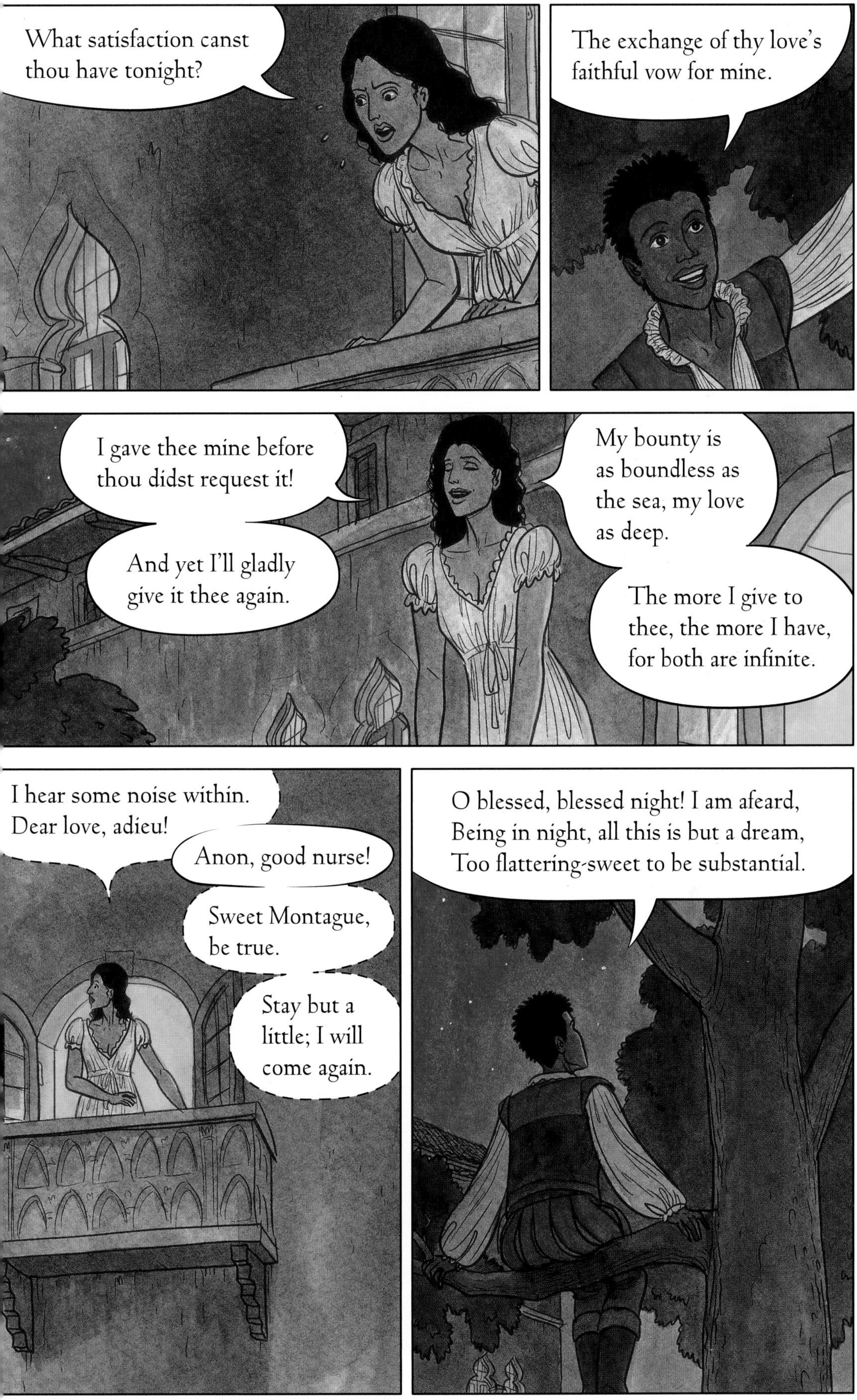
What satisfaction canst thou have tonight?
The exchange of thy love's faithful vow for mine.
I gave thee mine before thou didst request it!
And yet I'll gladly give it thee again.
My bounty is as boundless as the sea, my love as deep.
The more I give to thee, the more I have, for both are infinite.
I hear some noise within. Dear love, adieu!
Anon, good nurse!
Sweet Montague, be true.
Stay but a little; I will come again.
O blessed, blessed night! I am afeard, Being in night, all this is but a dream, Too flattering-sweet to be substantial.

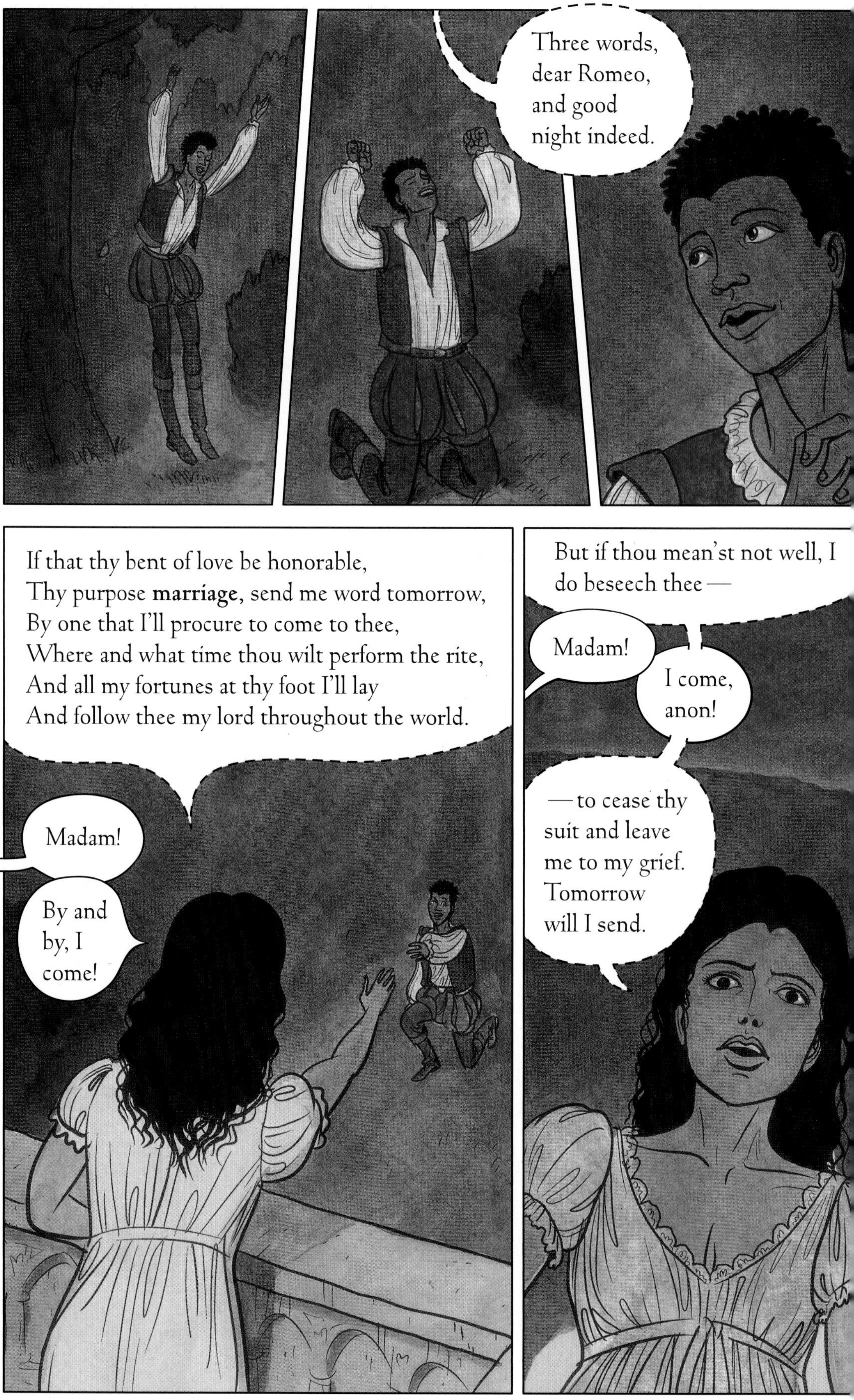
Three words, dear Romeo, and good night indeed.
If that thy bent of love be honorable, Thy purpose **marriage**, send me word tomorrow, By one that I'll procure to come to thee, Where and what time thou wilt perform the rite, And all my fortunes at thy foot I'll lay And follow thee my lord throughout the world.
Madam!
By and by, I come!
But if thou mean'st not well, I do beseech thee —
Madam!
I come, anon!
— to cease thy suit and leave me to my grief. Tomorrow will I send.

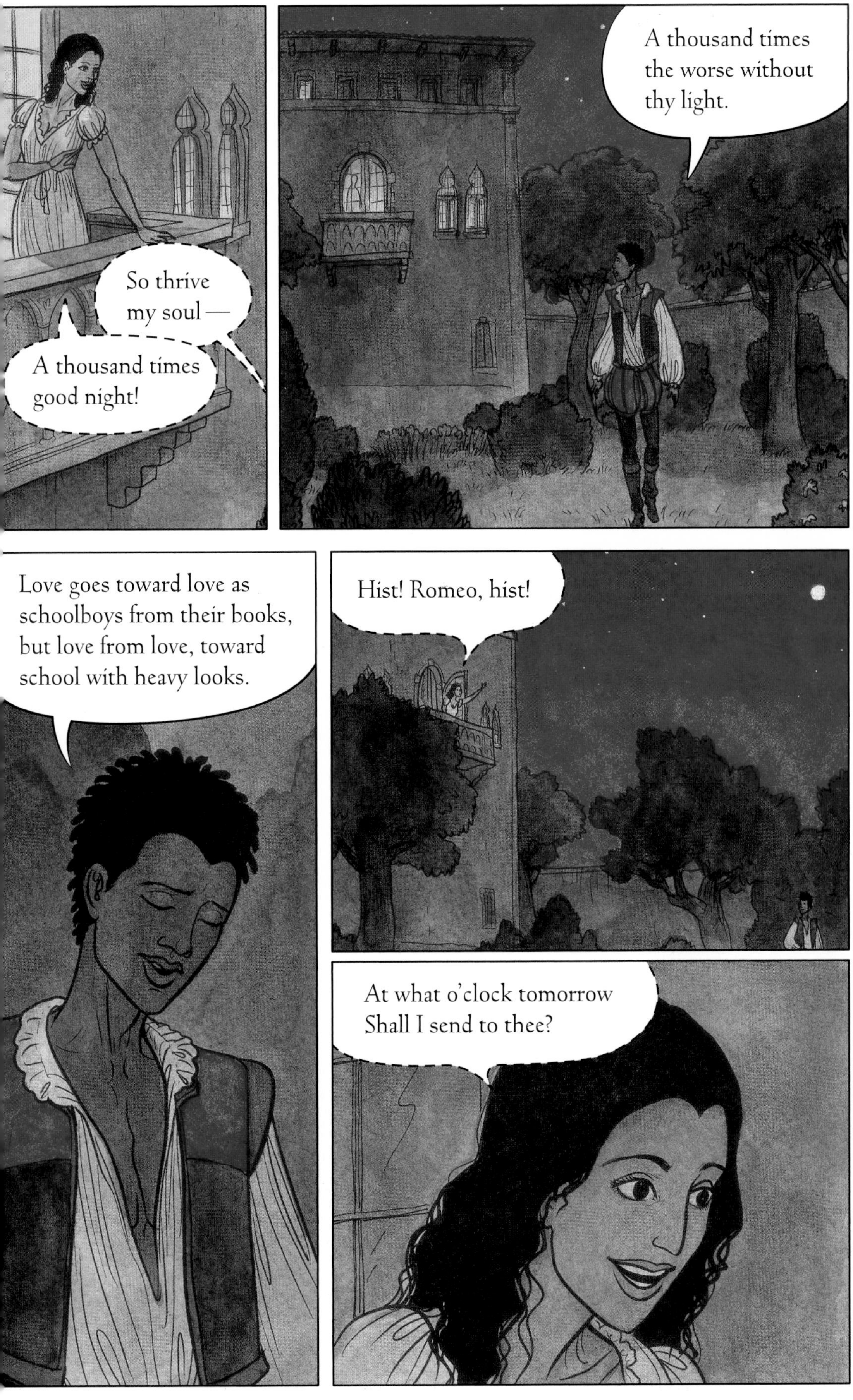
So thrive my soul —
A thousand times good night!
A thousand times the worse without thy light.
Love goes toward love as schoolboys from their books, but love from love, toward school with heavy looks.
Hist! Romeo, hist!
At what o'clock tomorrow Shall I send to thee?

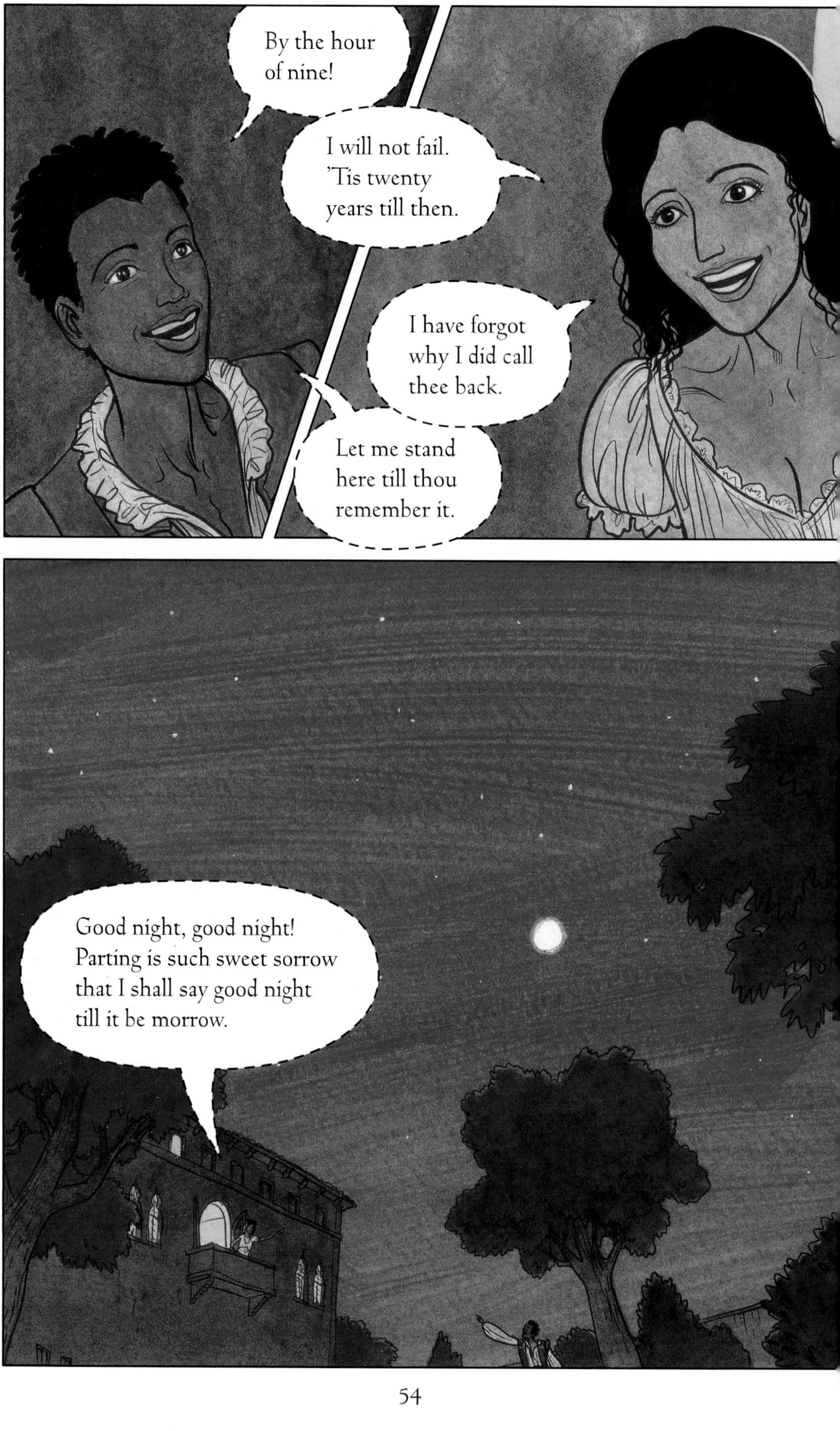
By the hour of nine!
I will not fail. 'Tis twenty years till then.
I have forgot why I did call thee back.
Let me stand here till thou remember it.
Good night, good night! Parting is such sweet sorrow that I shall say good night till it be morrow.

Scene 3 : The Franciscan Monastery of Friar Laurence

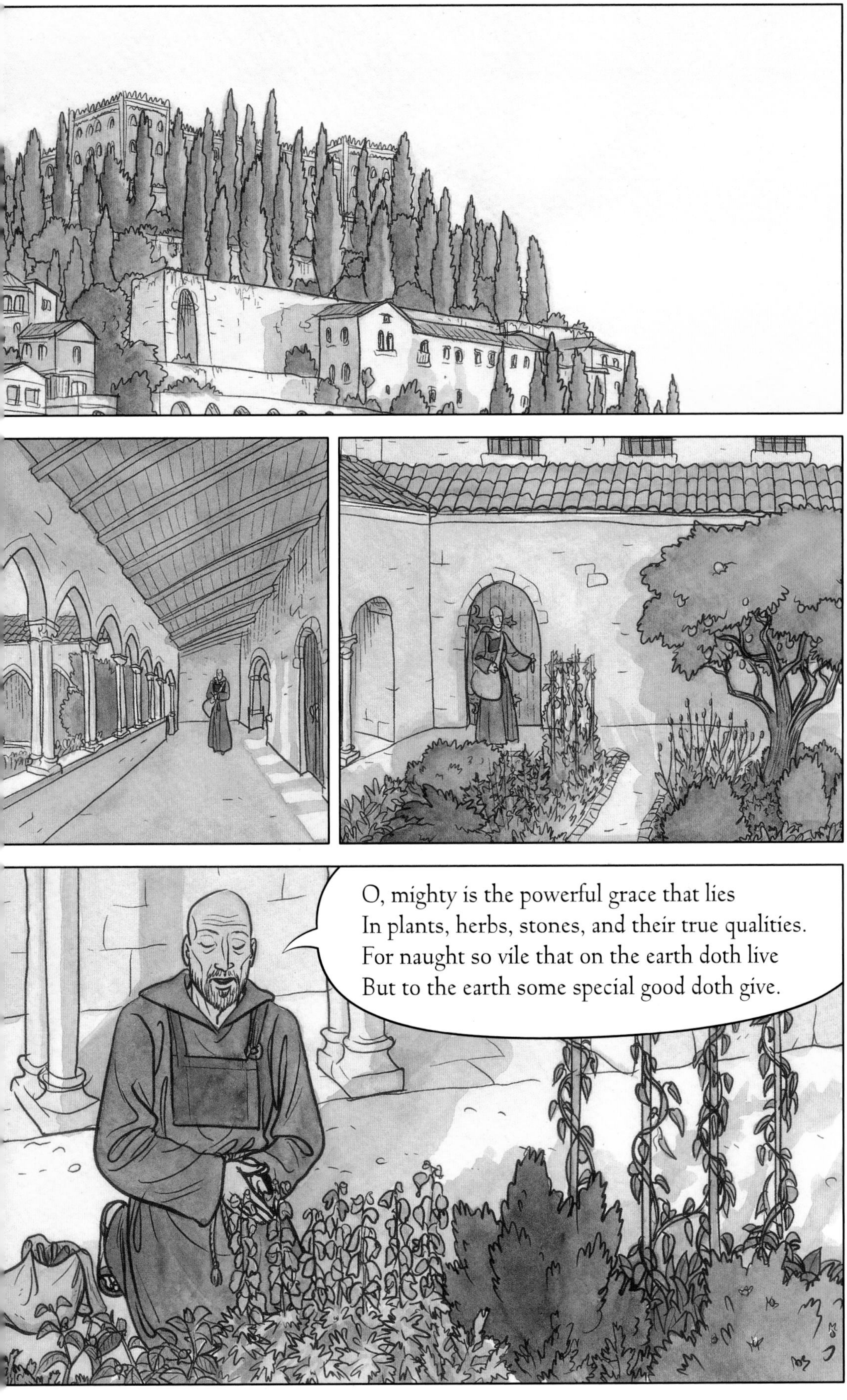
O, mighty is the powerful grace that lies
In plants, herbs, stones, and their true qualities.
For naught so vile that on the earth doth live
But to the earth some special good doth give.

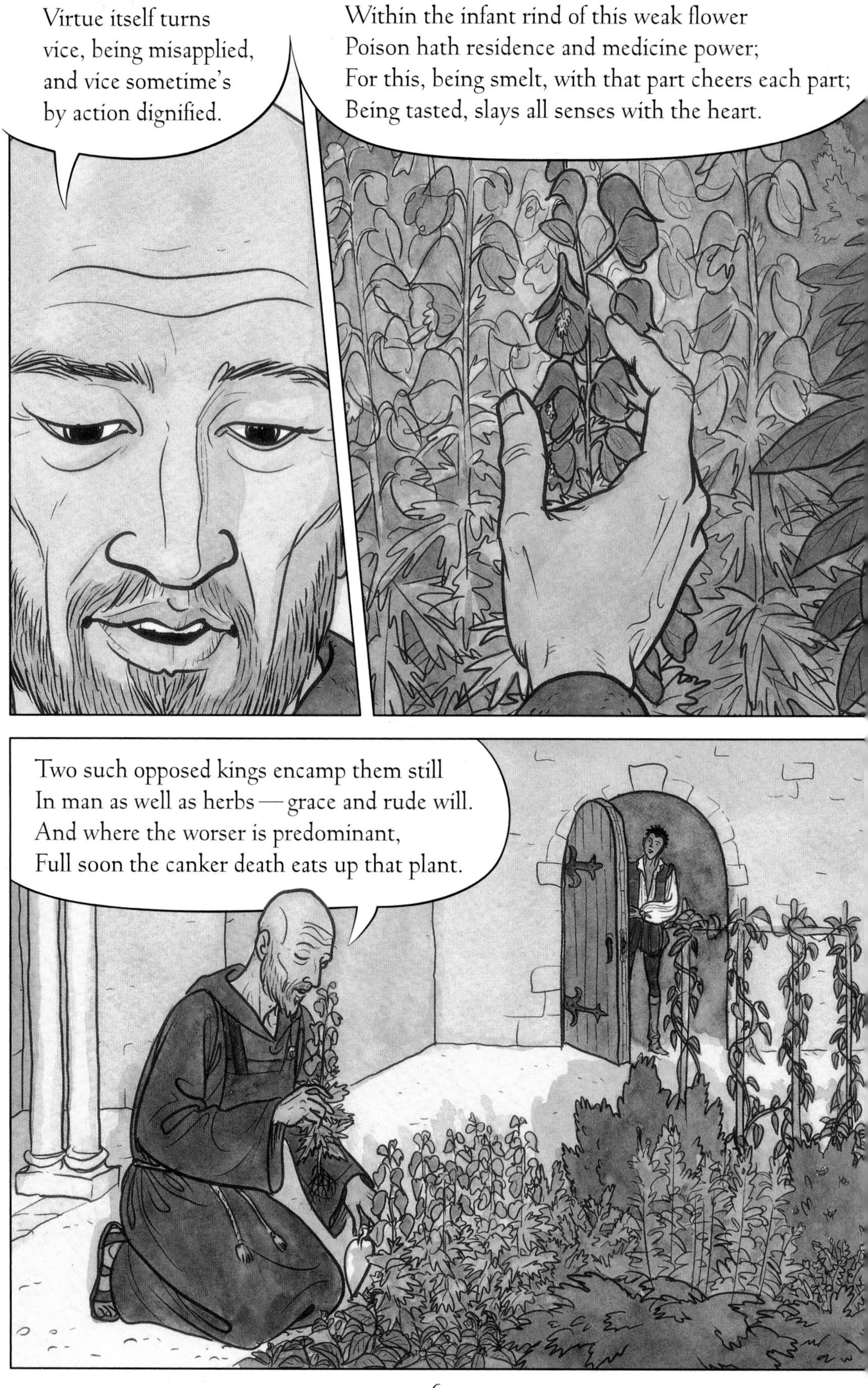
Virtue itself turns vice, being misapplied, and vice sometime's by action dignified.
Within the infant rind of this weak flower
Poison hath residence and medicine power;
For this, being smelt, with that part cheers each part;
Being tasted, slays all senses with the heart.
Two such opposed kings encamp them still
In man as well as herbs — grace and rude will.
And where the worser is predominant,
Full soon the canker death eats up that plant.

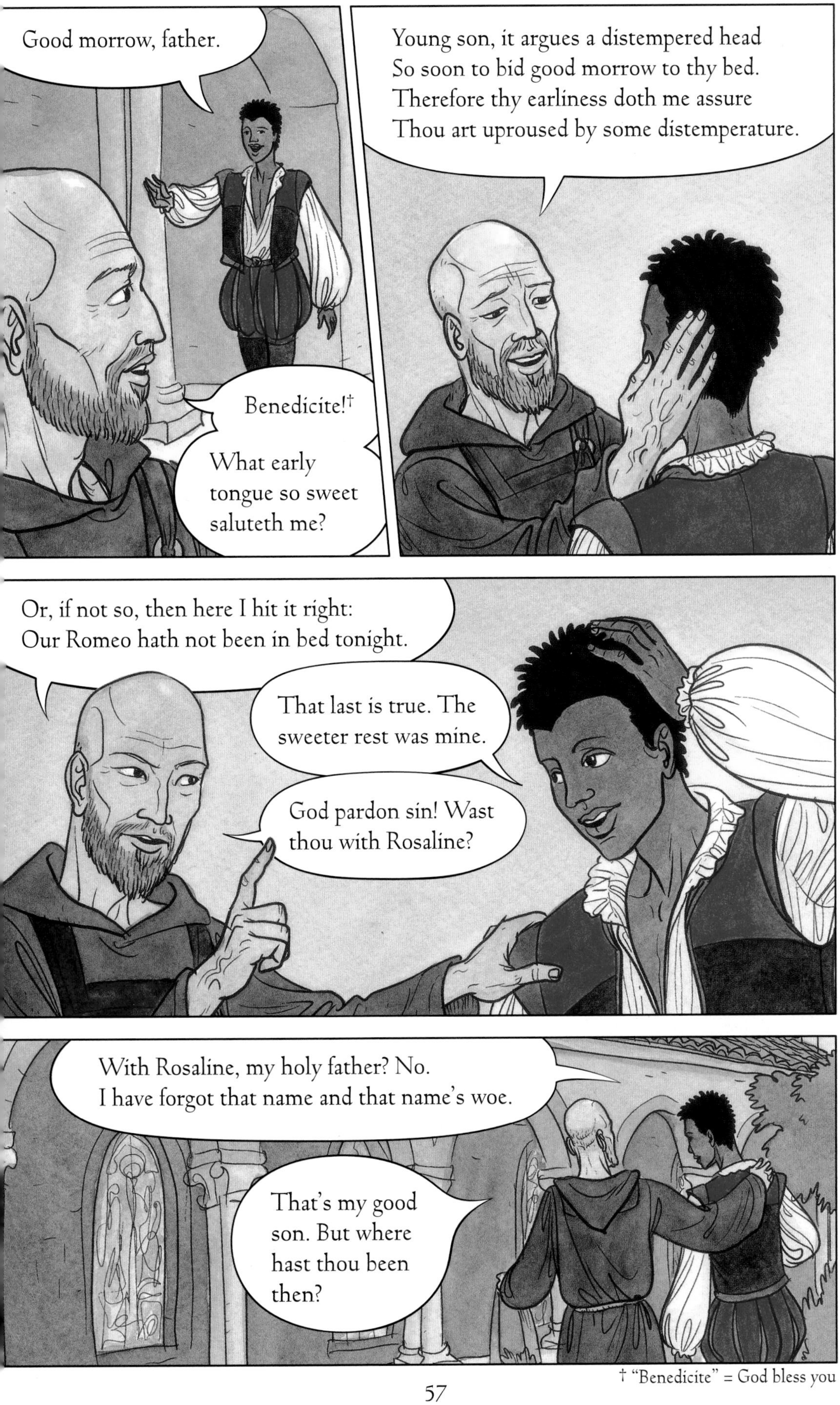
Good morrow, father.
Benedicite![†]
What early tongue so sweet saluteth me?
Young son, it argues a distempered head
So soon to bid good morrow to thy bed.
Therefore thy earliness doth me assure
Thou art uproused by some distemperature.
Or, if not so, then here I hit it right:
Our Romeo hath not been in bed tonight.
That last is true. The sweeter rest was mine.
God pardon sin! Wast thou with Rosaline?
With Rosaline, my holy father? No.
I have forgot that name and that name's woe.
That's my good son. But where hast thou been then?

† "Benedicite" = God bless you

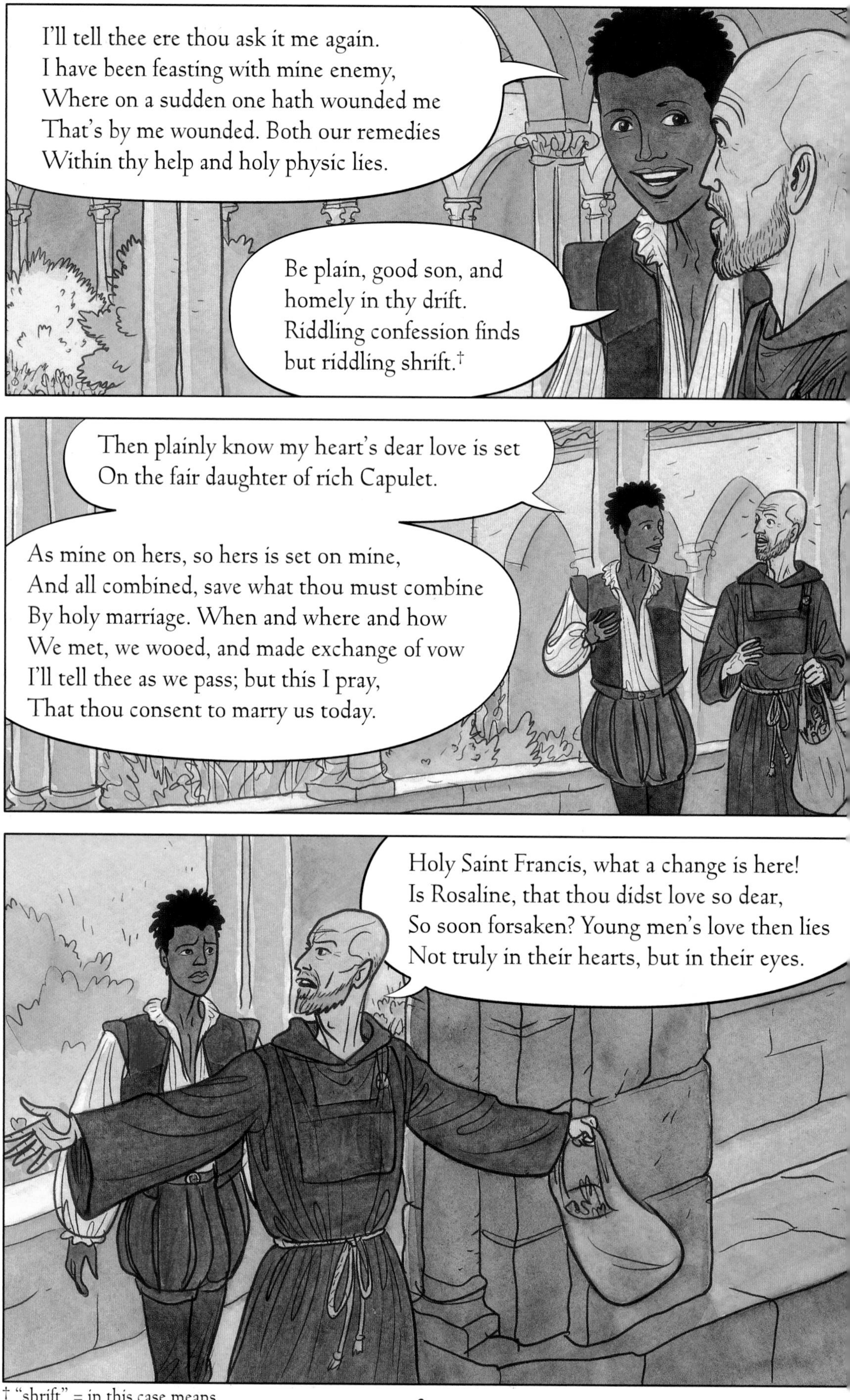
I'll tell thee ere thou ask it me again.
I have been feasting with mine enemy,
Where on a sudden one hath wounded me
That's by me wounded. Both our remedies
Within thy help and holy physic lies.
Be plain, good son, and
homely in thy drift.
Riddling confession finds
but riddling shrift.†
Then plainly know my heart's dear love is set
On the fair daughter of rich Capulet.
As mine on hers, so hers is set on mine,
And all combined, save what thou must combine
By holy marriage. When and where and how
We met, we wooed, and made exchange of vow
I'll tell thee as we pass; but this I pray,
That thou consent to marry us today.
Holy Saint Francis, what a change is here!
Is Rosaline, that thou didst love so dear,
So soon forsaken? Young men's love then lies
Not truly in their hearts, but in their eyes.

† "shrift" = in this case means
forgiveness after confession

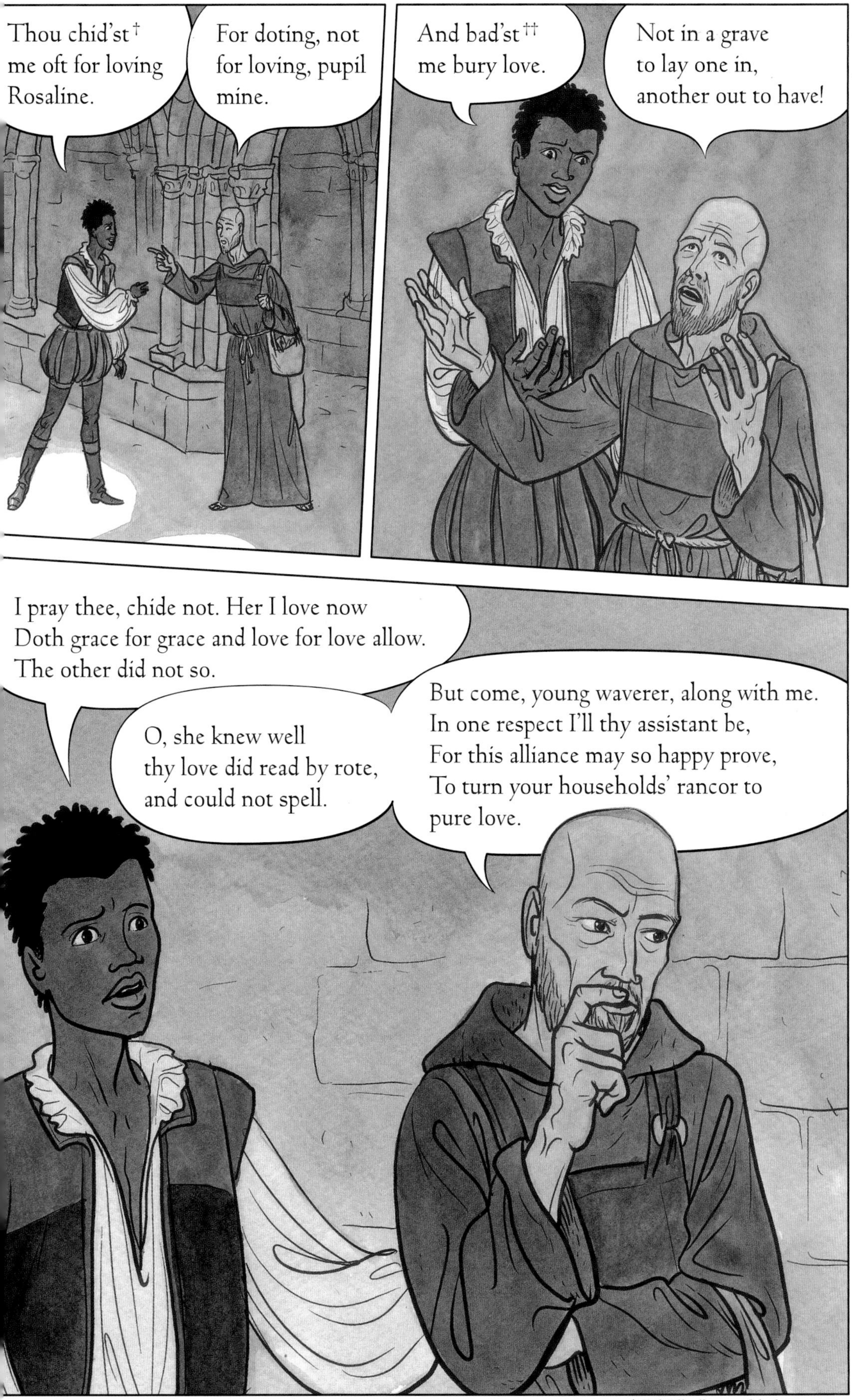
Thou chid'st† me oft for loving Rosaline.
For doting, not for loving, pupil mine.
And bad'st†† me bury love.
Not in a grave to lay one in, another out to have!
I pray thee, chide not. Her I love now Doth grace for grace and love for love allow. The other did not so.
O, she knew well thy love did read by rote, and could not spell.
But come, young waverer, along with me. In one respect I'll thy assistant be, For this alliance may so happy prove, To turn your households' rancor to pure love.

† "chid'st" = scolded
†† "bad'st" = asked, encouraged

Scene 4 : Bank of the Adige River

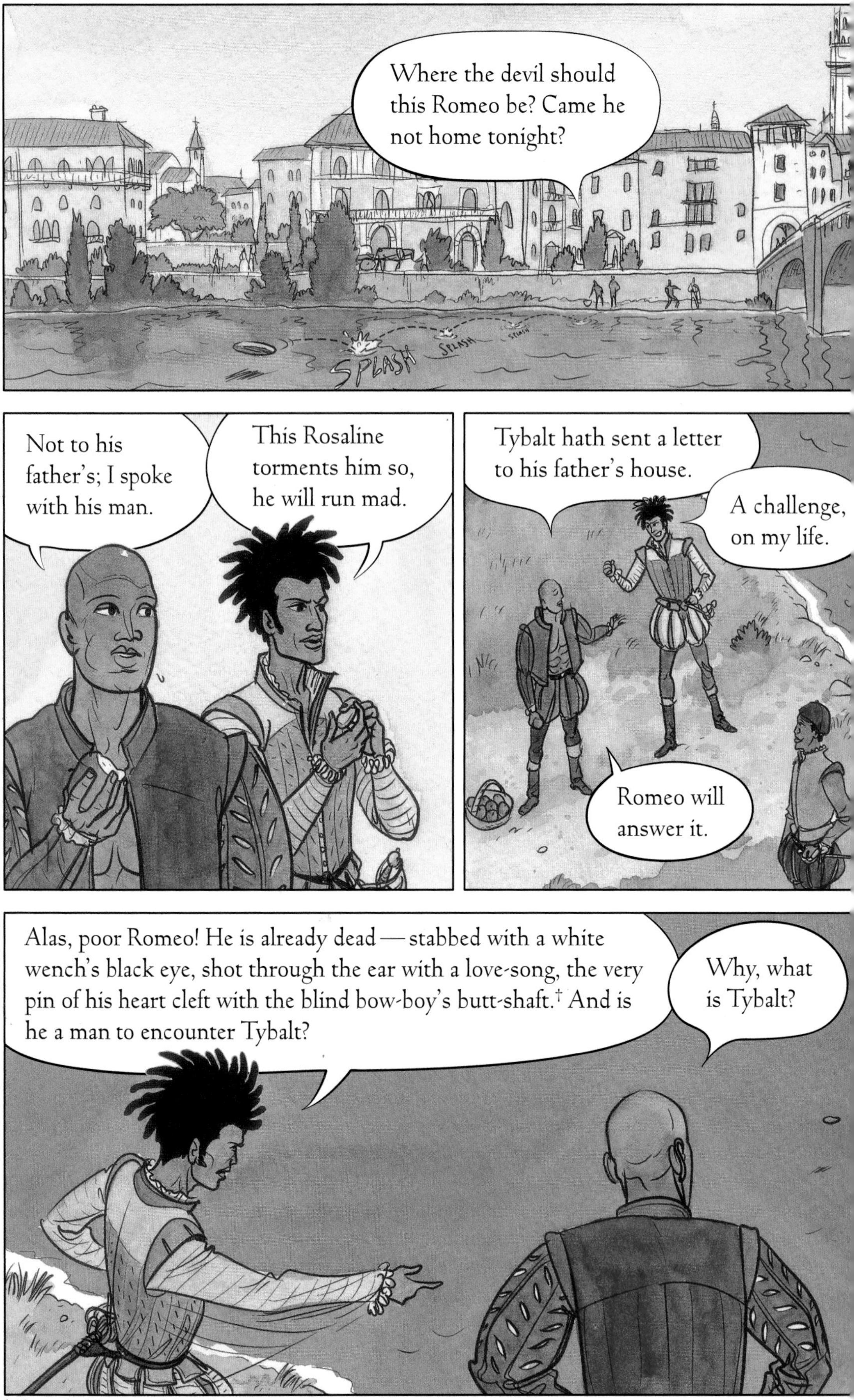

Where the devil should this Romeo be? Came he not home tonight?
SPLASH
SPLASH
Not to his father's; I spoke with his man.
This Rosaline torments him so, he will run mad.
Tybalt hath sent a letter to his father's house.
A challenge, on my life.
Romeo will answer it.
Alas, poor Romeo! He is already dead — stabbed with a white wench's black eye, shot through the ear with a love-song, the very pin of his heart cleft with the blind bow-boy's butt-shaft.† And is he a man to encounter Tybalt?
Why, what is Tybalt?

† "butt-shaft" = one of Cupid's blunt practice arrows

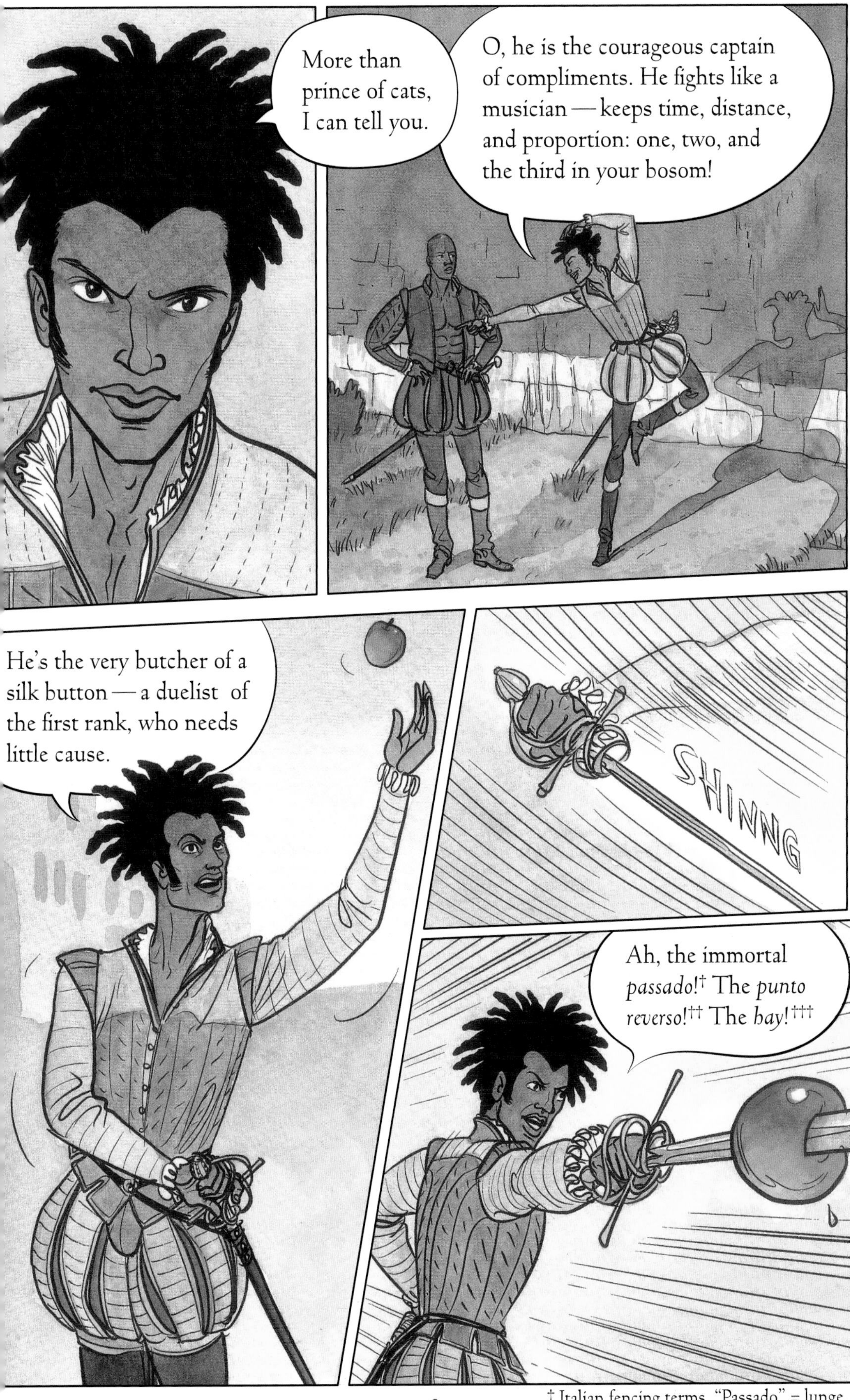
More than prince of cats, I can tell you.
O, he is the courageous captain of compliments. He fights like a musician — keeps time, distance, and proportion: one, two, and the third in your bosom!
He's the very butcher of a silk button — a duelist of the first rank, who needs little cause.
SHINNG
Ah, the immortal *passado*!† The *punto reverso*!†† The *hay*!†††

† Italian fencing terms. "Passado" = lunge,
†† "punto reverso" = backhand thrust,
††† "hay" = cry of victory on scoring a hit

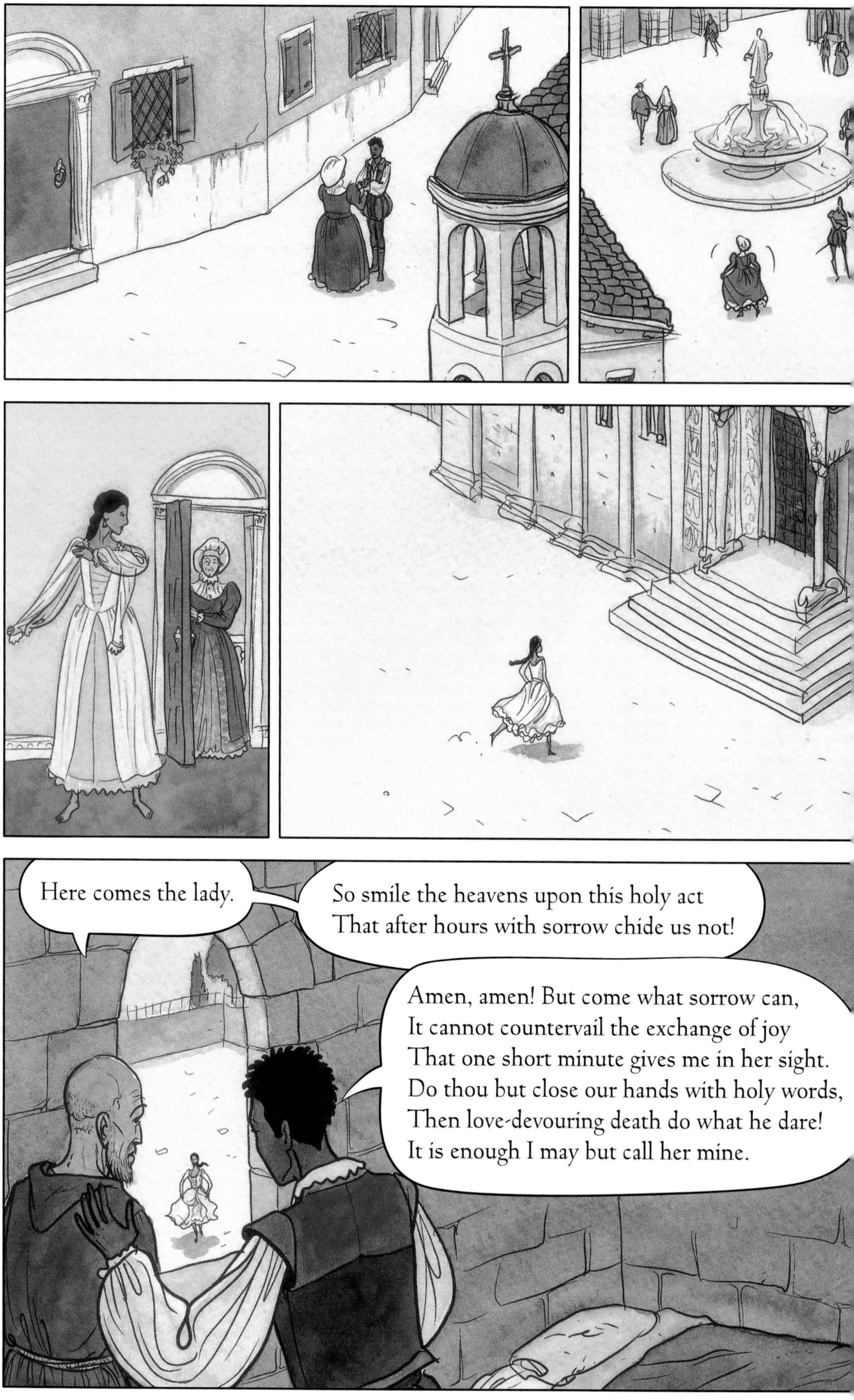
Here comes the lady.
So smile the heavens upon this holy act
That after hours with sorrow chide us not!
Amen, amen! But come what sorrow can,
It cannot countervail the exchange of joy
That one short minute gives me in her sight.
Do thou but close our hands with holy words,
Then love-devouring death do what he dare!
It is enough I may but call her mine.

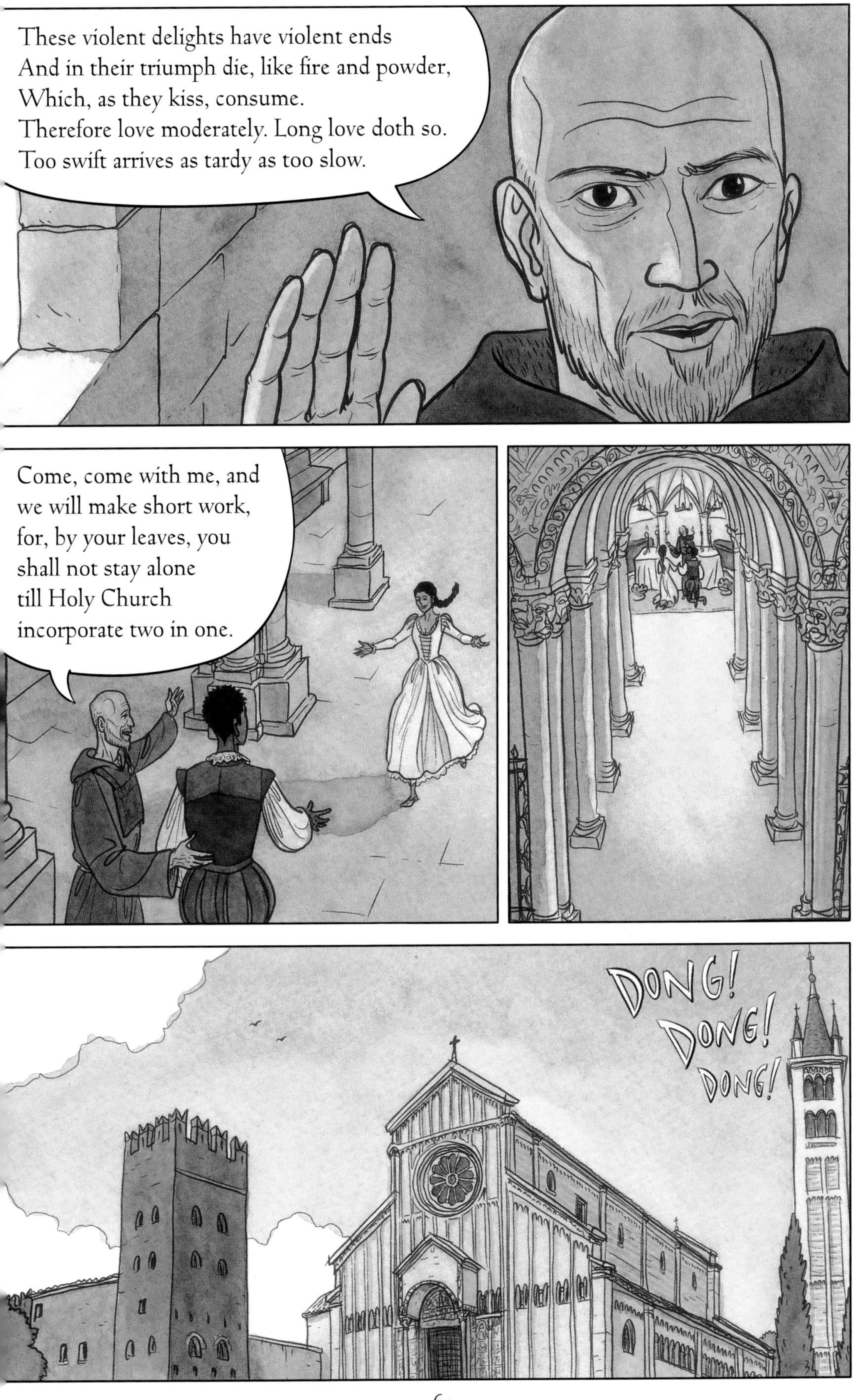
These violent delights have violent ends
And in their triumph die, like fire and powder,
Which, as they kiss, consume.
Therefore love moderately. Long love doth so.
Too swift arrives as tardy as too slow.
Come, come with me, and
we will make short work,
for, by your leaves, you
shall not stay alone
till Holy Church
incorporate two in one.
DONG!
DONG!
DONG!

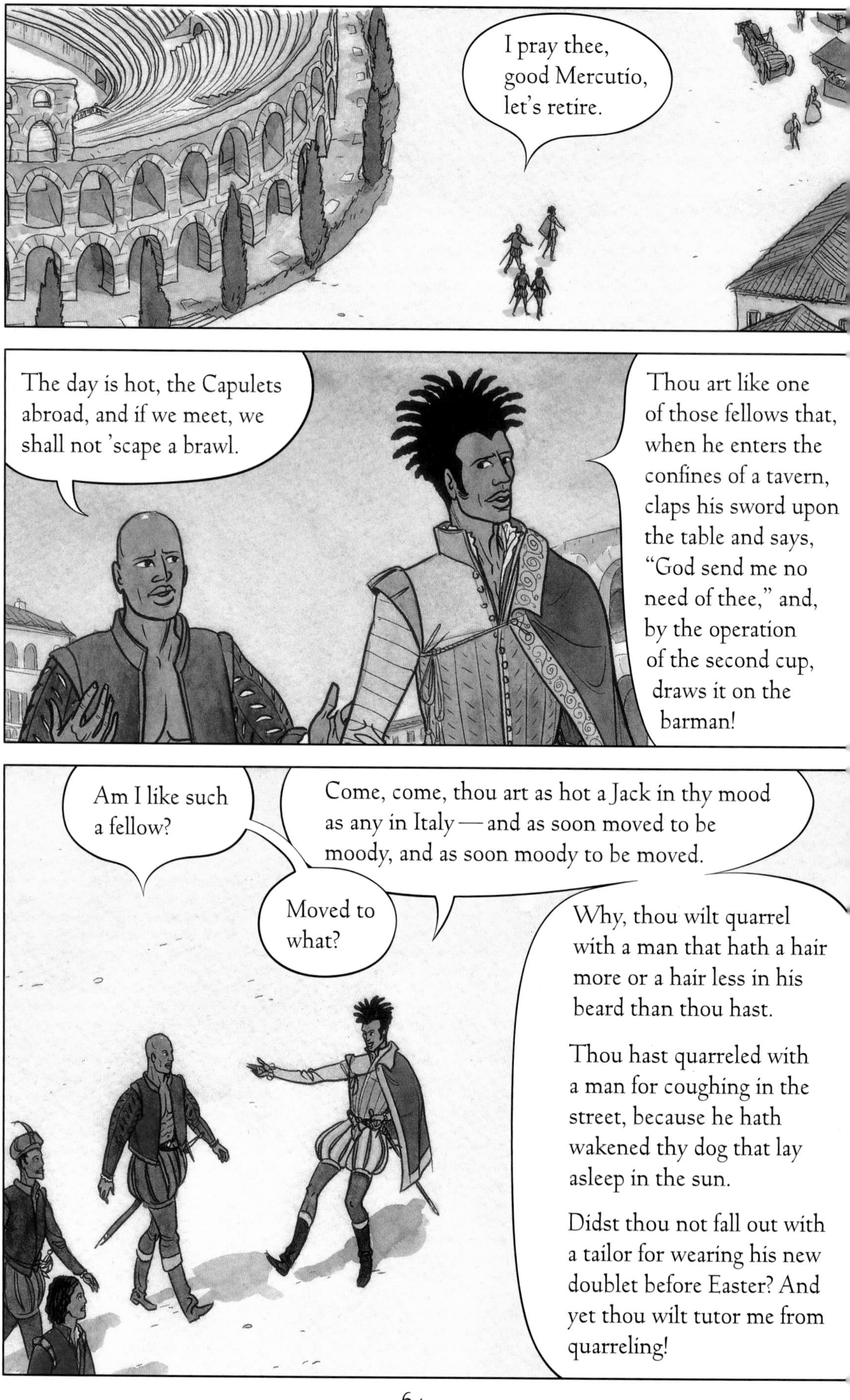
I pray thee, good Mercutio, let's retire.
The day is hot, the Capulets abroad, and if we meet, we shall not 'scape a brawl.
Thou art like one of those fellows that, when he enters the confines of a tavern, claps his sword upon the table and says, "God send me no need of thee," and, by the operation of the second cup, draws it on the barman!
Am I like such a fellow?
Come, come, thou art as hot a Jack in thy mood as any in Italy — and as soon moved to be moody, and as soon moody to be moved.
Moved to what?
Why, thou wilt quarrel with a man that hath a hair more or a hair less in his beard than thou hast.
Thou hast quarreled with a man for coughing in the street, because he hath wakened thy dog that lay asleep in the sun.
Didst thou not fall out with a tailor for wearing his new doublet before Easter? And yet thou wilt tutor me from quarreling!

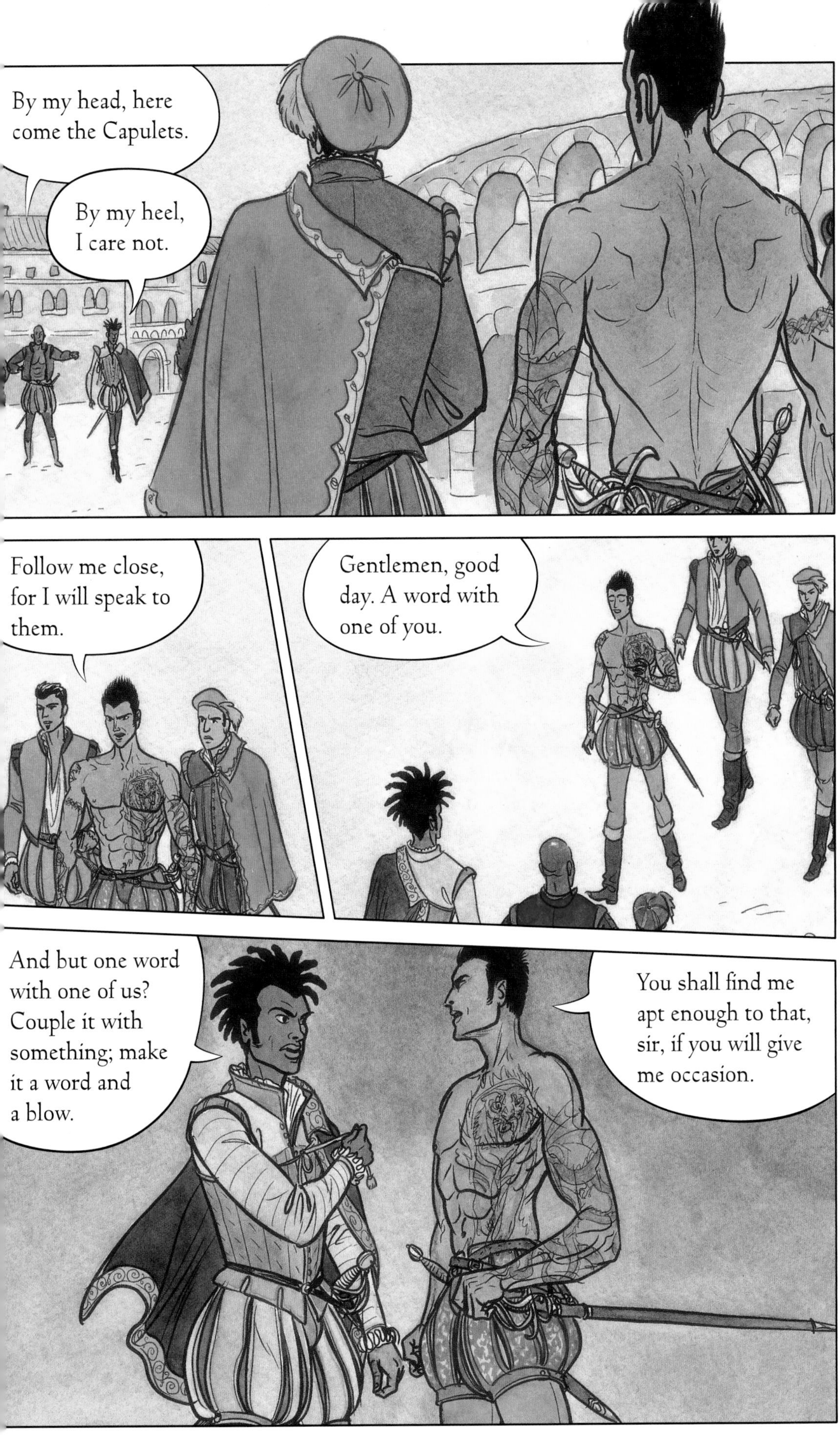
By my head, here come the Capulets.
By my heel, I care not.
Follow me close, for I will speak to them.
Gentlemen, good day. A word with one of you.
And but one word with one of us? Couple it with something; make it a word and a blow.
You shall find me apt enough to that, sir, if you will give me occasion.

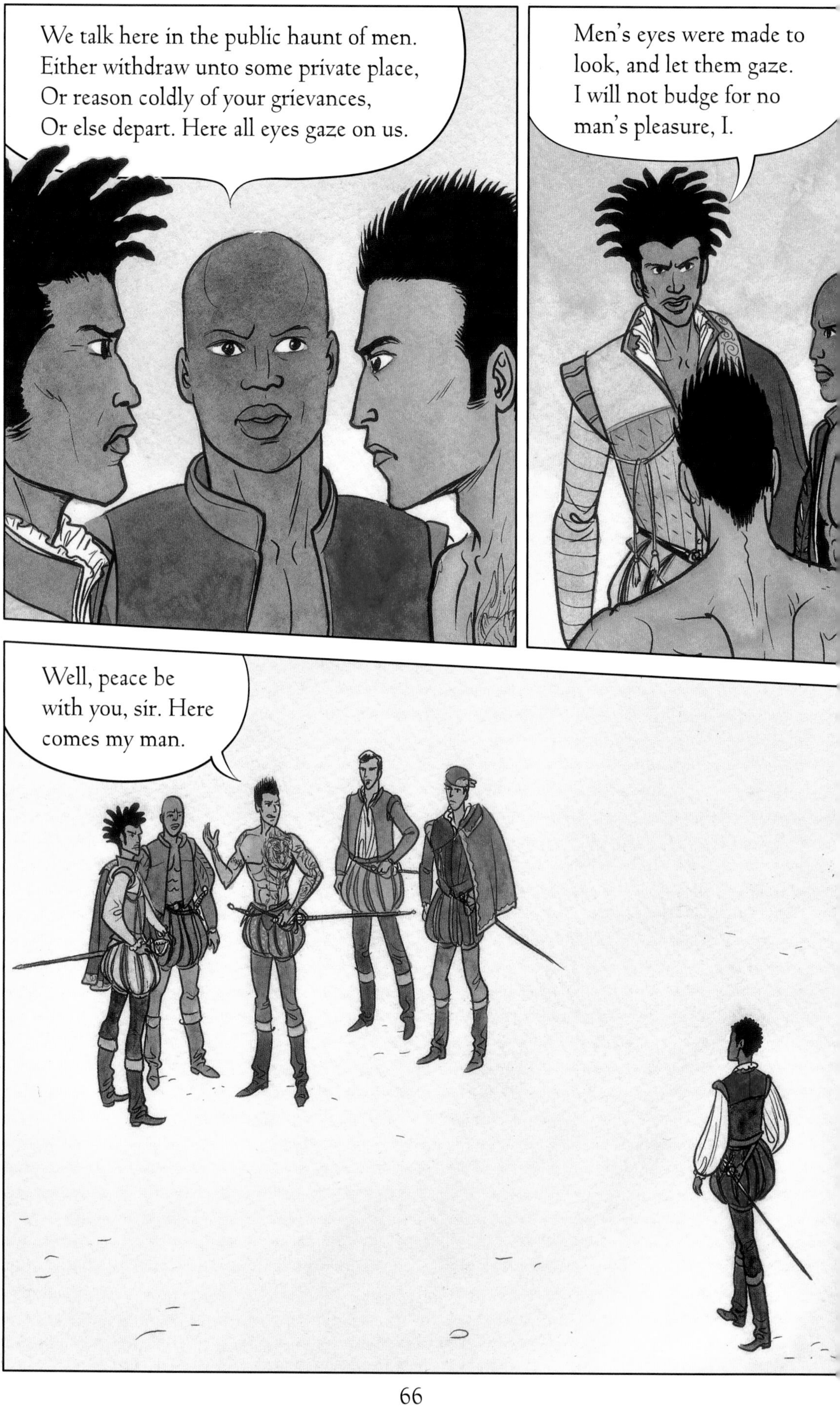
We talk here in the public haunt of men.
Either withdraw unto some private place,
Or reason coldly of your grievances,
Or else depart. Here all eyes gaze on us.
Men's eyes were made to look, and let them gaze. I will not budge for no man's pleasure, I.
Well, peace be with you, sir. Here comes my man.

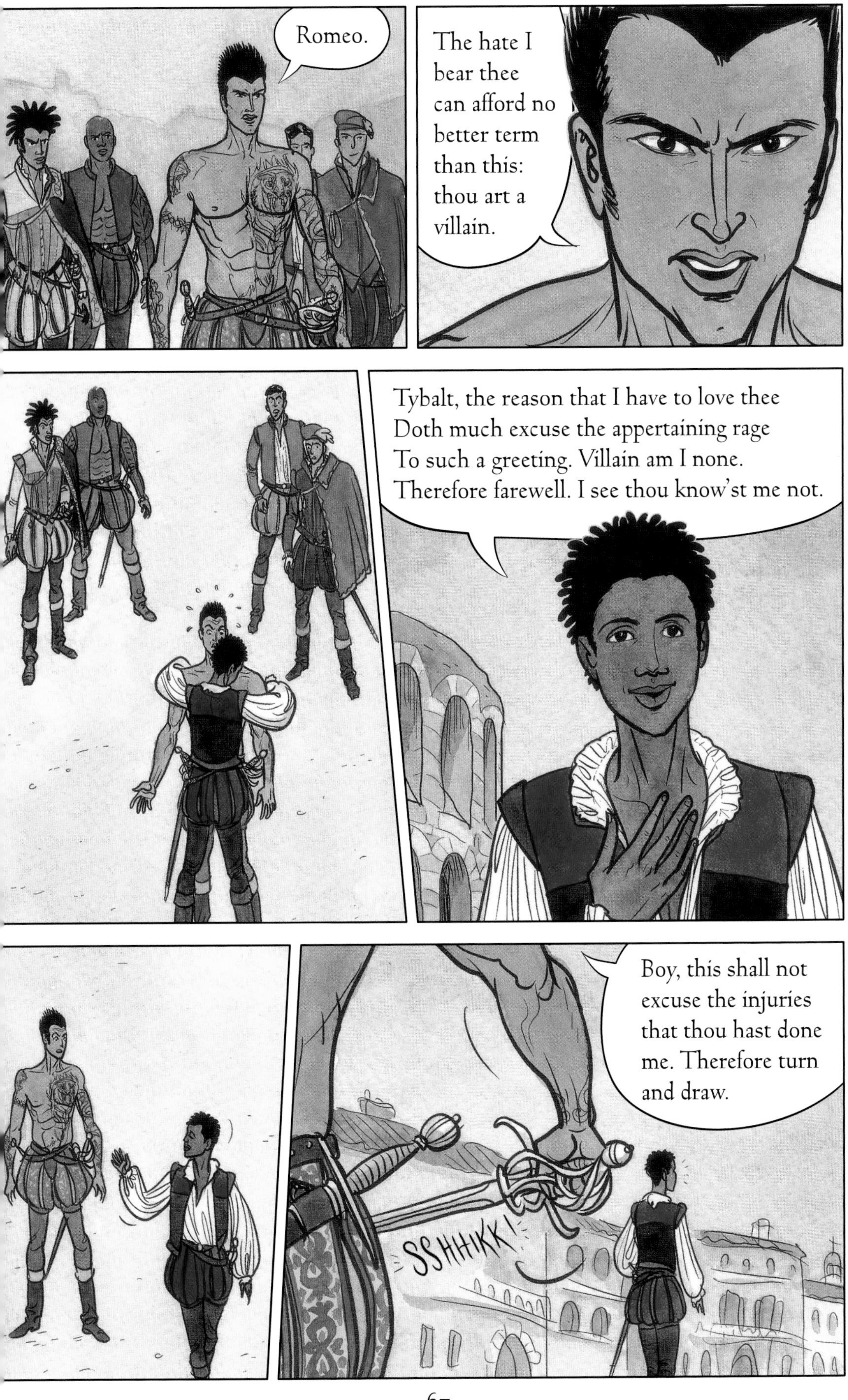
Romeo.
The hate I bear thee can afford no better term than this: thou art a villain.
Tybalt, the reason that I have to love thee Doth much excuse the appertaining rage To such a greeting. Villain am I none. Therefore farewell. I see thou know'st me not.
Boy, this shall not excuse the injuries that thou hast done me. Therefore turn and draw.
SSHHIKK!

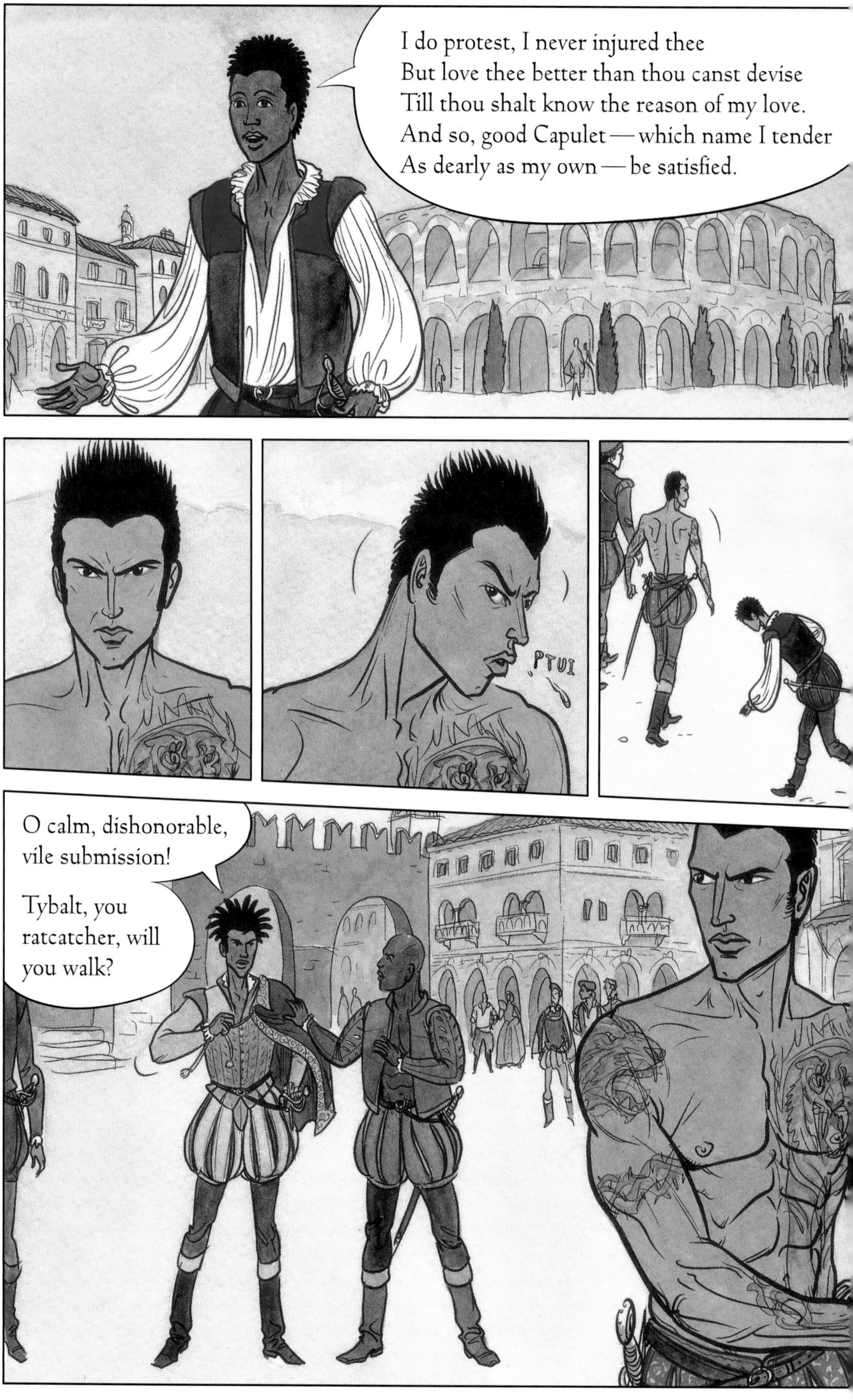
I do protest, I never injured thee
But love thee better than thou canst devise
Till thou shalt know the reason of my love.
And so, good Capulet — which name I tender
As dearly as my own — be satisfied.
PTUI
O calm, dishonorable, vile submission!
Tybalt, you ratcatcher, will you walk?

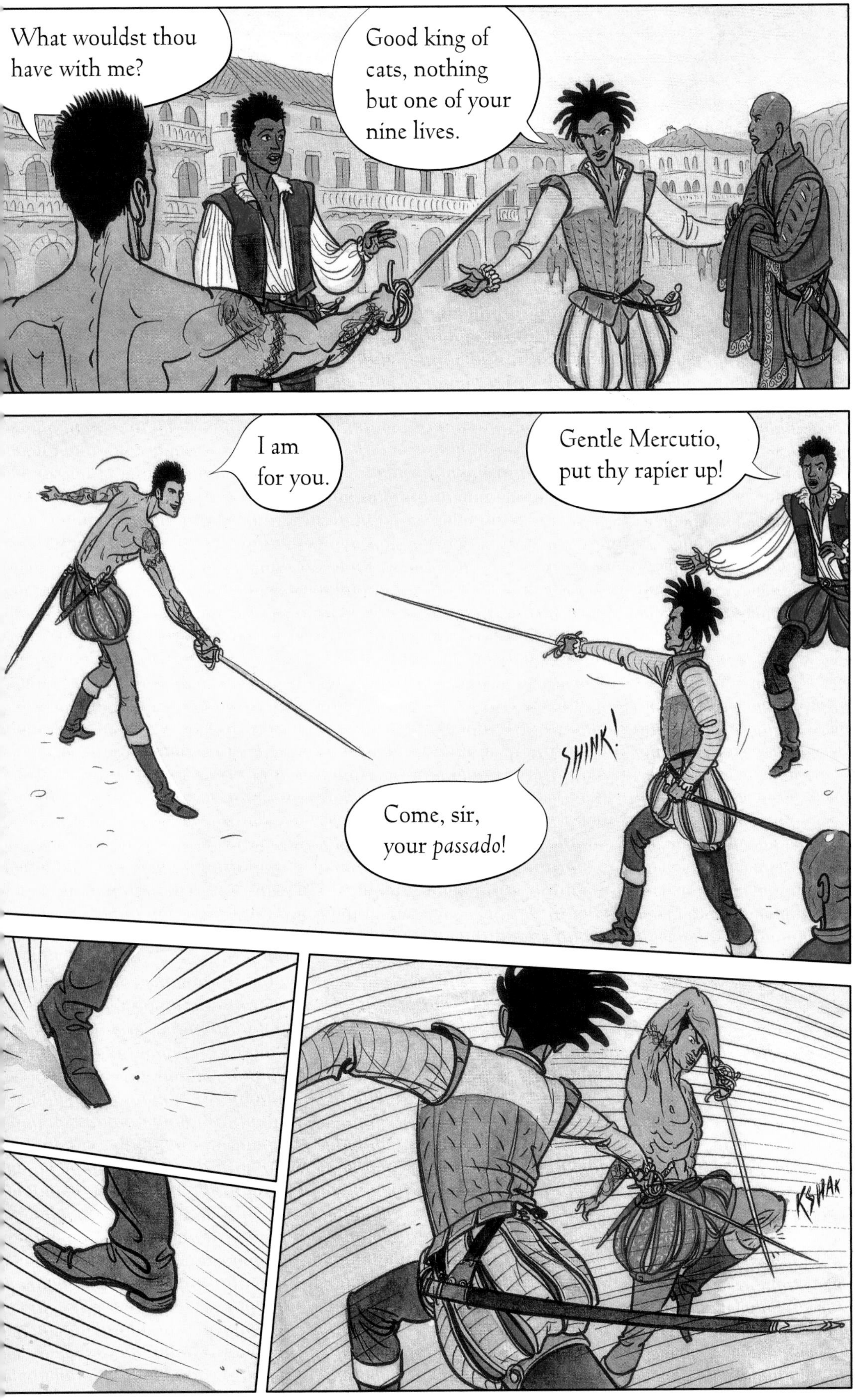
What wouldst thou have with me?
Good king of cats, nothing but one of your nine lives.
I am for you.
Gentle Mercutio, put thy rapier up!
SHINK!
Come, sir, your *passado*!
KSHAK

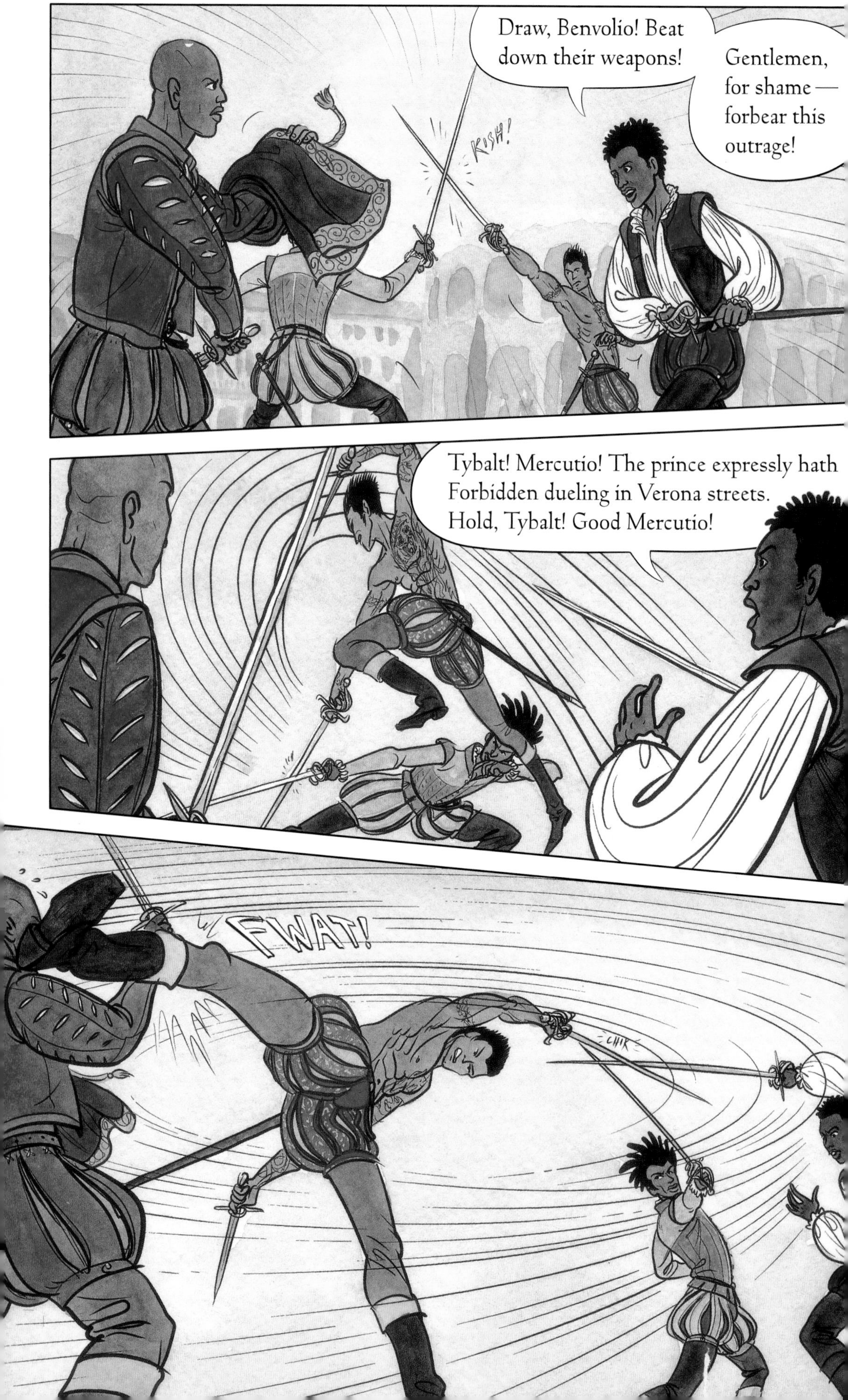
Draw, Benvolio! Beat down their weapons!
KRSH!
Gentlemen, for shame — forbear this outrage!
Tybalt! Mercutio! The prince expressly hath Forbidden dueling in Verona streets. Hold, Tybalt! Good Mercutio!
FWAT!
CHIK

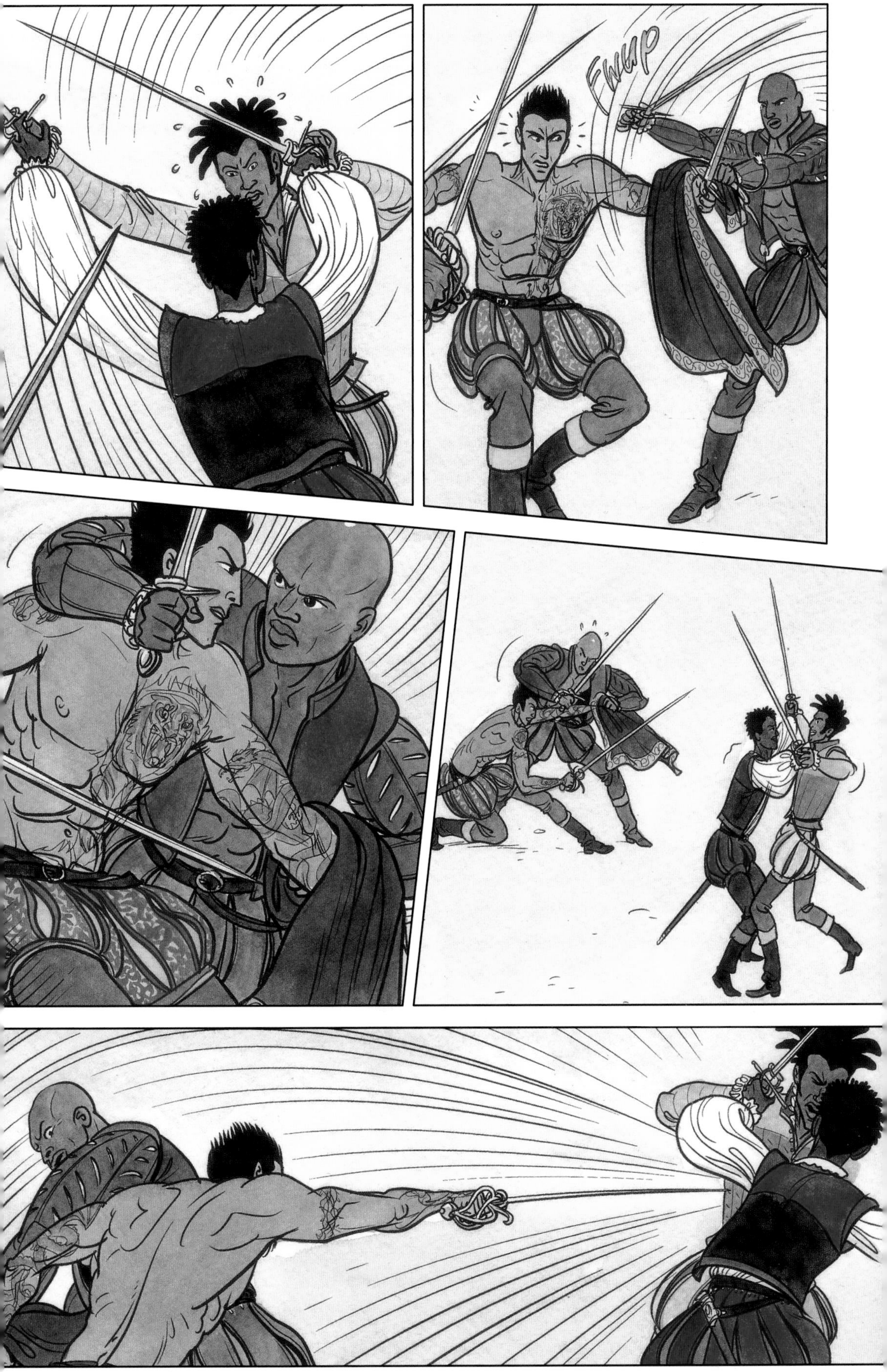
FWUP

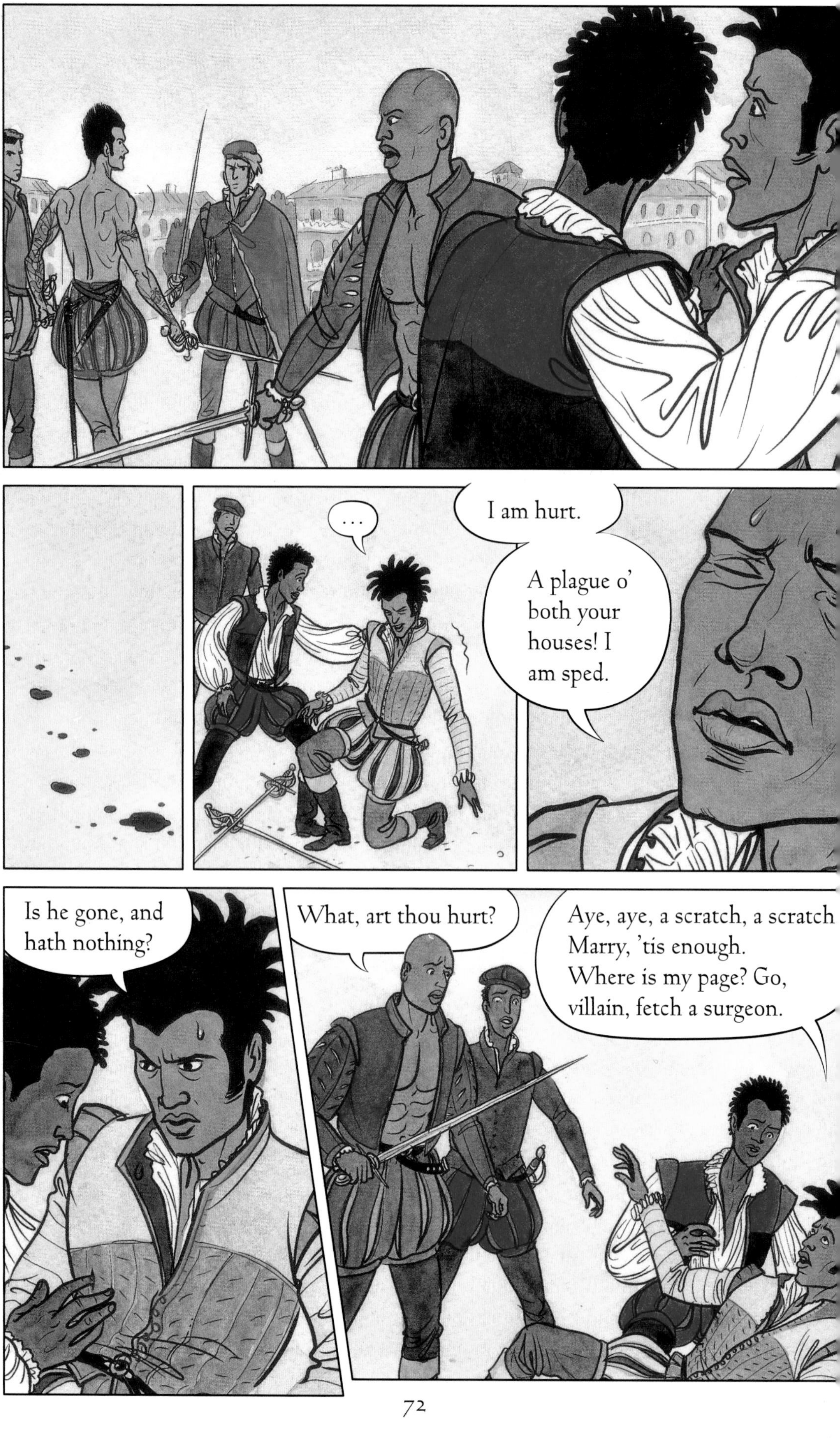

. . .
I am hurt.
A plague o' both your houses! I am sped.
Is he gone, and hath nothing?
What, art thou hurt?
Aye, aye, a scratch, a scratch
Marry, 'tis enough.
Where is my page? Go, villain, fetch a surgeon.

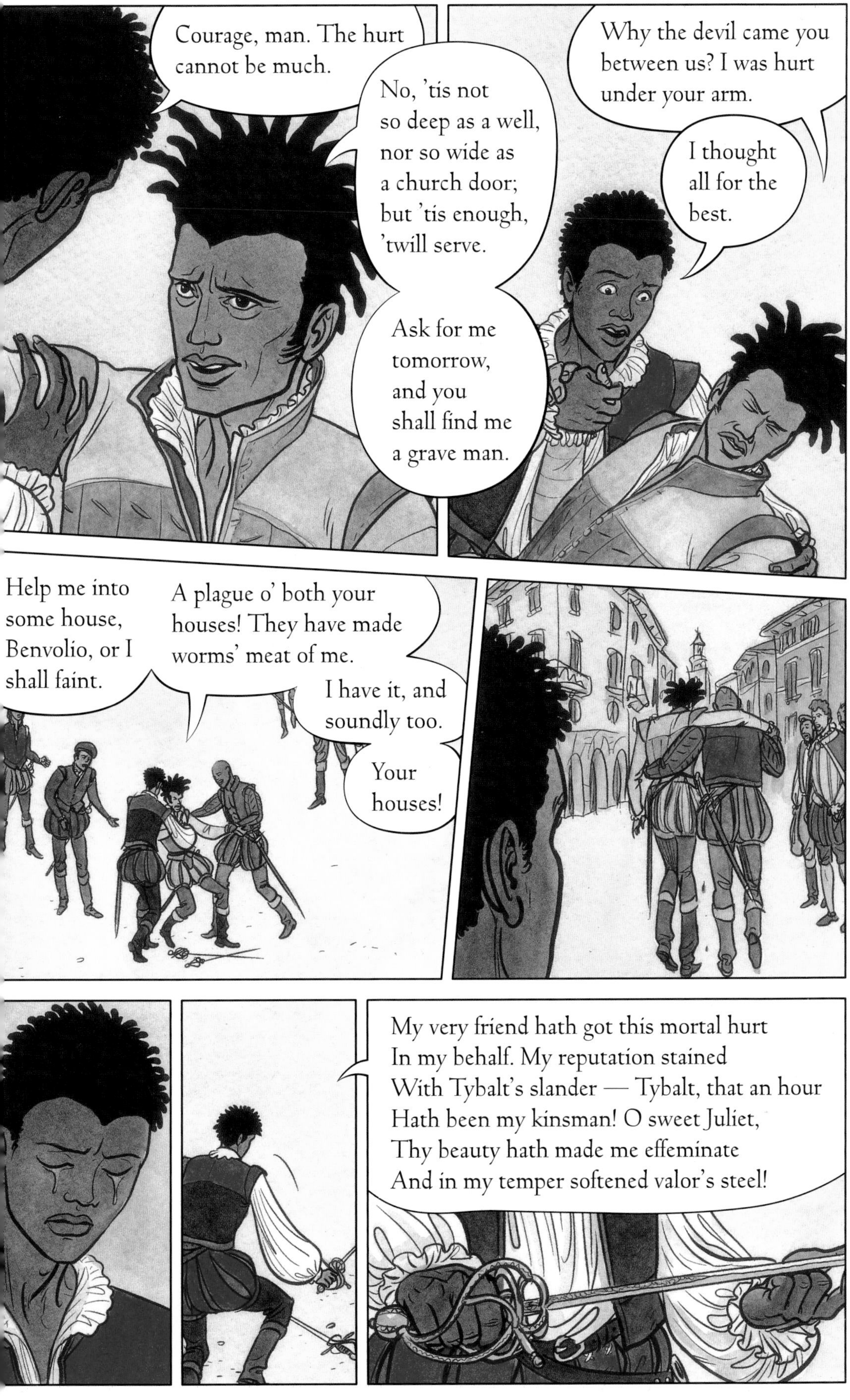
Courage, man. The hurt cannot be much.
No, 'tis not so deep as a well, nor so wide as a church door; but 'tis enough, 'twill serve.
Ask for me tomorrow, and you shall find me a grave man.
Why the devil came you between us? I was hurt under your arm.
I thought all for the best.
Help me into some house, Benvolio, or I shall faint.
A plague o' both your houses! They have made worms' meat of me.
I have it, and soundly too.
Your houses!
My very friend hath got this mortal hurt
In my behalf. My reputation stained
With Tybalt's slander — Tybalt, that an hour
Hath been my kinsman! O sweet Juliet,
Thy beauty hath made me effeminate
And in my temper softened valor's steel!

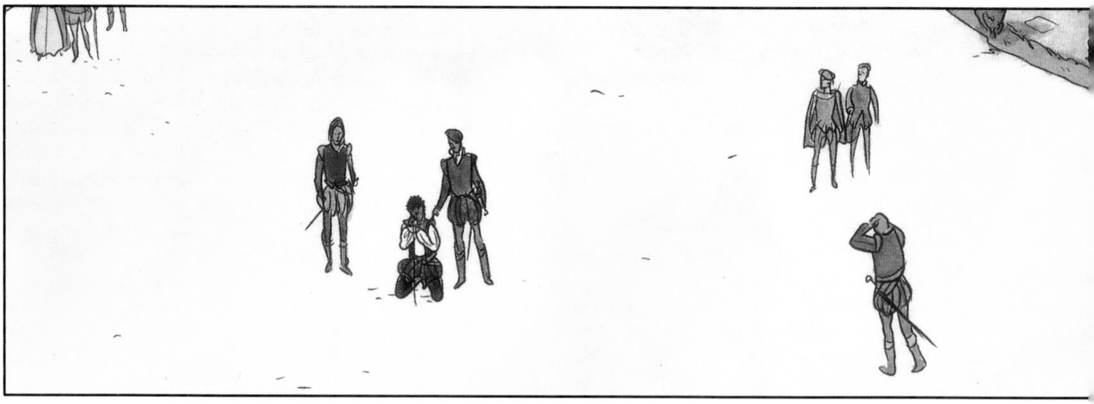

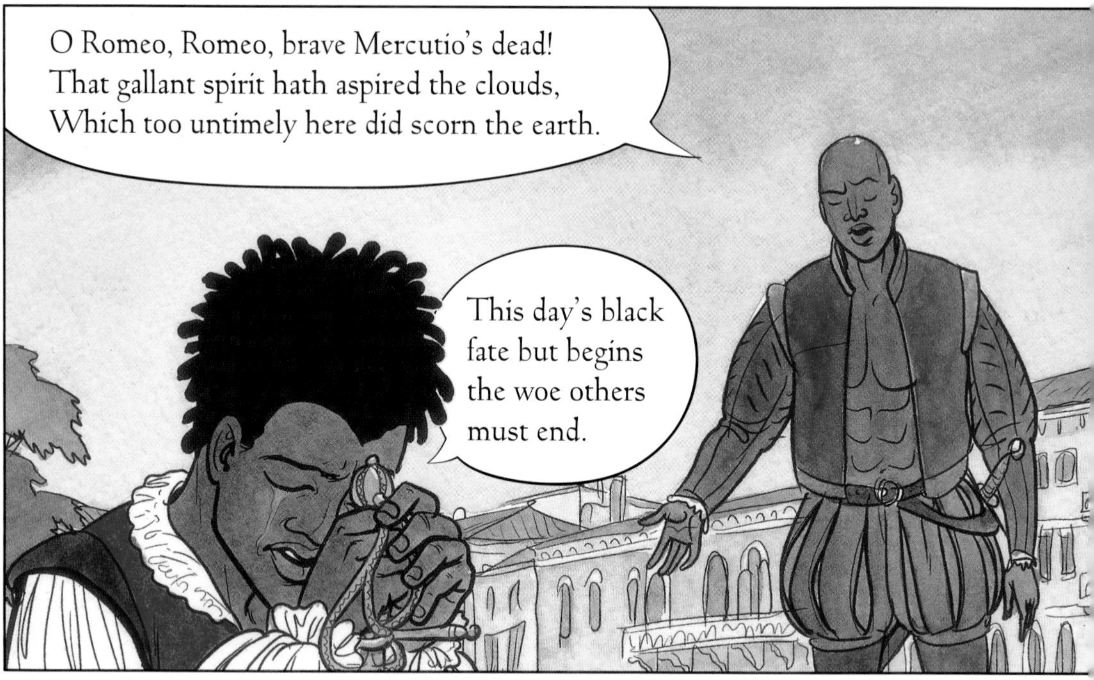

O Romeo, Romeo, brave Mercutio's dead!
That gallant spirit hath aspired the clouds,
Which too untimely here did scorn the earth.
This day's black fate but begins the woe others must end.

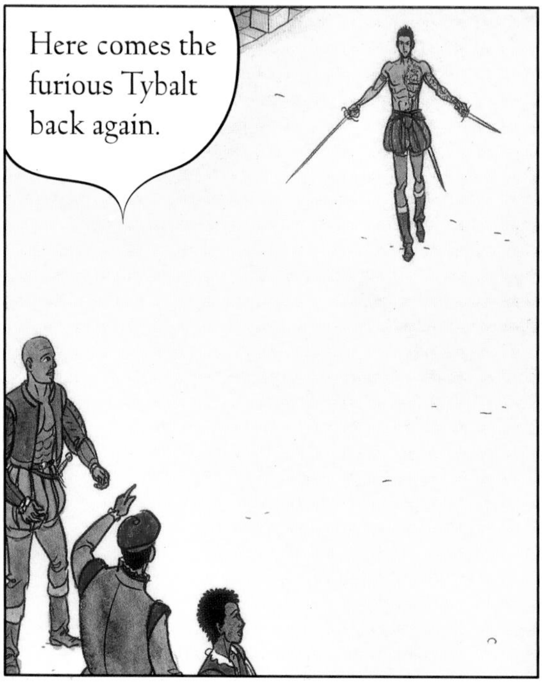

Here comes the furious Tybalt back again.

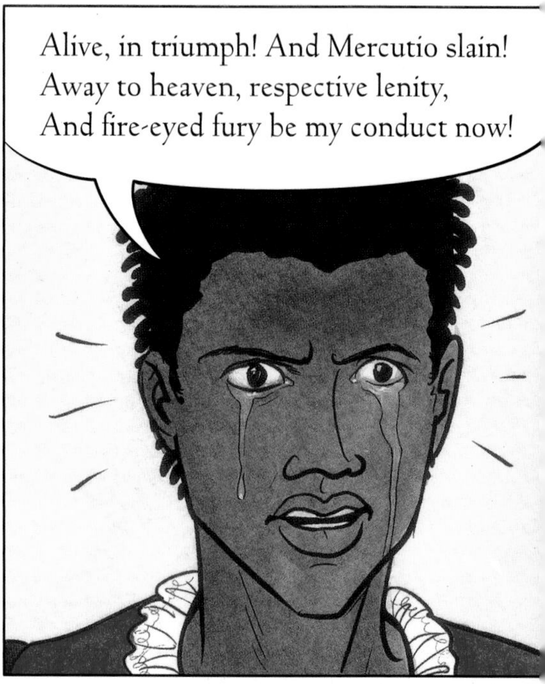

Alive, in triumph! And Mercutio slain!
Away to heaven, respective lenity,
And fire-eyed fury be my conduct now!

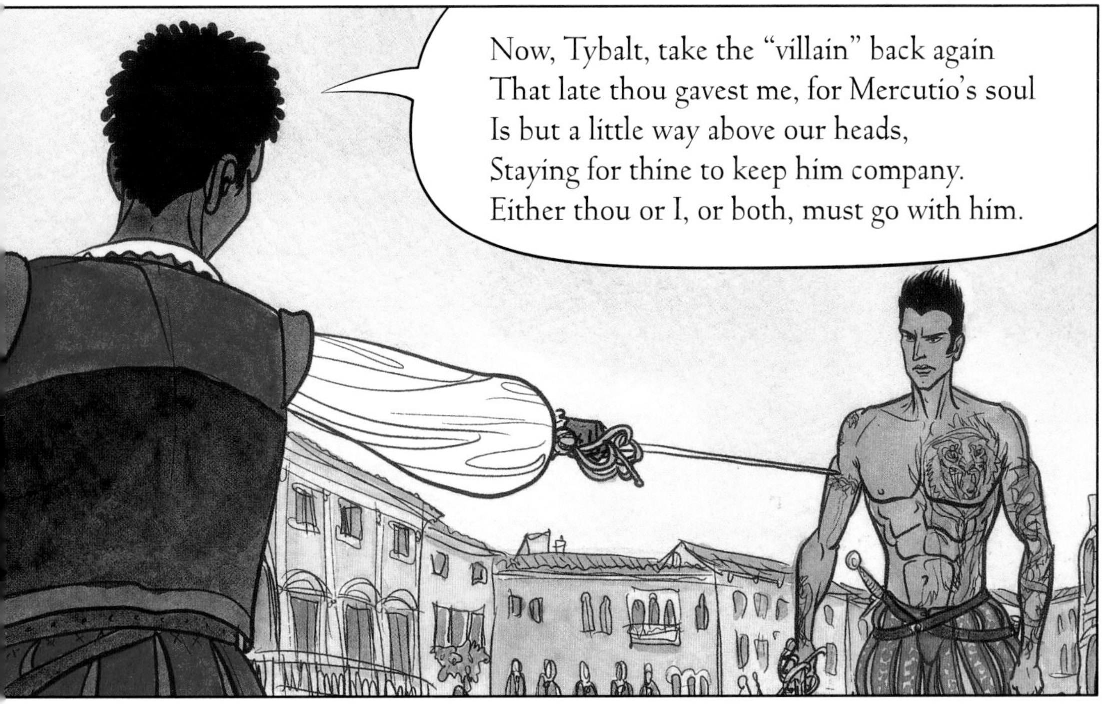
Now, Tybalt, take the "villain" back again
That late thou gavest me, for Mercutio's soul
Is but a little way above our heads,
Staying for thine to keep him company.
Either thou or I, or both, must go with him.

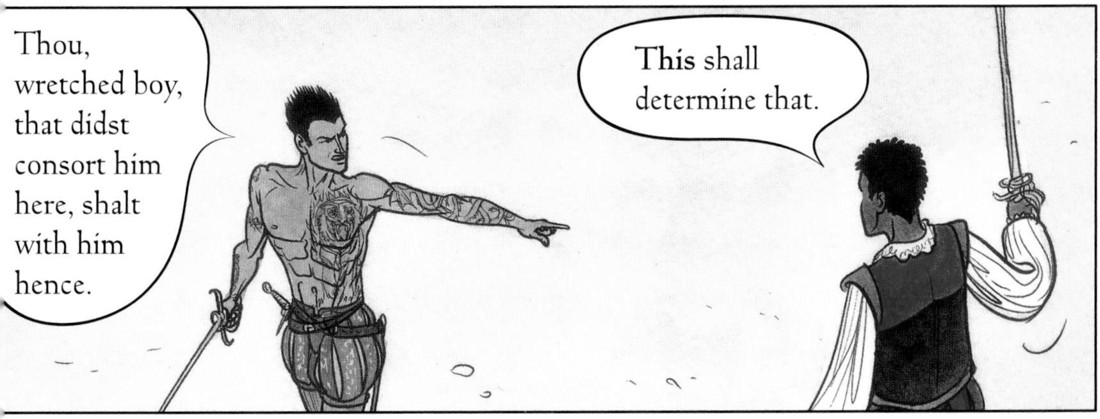
Thou, wretched boy, that didst consort him here, shalt with him hence.
This shall determine that.

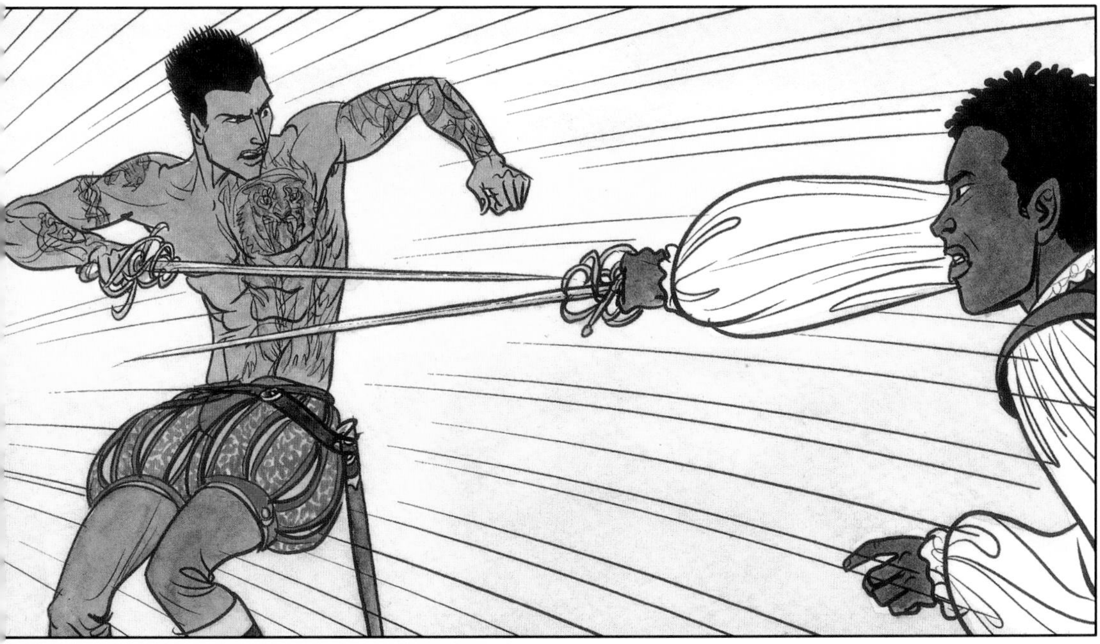

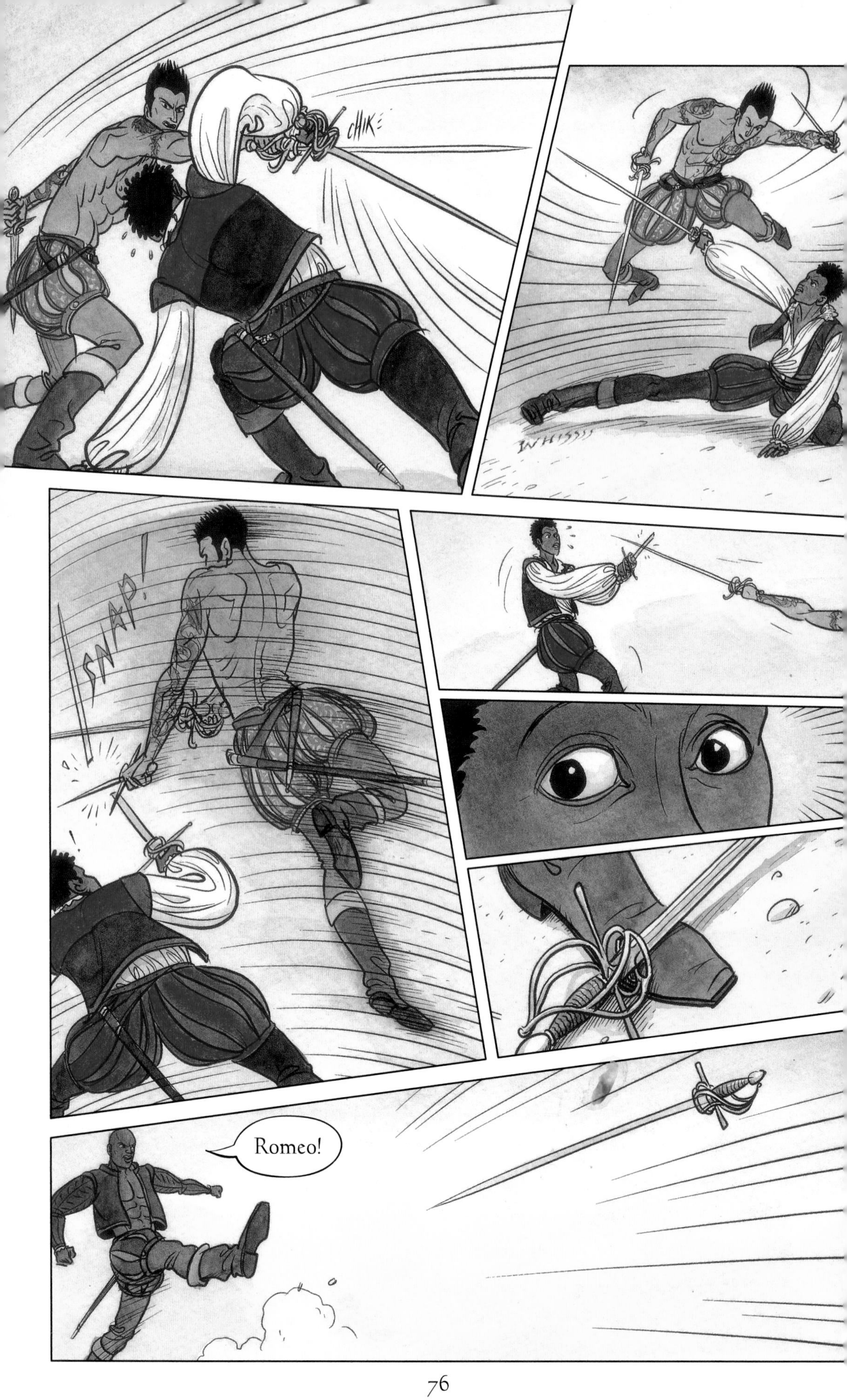
CHIK
WHISSSS
SNAP!
Romeo!

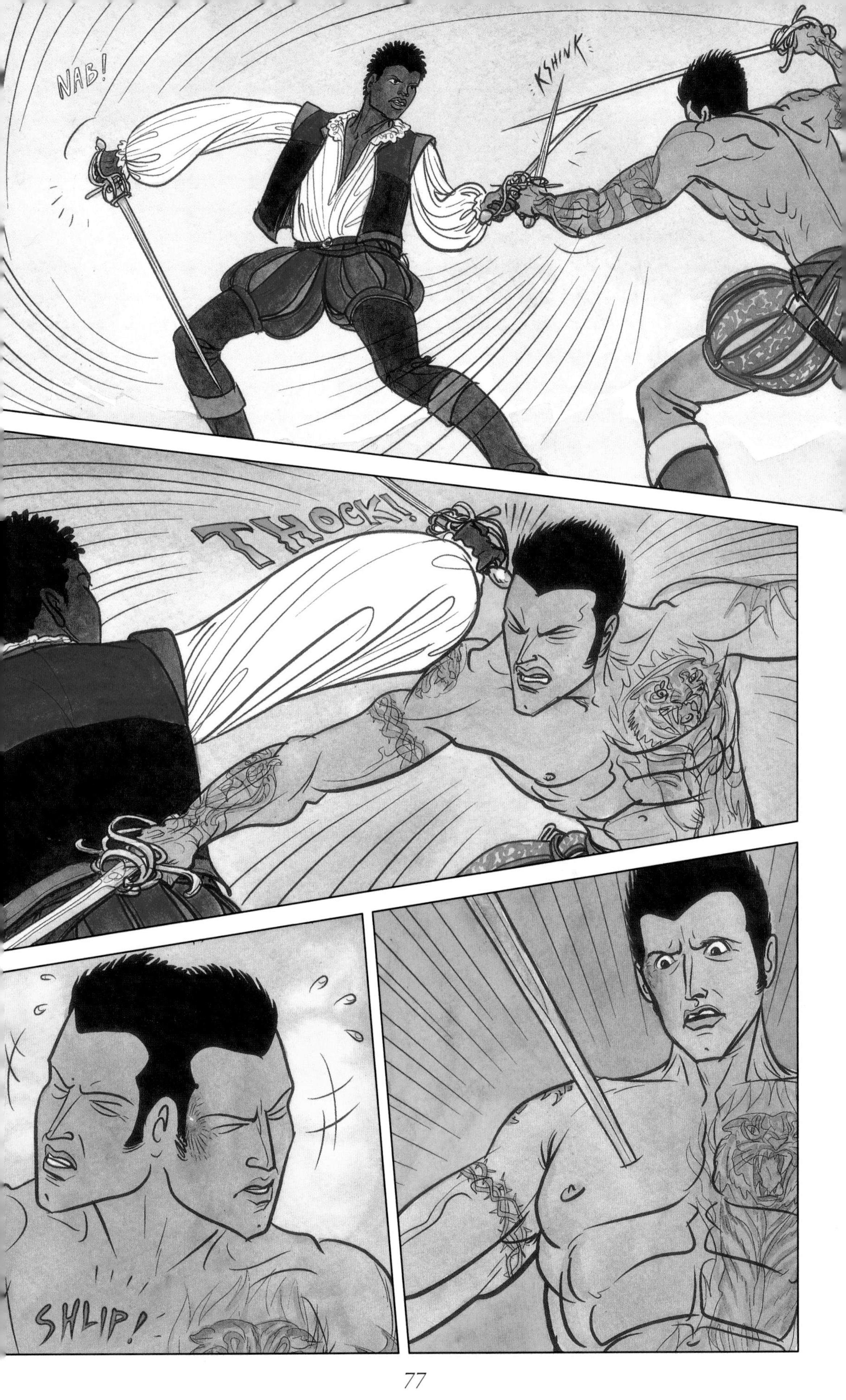
NAB!
KSHINK
THOCK!
SHLIP!

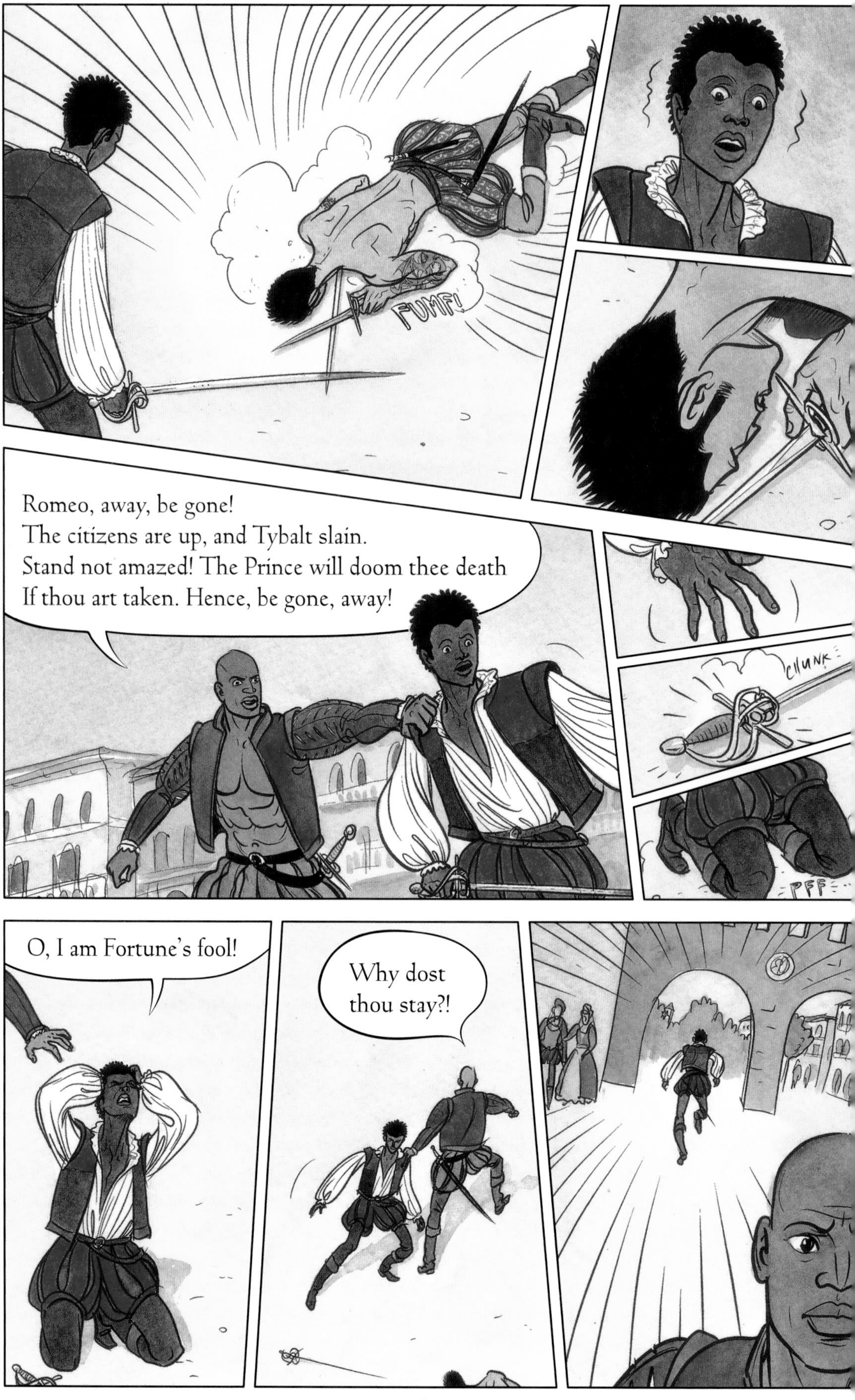
FUMF!
Romeo, away, be gone!
The citizens are up, and Tybalt slain.
Stand not amazed! The Prince will doom thee death
If thou art taken. Hence, be gone, away!
CHUNK
PFF
O, I am Fortune's fool!
Why dost thou stay?!

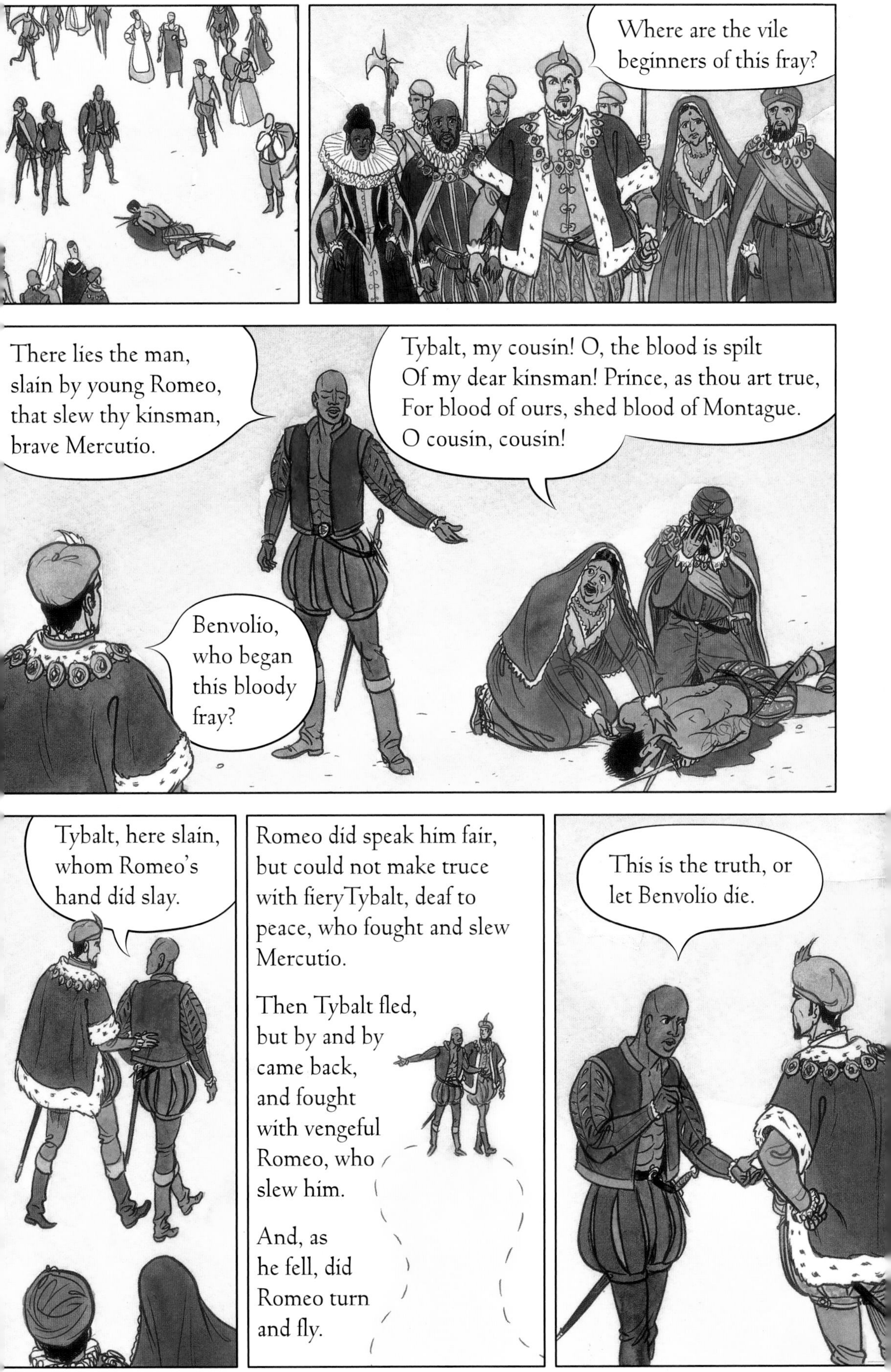
Where are the vile beginners of this fray?
There lies the man, slain by young Romeo, that slew thy kinsman, brave Mercutio.
Tybalt, my cousin! O, the blood is spilt
Of my dear kinsman! Prince, as thou art true,
For blood of ours, shed blood of Montague.
O cousin, cousin!
Benvolio, who began this bloody fray?
Tybalt, here slain, whom Romeo's hand did slay.
Romeo did speak him fair, but could not make truce with fieryTybalt, deaf to peace, who fought and slew Mercutio.
Then Tybalt fled, but by and by came back, and fought with vengeful Romeo, who slew him.
And, as he fell, did Romeo turn and fly.
This is the truth, or let Benvolio die.

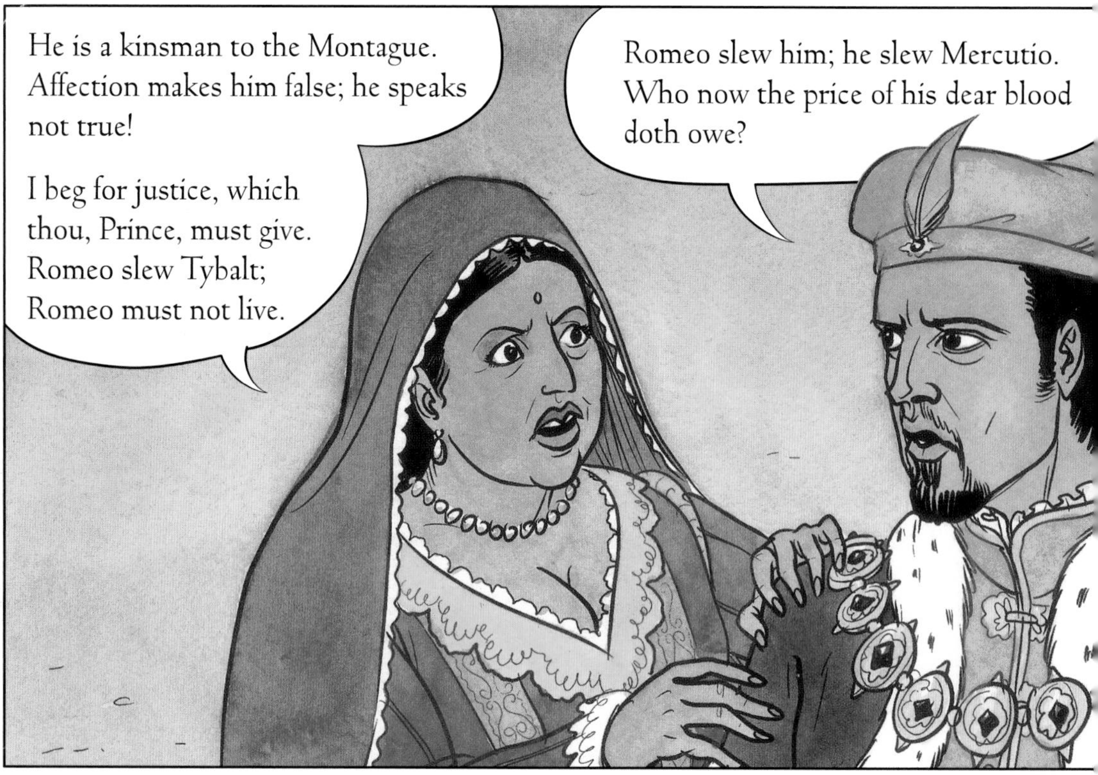
He is a kinsman to the Montague. Affection makes him false; he speaks not true!
I beg for justice, which thou, Prince, must give. Romeo slew Tybalt; Romeo must not live.
Romeo slew him; he slew Mercutio. Who now the price of his dear blood doth owe?

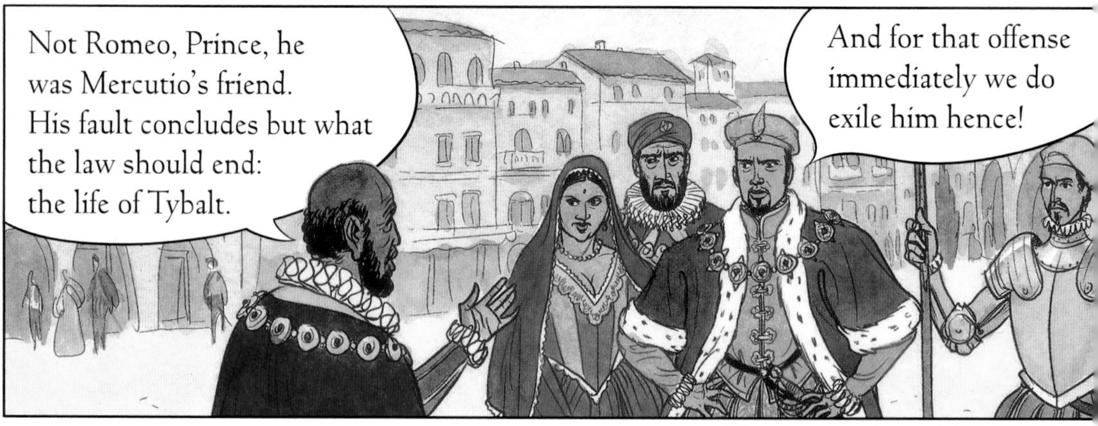
Not Romeo, Prince, he was Mercutio's friend. His fault concludes but what the law should end: the life of Tybalt.
And for that offense immediately we do exile him hence!

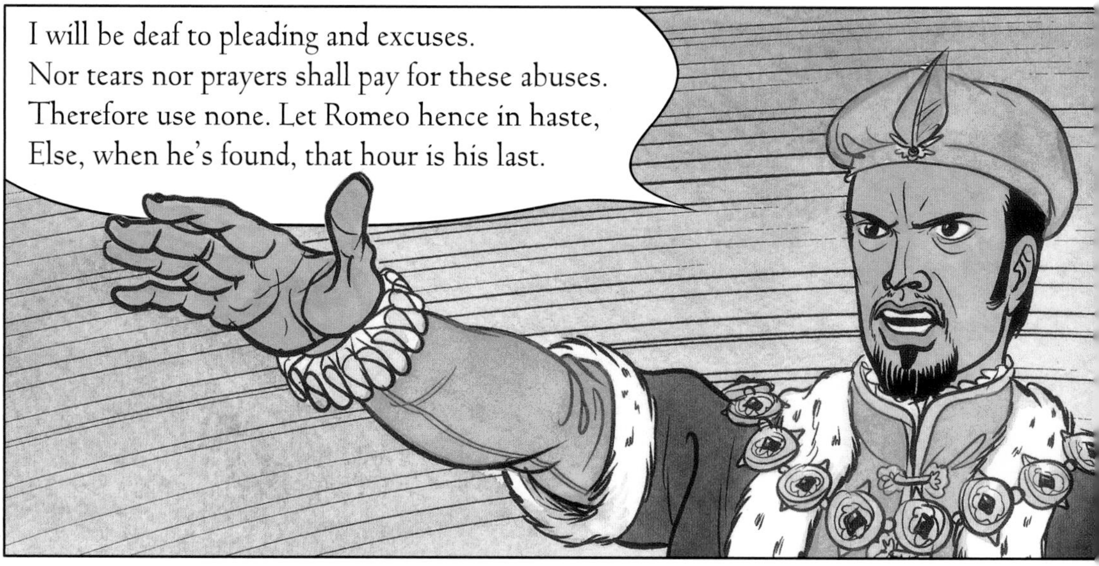
I will be deaf to pleading and excuses. Nor tears nor prayers shall pay for these abuses. Therefore use none. Let Romeo hence in haste, Else, when he's found, that hour is his last.

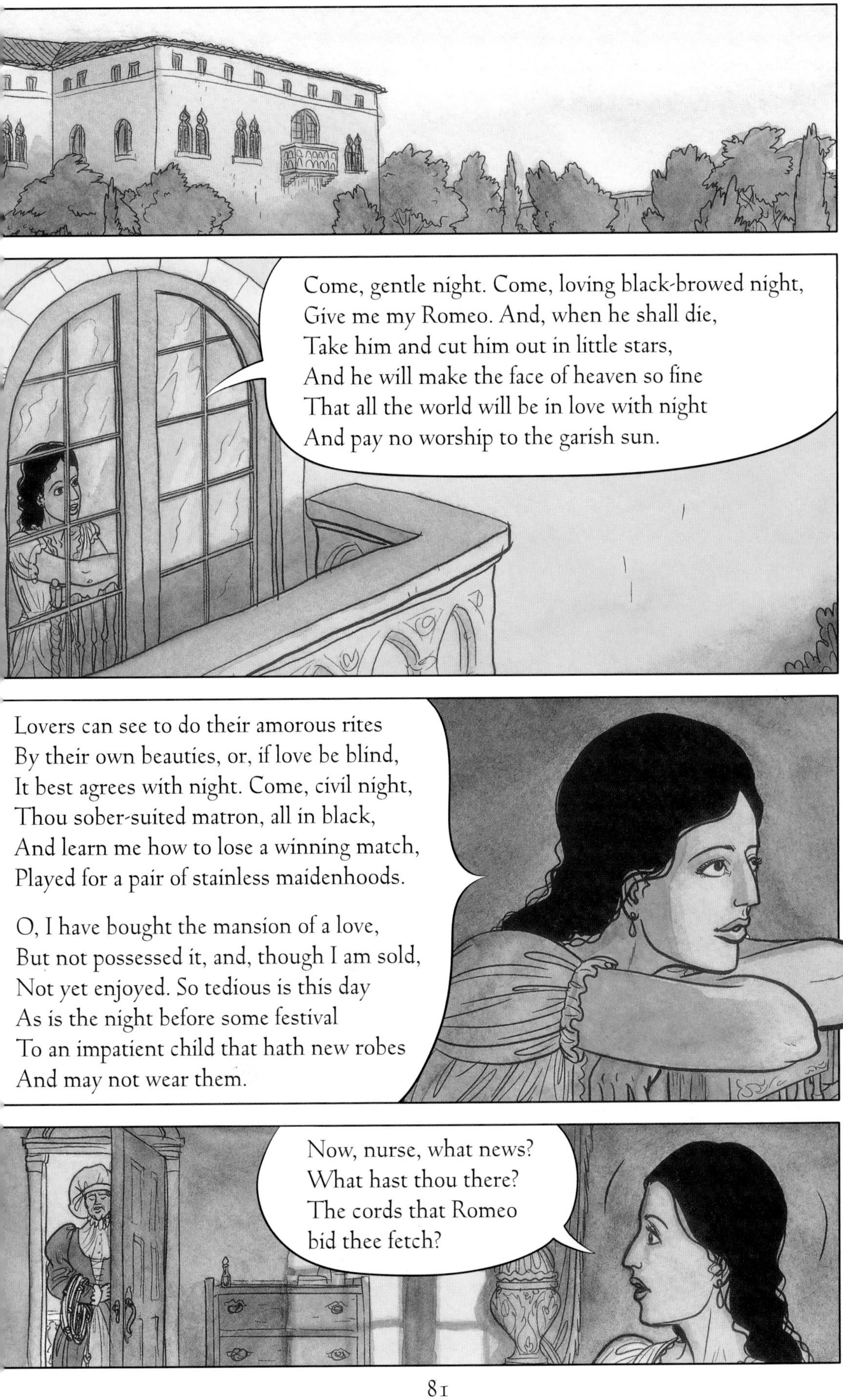
Come, gentle night. Come, loving black-browed night, Give me my Romeo. And, when he shall die, Take him and cut him out in little stars, And he will make the face of heaven so fine That all the world will be in love with night And pay no worship to the garish sun.
Lovers can see to do their amorous rites By their own beauties, or, if love be blind, It best agrees with night. Come, civil night, Thou sober-suited matron, all in black, And learn me how to lose a winning match, Played for a pair of stainless maidenhoods.
O, I have bought the mansion of a love, But not possessed it, and, though I am sold, Not yet enjoyed. So tedious is this day As is the night before some festival To an impatient child that hath new robes And may not wear them.
Now, nurse, what news? What hast thou there? The cords that Romeo bid thee fetch?

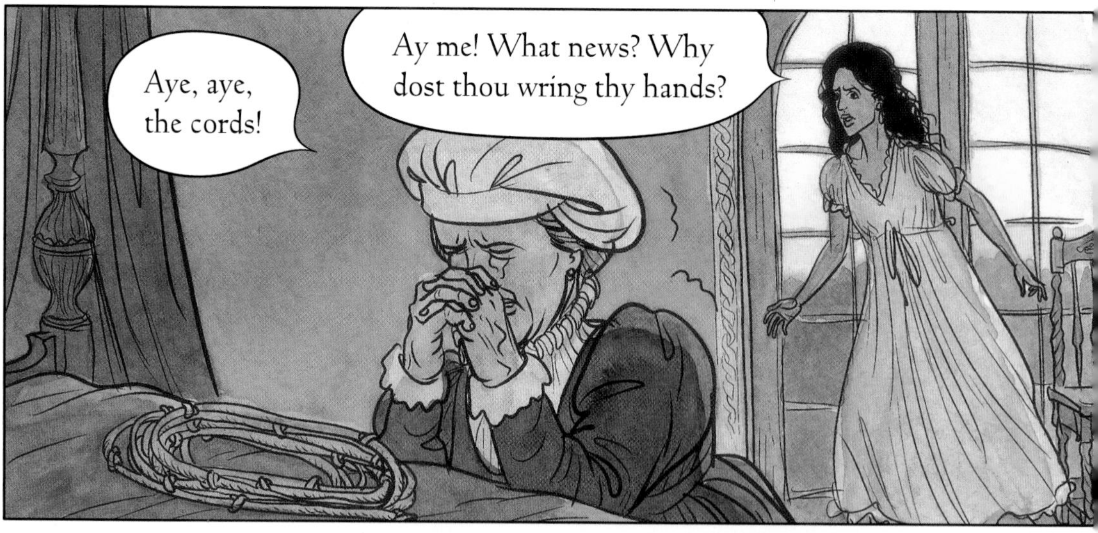
Aye, aye, the cords!
Ay me! What news? Why dost thou wring thy hands?

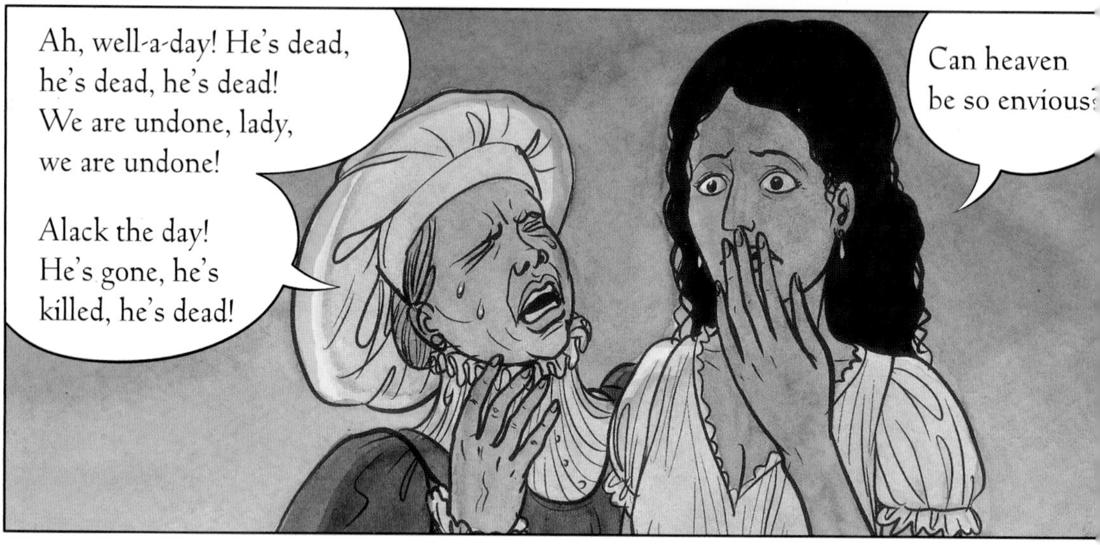
Ah, well-a-day! He's dead, he's dead, he's dead! We are undone, lady, we are undone!
Alack the day! He's gone, he's killed, he's dead!
Can heaven be so envious?

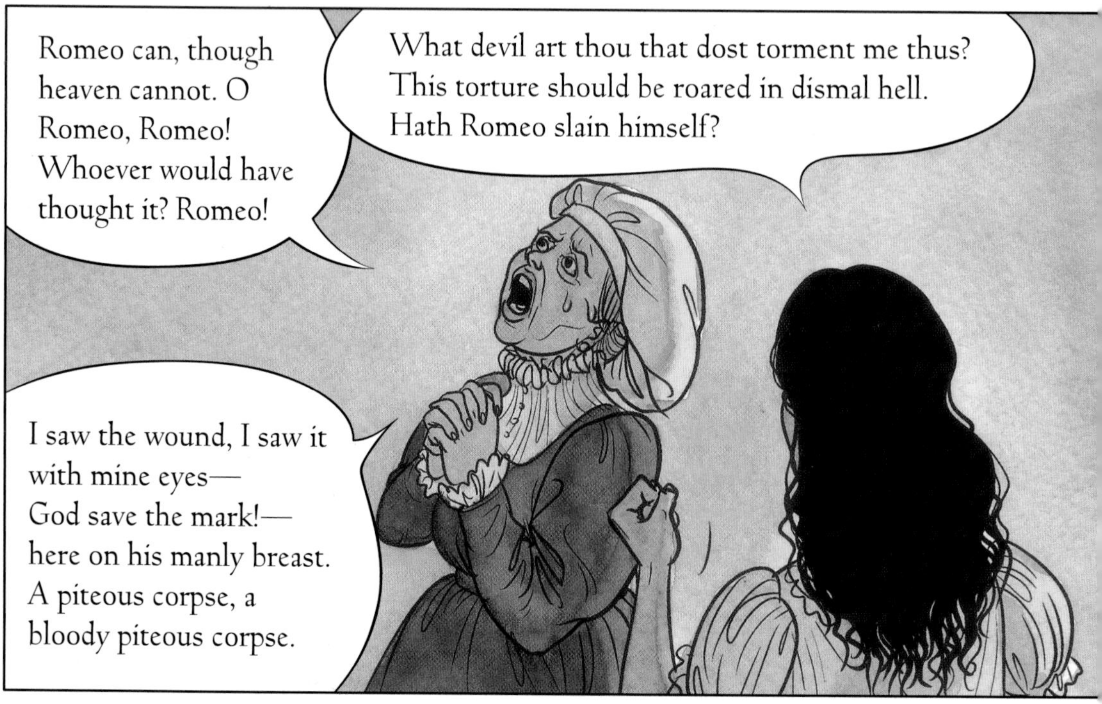
Romeo can, though heaven cannot. O Romeo, Romeo! Whoever would have thought it? Romeo!
What devil art thou that dost torment me thus? This torture should be roared in dismal hell. Hath Romeo slain himself?
I saw the wound, I saw it with mine eyes— God save the mark!— here on his manly breast. A piteous corpse, a bloody piteous corpse.

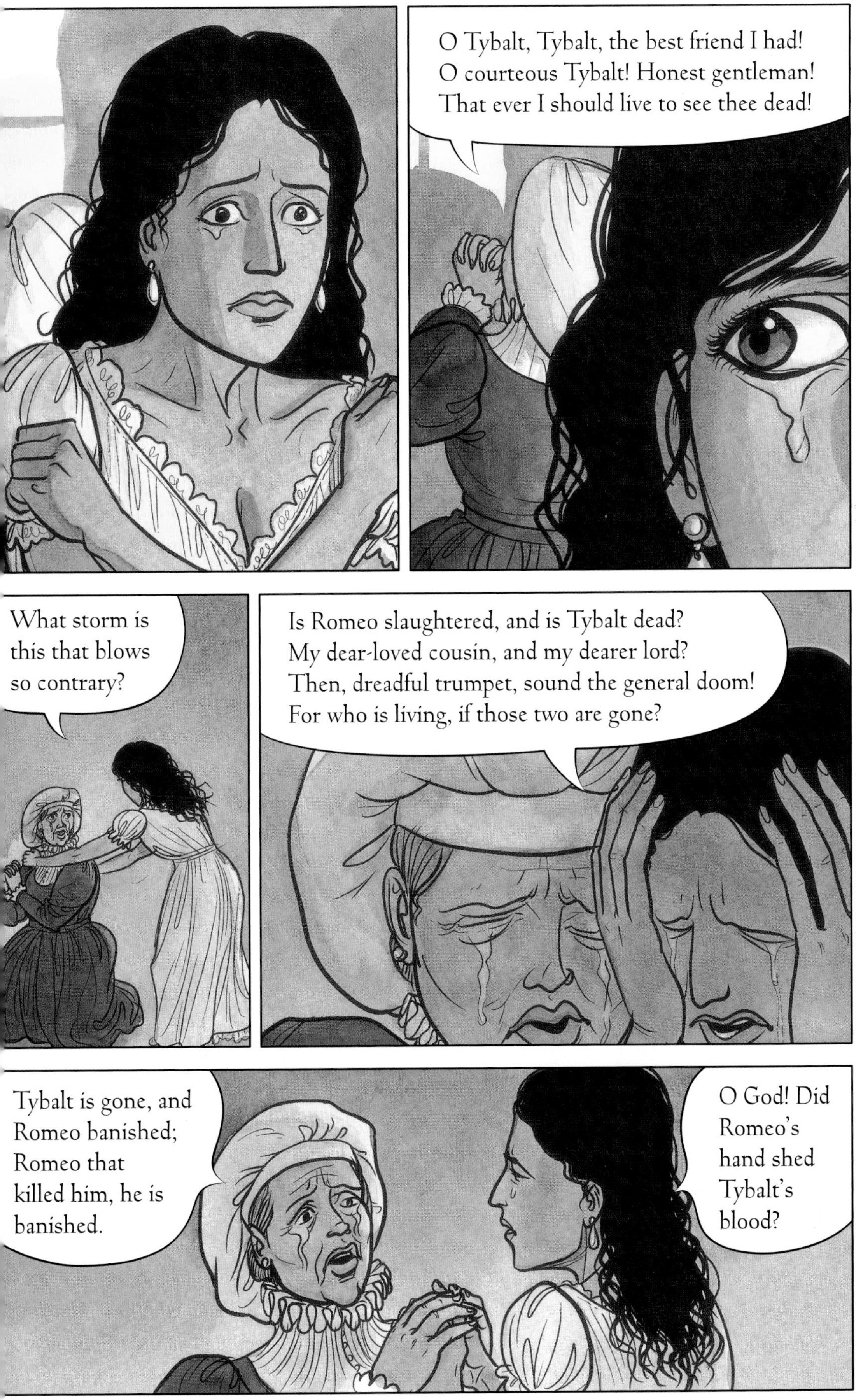

O Tybalt, Tybalt, the best friend I had! O courteous Tybalt! Honest gentleman! That ever I should live to see thee dead!
What storm is this that blows so contrary?
Is Romeo slaughtered, and is Tybalt dead? My dear-loved cousin, and my dearer lord? Then, dreadful trumpet, sound the general doom! For who is living, if those two are gone?
Tybalt is gone, and Romeo banished; Romeo that killed him, he is banished.
O God! Did Romeo's hand shed Tybalt's blood?

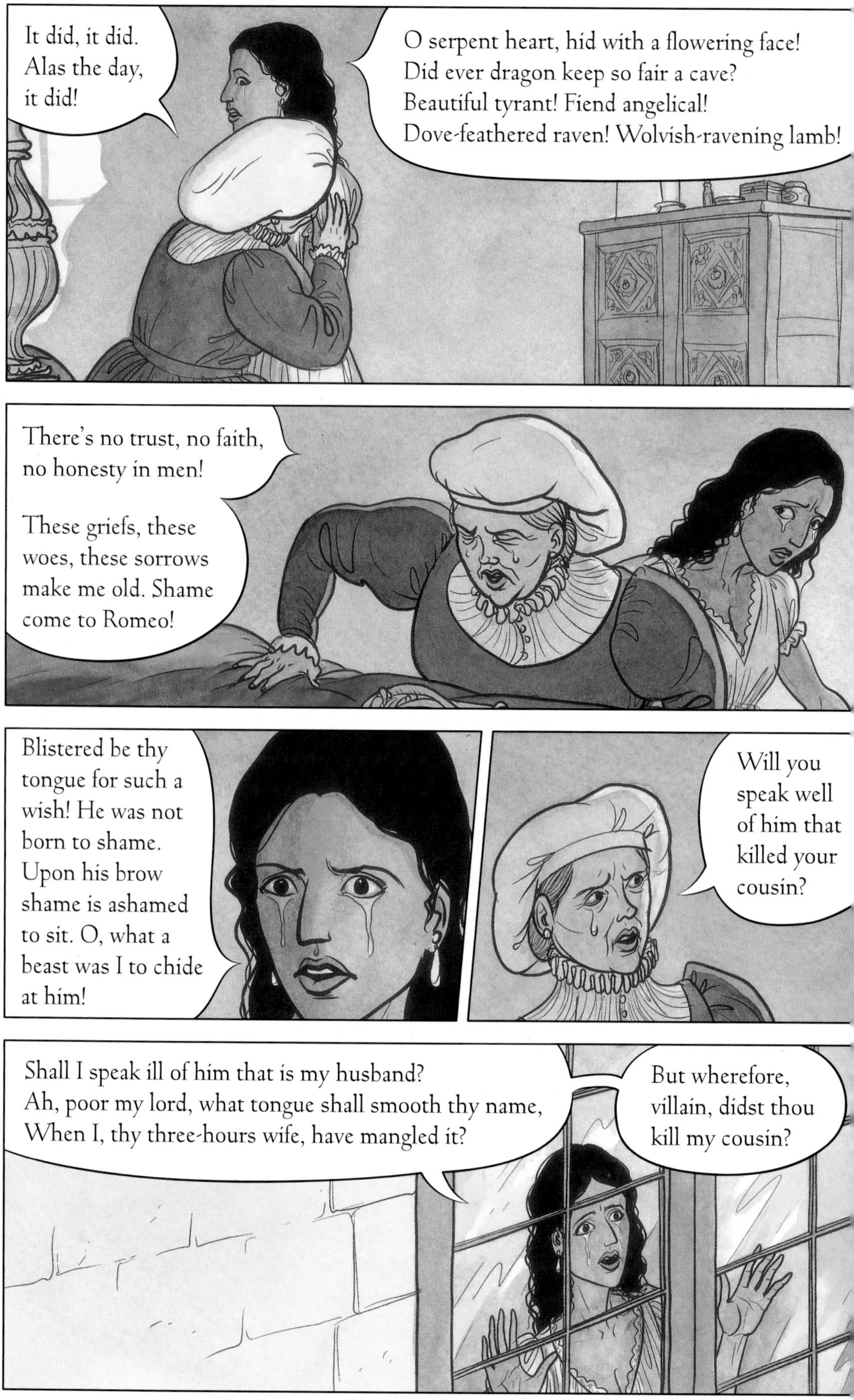
It did, it did. Alas the day, it did!
O serpent heart, hid with a flowering face! Did ever dragon keep so fair a cave? Beautiful tyrant! Fiend angelical! Dove-feathered raven! Wolvish-ravening lamb!
There's no trust, no faith, no honesty in men!
These griefs, these woes, these sorrows make me old. Shame come to Romeo!
Blistered be thy tongue for such a wish! He was not born to shame. Upon his brow shame is ashamed to sit. O, what a beast was I to chide at him!
Will you speak well of him that killed your cousin?
Shall I speak ill of him that is my husband? Ah, poor my lord, what tongue shall smooth thy name, When I, thy three-hours wife, have mangled it?
But wherefore, villain, didst thou kill my cousin?

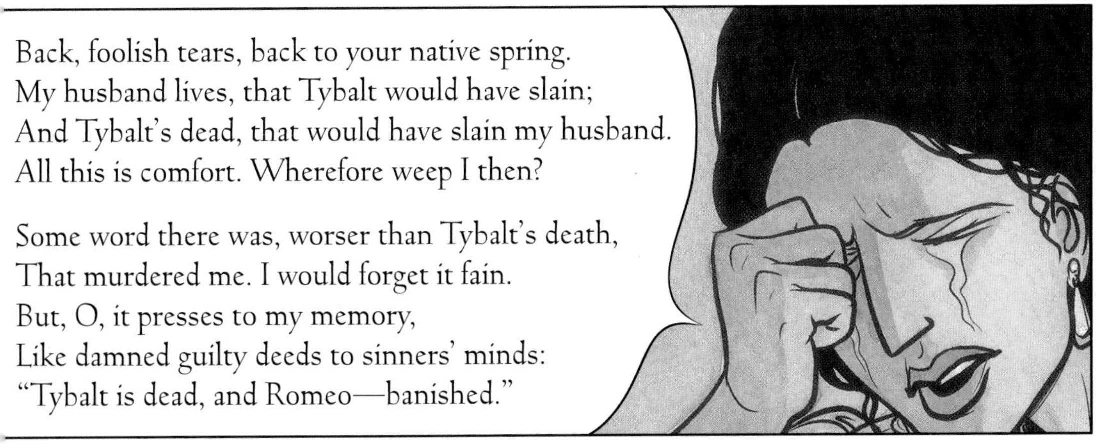
Back, foolish tears, back to your native spring.
My husband lives, that Tybalt would have slain;
And Tybalt's dead, that would have slain my husband.
All this is comfort. Wherefore weep I then?
Some word there was, worser than Tybalt's death,
That murdered me. I would forget it fain.
But, O, it presses to my memory,
Like damned guilty deeds to sinners' minds:
"Tybalt is dead, and Romeo—banished."

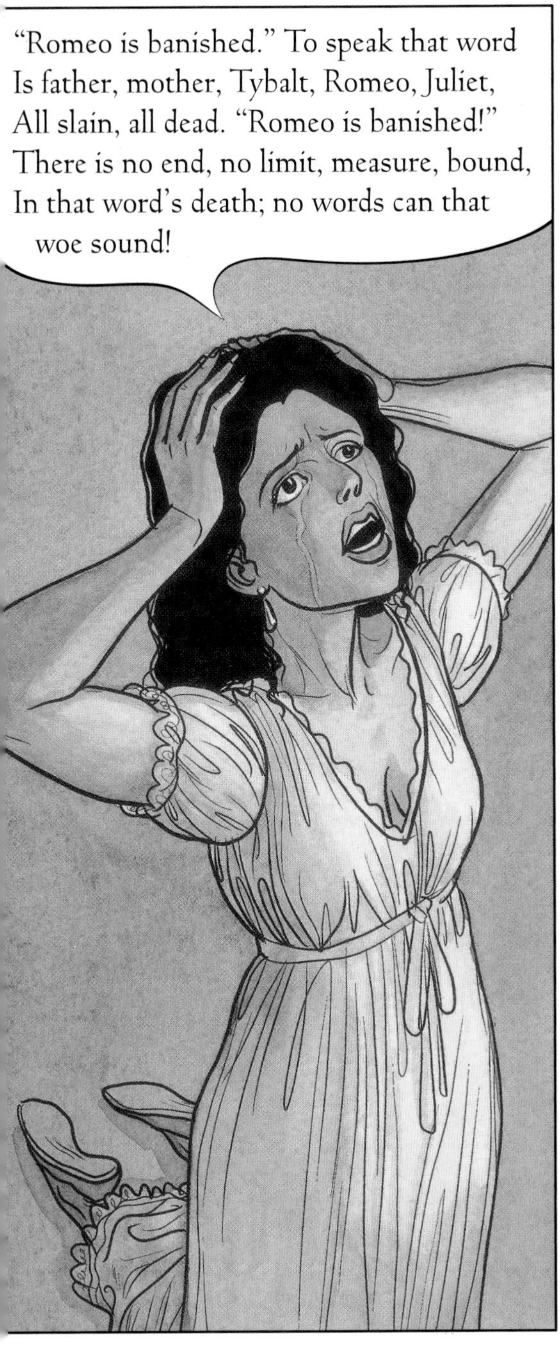
"Romeo is banished." To speak that word
Is father, mother, Tybalt, Romeo, Juliet,
All slain, all dead. "Romeo is banished!"
There is no end, no limit, measure, bound,
In that word's death; no words can that
woe sound!

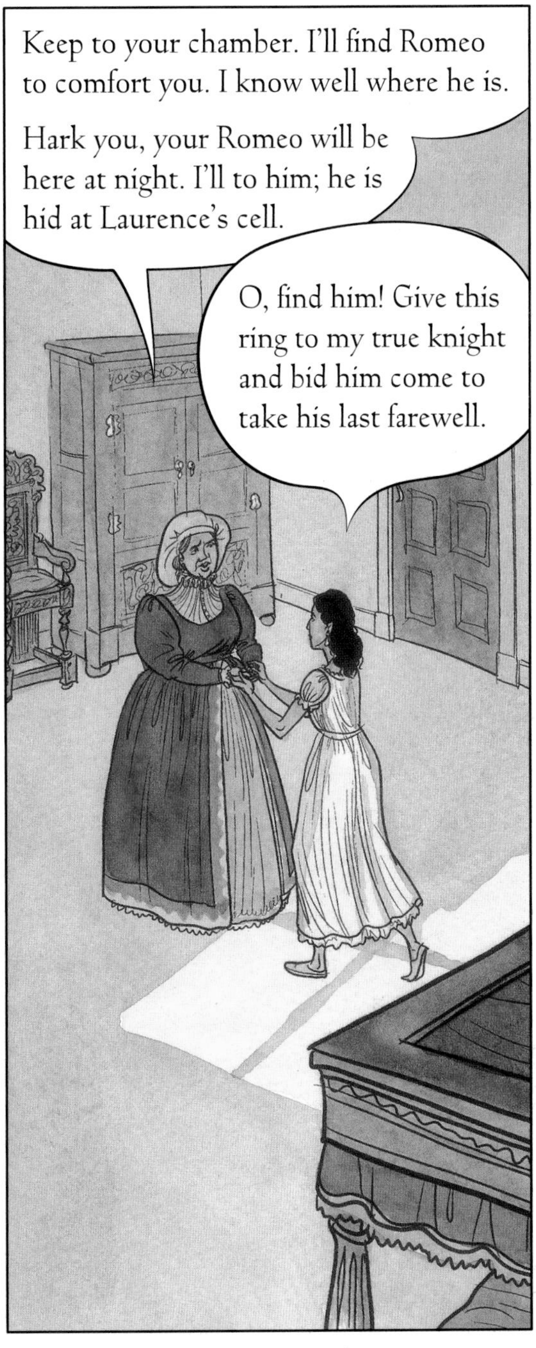
Keep to your chamber. I'll find Romeo to comfort you. I know well where he is.
Hark you, your Romeo will be here at night. I'll to him; he is hid at Laurence's cell.
O, find him! Give this ring to my true knight and bid him come to take his last farewell.

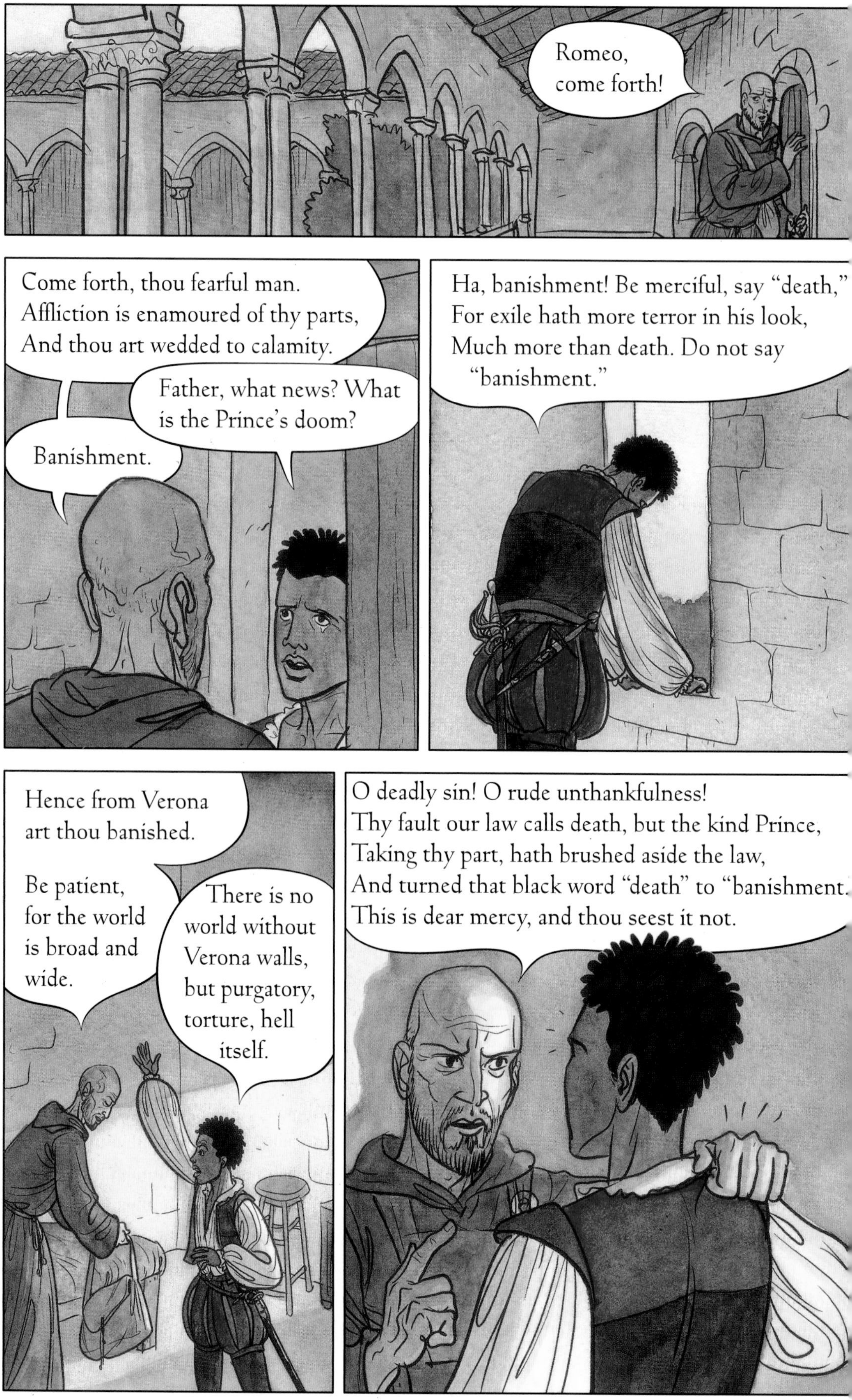
Romeo, come forth!
Come forth, thou fearful man. Affliction is enamoured of thy parts, And thou art wedded to calamity.
Father, what news? What is the Prince's doom?
Banishment.
Ha, banishment! Be merciful, say "death," For exile hath more terror in his look, Much more than death. Do not say "banishment."
Hence from Verona art thou banished.
Be patient, for the world is broad and wide.
There is no world without Verona walls, but purgatory, torture, hell itself.
O deadly sin! O rude unthankfulness! Thy fault our law calls death, but the kind Prince, Taking thy part, hath brushed aside the law, And turned that black word "death" to "banishment. This is dear mercy, and thou seest it not.

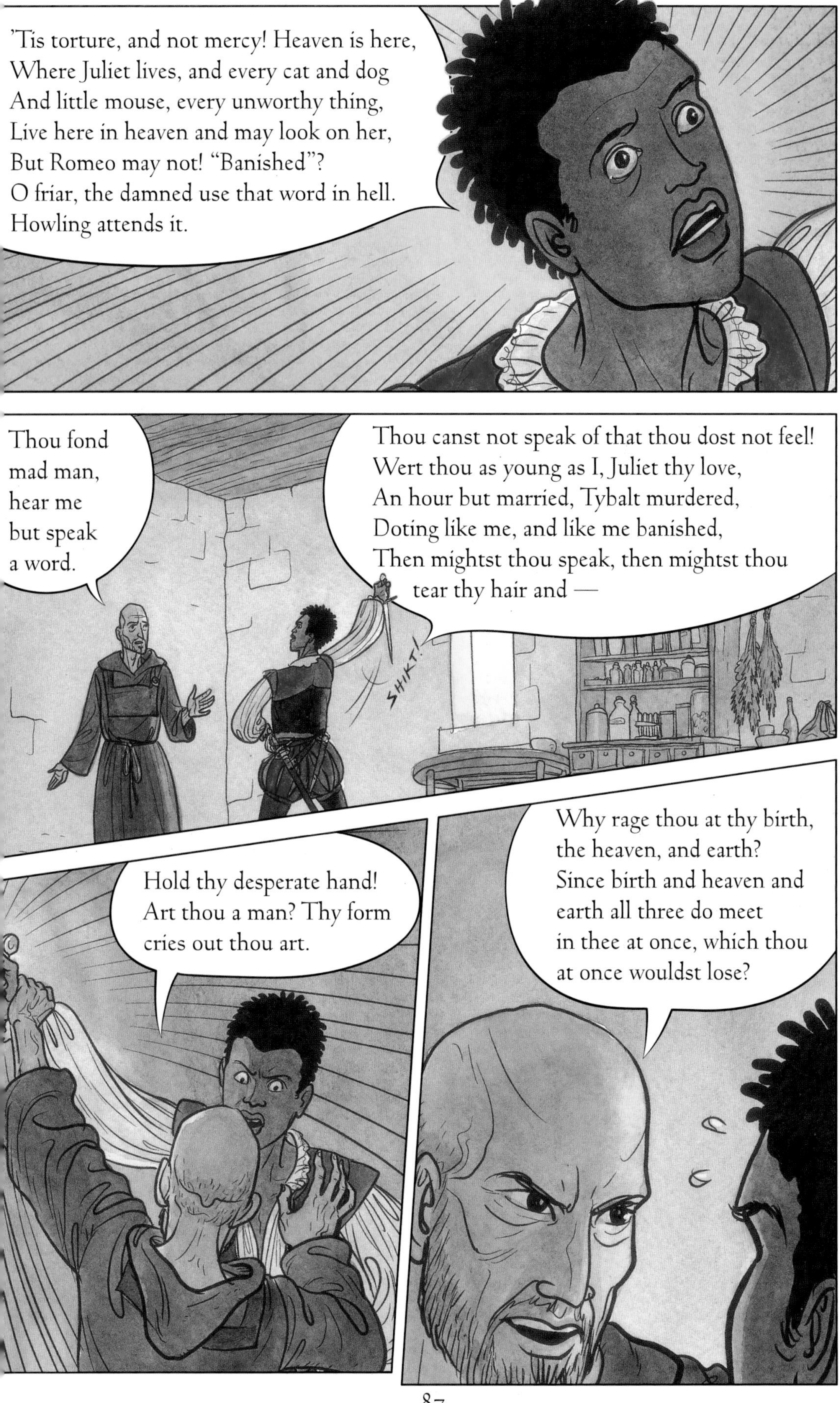
'Tis torture, and not mercy! Heaven is here, Where Juliet lives, and every cat and dog And little mouse, every unworthy thing, Live here in heaven and may look on her, But Romeo may not! "Banished"? O friar, the damned use that word in hell. Howling attends it.
Thou fond mad man, hear me but speak a word.
Thou canst not speak of that thou dost not feel! Wert thou as young as I, Juliet thy love, An hour but married, Tybalt murdered, Doting like me, and like me banished, Then mightst thou speak, then mightst thou tear thy hair and —
SHIKT!
Hold thy desperate hand! Art thou a man? Thy form cries out thou art.
Why rage thou at thy birth, the heaven, and earth? Since birth and heaven and earth all three do meet in thee at once, which thou at once wouldst lose?

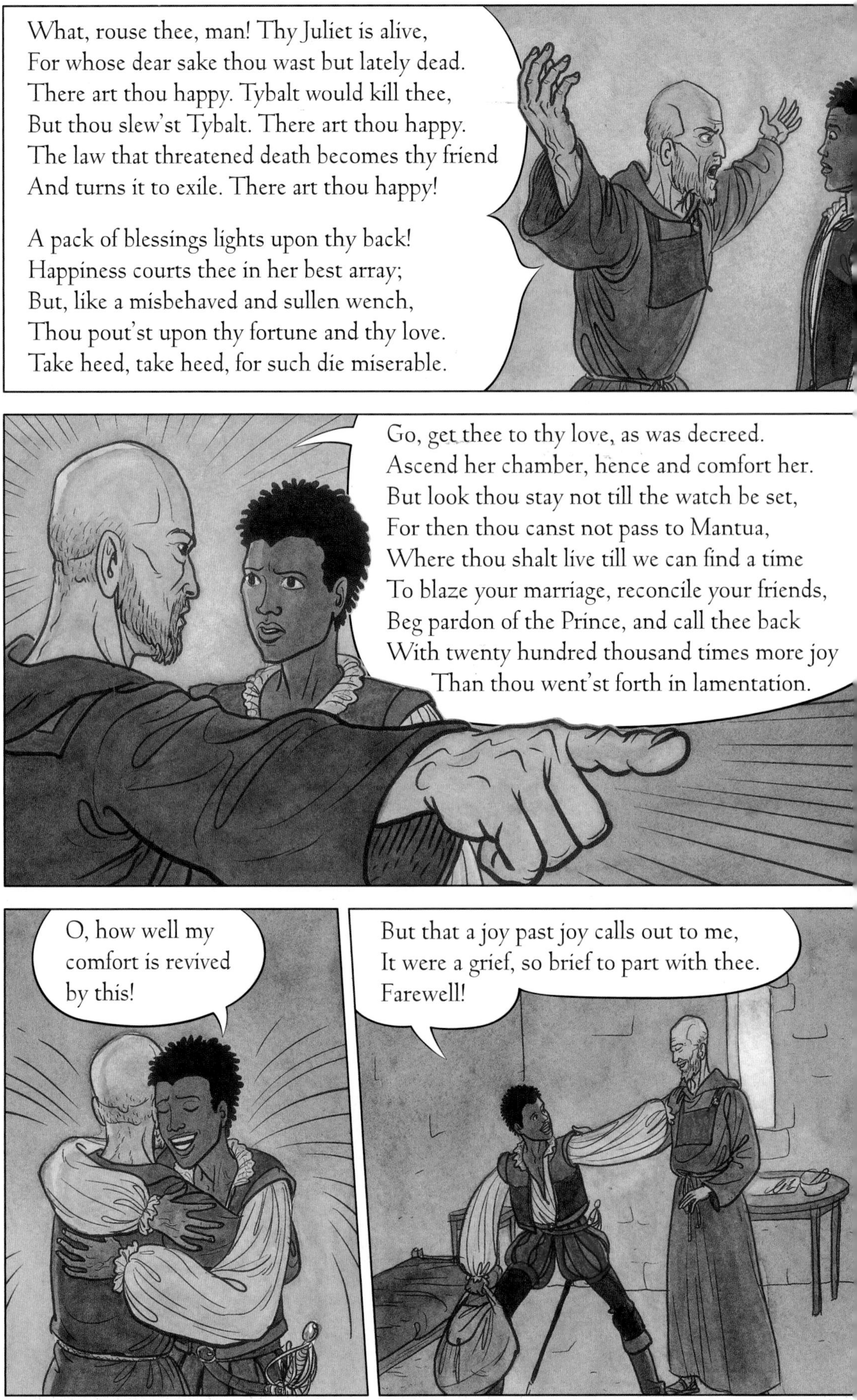
What, rouse thee, man! Thy Juliet is alive,
For whose dear sake thou wast but lately dead.
There art thou happy. Tybalt would kill thee,
But thou slew'st Tybalt. There art thou happy.
The law that threatened death becomes thy friend
And turns it to exile. There art thou happy!
A pack of blessings lights upon thy back!
Happiness courts thee in her best array;
But, like a misbehaved and sullen wench,
Thou pout'st upon thy fortune and thy love.
Take heed, take heed, for such die miserable.
Go, get thee to thy love, as was decreed.
Ascend her chamber, hence and comfort her.
But look thou stay not till the watch be set,
For then thou canst not pass to Mantua,
Where thou shalt live till we can find a time
To blaze your marriage, reconcile your friends,
Beg pardon of the Prince, and call thee back
With twenty hundred thousand times more joy
Than thou went'st forth in lamentation.
O, how well my comfort is revived by this!
But that a joy past joy calls out to me,
It were a grief, so brief to part with thee.
Farewell!

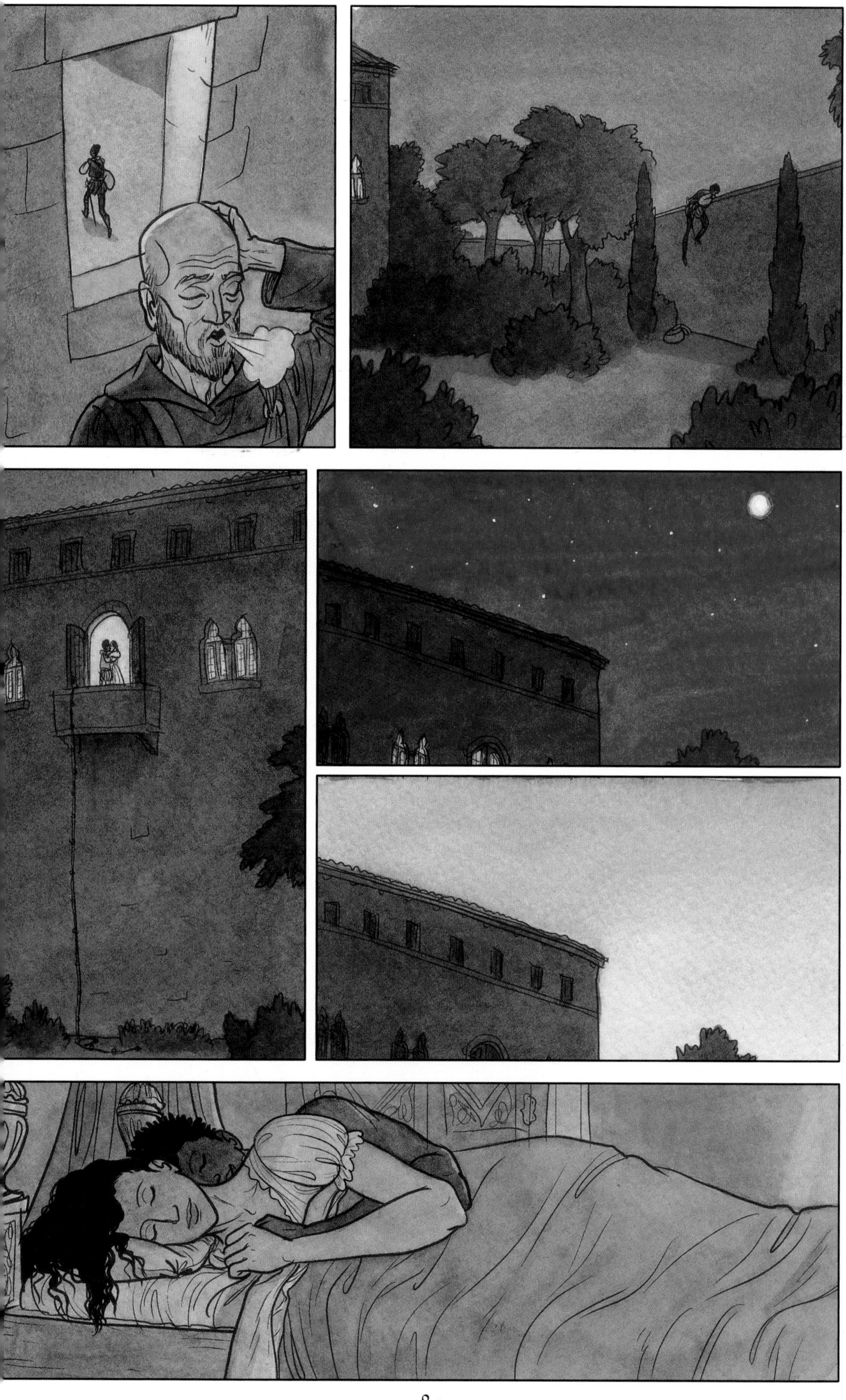

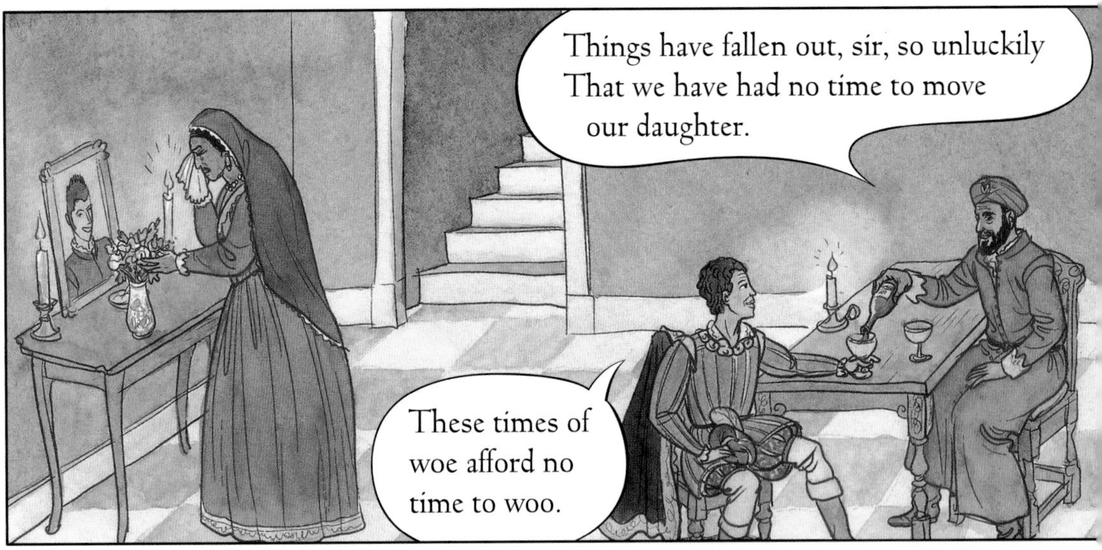
Things have fallen out, sir, so unluckily
That we have had no time to move our daughter.
These times of woe afford no time to woo.

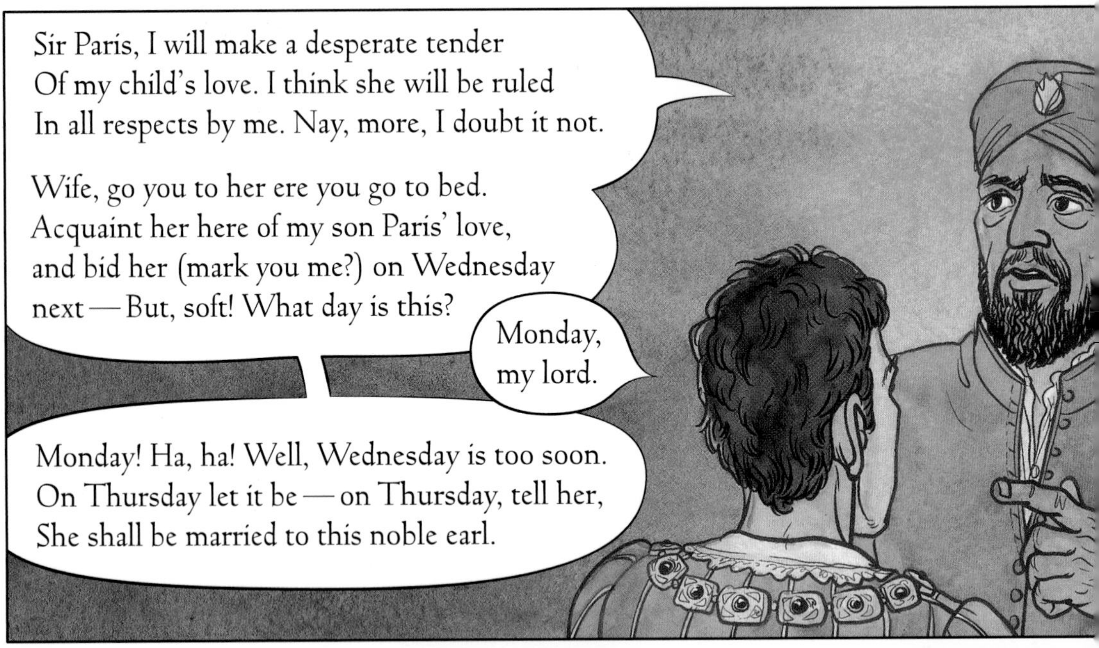
Sir Paris, I will make a desperate tender
Of my child's love. I think she will be ruled
In all respects by me. Nay, more, I doubt it not.
Wife, go you to her ere you go to bed.
Acquaint her here of my son Paris' love,
and bid her (mark you me?) on Wednesday next — But, soft! What day is this?
Monday, my lord.
Monday! Ha, ha! Well, Wednesday is too soon.
On Thursday let it be — on Thursday, tell her,
She shall be married to this noble earl.

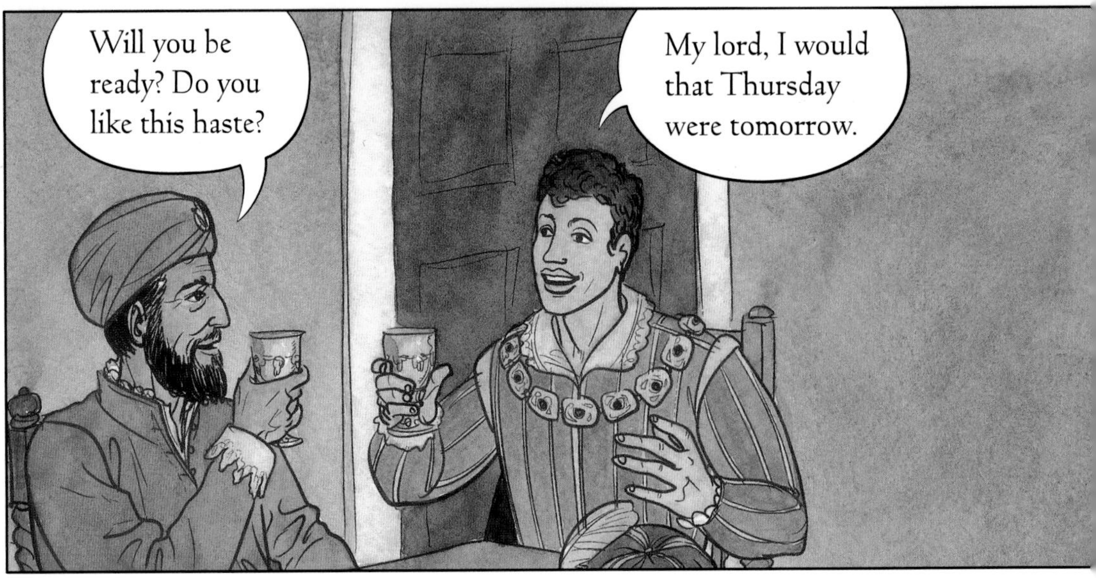
Will you be ready? Do you like this haste?
My lord, I would that Thursday were tomorrow.

Scene 5 : Juliet's Bedroom

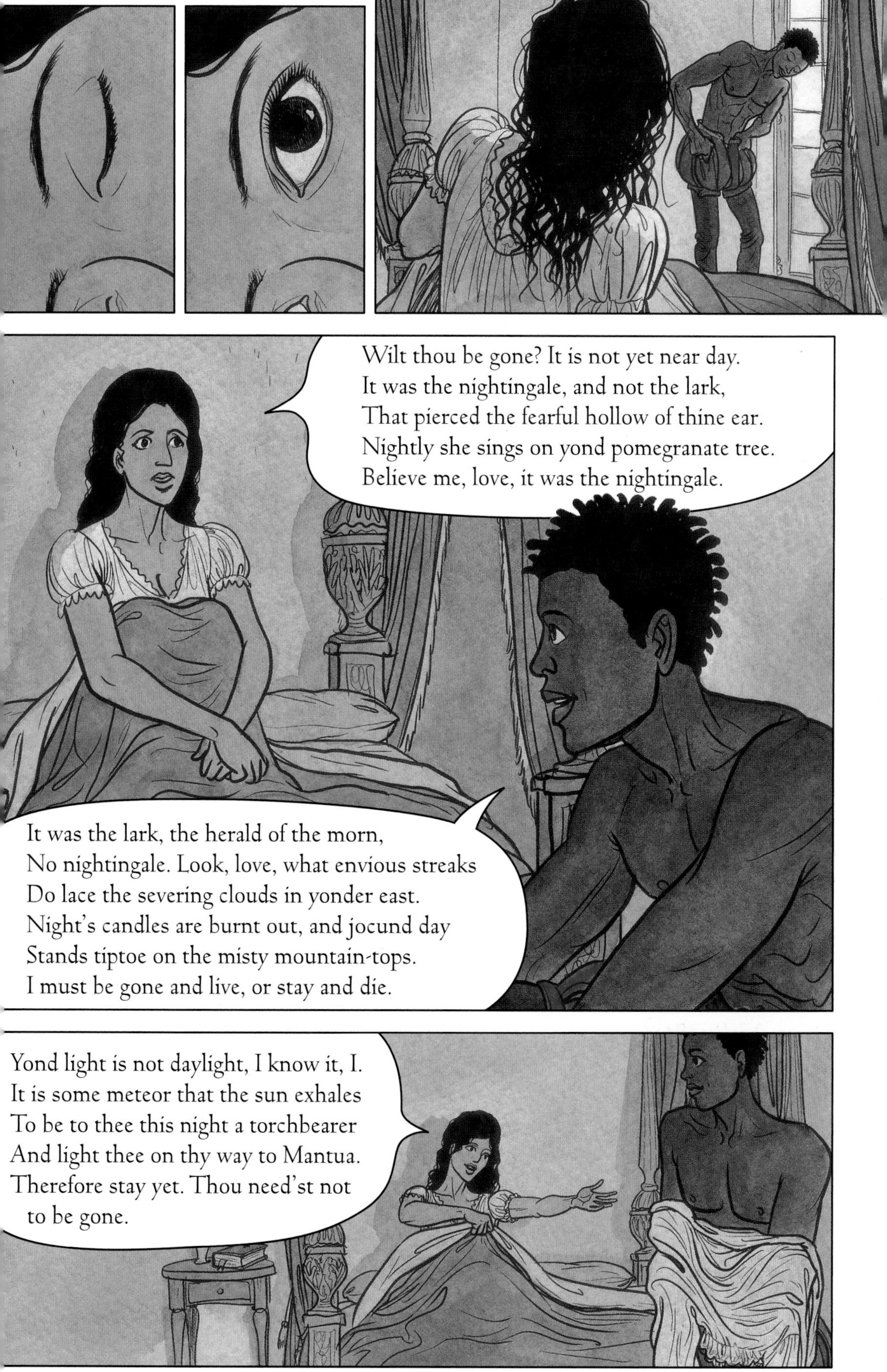
Wilt thou be gone? It is not yet near day. It was the nightingale, and not the lark, That pierced the fearful hollow of thine ear. Nightly she sings on yond pomegranate tree. Believe me, love, it was the nightingale.
It was the lark, the herald of the morn, No nightingale. Look, love, what envious streaks Do lace the severing clouds in yonder east. Night's candles are burnt out, and jocund day Stands tiptoe on the misty mountain-tops. I must be gone and live, or stay and die.
Yond light is not daylight, I know it, I. It is some meteor that the sun exhales To be to thee this night a torchbearer And light thee on thy way to Mantua. Therefore stay yet. Thou need'st not to be gone.

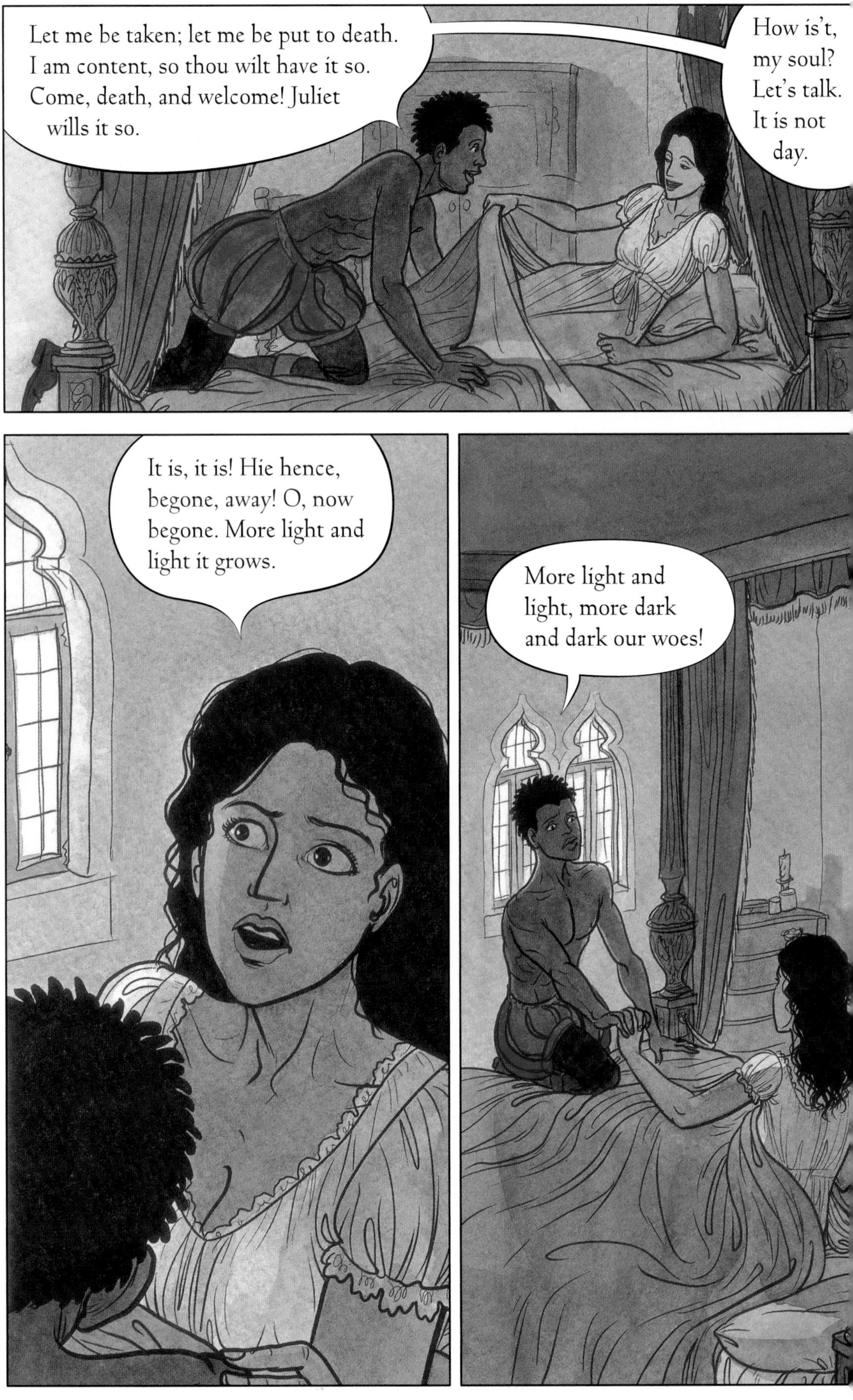
Let me be taken; let me be put to death. I am content, so thou wilt have it so. Come, death, and welcome! Juliet wills it so.
How is't, my soul? Let's talk. It is not day.
It is, it is! Hie hence, begone, away! O, now begone. More light and light it grows.
More light and light, more dark and dark our woes!

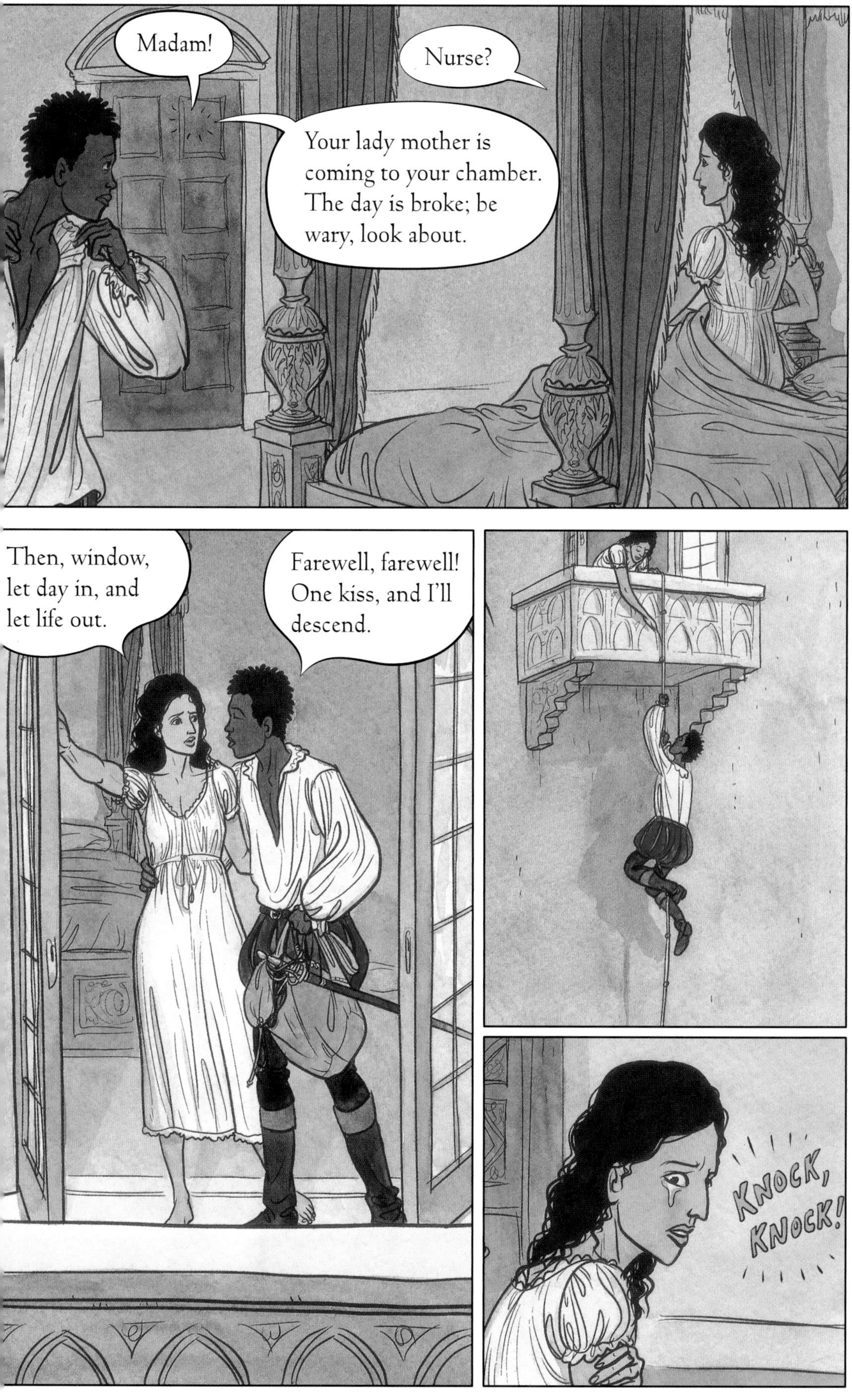
Madam!
Nurse?
Your lady mother is coming to your chamber. The day is broke; be wary, look about.
Then, window, let day in, and let life out.
Farewell, farewell! One kiss, and I'll descend.
KNOCK, KNOCK!

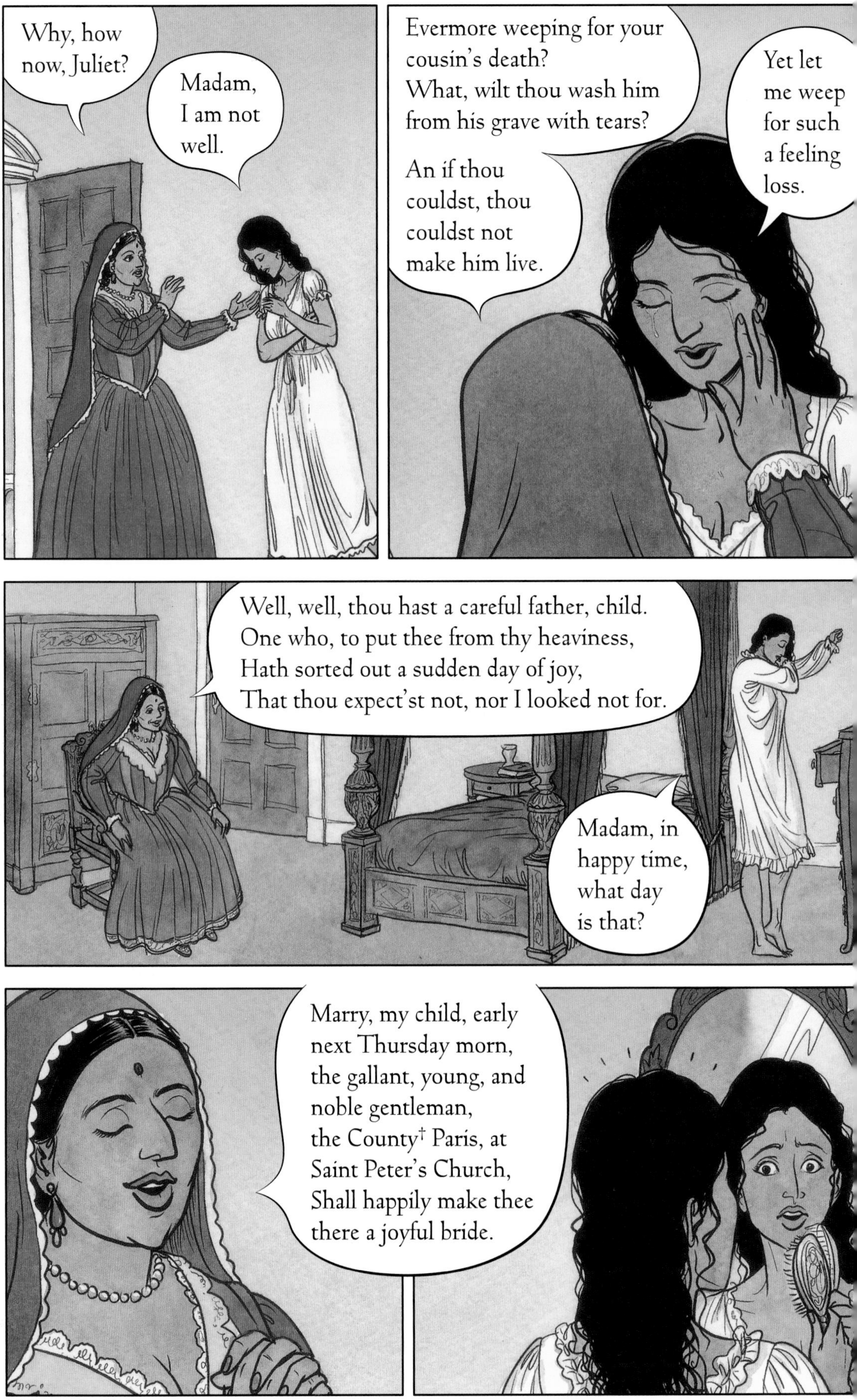
Why, how now, Juliet?
Madam, I am not well.
Evermore weeping for your cousin's death? What, wilt thou wash him from his grave with tears?
An if thou couldst, thou couldst not make him live.
Yet let me weep for such a feeling loss.
Well, well, thou hast a careful father, child. One who, to put thee from thy heaviness, Hath sorted out a sudden day of joy, That thou expect'st not, nor I looked not for.
Madam, in happy time, what day is that?
Marry, my child, early next Thursday morn, the gallant, young, and noble gentleman, the County† Paris, at Saint Peter's Church, Shall happily make thee there a joyful bride.

† "County" = Count

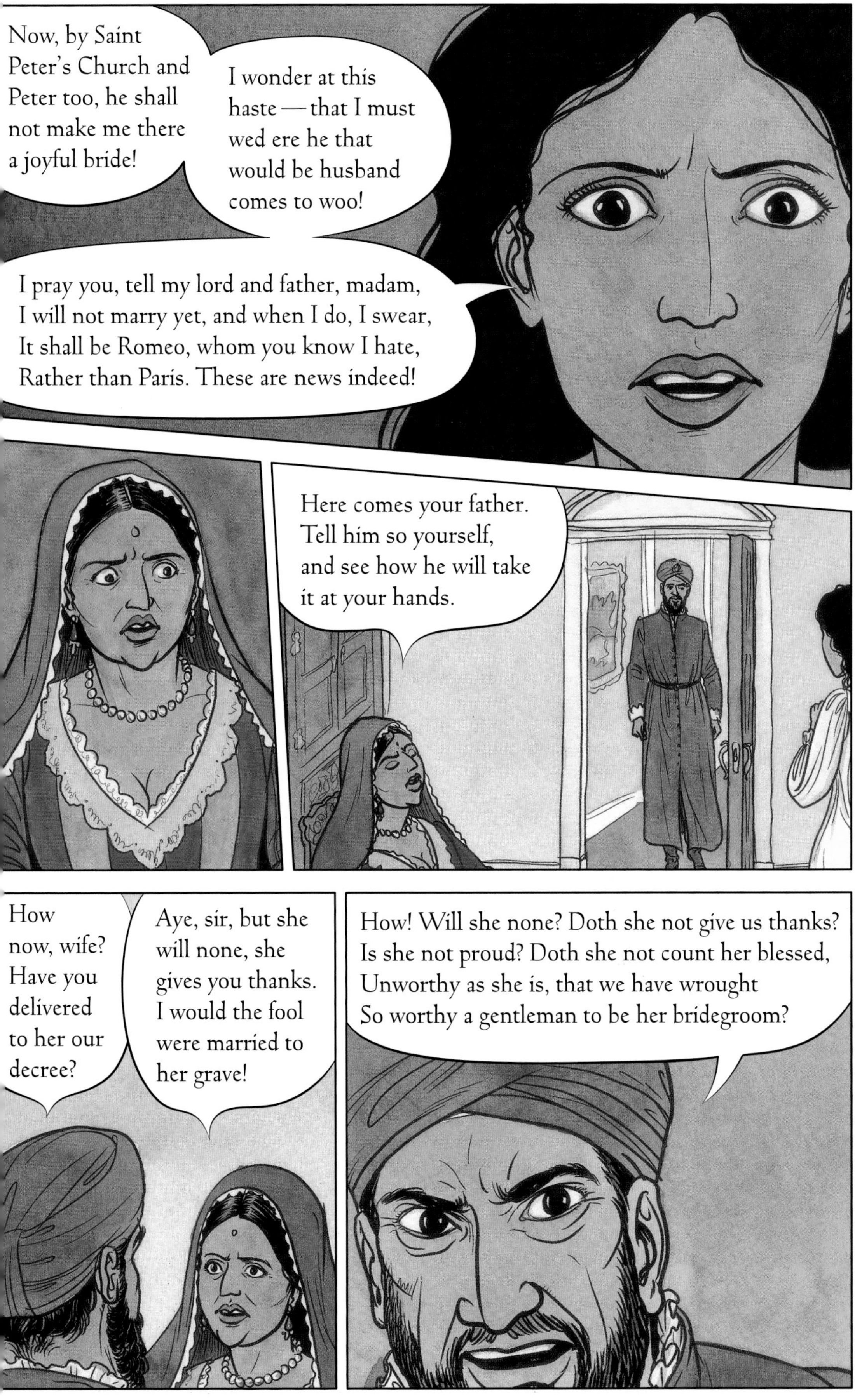
Now, by Saint Peter's Church and Peter too, he shall not make me there a joyful bride!
I wonder at this haste — that I must wed ere he that would be husband comes to woo!
I pray you, tell my lord and father, madam, I will not marry yet, and when I do, I swear, It shall be Romeo, whom you know I hate, Rather than Paris. These are news indeed!
Here comes your father. Tell him so yourself, and see how he will take it at your hands.
How now, wife? Have you delivered to her our decree?
Aye, sir, but she will none, she gives you thanks. I would the fool were married to her grave!
How! Will she none? Doth she not give us thanks? Is she not proud? Doth she not count her blessed, Unworthy as she is, that we have wrought So worthy a gentleman to be her bridegroom?

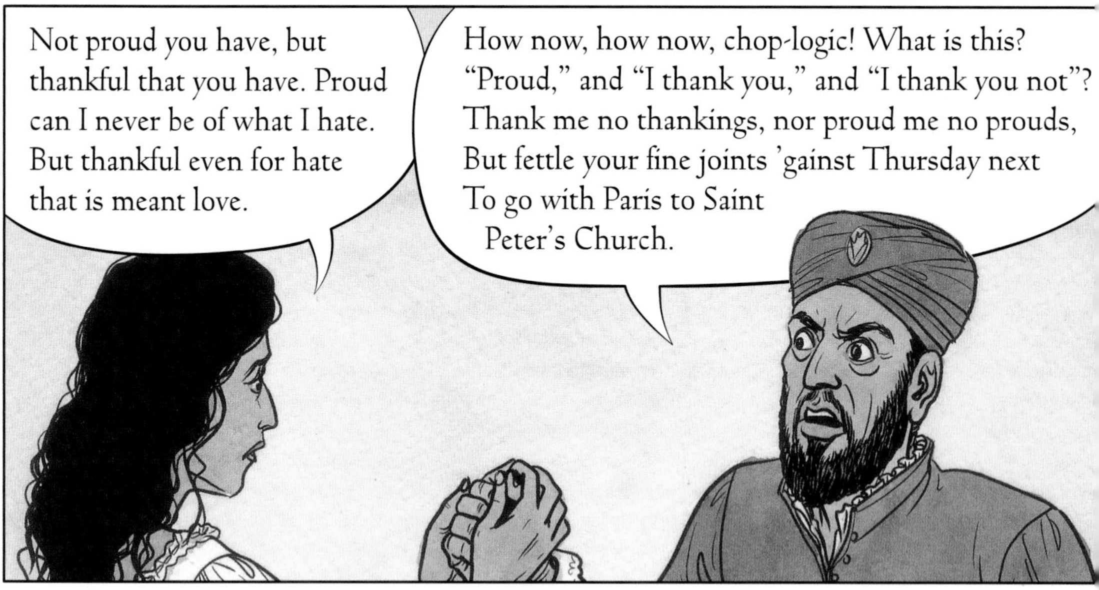
Not proud you have, but thankful that you have. Proud can I never be of what I hate. But thankful even for hate that is meant love.
How now, how now, chop-logic! What is this?
"Proud," and "I thank you," and "I thank you not"?
Thank me no thankings, nor proud me no prouds,
But fettle your fine joints 'gainst Thursday next
To go with Paris to Saint
Peter's Church.

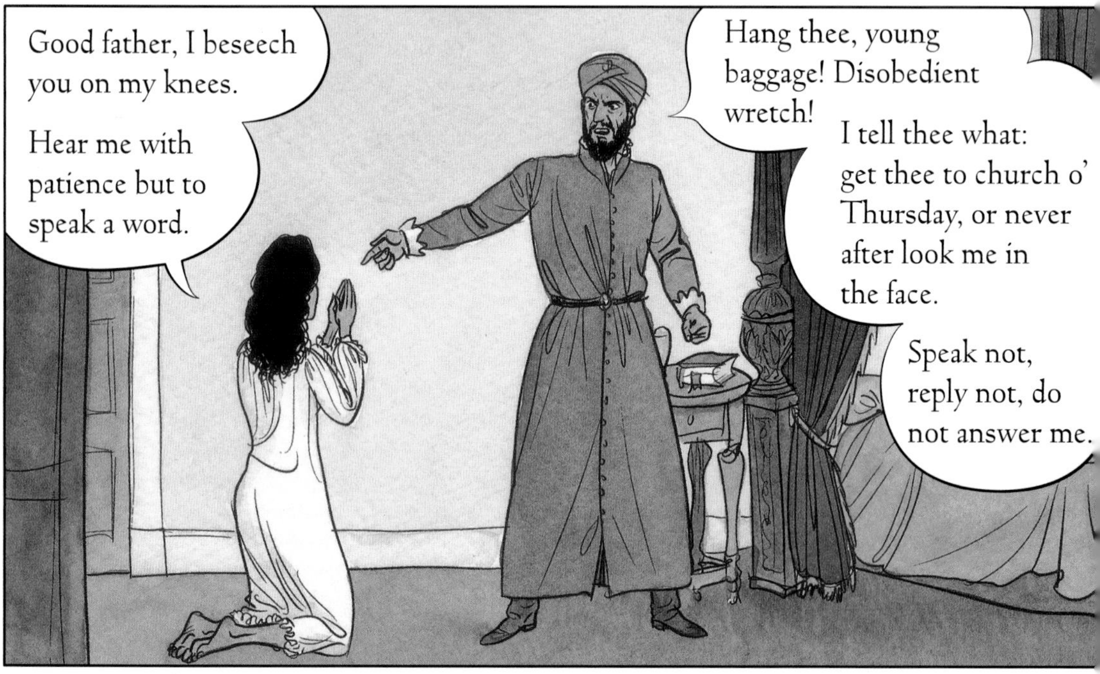
Good father, I beseech you on my knees.
Hear me with patience but to speak a word.
Hang thee, young baggage! Disobedient wretch!
I tell thee what: get thee to church o' Thursday, or never after look me in the face.
Speak not, reply not, do not answer me.

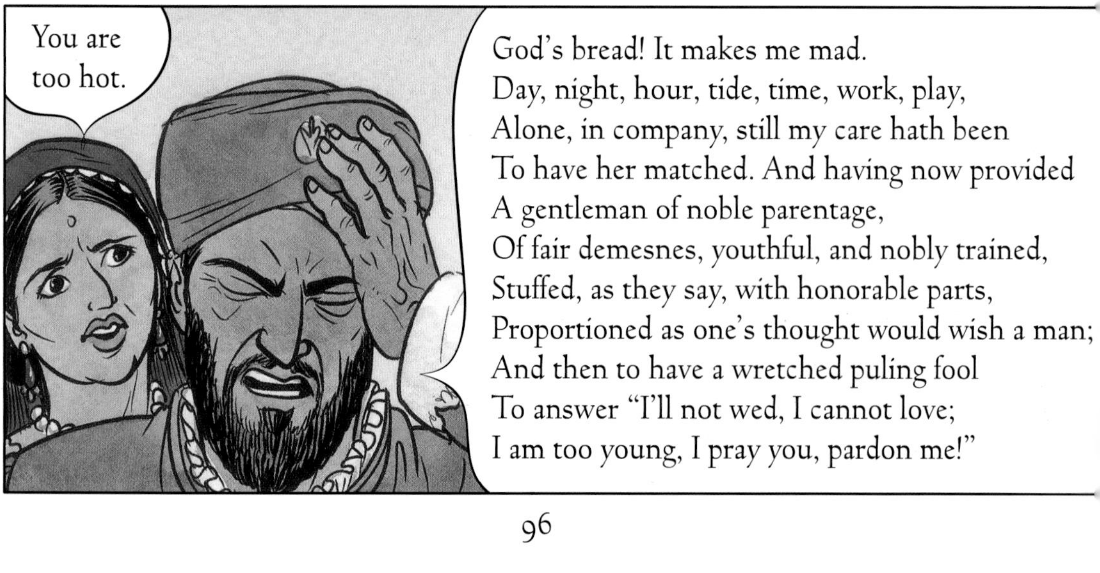
You are too hot.
God's bread! It makes me mad.
Day, night, hour, tide, time, work, play,
Alone, in company, still my care hath been
To have her matched. And having now provided
A gentleman of noble parentage,
Of fair demesnes, youthful, and nobly trained,
Stuffed, as they say, with honorable parts,
Proportioned as one's thought would wish a man;
And then to have a wretched puling fool
To answer "I'll not wed, I cannot love;
I am too young, I pray you, pardon me!"

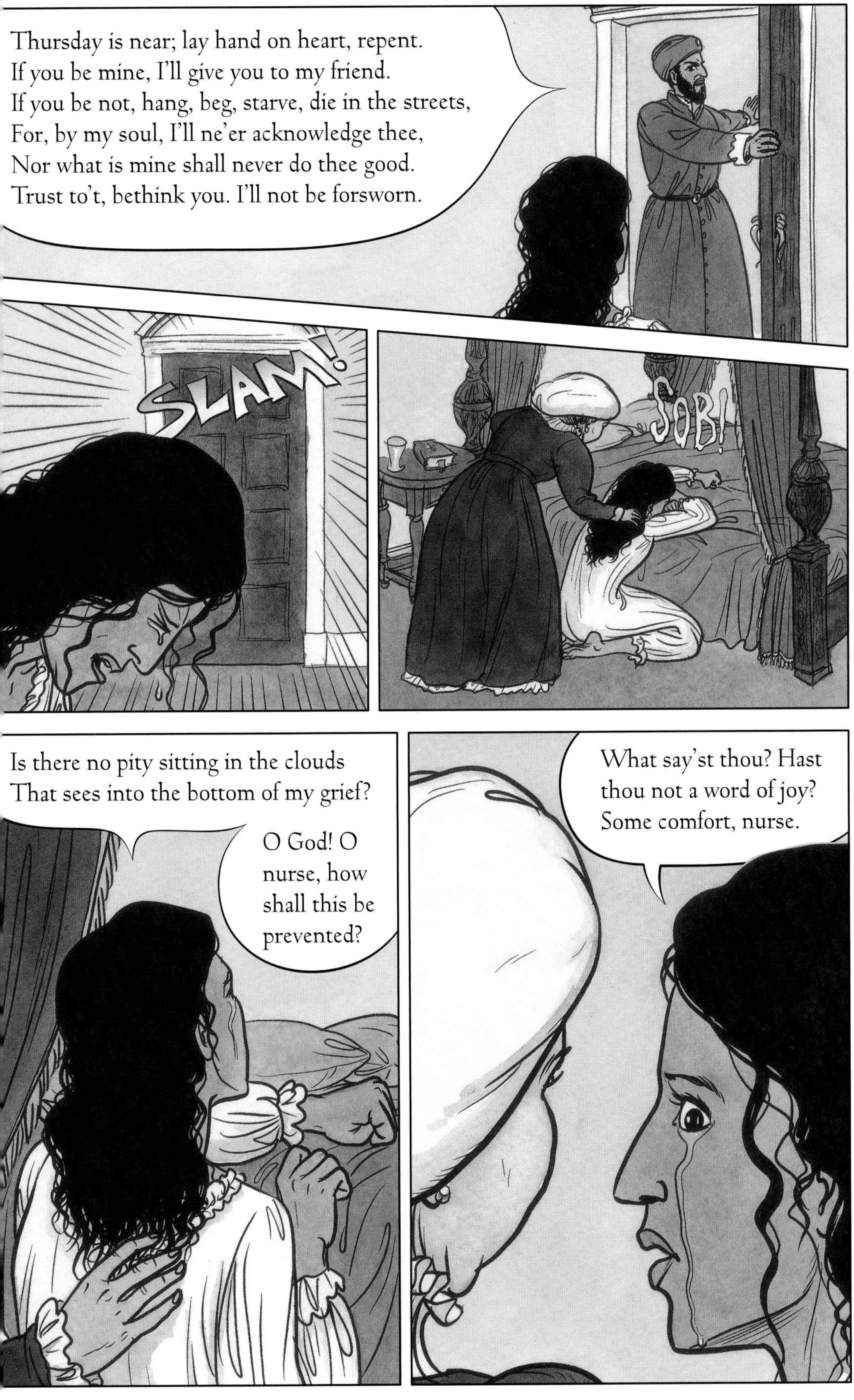
Thursday is near; lay hand on heart, repent. If you be mine, I'll give you to my friend. If you be not, hang, beg, starve, die in the streets, For, by my soul, I'll ne'er acknowledge thee, Nor what is mine shall never do thee good. Trust to't, bethink you. I'll not be forsworn.
SLAM!
SOB!
Is there no pity sitting in the clouds That sees into the bottom of my grief?
O God! O nurse, how shall this be prevented?
What say'st thou? Hast thou not a word of joy? Some comfort, nurse.

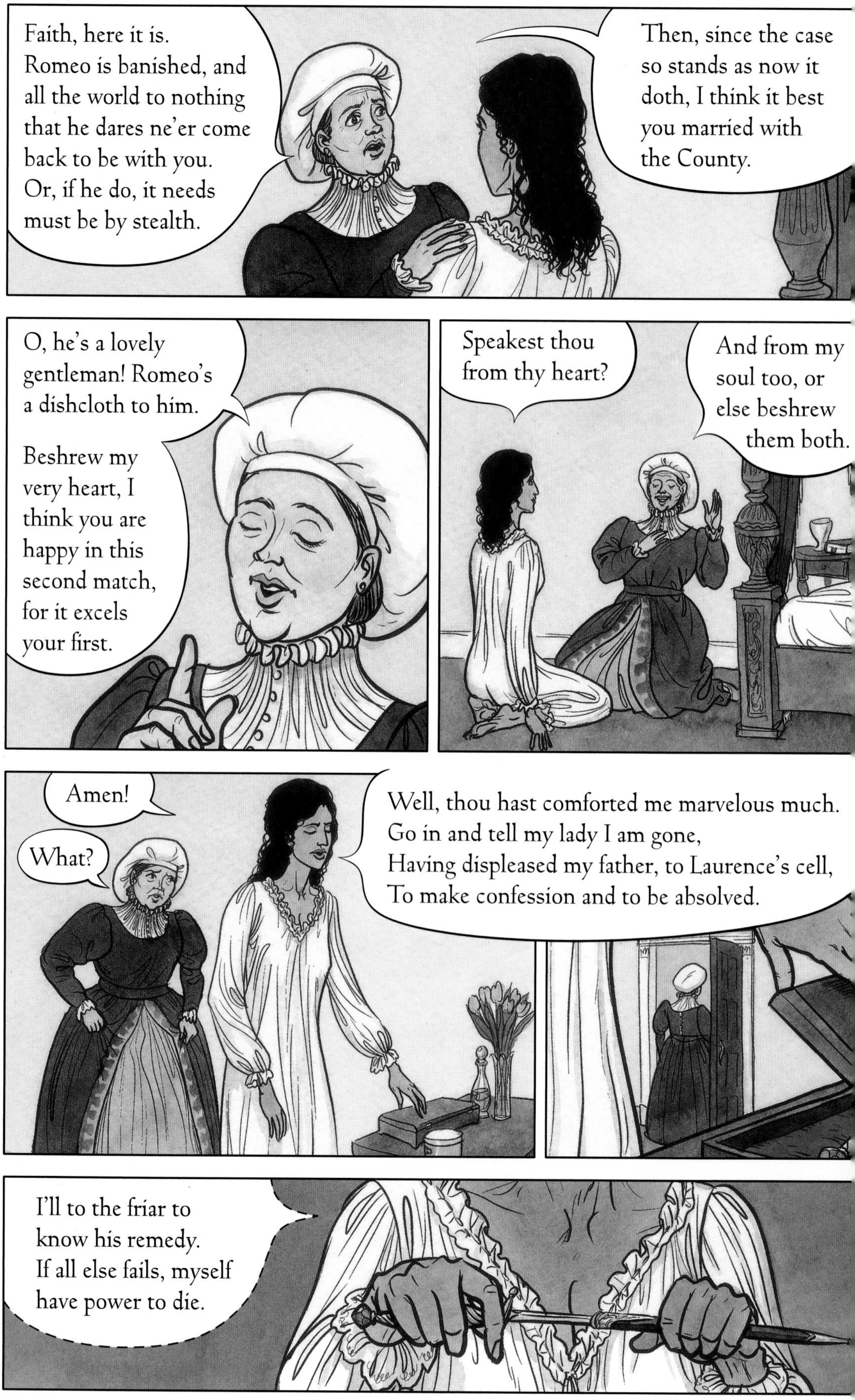
Faith, here it is. Romeo is banished, and all the world to nothing that he dares ne'er come back to be with you. Or, if he do, it needs must be by stealth.
Then, since the case so stands as now it doth, I think it best you married with the County.
O, he's a lovely gentleman! Romeo's a dishcloth to him.
Beshrew my very heart, I think you are happy in this second match, for it excels your first.
Speakest thou from thy heart?
And from my soul too, or else beshrew them both.
Amen!
What?
Well, thou hast comforted me marvelous much.
Go in and tell my lady I am gone,
Having displeased my father, to Laurence's cell,
To make confession and to be absolved.
I'll to the friar to know his remedy. If all else fails, myself have power to die.

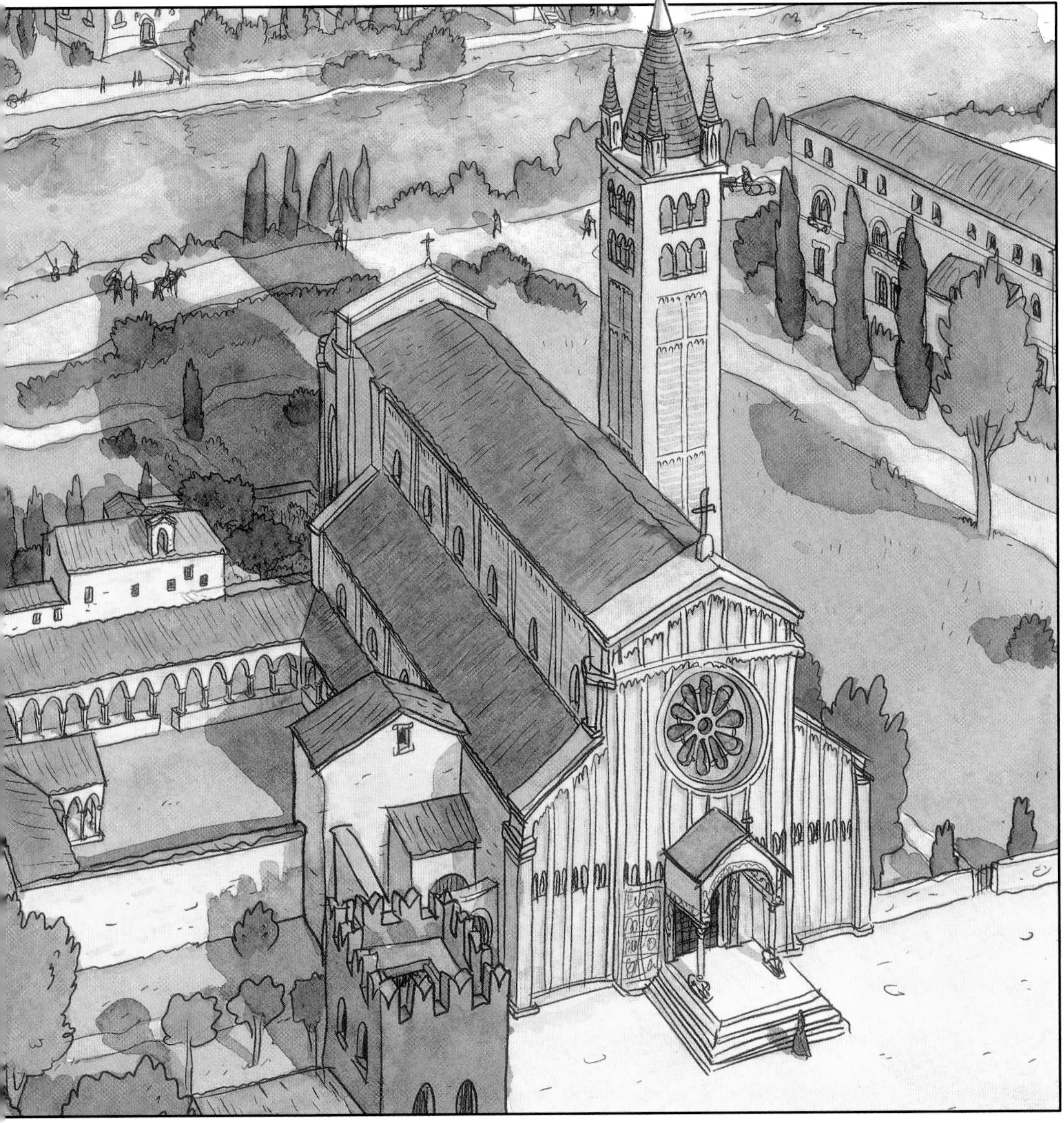

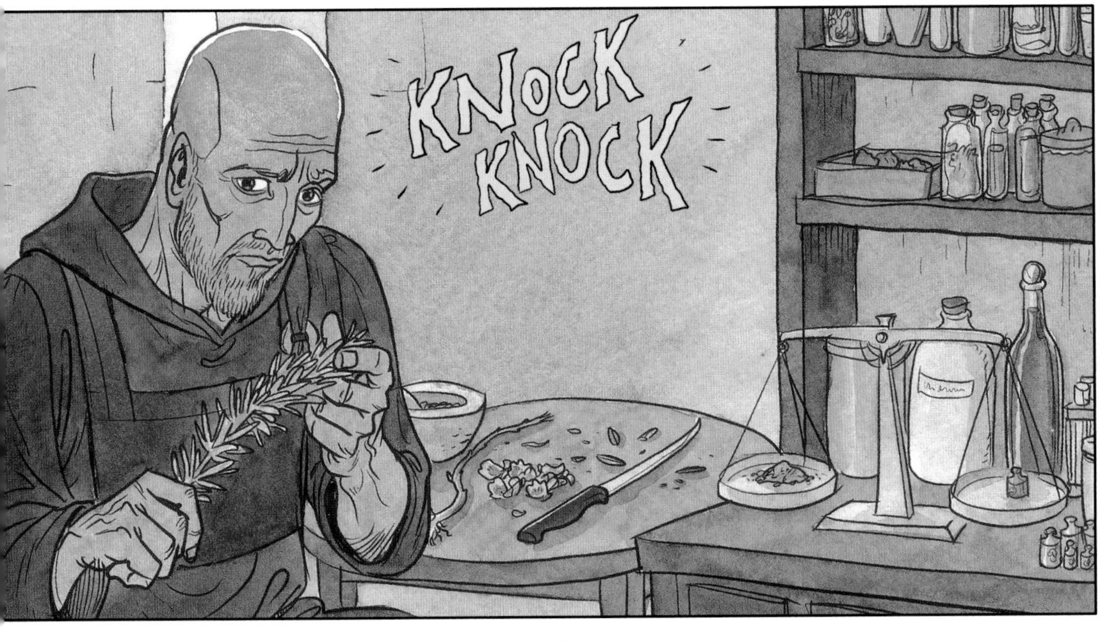
KNOCK KNOCK

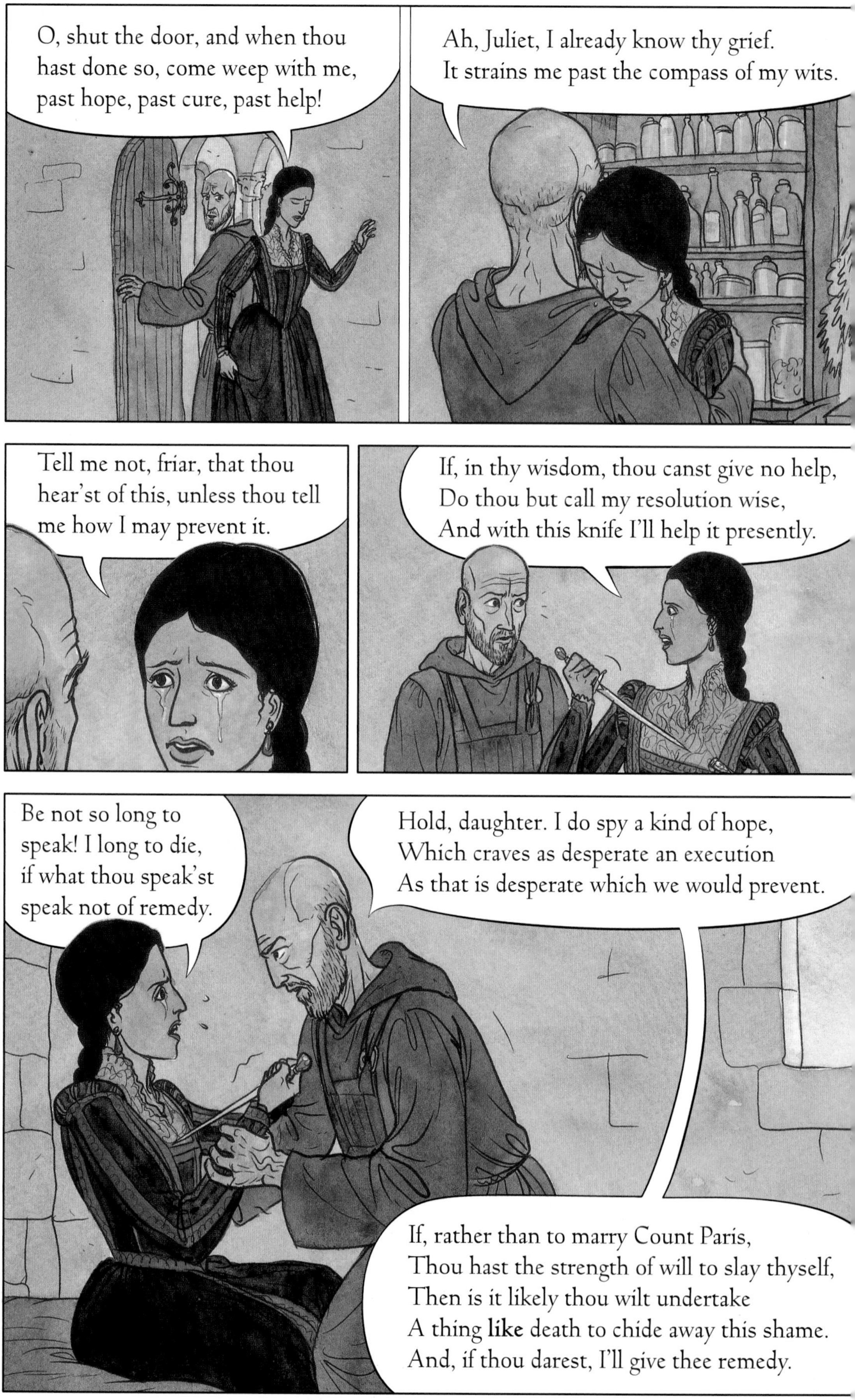
O, shut the door, and when thou hast done so, come weep with me, past hope, past cure, past help!
Ah, Juliet, I already know thy grief. It strains me past the compass of my wits.
Tell me not, friar, that thou hear'st of this, unless thou tell me how I may prevent it.
If, in thy wisdom, thou canst give no help, Do thou but call my resolution wise, And with this knife I'll help it presently.
Be not so long to speak! I long to die, if what thou speak'st speak not of remedy.
Hold, daughter. I do spy a kind of hope, Which craves as desperate an execution As that is desperate which we would prevent.
If, rather than to marry Count Paris, Thou hast the strength of will to slay thyself, Then is it likely thou wilt undertake A thing **like** death to chide away this shame. And, if thou darest, I'll give thee remedy.

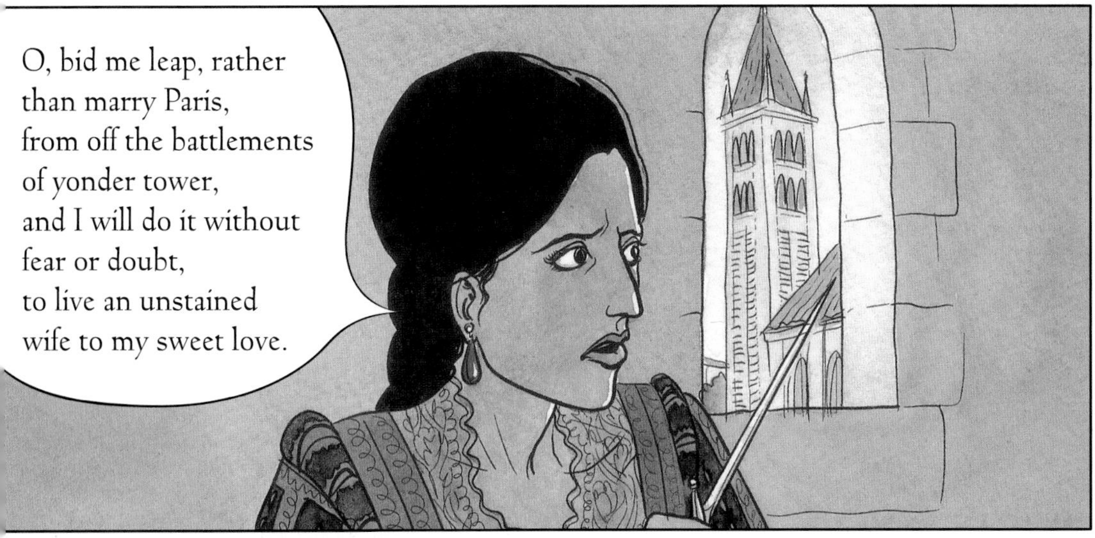
O, bid me leap, rather than marry Paris, from off the battlements of yonder tower, and I will do it without fear or doubt, to live an unstained wife to my sweet love.

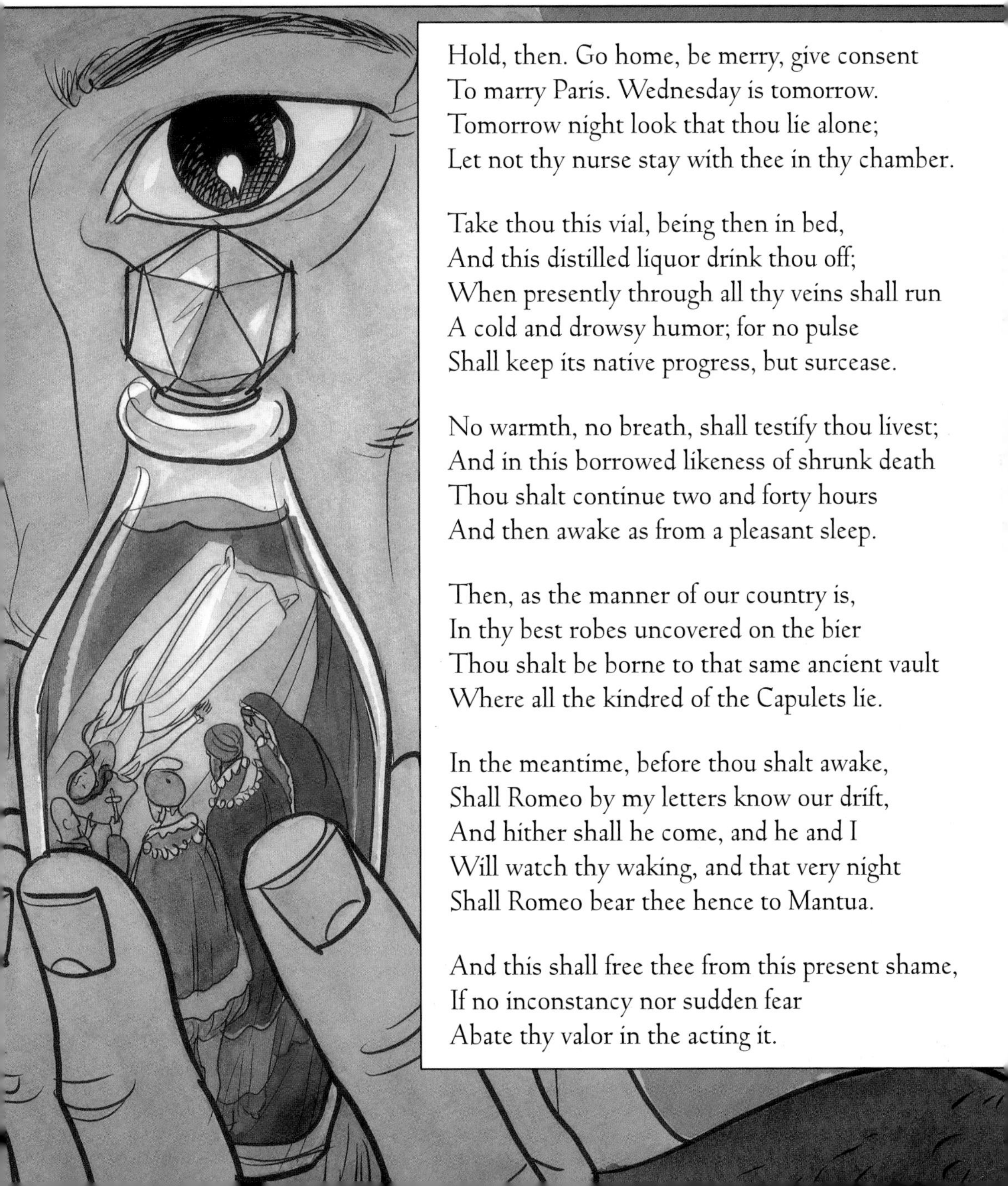
Hold, then. Go home, be merry, give consent
To marry Paris. Wednesday is tomorrow.
Tomorrow night look that thou lie alone;
Let not thy nurse stay with thee in thy chamber.
Take thou this vial, being then in bed,
And this distilled liquor drink thou off;
When presently through all thy veins shall run
A cold and drowsy humor; for no pulse
Shall keep its native progress, but surcease.
No warmth, no breath, shall testify thou livest;
And in this borrowed likeness of shrunk death
Thou shalt continue two and forty hours
And then awake as from a pleasant sleep.
Then, as the manner of our country is,
In thy best robes uncovered on the bier
Thou shalt be borne to that same ancient vault
Where all the kindred of the Capulets lie.
In the meantime, before thou shalt awake,
Shall Romeo by my letters know our drift,
And hither shall he come, and he and I
Will watch thy waking, and that very night
Shall Romeo bear thee hence to Mantua.
And this shall free thee from this present shame,
If no inconstancy nor sudden fear
Abate thy valor in the acting it.

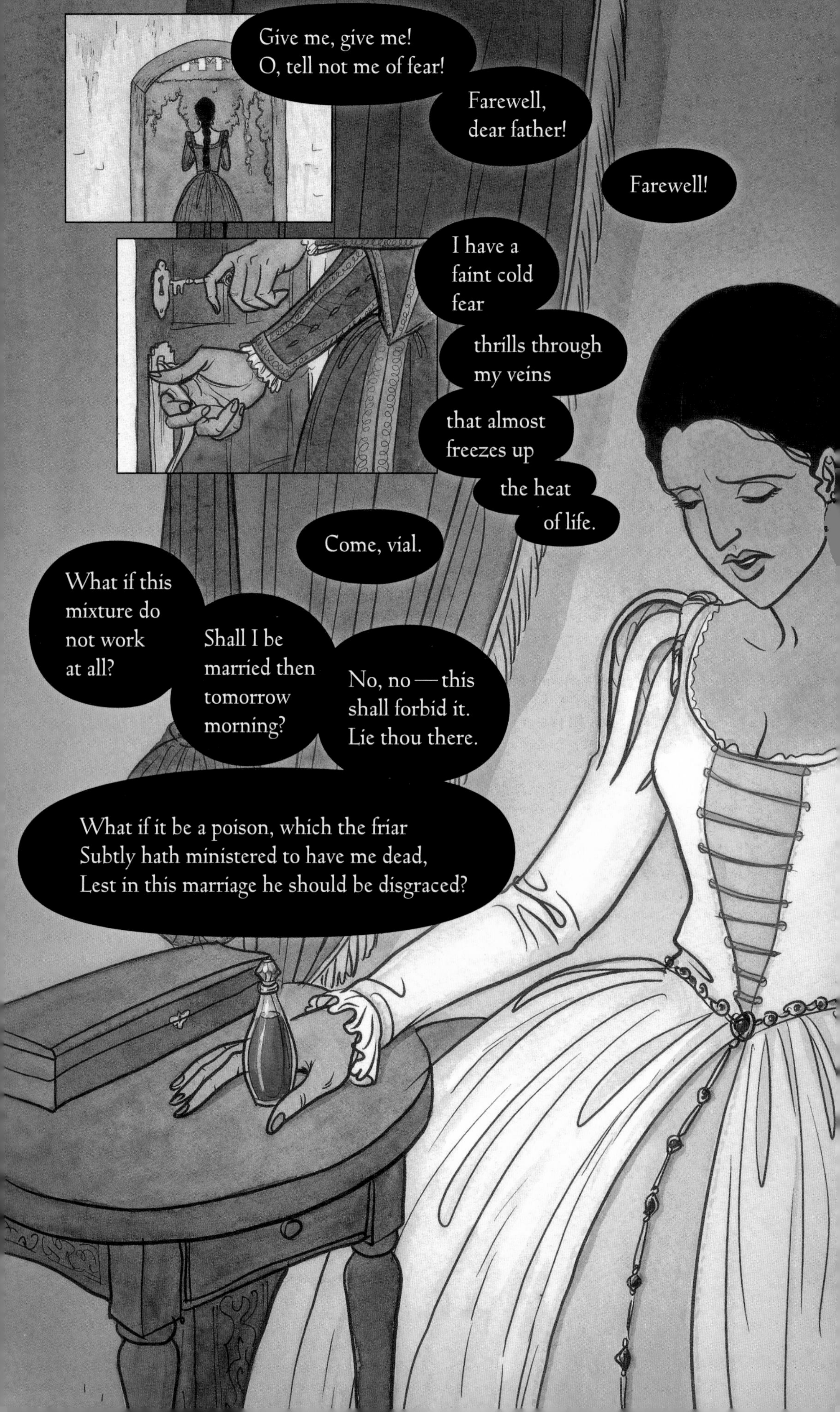
Give me, give me! O, tell not me of fear!
Farewell, dear father!
Farewell!
I have a faint cold fear
thrills through my veins
that almost freezes up
the heat
of life.
Come, vial.
What if this mixture do not work at all?
Shall I be married then tomorrow morning?
No, no — this shall forbid it. Lie thou there.
What if it be a poison, which the friar
Subtly hath ministered to have me dead,
Lest in this marriage he should be disgraced?

How if, when I am laid into the tomb,
I wake before the time that Romeo
Come to redeem me? There's a fearful point!
Shall I not then be stifled in the vault,
To whose foul mouth no healthsome air breathes in,
And there die strangled ere my Romeo comes?

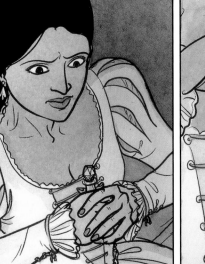

Romeo, I come! This do I drink to thee.

Hold, take these keys, and fetch more spices, nurse.
They call for dates and quinces in the pastry.
Come, stir, stir, stir! The second cock hath crowed, the curfew bell hath rung, 'tis three o'clock!
Look to the baked meats, good Angelica. Spare not for the cost.
Nurse! Wife! Go waken Juliet. Go and dress her up. I'll go and chat with Paris. Hie, make haste, Make haste. The bridegroom he is come already.
Alas, alas! Help, help! My lady's dead!

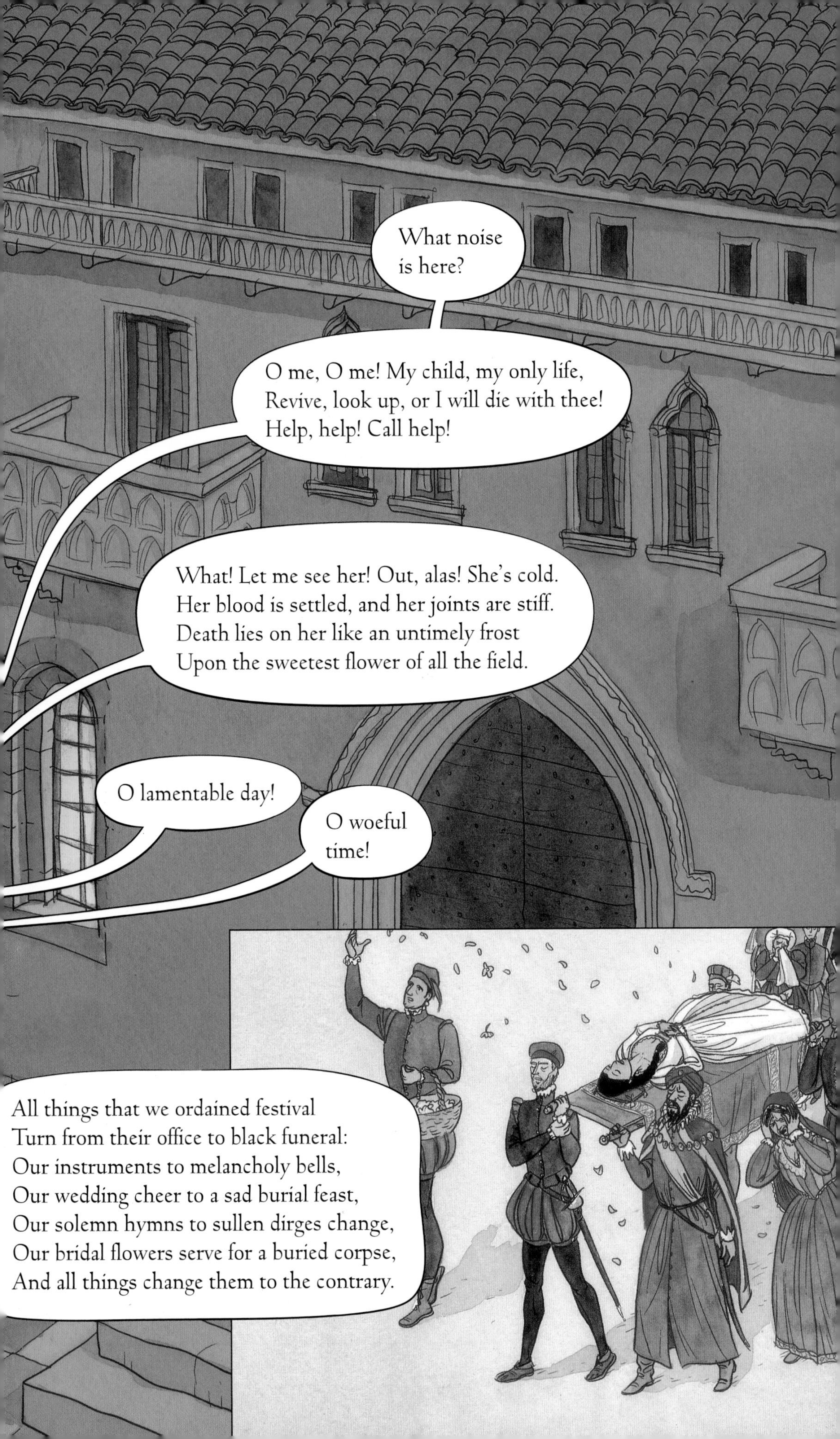
What noise is here?
O me, O me! My child, my only life, Revive, look up, or I will die with thee! Help, help! Call help!
What! Let me see her! Out, alas! She's cold. Her blood is settled, and her joints are stiff. Death lies on her like an untimely frost Upon the sweetest flower of all the field.
O lamentable day!
O woeful time!
All things that we ordained festival Turn from their office to black funeral: Our instruments to melancholy bells, Our wedding cheer to a sad burial feast, Our solemn hymns to sullen dirges change, Our bridal flowers serve for a buried corpse, And all things change them to the contrary.

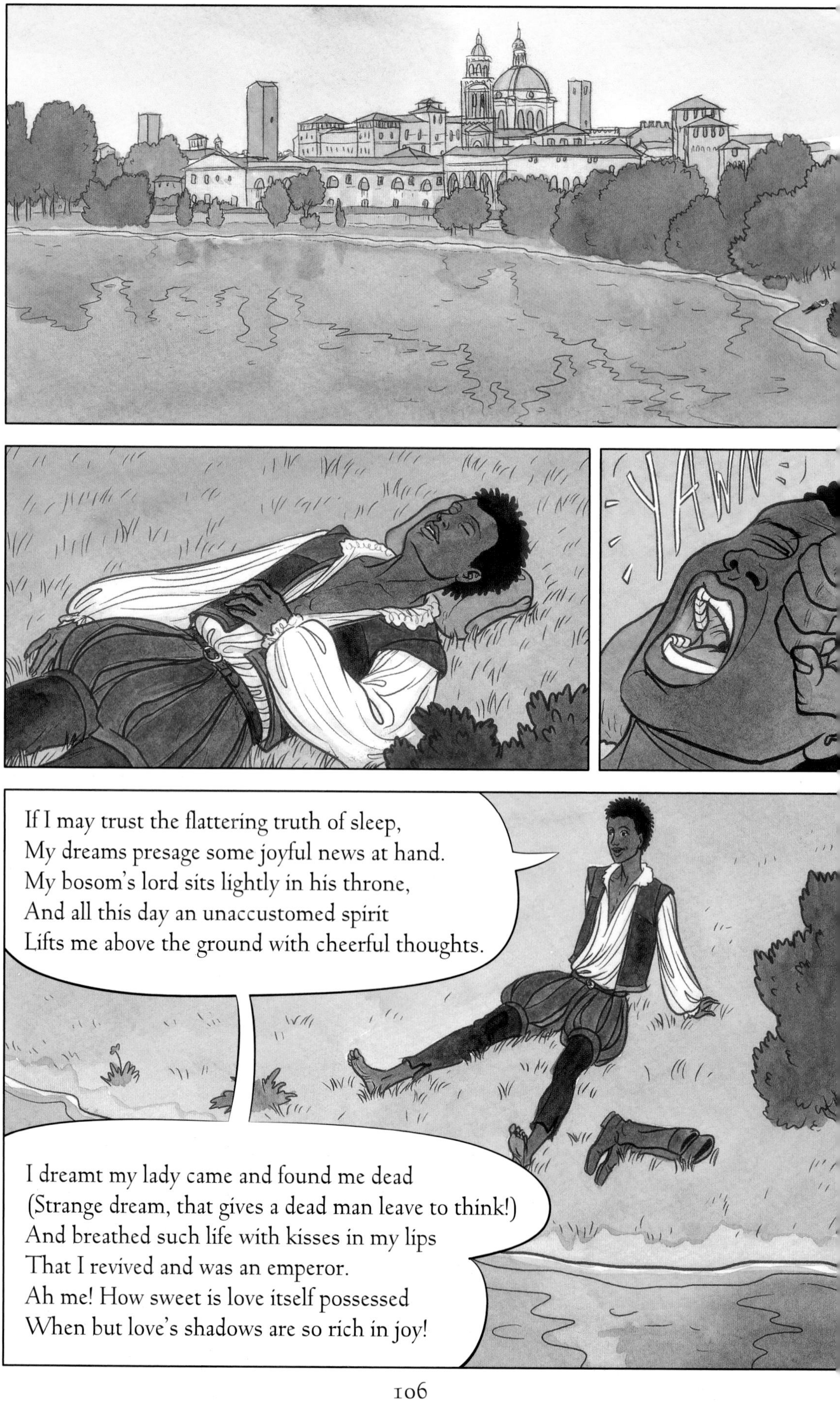
YAWN
If I may trust the flattering truth of sleep,
My dreams presage some joyful news at hand.
My bosom's lord sits lightly in his throne,
And all this day an unaccustomed spirit
Lifts me above the ground with cheerful thoughts.
I dreamt my lady came and found me dead
(Strange dream, that gives a dead man leave to think!)
And breathed such life with kisses in my lips
That I revived and was an emperor.
Ah me! How sweet is love itself possessed
When but love's shadows are so rich in joy!

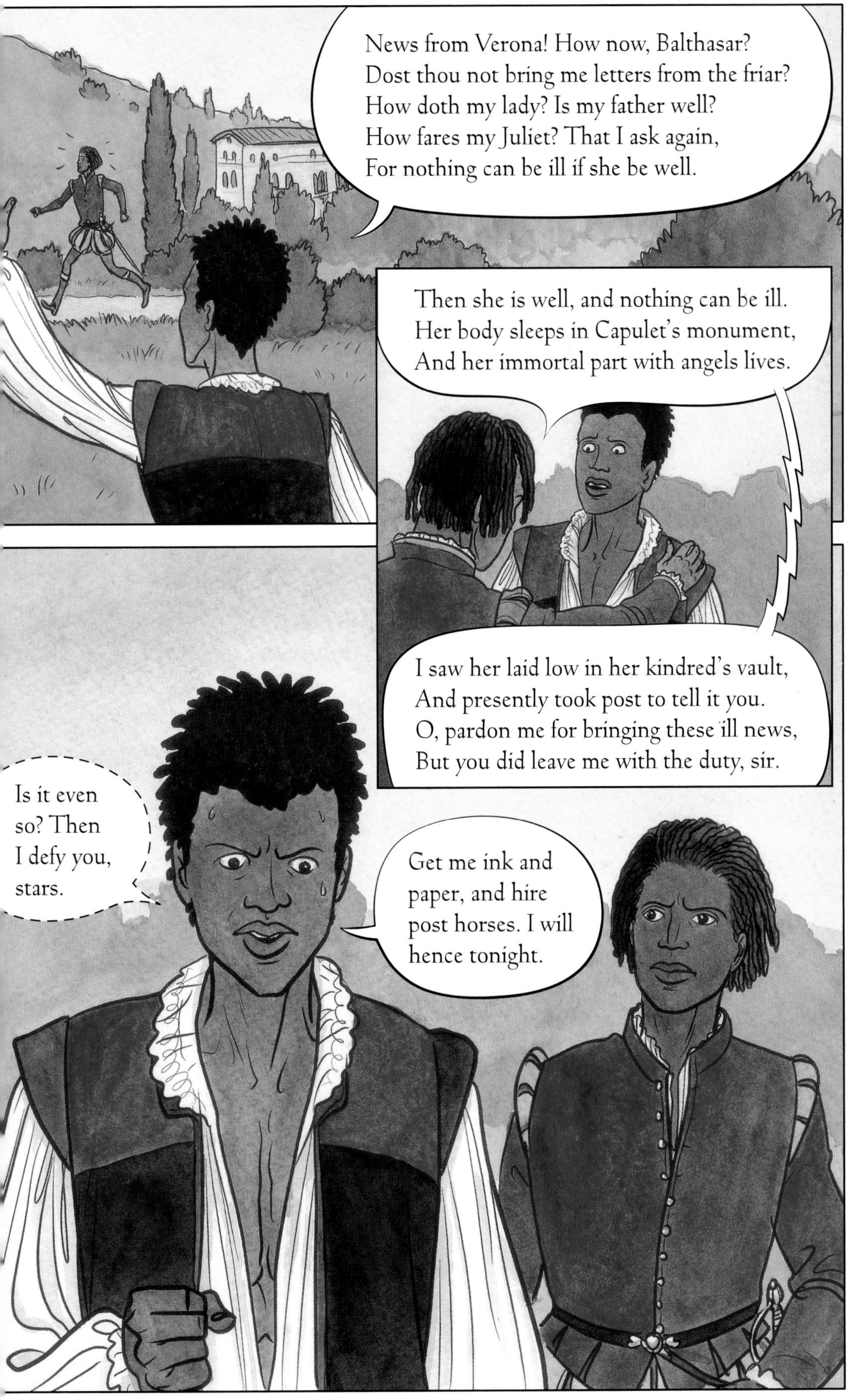
News from Verona! How now, Balthasar? Dost thou not bring me letters from the friar? How doth my lady? Is my father well? How fares my Juliet? That I ask again, For nothing can be ill if she be well.
Then she is well, and nothing can be ill. Her body sleeps in Capulet's monument, And her immortal part with angels lives.
I saw her laid low in her kindred's vault, And presently took post to tell it you. O, pardon me for bringing these ill news, But you did leave me with the duty, sir.
Is it even so? Then I defy you, stars.
Get me ink and paper, and hire post horses. I will hence tonight.

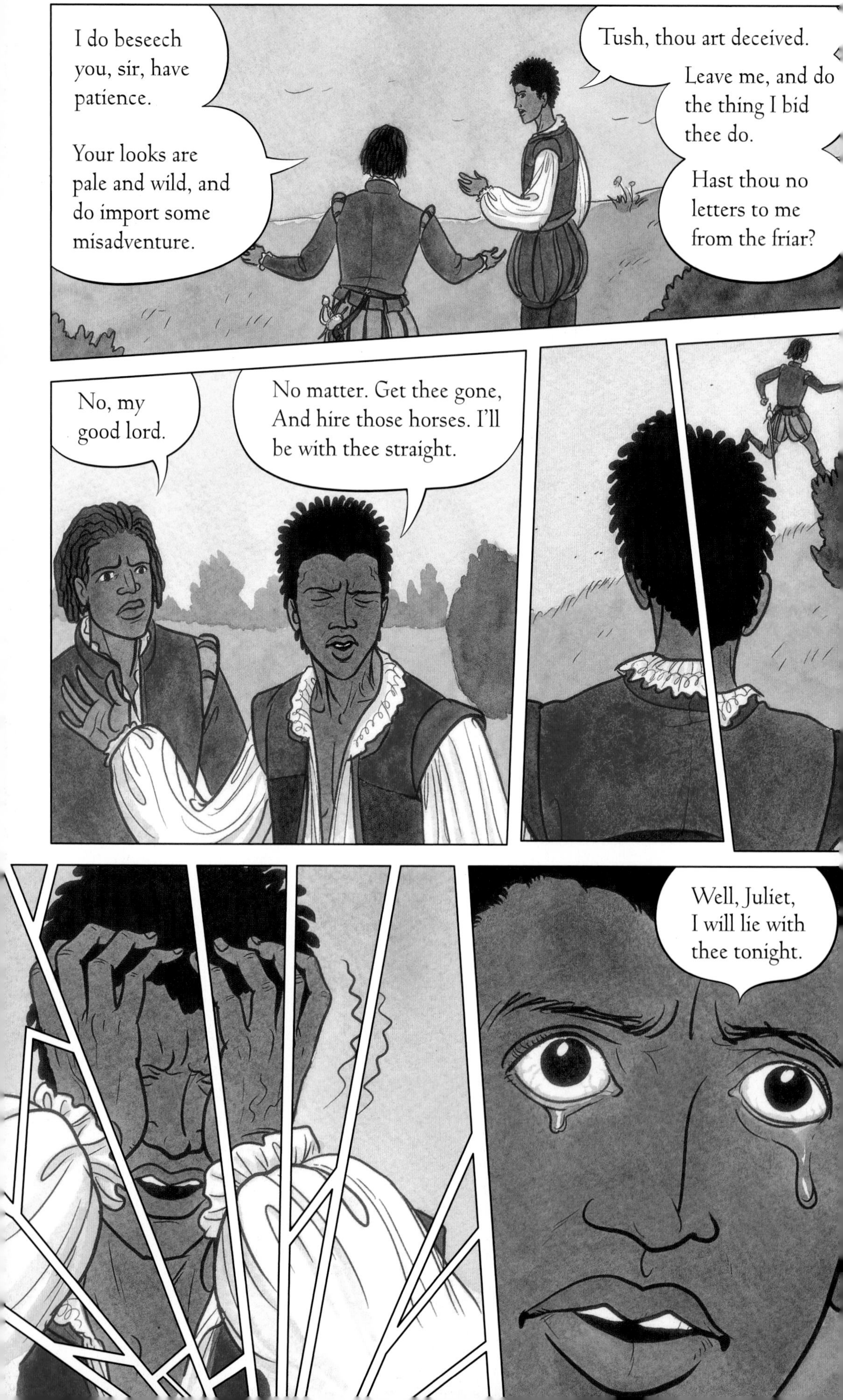
I do beseech you, sir, have patience.
Your looks are pale and wild, and do import some misadventure.
Tush, thou art deceived.
Leave me, and do the thing I bid thee do.
Hast thou no letters to me from the friar?
No, my good lord.
No matter. Get thee gone, And hire those horses. I'll be with thee straight.
Well, Juliet, I will lie with thee tonight.

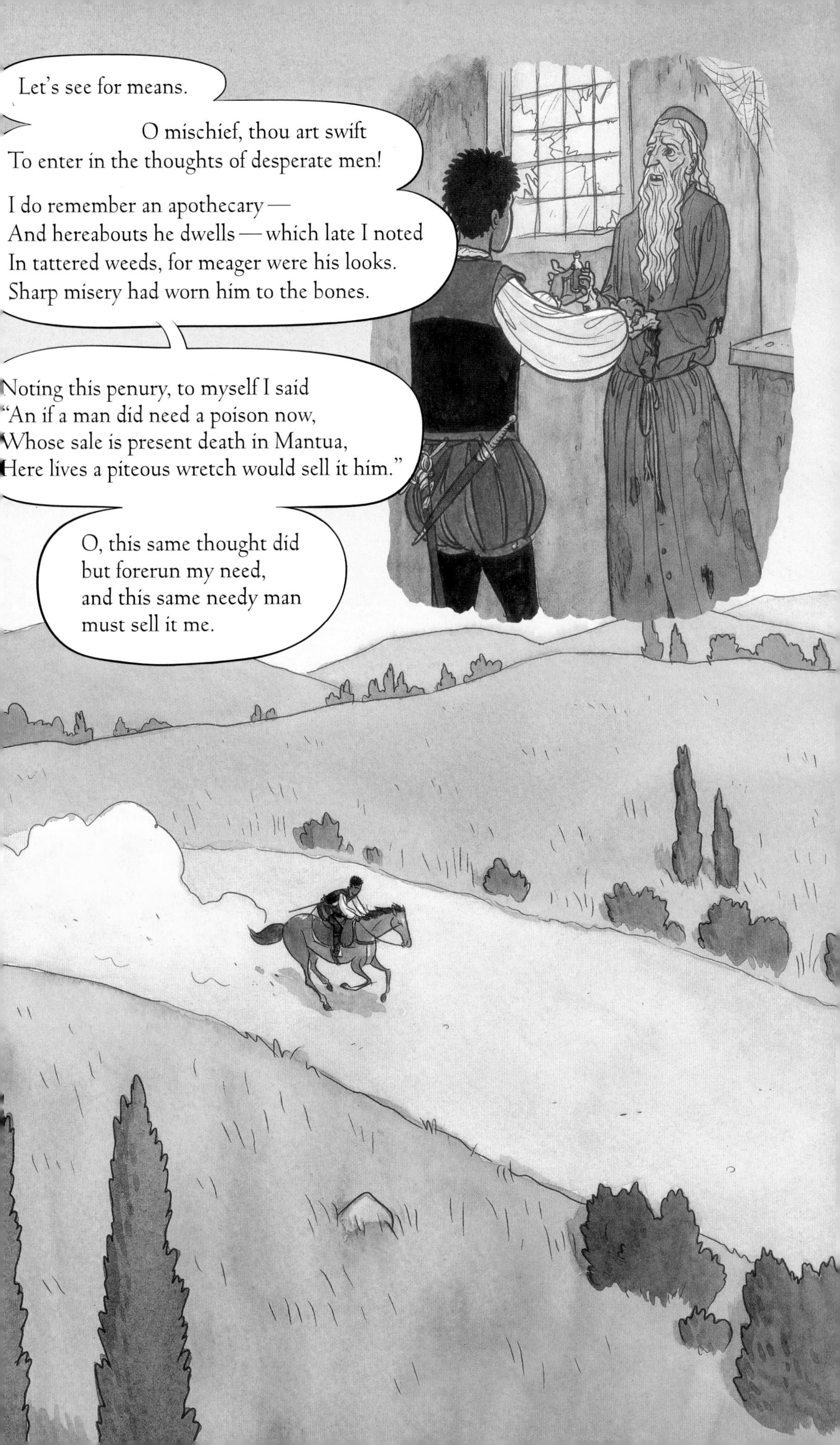

Let's see for means.
O mischief, thou art swift
To enter in the thoughts of desperate men!
I do remember an apothecary —
And hereabouts he dwells — which late I noted
In tattered weeds, for meager were his looks.
Sharp misery had worn him to the bones.
Noting this penury, to myself I said
"An if a man did need a poison now,
Whose sale is present death in Mantua,
Here lives a piteous wretch would sell it him."
O, this same thought did but forerun my need, and this same needy man must sell it me.

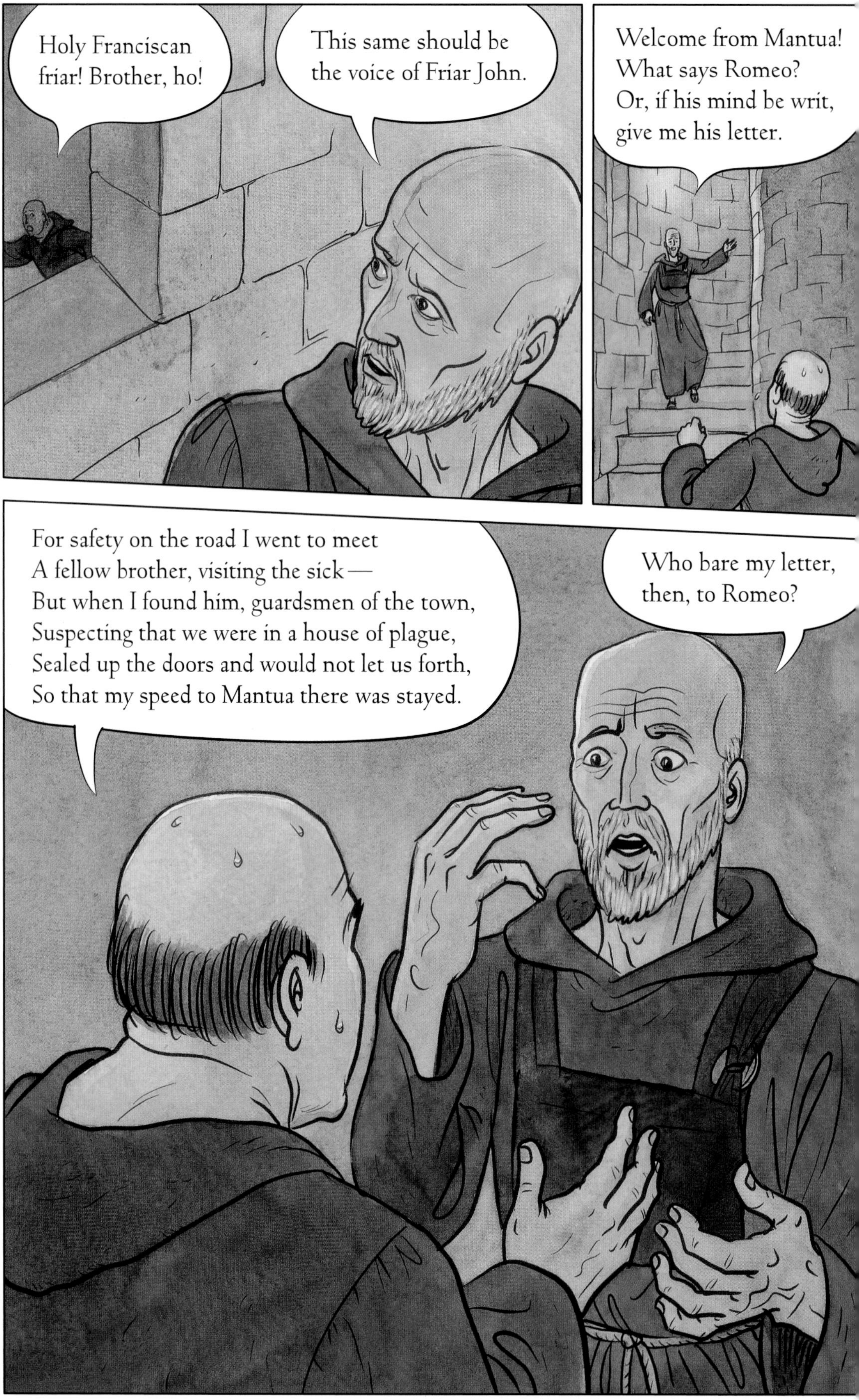
Holy Franciscan friar! Brother, ho!
This same should be the voice of Friar John.
Welcome from Mantua! What says Romeo? Or, if his mind be writ, give me his letter.
For safety on the road I went to meet
A fellow brother, visiting the sick—
But when I found him, guardsmen of the town,
Suspecting that we were in a house of plague,
Sealed up the doors and would not let us forth,
So that my speed to Mantua there was stayed.
Who bare my letter, then, to Romeo?

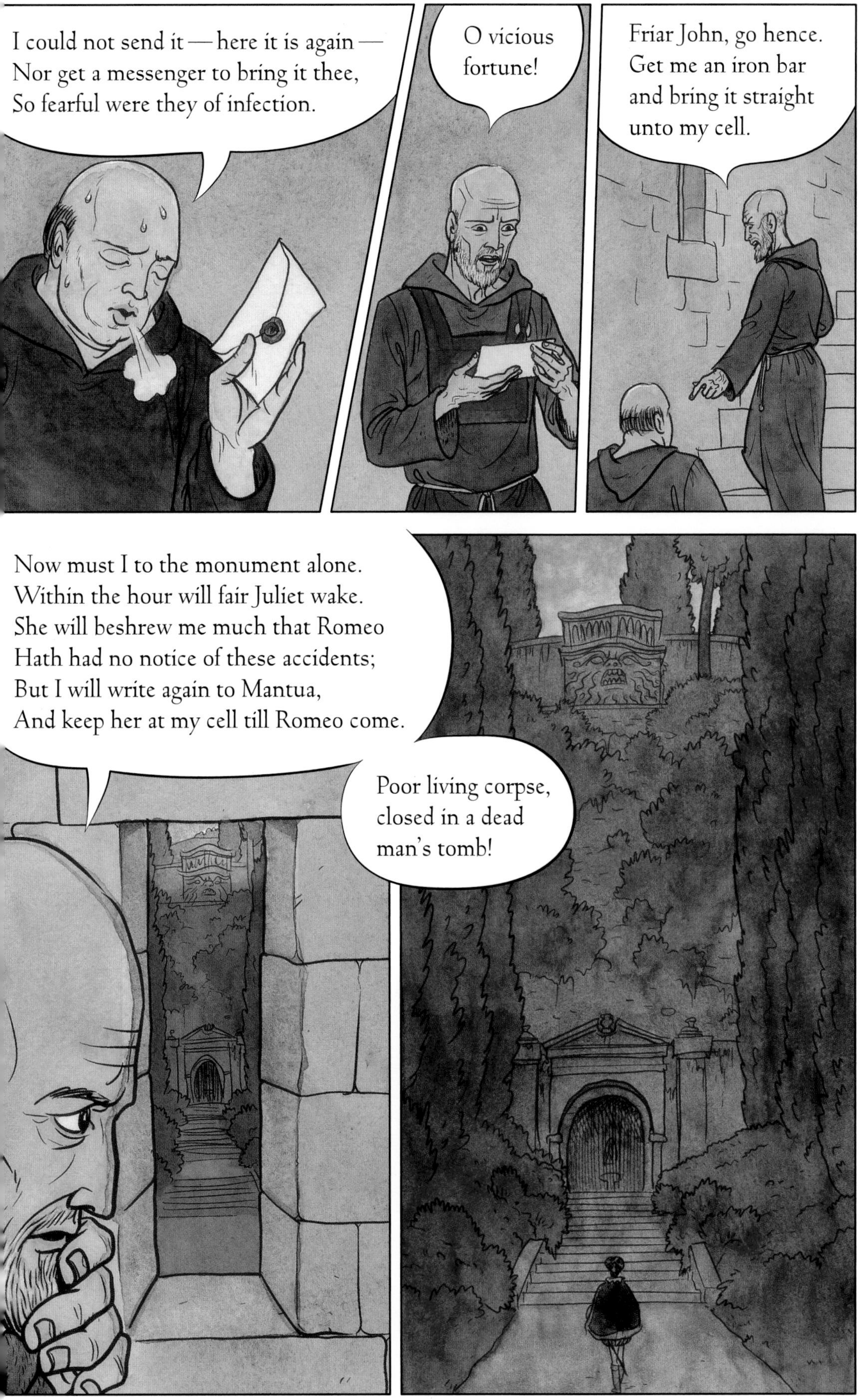

I could not send it — here it is again —
Nor get a messenger to bring it thee,
So fearful were they of infection.
O vicious fortune!
Friar John, go hence. Get me an iron bar and bring it straight unto my cell.
Now must I to the monument alone.
Within the hour will fair Juliet wake.
She will beshrew me much that Romeo
Hath had no notice of these accidents;
But I will write again to Mantua,
And keep her at my cell till Romeo come.
Poor living corpse, closed in a dead man's tomb!

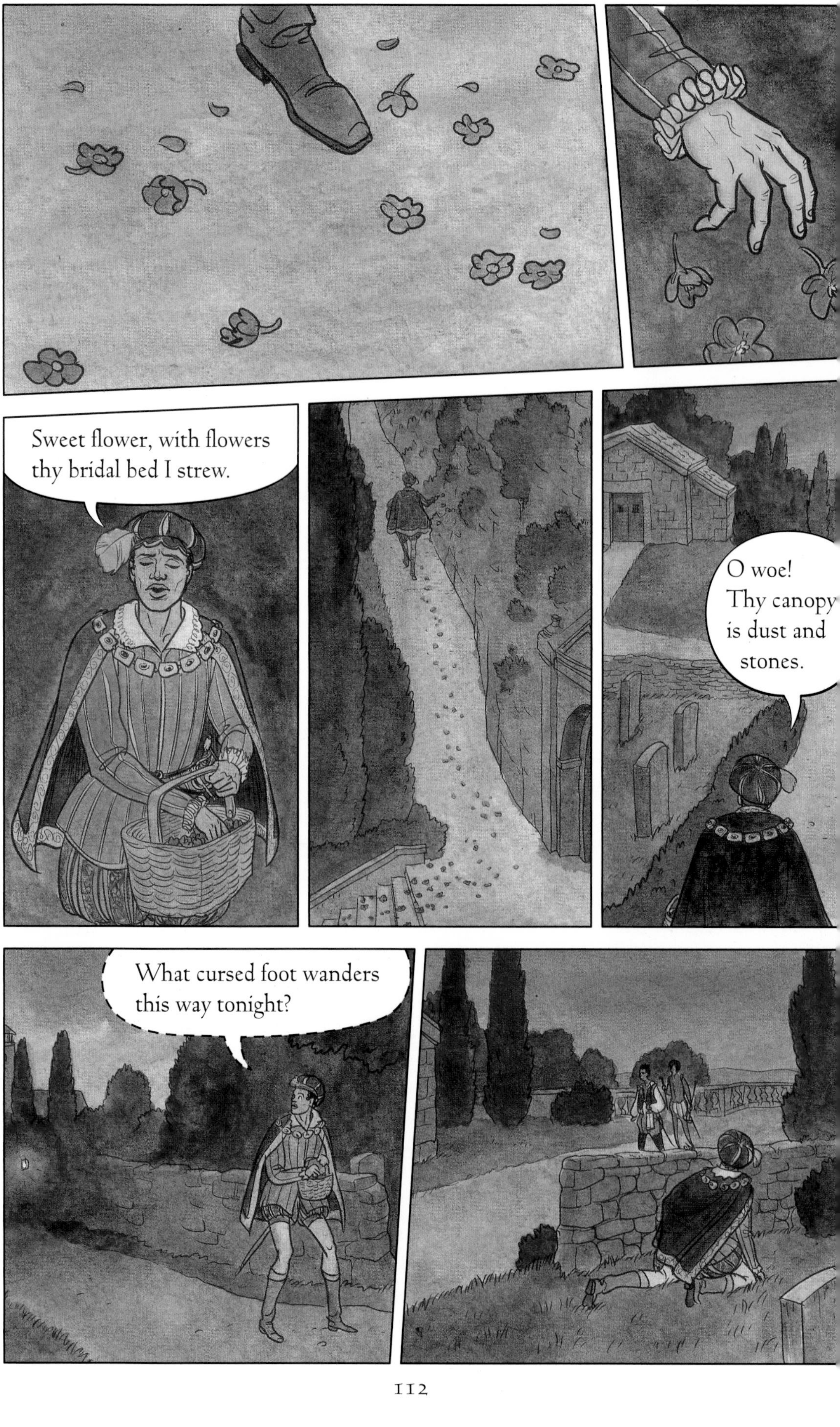
Sweet flower, with flowers thy bridal bed I strew.
O woe! Thy canopy is dust and stones.
What cursed foot wanders this way tonight?

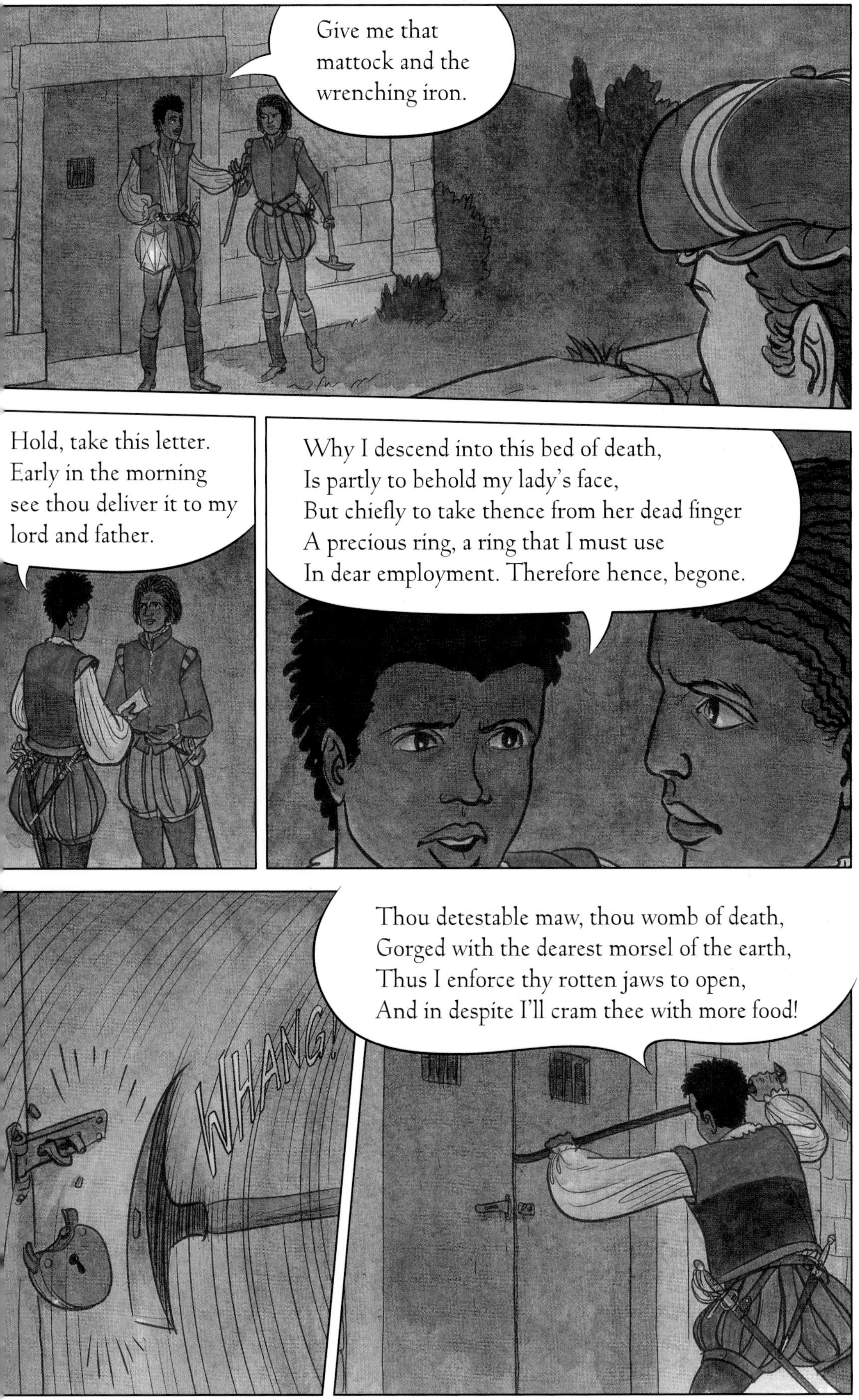
Give me that mattock and the wrenching iron.
Hold, take this letter. Early in the morning see thou deliver it to my lord and father.
Why I descend into this bed of death,
Is partly to behold my lady's face,
But chiefly to take thence from her dead finger
A precious ring, a ring that I must use
In dear employment. Therefore hence, begone.
WHANG!
Thou detestable maw, thou womb of death,
Gorged with the dearest morsel of the earth,
Thus I enforce thy rotten jaws to open,
And in despite I'll cram thee with more food!

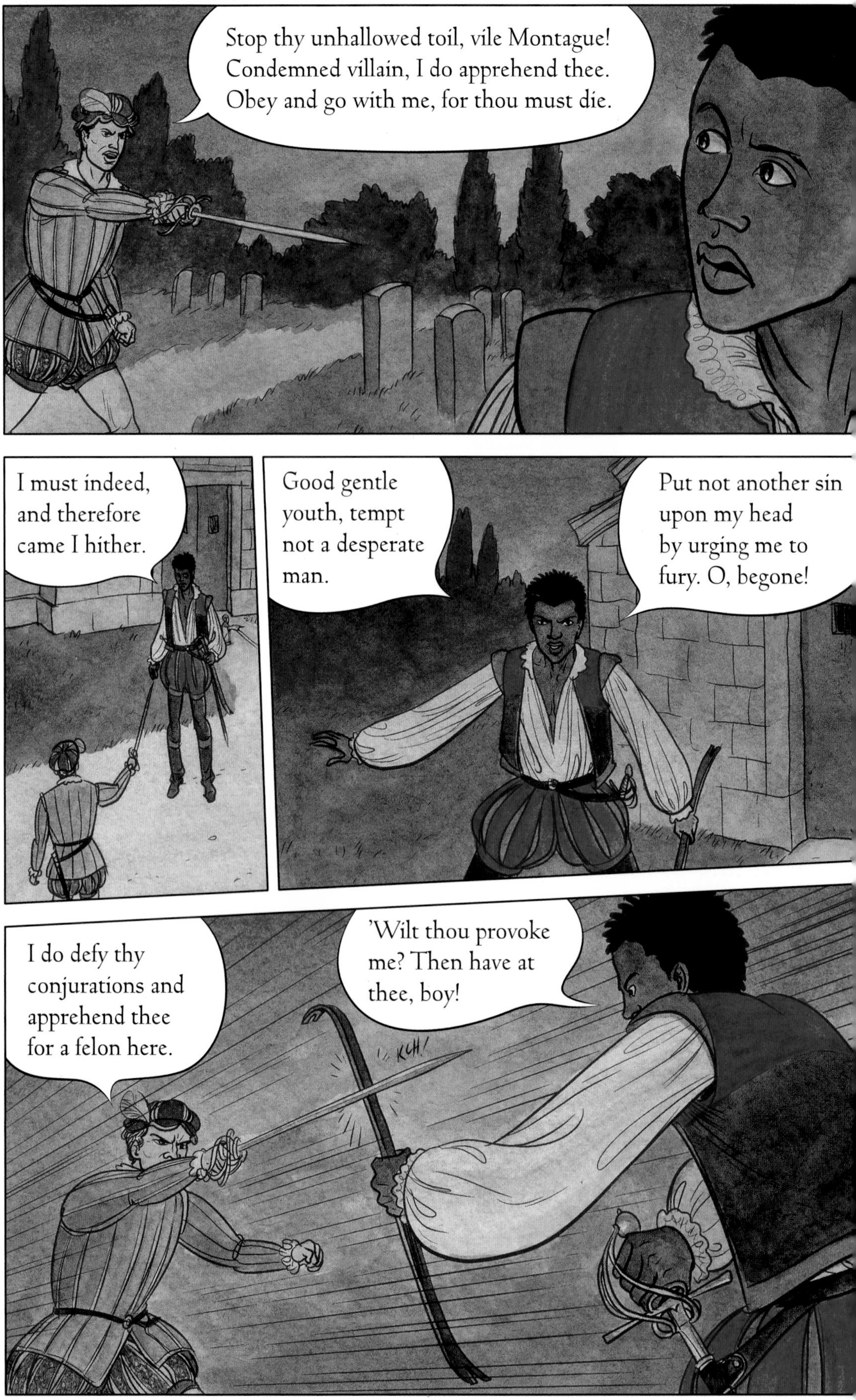
Stop thy unhallowed toil, vile Montague! Condemned villain, I do apprehend thee. Obey and go with me, for thou must die.
I must indeed, and therefore came I hither.
Good gentle youth, tempt not a desperate man.
Put not another sin upon my head by urging me to fury. O, begone!
I do defy thy conjurations and apprehend thee for a felon here.
'Wilt thou provoke me? Then have at thee, boy!
KCH!

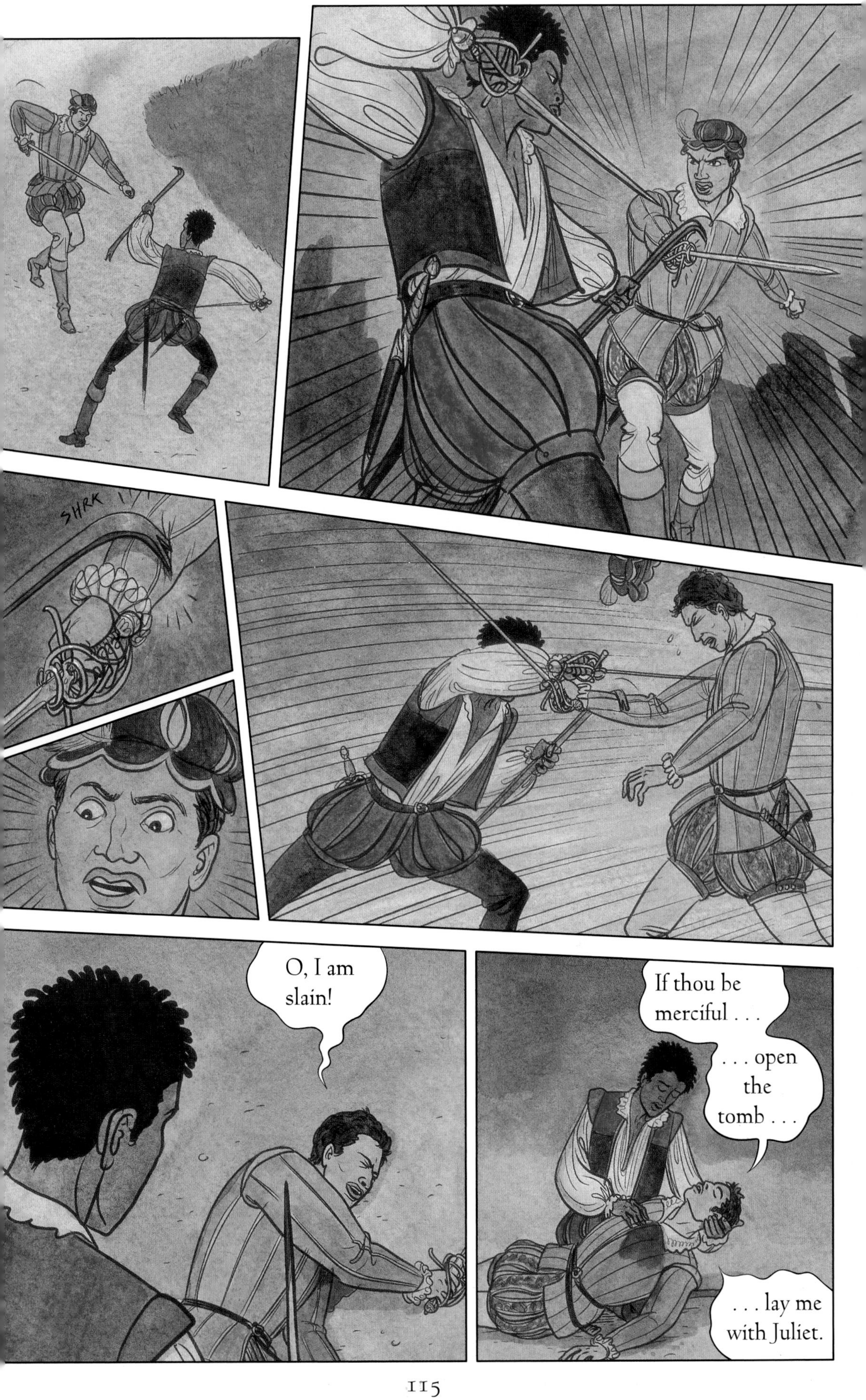
SHRK
O, I am slain!
If thou be merciful . . .
. . . open the tomb . . .
. . . lay me with Juliet.

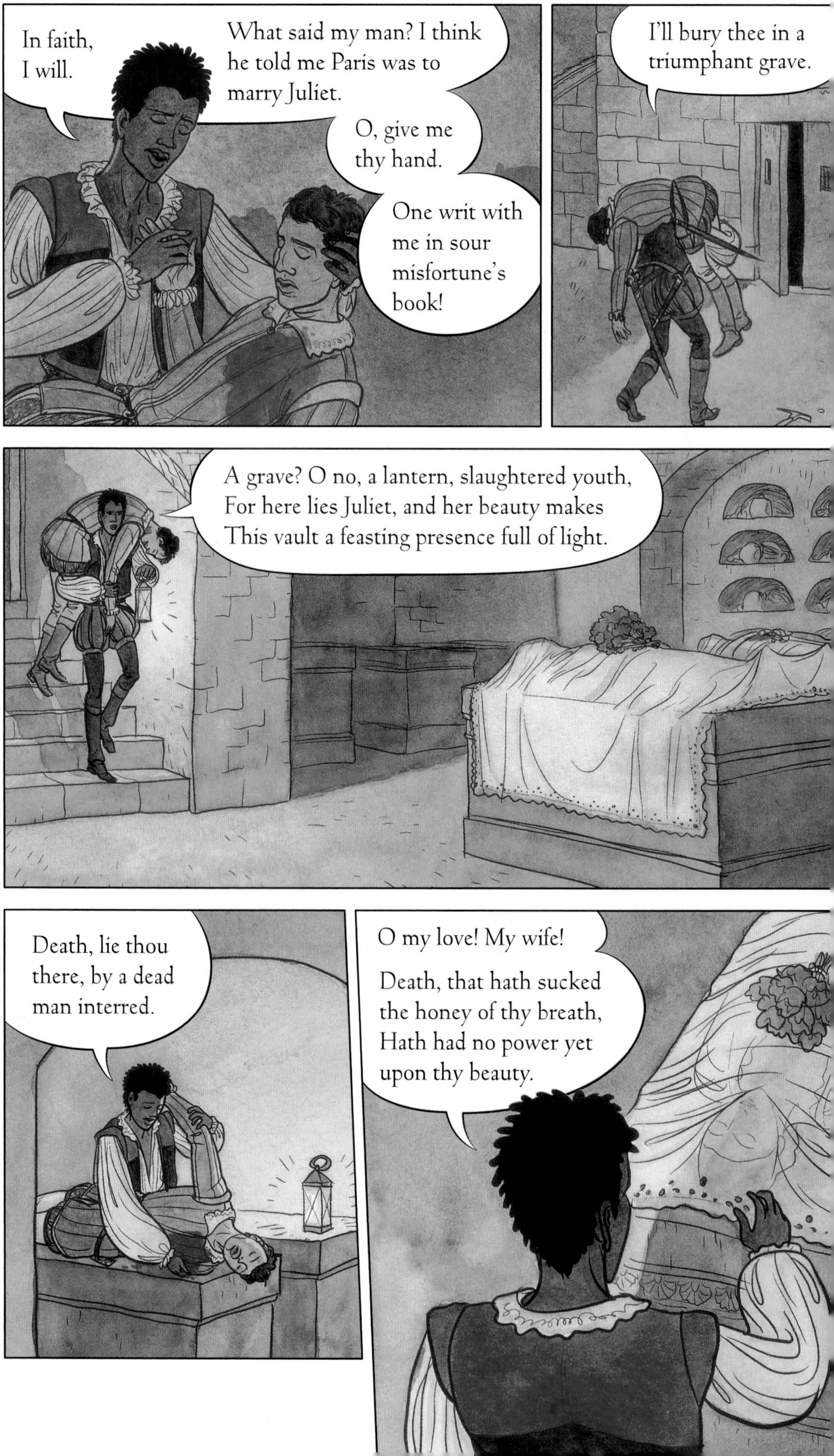

In faith, I will.
What said my man? I think he told me Paris was to marry Juliet.
O, give me thy hand.
One writ with me in sour misfortune's book!
I'll bury thee in a triumphant grave.
A grave? O no, a lantern, slaughtered youth, For here lies Juliet, and her beauty makes This vault a feasting presence full of light.
Death, lie thou there, by a dead man interred.
O my love! My wife!
Death, that hath sucked the honey of thy breath, Hath had no power yet upon thy beauty.

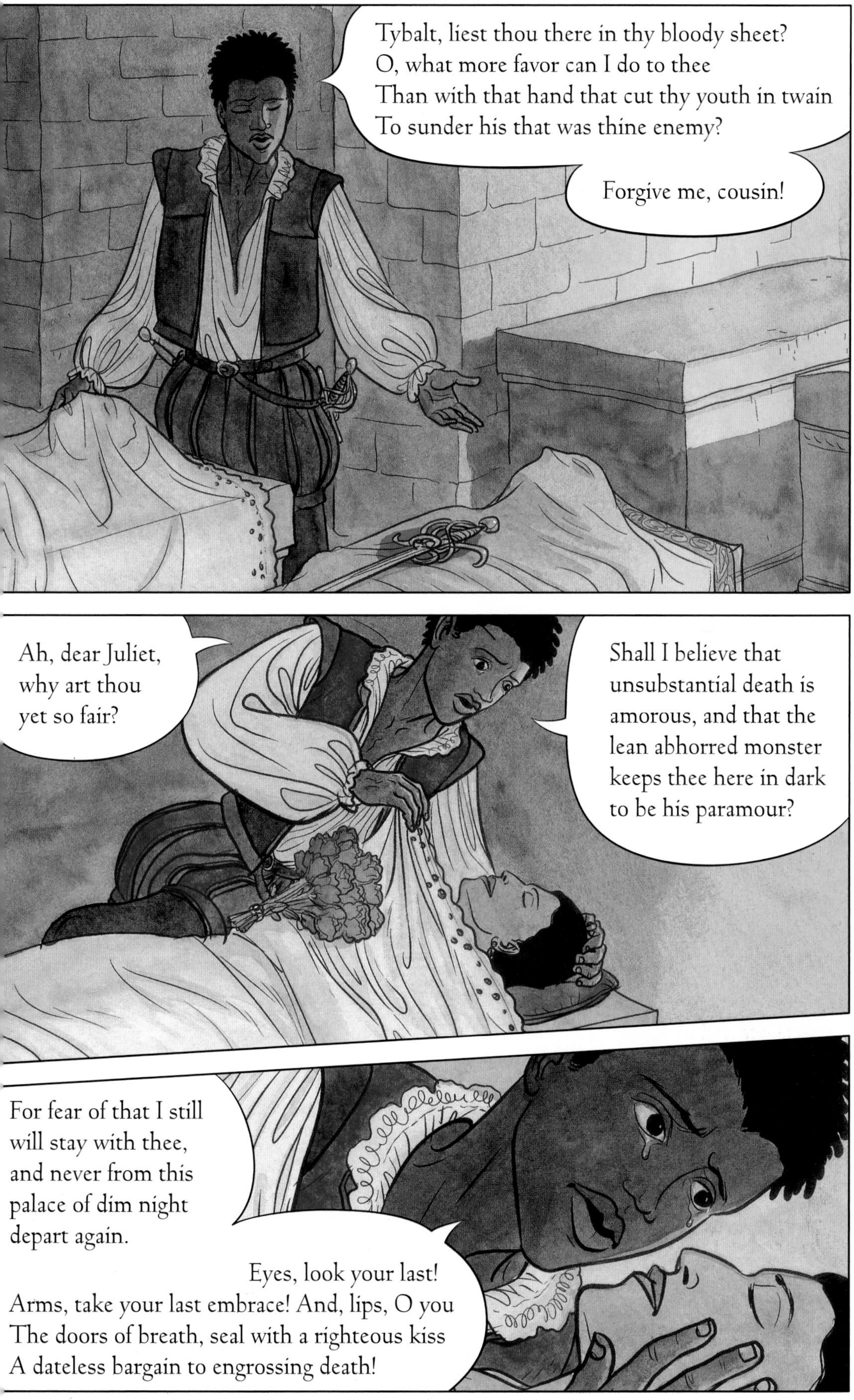

Tybalt, liest thou there in thy bloody sheet?
O, what more favor can I do to thee
Than with that hand that cut thy youth in twain
To sunder his that was thine enemy?
Forgive me, cousin!
Ah, dear Juliet, why art thou yet so fair?
Shall I believe that unsubstantial death is amorous, and that the lean abhorred monster keeps thee here in dark to be his paramour?
For fear of that I still will stay with thee, and never from this palace of dim night depart again.
Eyes, look your last!
Arms, take your last embrace! And, lips, O you
The doors of breath, seal with a righteous kiss
A dateless bargain to engrossing death!

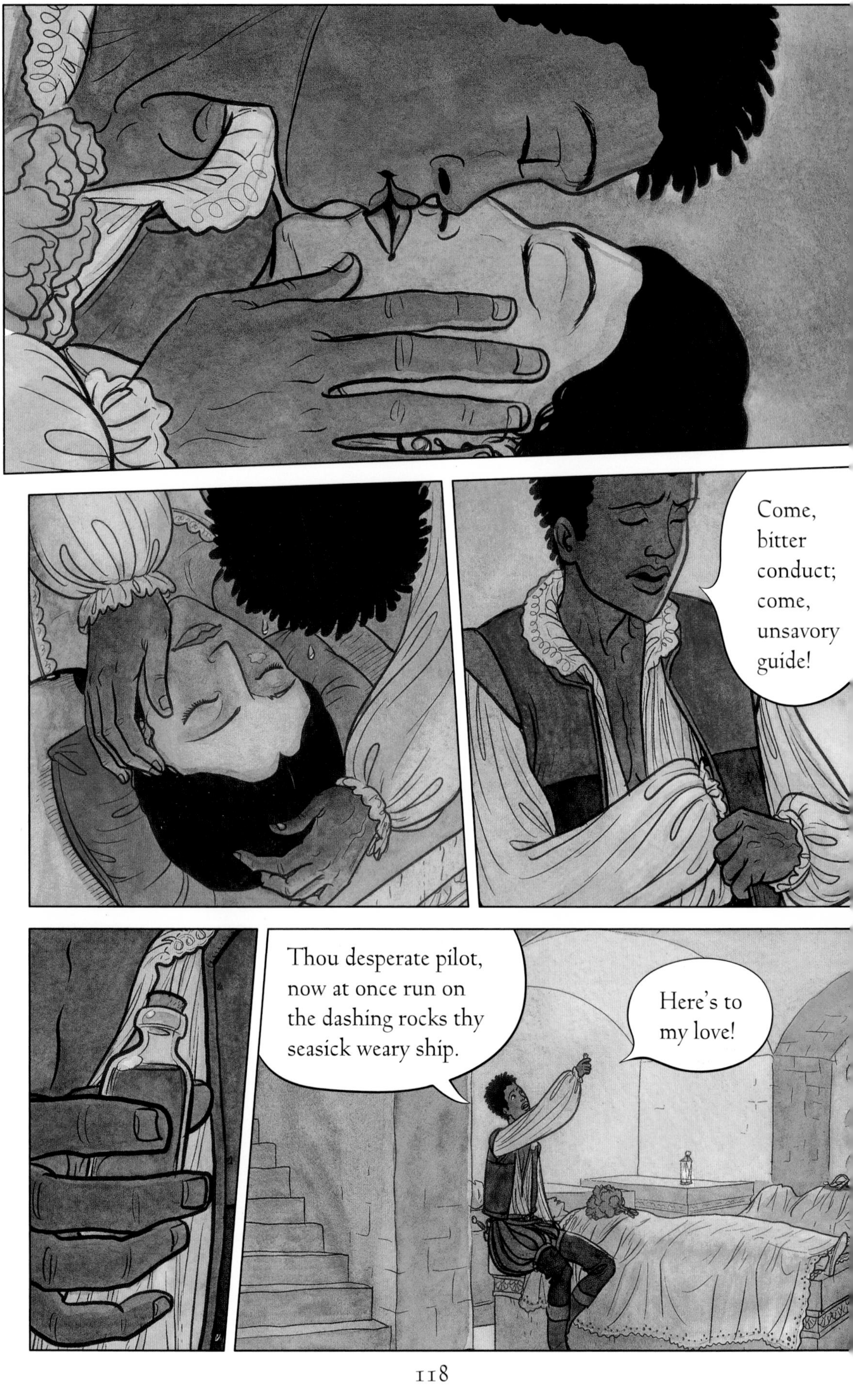
Come, bitter conduct; come, unsavory guide!
Thou desperate pilot, now at once run on the dashing rocks thy seasick weary ship.
Here's to my love!

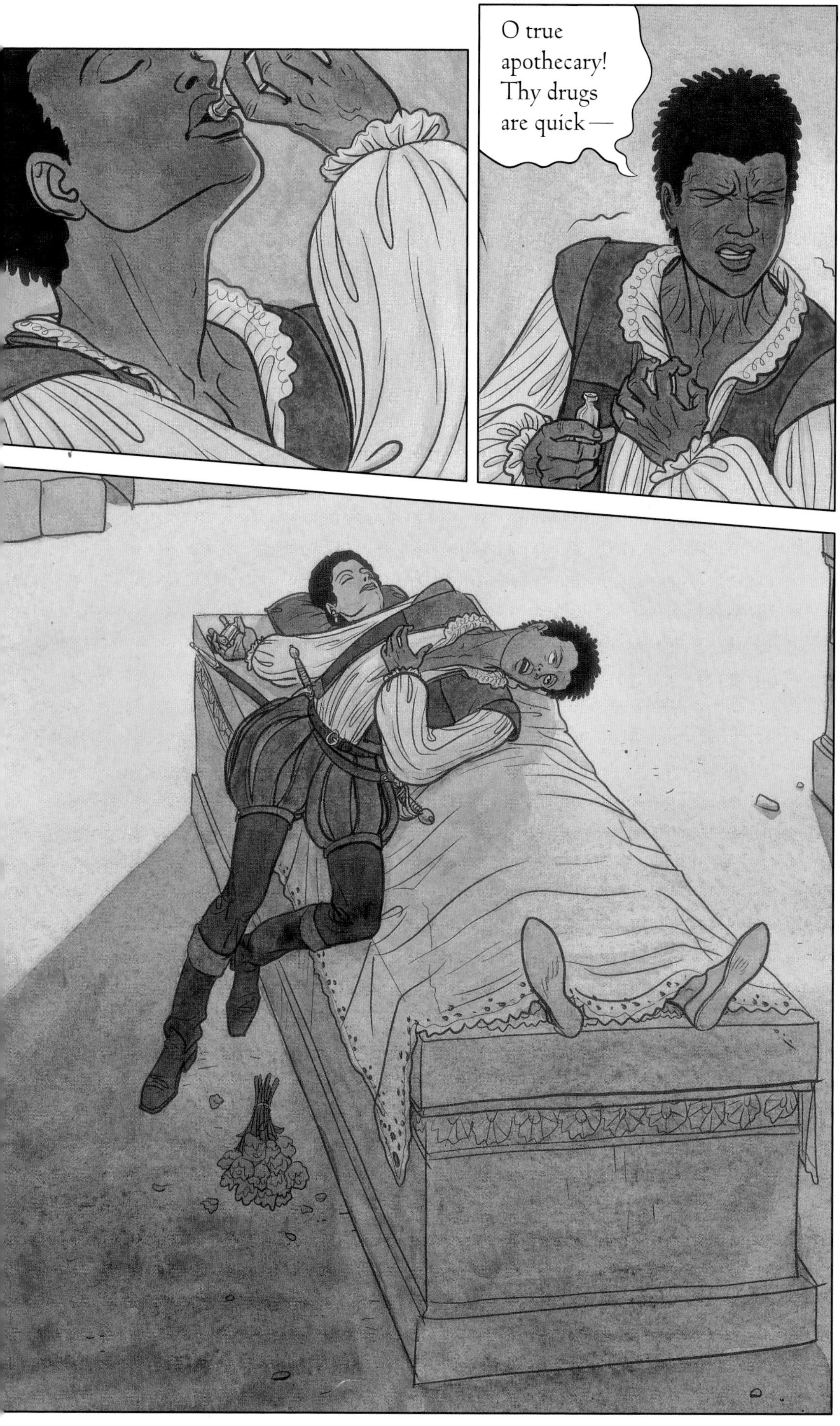
O true apothecary! Thy drugs are quick —

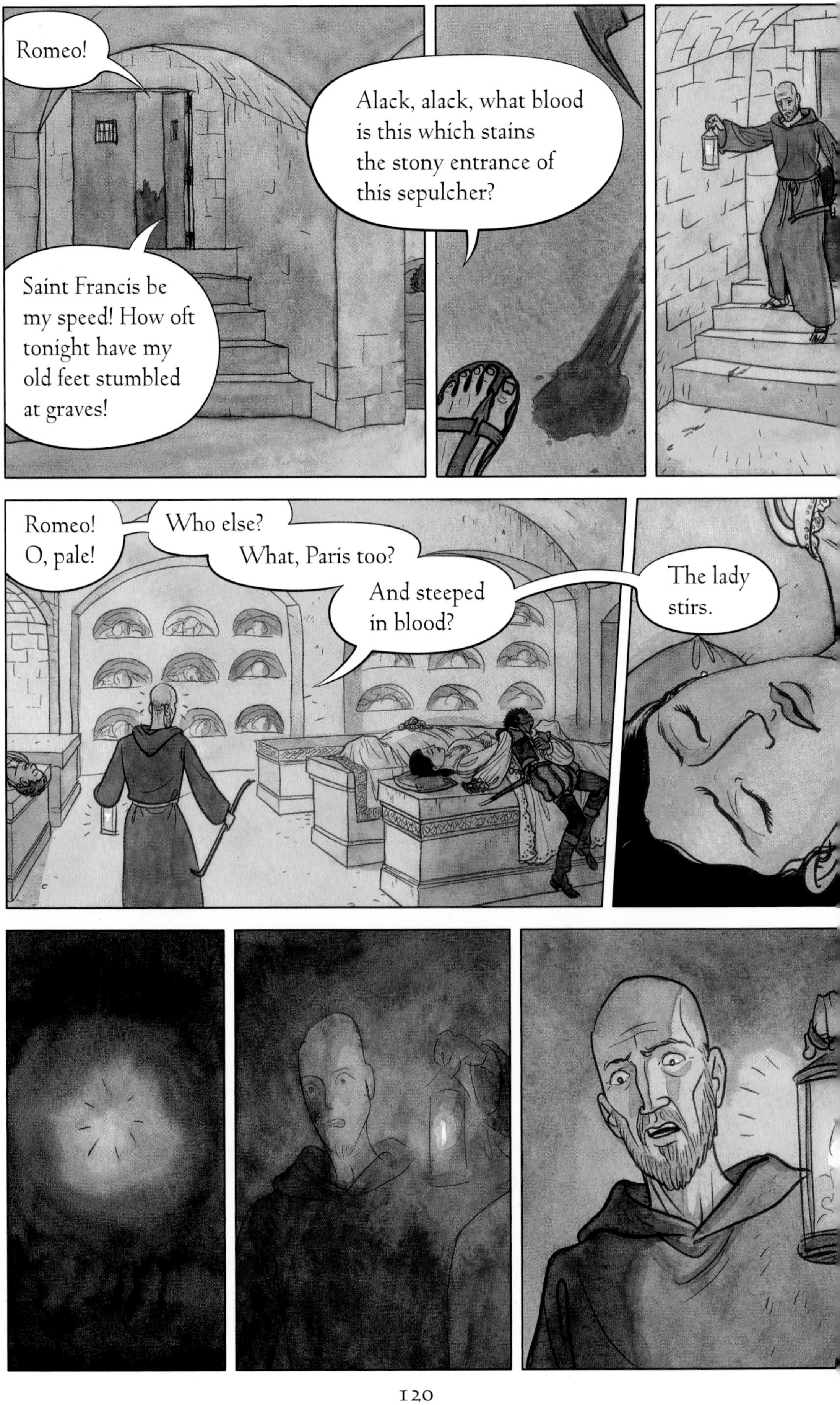
Romeo!
Saint Francis be my speed! How oft tonight have my old feet stumbled at graves!
Alack, alack, what blood is this which stains the stony entrance of this sepulcher?
Romeo! O, pale!
Who else?
What, Paris too?
And steeped in blood?
The lady stirs.

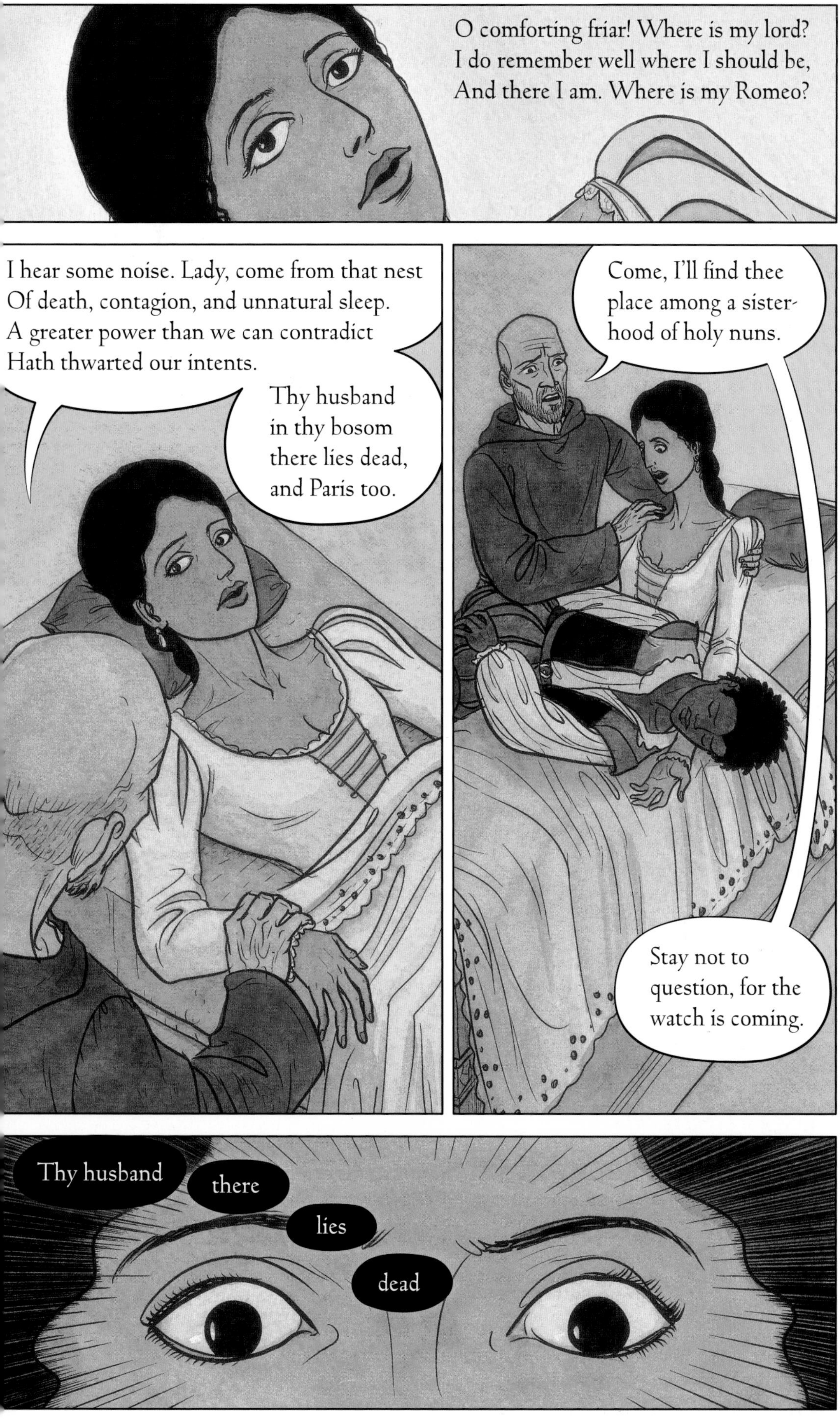
O comforting friar! Where is my lord?
I do remember well where I should be,
And there I am. Where is my Romeo?
I hear some noise. Lady, come from that nest
Of death, contagion, and unnatural sleep.
A greater power than we can contradict
Hath thwarted our intents.
Thy husband in thy bosom there lies dead, and Paris too.
Come, I'll find thee place among a sisterhood of holy nuns.
Stay not to question, for the watch is coming.
Thy husband
there
lies
dead

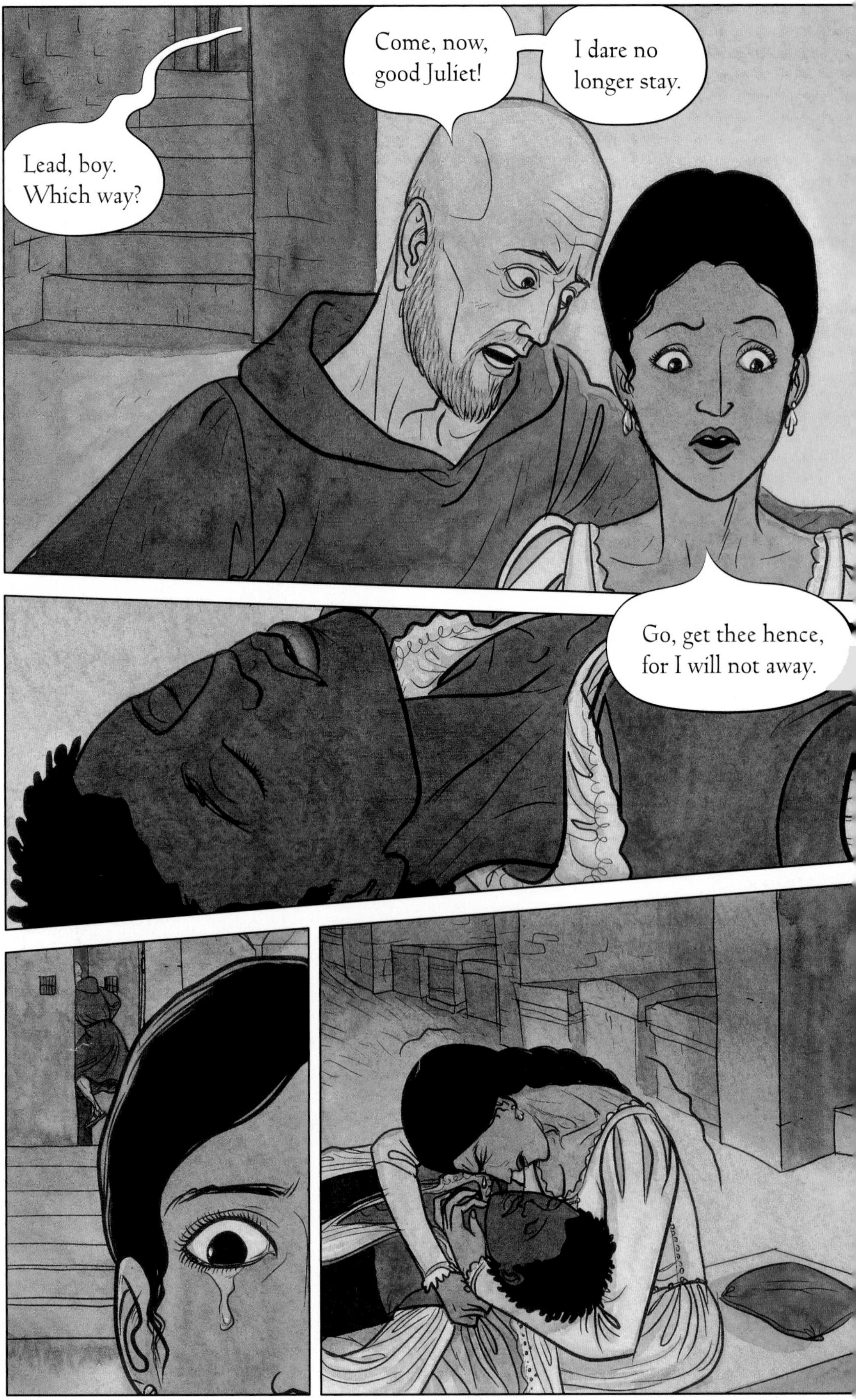
Lead, boy. Which way?
Come, now, good Juliet!
I dare no longer stay.
Go, get thee hence, for I will not away.

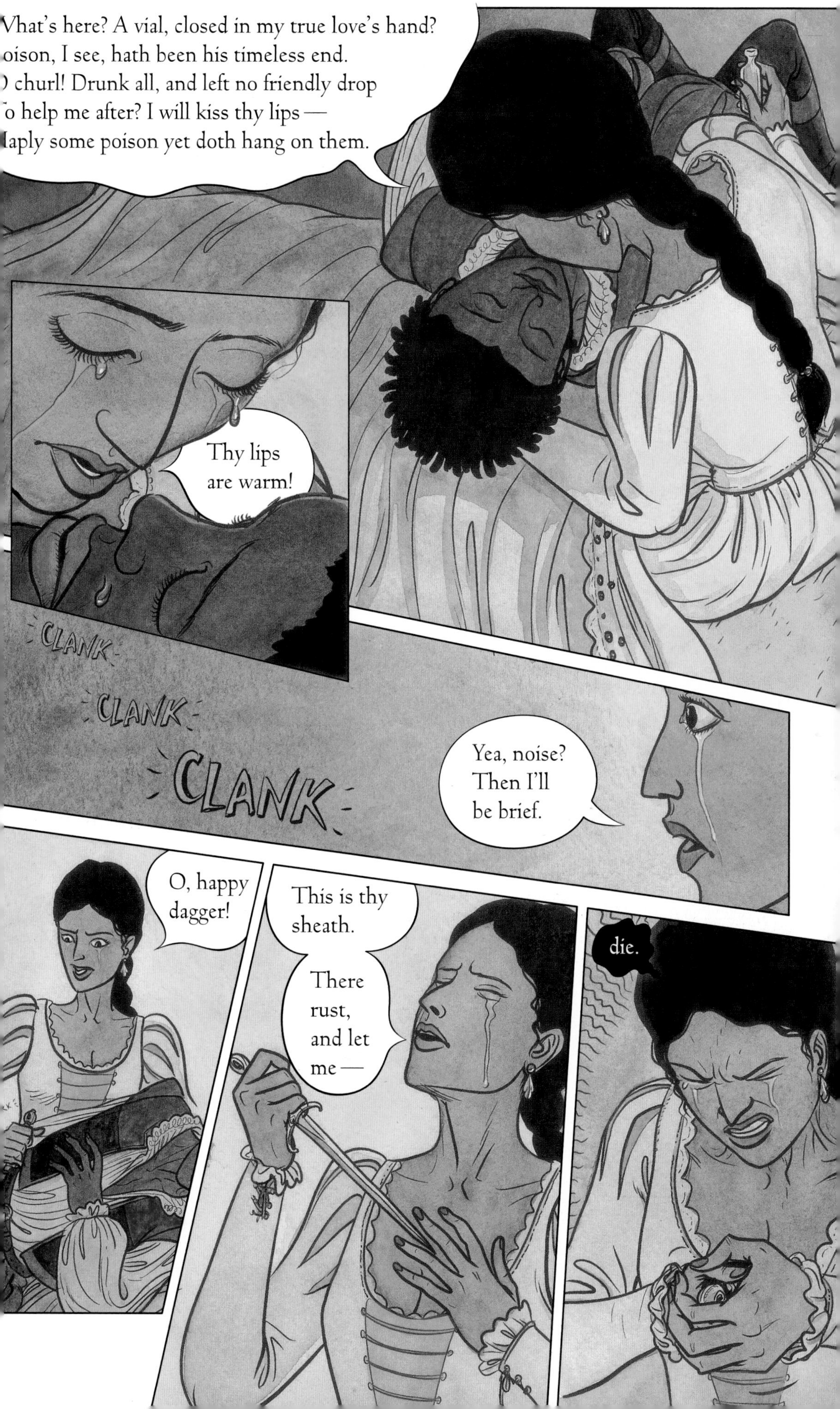
Vhat's here? A vial, closed in my true love's hand?
oison, I see, hath been his timeless end.
) churl! Drunk all, and left no friendly drop
'o help me after? I will kiss thy lips —
Iaply some poison yet doth hang on them.
Thy lips are warm!
CLANK
CLANK
CLANK
Yea, noise? Then I'll be brief.
O, happy dagger!
This is thy sheath.
There rust, and let me —
die.

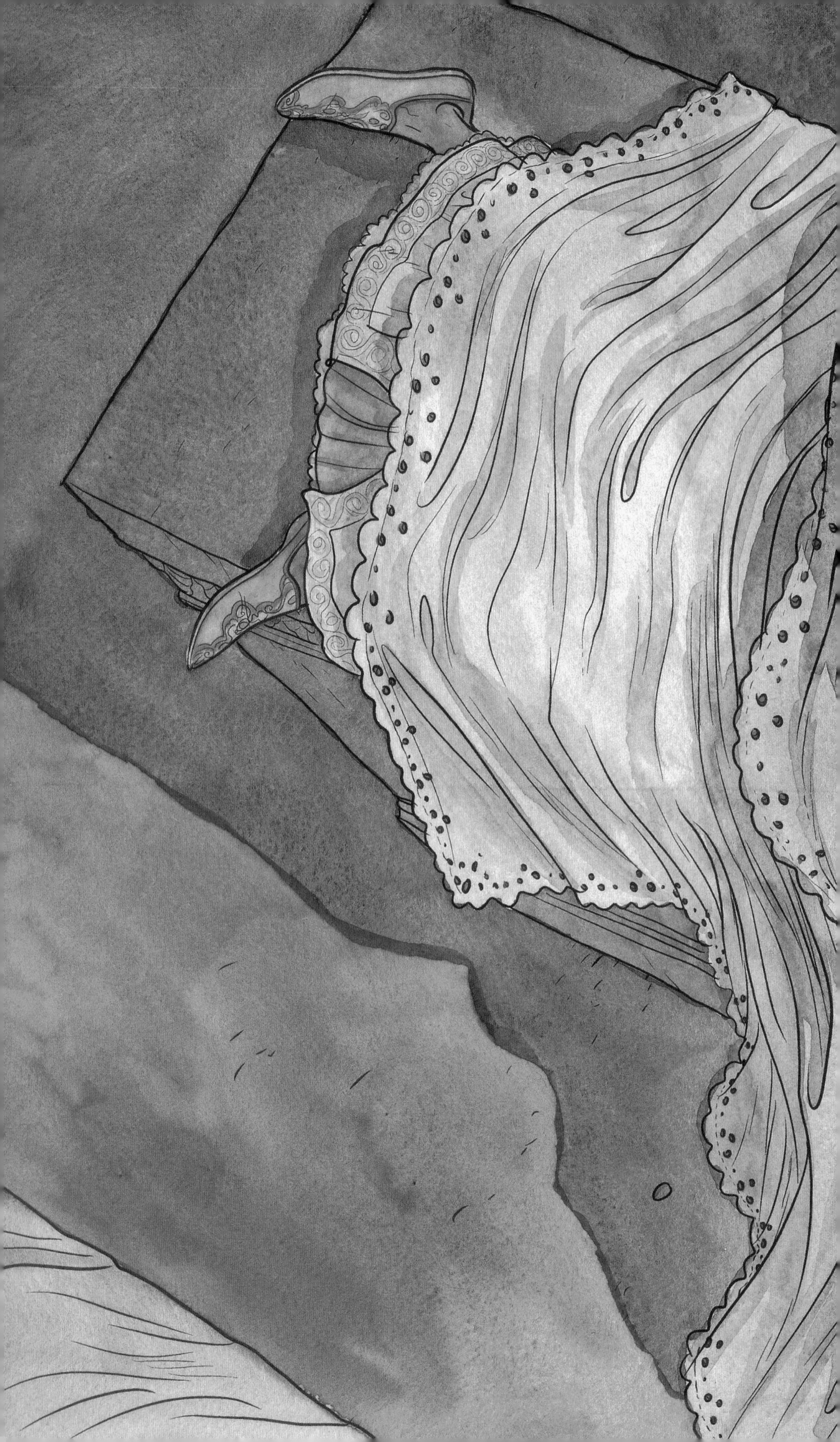

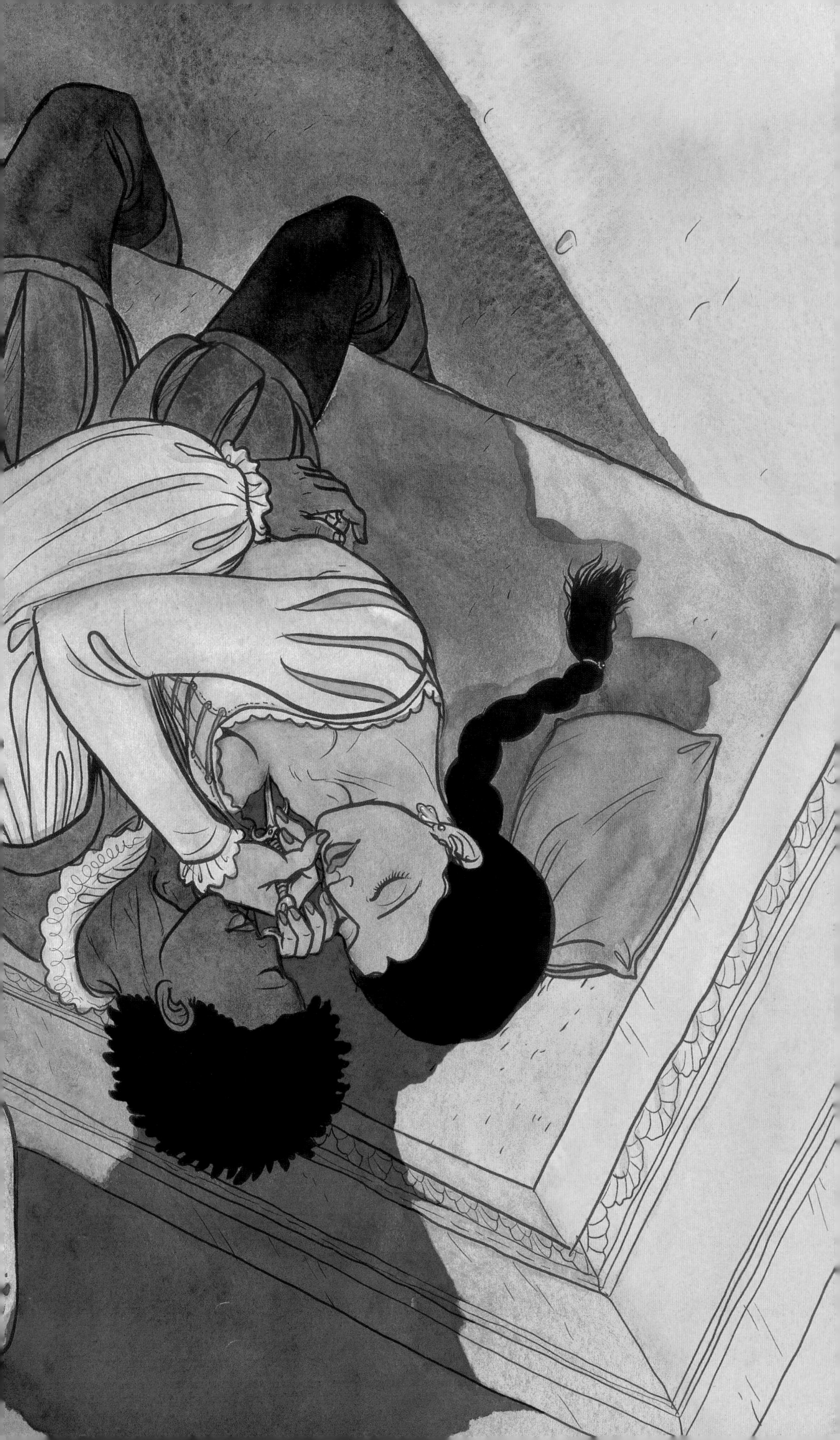

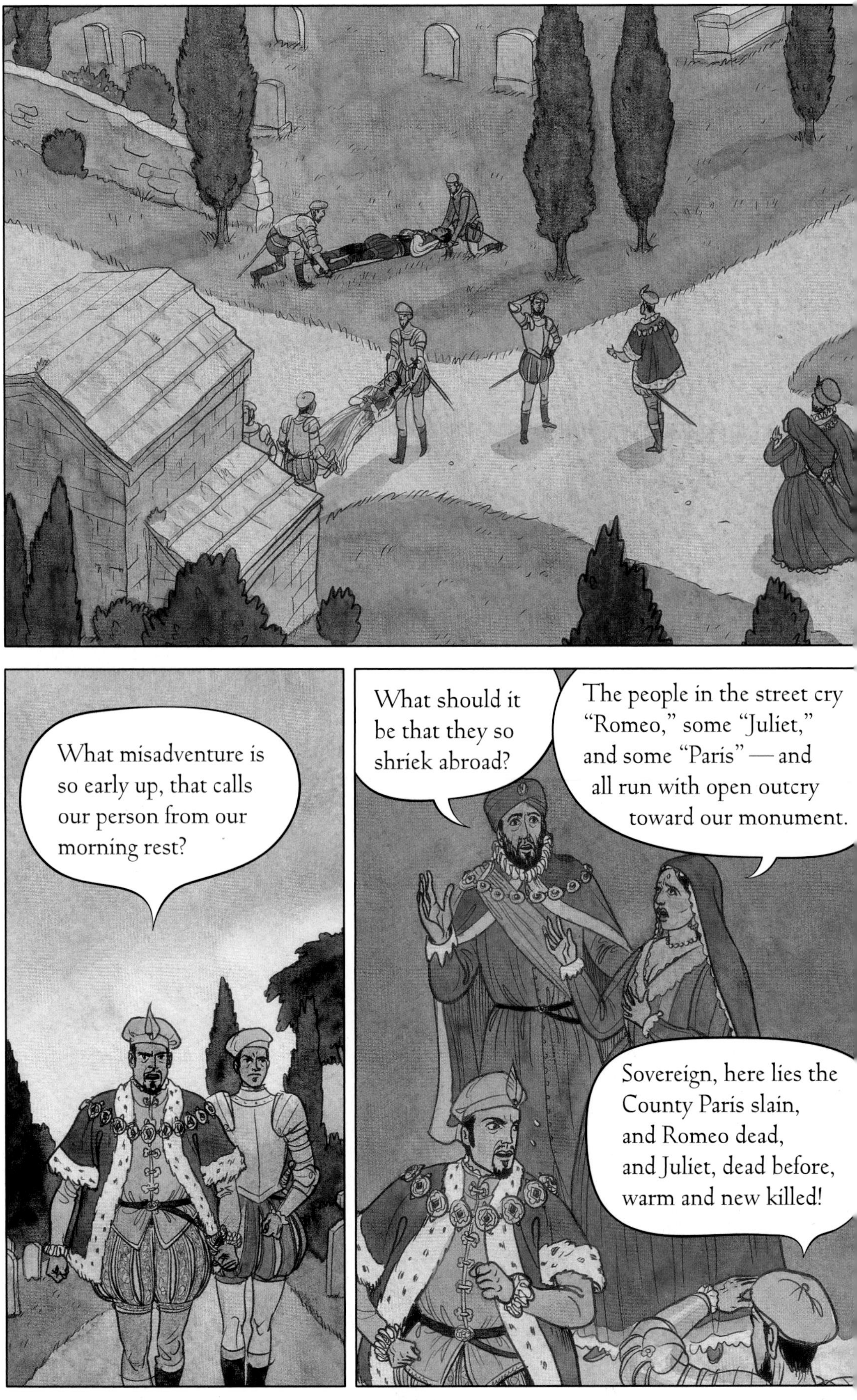
What misadventure is so early up, that calls our person from our morning rest?
What should it be that they so shriek abroad?
The people in the street cry "Romeo," some "Juliet," and some "Paris" — and all run with open outcry toward our monument.
Sovereign, here lies the County Paris slain, and Romeo dead, and Juliet, dead before, warm and new killed!

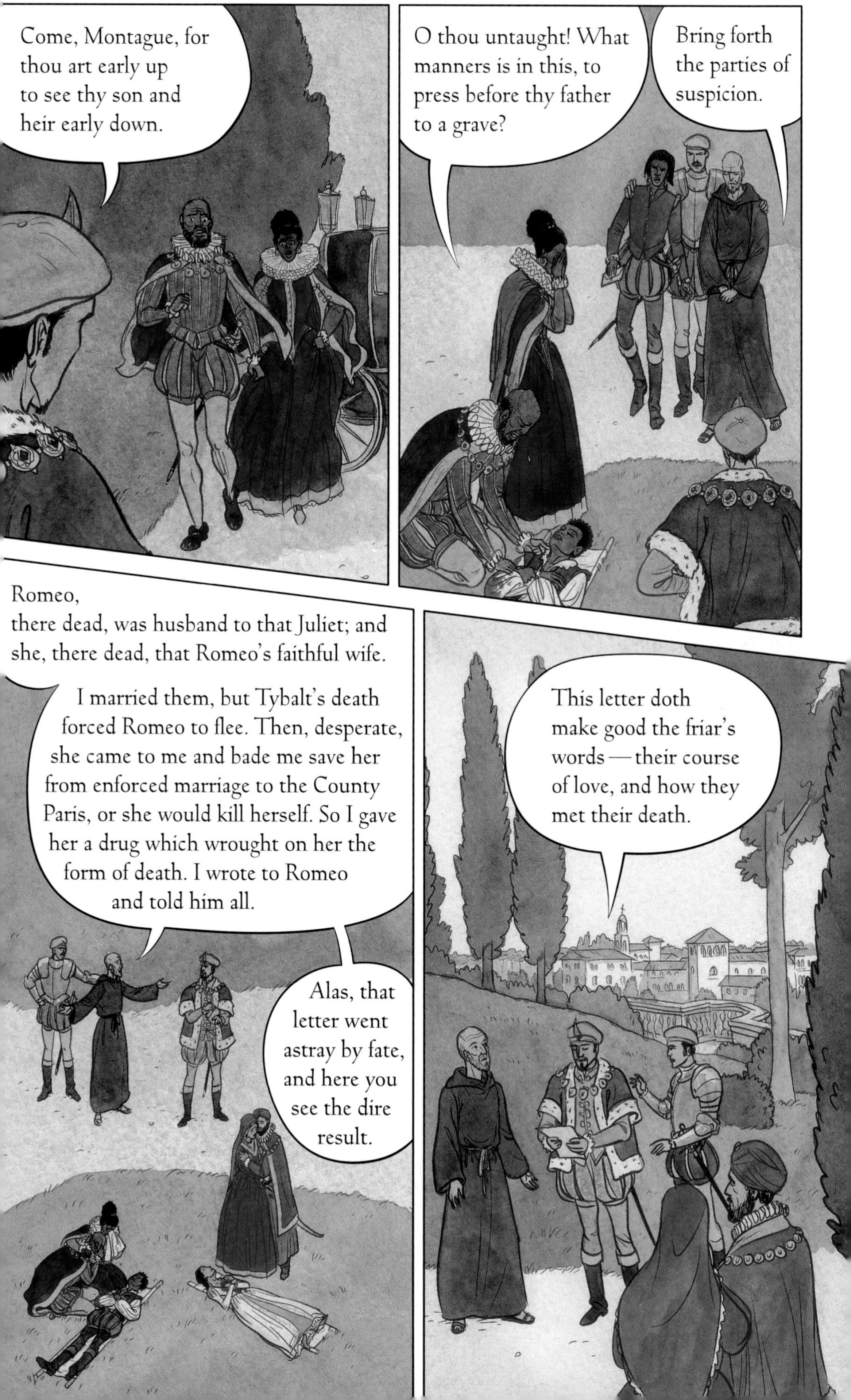
Come, Montague, for thou art early up to see thy son and heir early down.
O thou untaught! What manners is in this, to press before thy father to a grave?
Bring forth the parties of suspicion.
Romeo, there dead, was husband to that Juliet; and she, there dead, that Romeo's faithful wife.
I married them, but Tybalt's death forced Romeo to flee. Then, desperate, she came to me and bade me save her from enforced marriage to the County Paris, or she would kill herself. So I gave her a drug which wrought on her the form of death. I wrote to Romeo and told him all.
Alas, that letter went astray by fate, and here you see the dire result.
This letter doth make good the friar's words — their course of love, and how they met their death.

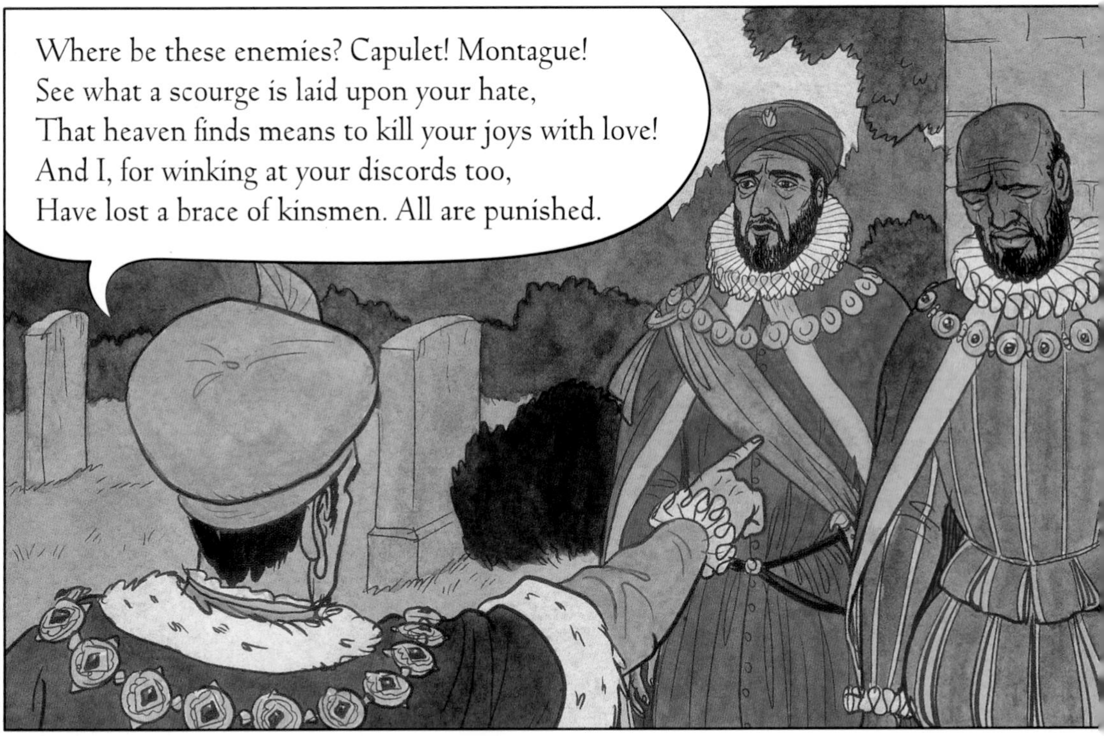
Where be these enemies? Capulet! Montague!
See what a scourge is laid upon your hate,
That heaven finds means to kill your joys with love!
And I, for winking at your discords too,
Have lost a brace of kinsmen. All are punished.

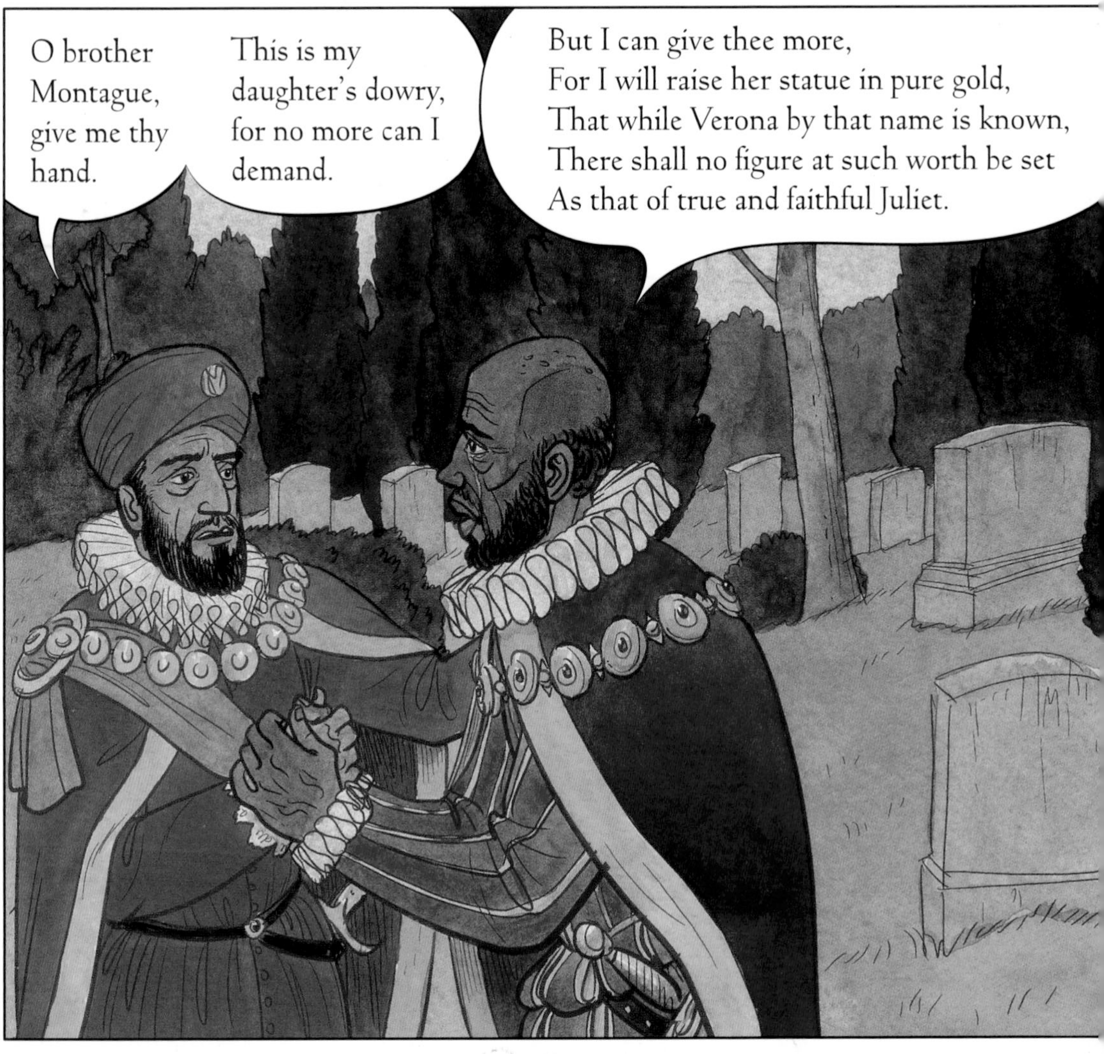
O brother Montague, give me thy hand.
This is my daughter's dowry, for no more can I demand.
But I can give thee more,
For I will raise her statue in pure gold,
That while Verona by that name is known,
There shall no figure at such worth be set
As that of true and faithful Juliet.

A glooming peace this morning with it brings.
The sun for sorrow will not show his head.
Go hence to have more talk of these sad things.
Some shall be pardoned, and some punished.
For never was a story of more woe
Than this of Juliet and her Romeo.

❧ AUTHOR'S NOTE ❧

The setting for this book is based closely on actual features of the city of Verona in northern Italy, but it is not one hundred percent historically accurate. In depicting the Verona of Shakespeare's time, I had to resort to considerable speculation, as there is little visual reference for the period. The historic architecture I've drawn here is historically plausible, but it's not a perfect re-creation of the city circa 1600.

I also took liberties with the city's geography so that I could spotlight my favorite parts in certain scenes. Basically, I pulled everything closer together—the Piazza delle Erbe (herb market square), the Capulet house, the Ponte Pietra (bridge), the entire hill of the Teatro Romano (Roman theater), San Zeno Basilica, and the Giusti Gardens. The Ponte Pietra made a picturesque centerpiece for my Verona. Originally a Roman bridge dating from 100 BC, it was damaged several times, most recently in World War II, but was accurately reconstructed using original materials.

A visitor to the supposed house and tomb of Juliet will find these quite picturesque but rather implausible and unsuitable for the scenes in which they appear in the play. The tomb is located in the basement of a building, rather than in a graveyard, and Juliet's famous balcony is directly next to the front door of a rather small house with no orchard or garden. However, the balcony itself has some interesting details, so I combined it with parts of Castelvecchio, the castle of the Scaligeri family, and the Palazzo Giusti, whose fabulous gardens were a highlight of my visit. From the formal Giusti Gardens you can walk up a path under the fearsome sculpted *mascherone* (mask) of a Green-Man-like face, past an ancient fountain, and up a switchback to the plateau above, which features beautiful views over the river and city. I situated the graveyard and the tomb of the Capulets up on this plateau (where, so far as I know, no graveyard ever existed) to get the picturesque scenes at the beginning and end of this book.

Likewise, I placed the San Zeno Basilica within sight of the Giusti Gardens and made it the scene of Romeo and Juliet's wedding. Tradition has it that San Zeno was probably where the young couple would have been married, if indeed such a young couple ever existed. The church is old enough and contains a cloister where Franciscan monks may have lived. I added an herb garden for Friar Laurence, and I based this on the Cloisters museum, which is near my home in New York and which features a beautiful and authentic medieval herb garden. I decided Friar Laurence's poisonous specimen would be a young monkshood plant, which features beautiful and slightly sinister-looking "hooded" flowers that are highly toxic if ingested. Later, in Act 4 Scene 1, he is seen dissecting rosemary, which was often used for medicinal purposes.

The colosseum that appears in the duel scene is one of the best-preserved Roman amphitheaters in Italy, dating from about the year AD 30, and is still used for concerts and performances. In 1117 an earthquake destroyed most of the outer ring and the topmost tier. I added some trees and turf where the outer ring would have stood.

The crenellated walls and towers that appear in various background scenes are more examples of the original Roman architecture that have survived thousands of years to the present day. Verona is still a very beautiful city, although the town center is now rather overrun with modern, trendy shops.

Along with the introduction of characters of different races into historical Verona, I took various liberties — or rather, had the characters take liberties — with their costumes. No self-respecting young woman of Shakespeare's time would cut her dress above the ankle or wear a short-sleeved nightshirt or go out without a hat, and tattoos were only to be found on sailors, never on gentlemen. This is all to show the rebellion of the younger generation against the older in a way that I hope makes immediate sense to a modern reader. The old folks wear their costumes in a historically correct manner, except for some cultural touches I added, like Capulet's Sikh turban or the Friar's *rakusu* (a ceremonial Buddhist garment). Since I cast the Capulets as an Indian family, I couldn't help making a *Bend It Like Beckham* reference by placing a portrait of "Babaji" (Guru Nanak Dev Ji, founder of the Sikh religion) prominently in the Capulet mansion.

I tried *not* to take too many liberties with the text, and in particular I decided not to change a few scenes that are often modified in other adaptations. The balcony scene, in most movies and some stage productions, has Romeo climbing up to embrace Juliet by means of a convenient tree or trellis. But the text contradicts this possibility, as Juliet's nurse must bring rope to allow Romeo to make the climb after their marriage. I decided to have Romeo climb a tree but not be able to reach the balcony. I think that's more symbolic anyway.

Then there is the problem of Friar Laurence. Why does this guy, whose advice through most of the play is sound and insightful, hatch such a bizarre plan? And then in the final scene, why does he run from the tomb, leaving the distraught and desperate Juliet alone? Indeed, his very presence in the scene has the potential to reduce the moment of tragic intimacy between Juliet and the dead (or dying, as in Baz Luhrmann's interpretation) Romeo; so some productions simply remove him from the scene. This has other complications, though, so ultimately I went with the original text and kept the friar in the tomb when Juliet wakes.

I started this book working from my dog-eared copy of the Folger Shakespeare's *Romeo and Juliet* from 1959, but later compared fine points of the Arden, Oxford, and updated Folger editions.

I've tried to use footnotes as little as possible, as I think they distract too much from the flow of the story, but I have added a few where I wanted to make sure certain terms are not misunderstood. In most cases I've provided a simple definition of the word or phrase as it is used in context, rather than the general definition. In some cases, to avoid adding footnotes, I've substituted a modern word for an archaic one, but only if it doesn't break the meter.

The text of this book is **not** the full text of the play. Although I have attempted to abridge it as sensitively and faithfully as possible, I am aware that I have edited arguably the greatest writer in the English language and that I have left "on the cutting-room floor," so to speak, many pages of incredibly exquisite material. There are some truly wonderful passages that, regretfully, I've left out. If you enjoyed this book and have not read the full play (as well as seen it staged), I hope you'll seek it out.

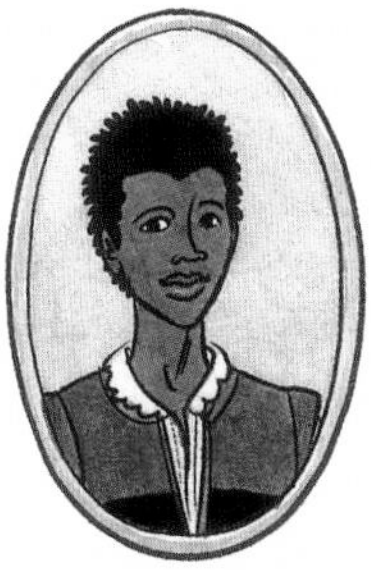 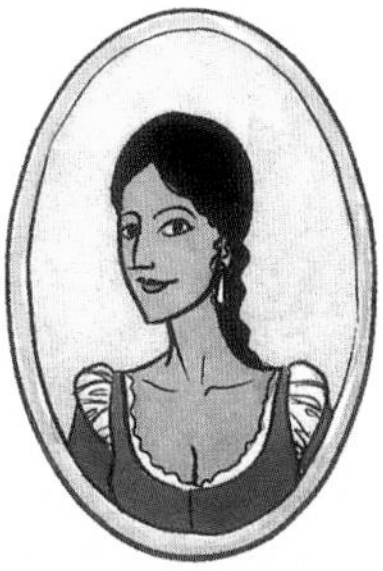

ACKNOWLEDGMENTS

I'd like to thank my amazing wife, Alison, for her help and input at every stage of this project.

I'd also like to thank the fine folks at Candlewick Press, especially my editor, Deb Noyes Wayshak, and my school & library marketing champions—Jenny Choy and Sharon Hancock. Gregg, Sherry, Lisa, Amanda, Carter, Becky, Liz, Laura, Anne, Jennifer, along with the many other folks who helped usher this book into the world, thank you all!

Thanks to Heather Glista, Hannah Purdy, and Kyle Bradley for providing reference materials and opinions on the costumes and architecture (though they are not responsible for any historical inaccuracies!). Thanks also to Deirdre Larkin, head gardener at the Cloisters, for information on poisonous flowers.

Thanks to my early readers Paul Crook and Mat MacKenzie for feedback. My parents were also among my early readers this time around, and they have my gratitude for this and so, so much more.

First edition 2013

Library of Congress Catalog Card Number 2012950561
ISBN 978-0-7636-5948-6 (hardcover)
ISBN 978-0-7636-6807-5 (paperback)

13 14 15 16 17 18 TLF 10 9 8 7 6 5 4 3 2 1
Printed in Dongguan, Guangdong, China

This book was typeset in Truesdell.
The illustrations were done in watercolor with digital elements.

Candlewick Press
99 Dover Street
Somerville, Massachusetts 02144

visit us at www.candlewick.com